THE
STOPOVER

OTHER TITLES BY T L SWAN

THE STOPOVER

THE MILES HIGH CLUB

T L SWAN

Montlake
Romance

Text copyright © 2019 by T L Swan
All rights reserved.

Published by Montlake Romance, Seattle

www.apub.com

Amazon, the Amazon logo, and Montlake Romance are trademarks of Amazon.com, Inc., or its affiliates.

ISBN-13: 9781542015875
ISBN-10: 1542015871

Cover design by @blacksheep-uk.com

Printed in the United States of America

*I would like to dedicate this book to the
alphabet,
for those twenty-six letters have changed my life.
Within those twenty-six letters I found myself,
and now I live my dream.
Next time you say the alphabet,
remember its power.
I do every day.*

Chapter 1

"Can you move?" a voice behind me growls.

Startled, I turn toward the man behind me in the line. "I'm sorry?" I say in a fluster. "Did you want to get past?"

"No. I want these fucking idiots at the desk to hurry up. I'm going to miss my damn plane." He sneers, and I smell the alcohol wafting off him. "They make me sick."

I turn back to the front. *Great, a drunk in the check-in line. Just what I need.*

Heathrow Airport is bustling. Bad weather has delayed most of the flights, and to be honest, I wish they would delay mine. Then I could turn around and go back to the hotel and sleep for a week.

I am not in the mood for this shit.

I hear the man turn and complain to the people behind him, and I roll my eyes. Why are people so damn rude?

For another ten minutes, I listen to him bitch, sigh, and moan until I can take it no longer. I turn to him. "They are working as fast as they can. There's no need to be rude," I snap.

"What?" he yells as he turns his anger on me.

"Manners are free," I mutter under my breath.

"Manners are free?" he cries. "What are you, a schoolteacher? Or just a raving bitch?"

I glare at him. *Oh, I dare all right.* I've just spent the last forty-eight hours in hell. I flew across the world to go to a wedding, only to watch my ex-boyfriend drape himself over his new girlfriend. I'm in the mood to cut somebody today.

Don't mess with me.

I turn back to the front as my fury begins to boil.

He kicks my suitcase at my feet, and I turn. "Stop it," I snap.

He gets right up in my face, and I wince at the smell of his breath. "I'll do whatever I fucking like."

I see security come through the lounge as they watch him. The staff has seen what's going on here and called for backup. I fake a smile. "Please don't kick my bag, sir," I say sweetly.

"I'll kick whatever I fucking like." He picks up my suitcase and throws it across the airport.

"What the hell?" I screech.

"Hey," the man behind us cries. "Don't touch her stuff. Security!" he says.

Mr. Drunk and Disorderly throws a punch at my savior, and a scuffle breaks out.

Security comes running in from everywhere, and I am pushed back as he throws punches and screams obscenities. Oh hell, I do not need this today.

Eventually they get him under control, and he is taken away in handcuffs. The kind security guard picks up my bag. "Sorry about that," he apologizes. "Come with me," he says as he unhooks the rope on the line.

"Thank you." I smile awkwardly at everyone else in the line. I hate jumping the queue, but at this point, I just don't care. "Great." I sheepishly follow him, and he takes me to a young man's counter. He looks up and smiles broadly. "Hello."

"Hi."

"Are you okay?" he asks.

2

"Yes, I'm fine. Thank you for asking."

"Look after her," the security guard tells the ticket man, and he gives us both a wink and disappears through the crowd.

"Identification, please?" the man asks.

I scramble through my purse and dig out my passport and pass it over; he smiles as he looks at the photo. Oh man, that's the worst photo in all of history. "Did you see me on *Most Wanted*?" I ask.

"Possibly. That photo: Is it even you?" He laughs.

I smile, embarrassed. "I hope not. I'm in trouble if it is."

He types in my details. "Okay, so we have you flying to New York today with a . . ." He stops typing and reads.

"Uh-huh. Preferably not next to that man."

"He won't be going anywhere today," he replies as he continues to type at a ridiculous speed. "Other than the lockup."

"Why would you get drunk before coming to the airport?" I ask. "He hasn't even been inside to the airport bars yet."

"You would be surprised by what goes on around here," he sighs.

I smile; this guy is nice.

He prints off my tickets. "I've upgraded you."

"What?"

"First class, as an apology for him mishandling your bag."

My eyes widen. "Oh, that's not necessary . . . really," I stammer.

He hands the tickets over and smiles broadly. "Enjoy your flight."

"Thank you so much," I gush.

He gives me a wink, and I could just reach over and hug him. But of course I won't. I'll pretend that cool things like this happen to me every day.

"Thanks again." I smile.

3

"You have access to the VIP lounge, which is located on level one. Lunch and drinks are on the house in there. Have a safe flight." With one last smile, he looks back to the line. "Next, please."

I walk through the baggage checks with a huge goofy grin on my face.

First class—just what the doctor ordered.

Three hours later, I walk onto the plane like a rock star. I didn't end up going into the VIP lounge because, well . . . I look like crap. My long dark hair is up in a high ponytail, and I'm wearing black leggings, a baggy pink sweater, and tennis shoes, but I did fix my makeup a little, so that's something. If I had known I was going to be upgraded, I would have at least tried to look the part and worn something swanky instead of looking like a homeless person. But anyway . . . who cares? It's not like I'm going to see anyone I know.

I hand my ticket over to the flight attendant. "Just through the left aisle and to the right."

"Thanks." I look at my ticket and walk through the plane and see my number.

1B.

Damn it, I don't have a window. I get to my seat, and a man sitting next to the window turns to me. Big blue eyes greet me, and he smiles. "Hello."

"Hi," I say.

Oh no . . . I'm sitting next to God's gift to women . . . only he's hotter.

I look like shit. *Fuck it.*

I open the overhead, and he stands. "Here, let me." He takes my bag from me and carefully places it up. He's tall and built and wearing blue jeans and a white T-shirt; he smells like the best aftershave in history.

"Thanks," I murmur as I pull my hand through my ponytail, trying to smooth out the knots. I mentally kick myself for not wearing something better.

"Do you want the window seat?" he asks.

I stare at him as my brain misfires.

He gestures to the seat beside the window.

"You don't mind?" I frown.

"Not at all." He smiles. "I fly all the time. You can have it."

I force a smile. "Thanks." That was code for "I know you got upgraded, you poor homeless person, and I feel sorry for you." I sit down in my seat and look nervously out the window, with my hands clasped in front of me on my lap.

"Are you going home?" he asks.

I turn to him. *Oh, please don't talk to me. You make me nervous just sitting there.* "No, I've been at a wedding, and I have a job interview in New York on the way home. I'm only there for the day, and then I fly out again to LA. I live there."

"Ah." He smiles. "I see."

I stare at him for a moment; I should ask him a question now. "Are . . . you going home?" I say.

"Yes."

I nod, unsure what to say next, so I choose the lame option and stare back out the window.

The attendant walks around with a bottle of champagne and glasses.

Glasses. Since when do airlines give you a real glass?

Oh right, first class. I knew that.

"Would you like some champagne to take off with, sir?" the flight attendant asks him. I notice that her name tag says JESSICA.

"That would be lovely." He smiles and turns to me. "Make that two, please."

I frown as she pours two glasses of champagne and passes one to him and one to me. "Thank you." I smile.

I wait for Jessica to move out of earshot. "Do you always order drinks for other people?" I ask.

He looks surprised by my statement. "Did it bother you?"

"Not at all," I huff. Damn this Mr. Fancy Pants for thinking he can order for me. "I do like to order my own drinks, though."

He smiles. "Well, you can order the next ones, then." He raises his glass to me and smirks; then he takes a sip. He seems amused by my annoyance.

I stare at him deadpan. This could be victim number two of my cutting today. I am not in the mood for some rich old bastard to boss me around. I sip my champagne as I look out the window. Well, he's not really old. Maybe mid- to late thirties. I mean, old compared to me; I'm twenty-five. But whatever.

"I'm Jim," he says as he holds his hand out to shake mine.

Oh God, now I have to be polite. I shake his hand. "Hi, Jim. I'm Emily."

His eyes dance with mischief. "Hello, Emily."

His eyes are big, bright blue, and dreamy, the kind I could get lost in. But why is he looking at me like that?

The plane begins to travel slowly down the runway, and I look between the earphones and armrest. Where do these plug in? They're high tech, the kind that overconfident YouTubers use. They don't even have a cord. I look around. *Well, this is stupid. How do I plug them in?*

"They're Bluetooth," Jim interrupts me.

6

"Oh," I mutter, feeling stupid. Of course they are. "Right."

"You haven't flown first class before?" he asks.

"No. I got an upgrade. Some weirdo threw my bag across the airport when he was drunk. I think the guy at the desk felt sorry for me." I give him a lopsided smile.

He rolls his lips as if amused and sips his champagne; his eyes linger on my face as if he has something on his mind.

"What?" I ask.

"Perhaps the guy at the desk thought you were gorgeous and upgraded you to try to impress you."

"I hadn't thought of that." I sip my champagne as I try to hide my smile. That's an odd thing to say. "Is that what you would do?" I ask. "If you were at the desk, would you upgrade women to impress them?"

"Absolutely."

I smirk.

"Impressing a woman you're attracted to is crucial," he continues.

I stare at him as I try to get my brain to keep up with the conversation. Why does that statement sound flirty? "And do tell . . . how would you impress a woman you're attracted to?" I ask, fascinated.

His eyes hold mine. "Offer her a window seat."

The air crackles between us, and I bite my lip to hide my goofy smile.

"You're trying to impress me?" I ask.

He gives me a slow, sexy smile. "How am I doing?"

I smirk, unsure what to say.

"I'm simply saying that you're attractive, nothing more and nothing less. Don't read into it. It was a statement, not a question."

"Oh." I stare at him, lost for words. What do I even say to that? Statement, not a question . . . huh? Don't read into it. This guy is weird . . . and utterly gorgeous.

The plane begins to take off with speed, and I hold on to my armrests and scrunch my eyes shut.

"You don't like takeoffs?" he asks.

"Do I look like I like takeoffs?" I wince as I hang on for dear life.

"I love them," he replies casually. "I love the feeling of power as it surges forward. That g-force throwback."

Okay . . . why is everything coming out of his mouth sounding sexual?

God, I need to get laid . . . stat.

I exhale and stare out the window as we go higher and higher. I don't have the energy for this guy to play cute today. I'm tired, I'm hungover, I look crappy, and my ex is a douche. I want to go to sleep and wake up next year.

I decide I'll watch a movie. I begin to flick through the choices on the screen in front of me.

He leans over and says, "Great minds think alike. I'm watching a movie too."

I fake a smile. *Just stop being all hot and in my space. You're probably married to a vegan yoga nut who does meditation and shit.*

"Great," I mutter deadpan. I should have flown coach; at least I wouldn't have had to inhale the scent of beautiful man for eight long, sexless hours.

I scroll through my screen and then narrow it down to my choices.

How to Lose a Guy in 10 Days.

Pride and Prejudice.

The Heat.

Jumanji . . . well, that has the Rock in it—it has to be good.

8

Notting Hill.
The Proposal.
50 First Dates.
Bridget Jones's Diary.
Pretty Woman.
Sleepless in Seattle.
Magic Mike XXL.

I smile at the choices, all of my favorites lined in a row; this flight is going to be a dream. I haven't seen the sequel to *Magic Mike* yet, so I might start with that one. I glance over to look at what Jim has picked, and I see the heading come up.

Lincoln.

Ugh . . . a political movie. Who watches that stuff for fun? I should have known he'd be boring.

He reaches up and taps the screen, and I catch sight of his watch. A chunky silver Rolex. Ugh, and he has money too.

Typical.

"What are you going to watch?" he asks.

Oh no . . . I don't want to appear ditzy. "I'm not sure yet," I reply. *Damn you . . . I want to watch men strip.* "What are you watching?" I ask.

"*Lincoln.* I've been meaning to see it for a long time."

"Sounds boring," I say.

He smiles at my answer. "I'll let you know." He puts his earphones on and begins to watch his movie, and I scroll through my choices again. I really want to watch *Magic Mike XXL.* Does it matter if he sees? No . . . that's just embarrassing. It makes me look desperate.

Who am I kidding? I am desperate. I haven't seen a dick in over a year.

I tap on *The Proposal.* I'll swap one fantasy for another. I've always dreamed of having Ryan Reynolds as my personal assistant.

The movie begins, and I smile at the screen. I love this movie. No matter how many times I watch it, I always laugh. Gammy is my favorite.

"You're watching a romance?" he asks.

"A rom-com," I reply. For God's sake, this guy is nosy.

He smirks as if he's better than me.

"More champagne?" the flight attendant asks.

Blue Eyes looks over at me. "Here's your chance to order for us."

I stare at him flatly; all right, he's beginning to piss me off now. "We'll have two, please."

"What do you like about rom-coms?" he asks as he keeps his eyes on the screen in front of him.

"Men who don't talk during movies," I whisper into my champagne glass.

He smiles broadly to himself.

"What do you like about . . ." I pause because I don't even know what *Lincoln* is about. "Political films?" I ask. "The fact that they're boring as all hell?"

"I just like true stories, regardless of what they are."

"So do I," I reply. "That's why I like romance. Love is true."

He chuckles into his glass as if amused.

I glance over at him. "What does that mean?"

"Rom-coms are as far from reality as you can get. I bet you're the type who reads trashy romance novels too."

I stare at him flatly. I think I hate this man. "I am, actually . . . and if you must know, I'm watching *Magic Mike XXL* after this so I can watch gorgeous men take their clothes off." I sip my champagne in annoyance. "And I'll smile through the whole damn thing, regardless of your snooty judgment."

He laughs out loud, and it's deep and strong and does things to my stomach.

I put my headphones back on and pretend to focus on my screen. I can't, though, because I just totally embarrassed myself, and I can feel myself blushing.

Stop talking.

Two hours later, I sit and stare out the window. My movie is over, but his scent is not. It's surrounding me, taunting me with things that I shouldn't be thinking about.

How does he smell so good?

Unsure what to do without seeming awkward, I decide I'll take a nap, try to sleep through the next few hours, but first I need to go to the bathroom. I stand. "Excuse me."

He moves his legs a little but not enough for me to fit through, and I have to lean over him to get past. I stumble and fall and put my hand on his thigh; it's large and hard to my touch. "I'm so sorry," I stammer, embarrassed.

"That's fine." He smirks up at me. "More than fine."

I stare at him for a moment. *Huh?*

"There's a method to my madness."

I frown. What does that mean? I make my way past him and go to the bathroom, and then I walk around and stretch my legs a little as I ponder that statement. I'm stumped—I've got nothing. "What did you mean by that?" I ask as I fall back into my seat.

"Nothing."

"Did you give me the window seat so I would have to climb over you?"

He tilts his head to the side. "No, I gave you the window seat because you wanted it. Climbing over me was just an added bonus."

I stare at him as I struggle to respond. Am I imagining this? Older rich guys don't usually speak to me like this . . . at all. "Are you flirting with me, Jim?" I ask.

He gives me a slow, sexy smile. "I don't know. Am I?"

"I asked you first, and don't answer my question with a question."

He smirks as he turns his attention back to the television screen. "This is probably where you should start flirting back . . . Emily."

I feel my cheeks flush with embarrassment as I try to hide my stupid smile. "I don't flirt. I either want a man or I don't," I announce.

"Is that so?" he says as if fascinated. "And how long after you meet a man do you make that decision?"

"Instantaneously," I lie. That's not true, but I'll pretend. Faking confidence is my superpower.

"Really?" he whispers as the flight attendant walks past us. "Excuse me, can we have two more champagnes, please?" he asks her.

"Of course, sir."

His eyes come back to meet mine. "Well, do tell. What was your first impression of me?"

I pretend to look around for Jessica the flight attendant. "You may need something stronger to drink to hear this, Jim. You're not going to like it."

He laughs out loud, and I find myself smiling broadly as I watch him.

"What's funny?" I ask.

"You are."

"Why am I funny?" I frown.

"This sense of righteousness that you have."

12

"Oh, like you don't have that too . . . Mr. I'll Have Two Champagnes."

Our drinks arrive, and he smiles as he passes mine to me. His eyes linger on my face as he takes a sip. "What were you doing in London?"

"Ugh." I roll my eyes. "I flew over for a friend's wedding, and to be honest, I wish I hadn't gone."

"Why not?"

"My ex was there with his new squeeze, and he was being over-the-top affectionate with her to piss me off."

"Which worked, obviously," he adds as he tilts his glass toward me.

"Hmm." I sip my drink in disgust. "Just a little."

"What did she look like?"

"Long bleached-blonde hair and huge silicone lips and boobs and eyelashes and fake tan and everything I'm not."

"Hmm." He listens intently.

"Like Backseat Barbie on crack."

He chuckles. "Everyone loves a Backseat Barbie."

I look over at him in disgust. "This is probably where you should tell me that all men hate Backseat Barbies, Jim. Don't you know anything about polite plane-conversation etiquette?"

"Obviously not." He frowns as he considers my statement. "Why would I do that?"

I widen my eyes to accentuate my point. "To be nice."

"Oh, right." He frowns as if bracing himself to lie. "Emily . . . all men are repulsed by Backseat Barbies."

I smile as I tip my glass to him. "Thank you, Jim."

"Although . . ." He pauses for a moment. "If they give good head . . ."

What the hell?

I snort my champagne up my nose and choke. That's the last thing I ever expected to hear come out of his mouth. "Jim," I splutter as it sprays everywhere.

He laughs as he grabs his napkins and hands them over, and I wipe the drink dribbling from my chin.

"Men who look like you are not supposed to talk about head." I cough.

"Why not?" he asks incredulously. "And what do you mean, men who look like me?"

"All serious and stuff."

He looks at me deadpan. "Define *stuff*."

"You know, older, rich, and bossy."

His eyes dance with delight. "And what gives you the impression that I'm rich and bossy?"

I exhale in an overexaggerated way. "You look rich."

"How do I?"

"Your fancy watch. The cut of your shirt." I glance down at his shoes. "I've never seen shoes like that before. Where did you even get those?"

"In a shop, Emily." He looks at his watch. "And I'll have you know that this watch was a gift from a girlfriend."

I roll my eyes. "I bet she's a vegan yoga nut."

He smirks.

"I know your type of woman."

"Really." He leans closer. "Please go on—this character analysis is fascinating."

I smile as a little voice from my subconscious screams, *Stop drinking, fool!* "I'm assuming you live in New York."

"Correct."

"In an apartment."

"Affirmative."

"You probably work at some ritzy company."

14

He smiles; he likes this game. "Perhaps."

"You would have a girlfriend or . . ." I glance down. "You don't wear a wedding ring . . . so perhaps you cheat on your wife when you travel for work?"

He chuckles. "You really should make a profession out of this. I'm amazed at the accuracy."

I like this game too; I smile broadly. "What do you think about me?" I ask. "What was your first impression when I walked onto the plane?"

"Well." He frowns as he considers the question. "Do you want the politically correct version?"

"No. I want the truth."

"Right . . . well, in that case, I noticed your long legs and the curve of your neck. The dimple in your chin. You are the most attractive woman I've seen in a long time, and when you smiled, it brought me to my feet."

I smile softly as the air swirls between us.

"And then you spoke . . . and ruined everything."

What?

I burst out laughing. "I ruined everything? How did I ruin everything?"

"You're bossy, with a sarcastic snark."

"What's the problem with that?" I stammer in outrage.

"Well, I'm bossy and sarcastic." He shrugs.

"And?"

"And I don't want to date myself. I like sweet, demure girls, the ones who do what I say."

"Ugh." I roll my eyes. "The ones who clean the house and have sex on Saturdays."

"Precisely."

I laugh and hold my glass up to clink with his. "You're not bad for a boring old guy with weird shoes."

He laughs. "And you're not bad for a young, hot smart-ass."

"Do you want to watch *Magic Mike XXL* with me?" I ask.

"I suppose, although I should let you know . . . I am an ex-stripper myself, so this is nothing new for me."

"Really?" I try to hide my smile. "You're good on a pole?"

His eyes hold mine. "My pole work is the best in the country."

The air crackles between us, and I have to concentrate on stopping my inebriated mouth from saying something slutty.

He pushes the screen and taps through to *Magic Mike XXL* . . . and I smile broadly. This man is so unexpected.

First class is definitely the way to fly.

Six hours later

"Okay, next question. The weirdest place you've ever had sex?" he whispers.

I smirk. "You can't ask me that."

"Yes, I can. I just did."

"It's rude."

"Says who?" He looks around. "It's just a question, and nobody is listening."

Jim and I have talked and whispered and laughed our way through the entire flight. "Hmm." I think out loud. "That's a tough one."

"Why?"

"I'm on a bit of a drought at the moment. I can hardly remember any sex."

"How long?" He frowns.

"Oh." I look to the ceiling as I think. "I haven't had sex in like . . . eighteen months."

His face falls in horror. "What?"

"It's lame, isn't it?" I wince.

"Very. You need to up your game. They're very bad statistics, indeed."

"I know." I giggle. Boy . . . we're so tipsy. "Why am I telling you all this stuff?" I whisper. "You're just some random guy I met on a plane."

"Who happens to be very interested in the subject."

"Why is that?"

He leans in and whispers to me so that the flight attendants can't hear us. "I don't understand how someone as hot as you doesn't get fucked three times a day."

I stare at him as I feel a tingle all the way to my toes. *Stop it.* This guy is too old for me and so not my type.

His eyes drop to my lips, and the air between us zaps with electricity.

"How long are you in New York?" he asks.

I watch his tongue dart out and lick his bottom lip in slow motion. I can almost feel it between my . . . "Just the afternoon. I have my interview at six tonight, and then I catch the last flight out," I whisper.

"Can you change your flight?"

Why? "No."

He smirks as he watches me, and it's obvious he's imagining something.

"What?" I smile.

"I wish we were on a private jet."

"Why is that?"

His eyes drop to my lips once more. "Because I'd break that drought of yours and initiate you into the Miles-High Club."

I get a visual of climbing on top of him, right here, right now. "It's Mile-High Club . . . not *Miles*," I whisper.

"No . . . it's Miles." He smirks as his eyes darken. "Trust me—it's Miles."

17

Something inside me snaps, and suddenly I want to say something crazy and out of the ordinary. I lean forward and whisper in his ear, "You know, I've never fucked a stranger before."

He inhales sharply as his eyes hold mine. "Do you want to fuck a stranger?" he murmurs as arousal thrums between us.

I stare at him. This is so out of character for me.

This man makes me . . .

"Don't be shy," he whispers. "Tell me, if we were alone right now . . ." He pauses as he chooses his words. "What would you give me, Emily?"

My eyes search his, and maybe it's the alcohol or the lack of sex or the fact that I know I'll never see him again . . . or perhaps I'm just a total ho. "Me," I breathe. "I would give you me."

Our eyes lock, and as if forgetting where we are, he leans forward and cups my face in his hand. His eyes are so blue, and a wave of arousal sweeps through me at his touch.

I want this man.

I want all of this man . . . every last drop.

"Hot towel?" Jessica the flight attendant asks.

We jump back from each other, embarrassed. What must they think of us? They've been watching us flirt shamelessly for the entire trip.

"Thank you," I stammer as I take the towel from her.

"There's a snowstorm in New York, and we're going to circle for a while to see if we can land," she says.

"What happens if we can't?" Jim asks.

"We will fly on to Boston and have an emergency layover for the night. You will be accommodated in a hotel, of course. We'll know in the next ten minutes. I'll keep you updated."

"Thank you."

She walks off to the other side of the plane and out of ear-shot, and Jim leans over and whispers, "I hope New York freezes the fuck over."

Nerves dance in my stomach. "Why is that?"

"I have plans for us," he whispers darkly.

I stare at him as my brain misfires. I've been prick teasing like a pro, but I'm really not that kind of girl. It's easy to be brave and slutty when there's no chance of anything happening. I begin to perspire. Why did I get so damn tipsy? Why did I tell him about my drought? *That's supposed to be kept private, fool.*

"Another drink?" Jim whispers.

"I can't—I have a job interview this afternoon."

"That won't be happening."

"Don't say that," I stammer. "I want this job."

"Good evening, passengers; this is the captain speaking." A voice comes over the loudspeaker, and I close my eyes. *Shit.*

"Due to a snowstorm in New York, we will be flying on to Boston tonight and staying there. We will return to New York early in the morning. Sorry for any inconvenience this has caused, but safety is our priority."

My eyes meet Jim's, and he gives me a slow and sexy smile and raises his eyebrow.

Oh no.

Chapter 2

"Don't look so excited." He smirks.

"Jim . . . ," I stammer. Oh hell, how do I say this? "I'm not really the kind of girl who . . ." My voice trails off.

"Who fucks on first dates?" he says, finishing my sentence.

"Yes." I wince at the crudeness of that statement. "I just don't want you to think . . ."

"I know. I wouldn't," he replies curtly. "I don't."

"Good." Relief fills me. "I was being flirty when I thought we were getting off and never seeing each other again."

"Right." He smirks in amusement.

"Not that I don't think you're great," I add. "Because if I were that kind of girl, I would totally be into you. We would be fucking like . . ." I pause as I try to think of an analogy.

"Rabbits?" he offers.

"Yes."

He holds both hands in the air. "I understand; platonic humans only."

I smile broadly. "I'm so glad you understand."

He slams me up against the wall as he struggles to pull my skirt up over my hips, and his open mouth ravages my neck. "Door," I pant. "Open the damn door."

Oh God . . . I've never felt this chemistry with anyone before. We've laughed and danced and kissed our way around Boston, and somehow he makes me feel at ease. It's as if I do this type of thing every day, and it's completely natural. The weird thing is, it feels right. The spontaneity of the situation I find myself in has me feeling all brave. This man is witty and funny and dirty as all hell, and in my opinion—which, in truth, could be totally screwed over with alcohol consumption at the moment—he's worth the risk . . . because I know I will never get the opportunity to be with a man like him again.

I've died and gone to layover bad-girl heaven.

Jim fumbles with the key, and we stumble into my room. Then he throws me onto the bed.

My chest rises and falls as we stare at each other, and the air between crackles with electricity.

"I'm not this kind of girl," I remind him.

"I know," he breathes. "I wouldn't want to corrupt you."

"But there is a drought," I whisper. "So . . . so dry."

He raises his eyebrows as he pants along with me. "This is true."

I stare at him for a moment as I try to clear my arousal fog. My sex is throbbing and pleading for his body. "It would be a shame to . . ." My voice trails off.

"I know." He licks his lips in appreciation as his eyes roam over my body. "Such a fucking shame."

He takes his shirt off over his shoulders, and my breath catches. He has a broad, muscular chest with olive skin and a scattering of hair that runs from his navel and disappears down into his pants. His hair is dark, and his eyes are a brilliant blue—but it's the power behind them that has me aching for him to take me. There's an edge to his touch that I've never felt before.

He's all male and pure domination. There's no mistaking who's in charge here.

Something about this man has opened up another side of me that I didn't know existed. I know he could have any woman in the world he wants.

And at this moment, he wants me.

There's no denying the chemistry between us; it's raw, honest, and all-consuming. He's hardly touched me, and I already know that this night is special.

Maybe fate has dealt me an ace for a change.

With his eyes locked on mine and in slow motion, he unzips his pants and pulls his dick out. It's big and hard, and my chest rises and falls as I watch him. My heart is in overdrive. Is this really happening?

Oh. My. God.

He begins to slowly stroke himself, and my mouth falls open as I stare, transfixed.

I've never had a man touch himself in front of me before.

Holy fucking shit. This is off the hook.

He lifts one of his feet to the bed and really begins to let himself have it. The muscles in his shoulders and arms flex as he jerks himself hard, and my insides ripple in pleasure as I imagine it's me doing it for him.

This is like reality porn . . . only ten times better.

What the hell am I doing here? I'm a good girl, and good girls don't do bad things with men like this.

We don't know the same people, we don't live in the same city, and I may never see him again, and there's an unexpected freedom in that. I can be different.

Whoever he wants me to be.

His eyes are locked on mine, and his jaw clenches. "Get over here and suck my cock, Emily," he murmurs darkly.

God, yes. I thought he'd never ask. I scurry to my knees, desperate to please him.

I don't know anything about this guy, but I do know that at this moment, I want to be the best sex he's ever had. I take him in my mouth as I pretend to be the deep-throat champion of the world. I fist him hard as my hand follows my lips.

It's been so long, and I feel my sex clench, my orgasm close just from the taste of his preejaculate.

"Fuck . . . so good," I murmur around him. "The taste of you is going to make me come."

He tips his head back to the sky and closes his eyes. "Naked. I need you fucking naked," he growls with urgency. He drags me off the bed and in one moment has my skirt and panties on the floor. He pulls my shirt off over my head and throws my bra to the side.

Then he stops still . . . and in slow motion, with his hands clenched by his sides, his eyes drop down my body. He drinks me in, and I feel the heat as his gaze skims my skin.

My world stops spinning, and I stand before him naked and vulnerable, waiting for his approval.

This is new for me. I've never been with a man who's so dominant and commanding. His eyes, his voice, his every touch reminds me of who I am with and how much his pleasure means to me.

I feel like I want to rise to the challenge, and the primal urge to satisfy him is taking me over.

When his eyes meet mine again, they're blazing with desire. An undercurrent of darkness and tenderness runs between us. Perhaps I've forgotten how a man looks at a woman when every ounce of his being wants her. Because I swear to God, I've never seen this look before in my life.

"On your back," he murmurs.

My face falls in fear.

He takes me in his arms and kisses me deeply as he holds my face in his hands. "What is it?" he breathes.

"It's . . . it's been a long time," I pant.

"I'll take care of you, baby," he whispers softly, which eases my fears. His mouth takes mine, his tongue slowly sliding through my open lips with just the right amount of suction.

My knees nearly buckle underneath me.

He lays me down and spreads my legs and smiles darkly as he kisses his way down my body.

I stare at the ceiling as I try to control my erratic breathing; no amount of alcohol could have prepared me for this. He lifts my legs and puts my feet onto his strong shoulders and then drops my knees wide.

I am completely open for him, and he takes me with no reservations and sucks hard.

I buck off the bed. "Ah!" I cry.

But he gives me no mercy as he drives three of his thick fingers into my sex and begins to pump me hard.

Shit . . . can't we ease into it, at least?

His tongue is on my clitoris, and his fingers are on my G-spot. *What the actual hell is going on here?* My body begins to quiver like a puppet . . . his puppet.

The man's a god.

My legs lift off his shoulders by themselves, and I convulse as a freight train of an orgasm rips through me.

That took approximately five seconds. *Oh hell. How embarrassing. Way to act cool.* He chuckles as if he's proud, and I throw the back of my forearm over my eyes to hide my face in shame.

He pulls my arm away and takes my jaw in his hand and drags my face back to his. "Don't hide from me, Emily. Not ever," he commands.

My eyes search his. This is too full on . . . too much. This guy is too intense.

"Answer me."

"What do you want me to say?" I whisper.

"Say yes so that I know you understand."

The air crackles between us. "Yes," I breathe. "I understand."

"Good girl," he whispers as he leans in and kisses me again. His tongue is soft stroking perfection, and my legs open by themselves once more. He gets up and takes four condoms from his wallet, opens one, and hands it to me. "Put it on me."

I take it from him and bend to kiss him softly on his dick before I roll the condom on. "You're very bossy." I smirk.

He smiles broadly as he falls onto his back, pulls me over him, and drags my face to his. "You'll fuck me first," he murmurs against my lips, "and then I'll fuck you when you're warmed up."

I smile against his mouth. "I only fuck once, big boy, and then I fall asleep."

He gives me a slow, sexy smile.

I straddle his large body as our kisses become desperate. His thick cock is up against his stomach, and he holds it in the air and guides my hips down over him.

Oh, the burn—he's big.

"Ow," I whimper.

"It's okay," he whispers. "Wiggle from side to side."

He cups my breasts in his hands as he stares up at me in what seems like awe.

25

I smile down at him. "What?"

"From the moment I saw you on the plane today, I wanted you riding my cock."

I giggle down at him. "Do you always get what you want?"

"Always." He grabs my hips and slams me down, and our mouths fall open in pleasure.

Oh . . . he's . . .

"So fucking tight," he grinds out.

With our eyes locked, he slowly moves me up and down, and I can feel every vein on his thick shaft.

His eyes are hooded as he looks up at me, and I lean forward and kiss him softly. "Do you know how perfect you feel inside me?" I whisper, and then I lick his open mouth.

His eyes roll back in his head. "You are one hot fuck." He picks me up by the hip bones and slams me back down on his cock, and I laugh out loud at the overwhelming sensation of being filled to the hilt.

"God, fill me up," I moan. "Give it to me," I beg. I love how he's losing control. It's making me crazy. And then as if in some kind of alternate universe, my mouth latches on to his neck, and I suck hard as I ride him.

He hisses, and as if he's completely losing control, he bucks me off and pulls out and throws me onto my back. He lifts my legs over his shoulders and slams in deep—so deep that the air is knocked from my lungs.

I smile. So he likes dirty talk, does he? Well, that just happens to be my specialty.

Game on.

I hold his face in my hands. "God, you've got a beautiful cock," I whisper. "Is it weeping for me, baby?" I whisper as I clench around him. "I can feel your pulse in it."

He gives me a slow, sexy smile as he pumps me. "I'm going to rip this condom off and blow in your dirty mouth in a minute."

"Please." I laugh as he pumps me hard, and in a moment of perfect clarity, he turns his head and tenderly kisses my inner ankle. We stare at each other as something intimate runs between us. A closeness that the reality of the situation shouldn't allow. "Don't look at me like that," I whisper to break the seriousness of the moment, "or I'm going to give you another hickey."

His eyes widen. "I better not have a fucking hickey, Emily."

I laugh out loud as I look at the huge purple welt rising on his neck. *God, what the hell?* I've been reading way too many vampire romances. "Will you be in trouble with your mother?" I tease.

He laughs and slams into me and hits just the right spot, and I moan. Oh . . . this man knows his way around a woman's body.

Every touch is perfectly placed and magnified. He knows exactly how to take me apart at the seams. He lifts my hip with his hand and circles deep, and my body takes on its own agenda because I need to come. Hard.

"Fuck me," I beg. "Give me that beautiful cock of yours. Harder," I moan. "Fuck, I need it harder."

His eyes close in pleasure, and he pumps me at piston pace. I grab on to him as tightly as I can as I convulse. He holds himself deep and cries out into my neck, and I feel his cock jerk as it releases.

We pant as we cling to each other, wet with perspiration, our hearts racing wildly together, and he smiles up against my cheek as if remembering something.

"What?"

"Welcome to the Miles-High Club, Emily."

I giggle as I kiss him. "First class is the only way to fly."

Jim smiles sexily down at me as I lie naked in bed. He's dressed, and his bag is packed and by the door. "I have to go."

I screw up my face and hold out my arms. "No, don't leave me," I tease in a whiny voice.

He chuckles as he bends and takes me into his arms one last time. We're not on the same plane back to New York this morning; his flight leaves early, and mine leaves late. He kisses me softly. "What a night," he whispers.

I smile as his head drops to the crook of my neck, his teeth nipping down toward my collarbone. "I won't be walking for a month—actually, a year," I mutter dryly.

He bends and bites my nipple hard, and I jump. Then he comes back up, and his eyes meet mine.

I cup his handsome face. "I had an incredible night."

He smiles softly. "Me too."

I reach up and put my finger on the huge hickey on his neck, and his fingers go to it too. "What the fuck were you thinking?"

"I have no idea what came over me." I giggle. "Your dick was too good, turned me into an animal."

He bites me again. "How am I supposed to get on a plane with a huge-ass hickey on my neck?" he scolds. "If you knew how many important meetings I have this week, Emily . . ."

We both laugh, and then his face falls as he watches me. I'm not joking—I don't want him to leave me. This man is everything I'm not looking for, but he's somehow ticking every box.

What if I never see him again?

How am I supposed to move on from a night like this, erase it from my memory bank, and pretend it never happened? I close my eyes in disgust with myself. This is why I don't do one-night stands. I'm not cut out for sex without strings—it's not who I am. I will never be that person.

I hate that he is.

"Actually, I have a scarf in my bag. Do you want it?" I ask.

"Yes," he snaps.

I climb out of bed and go to my suitcase and begin to rummage through it. He takes the opportunity and stands behind me and grabs my naked hip bones in his hands and pumps me with his hips. I stand and turn to face him. "I'm not even joking now—stay another night."

He traces his finger down my face and cups my jaw in his hand as our eyes lock.

"I can't," he whispers, his eyes searching mine . . . with something unspoken.

Does he have someone at home? Is that why he hasn't asked for my number? Uneasiness fills me. I'm not made for this one-night stand crap.

I turn my back on him and dig out the scarf and hand it over. It's cream and cashmere, and it's initialed.

E.F.

My mother's tennis group gave it to me as a gift when I finished college. I did love it . . . but oh well.

He frowns as he looks down at the embroidered letters, and I take it from him and wrap it around his neck to cover the huge purple bruise. I smirk as I look at it. I didn't even know how to give a hickey. I must have really been in the moment.

"What does the *F* stand for?" he asks.

"Fuck bunny." I smile to cover my disappointment. I don't want him to know that his last comment upset me.

He chuckles and grabs me roughly into his arms and walks me back toward the bed. "What an apt description that is." He takes my leg and wraps it around his waist, and we share one last lingering kiss.

"Goodbye, my beautiful fuck bunny," he whispers.

I run my fingers through his hair as I stare at his gorgeous face. "Goodbye, Blue Eyes."

He picks the scarf up and inhales deeply. "This smells like you."

"Put it on every time you jerk off." I smile sweetly. "Imagine it's me doing all the work."

His eyes flicker with excitement. "You know, for someone who hasn't had sex for eighteen months, you're a fucking sex maniac."

I giggle. "I'll go back to my drought now. It's safe there . . . and I can walk unassisted."

His face falls, and I feel like he wants to say something but is stopping himself.

"You're going to miss your plane." I fake a smile.

We kiss once more, and I hold him tight, and God, he really is incredible.

He stands, and with one last lingering look at me lying naked in the bed, he turns and walks out.

I smile sadly at the door he just left through. "Yes, sure, you can have my number," I whisper into the silence.

But he didn't want it. He's gone.

Twelve months later

I exhale and put my hand over my heart as I stand on the curbside and look up at the glass skyscraper in front of me. My phone rings, and the name *Mom* lights up the screen. "Hello, Mom." I smile. I get a vision of my beautiful mother. She has a perfect blonde bob and flawless skin, and she's always immaculately dressed. If I can look half as good as her at her age, I will be winning at life. I miss her already.

"Oh, darling, I just called to wish you good luck."

"Thank you." I tap my toe, unable to stand still. "I'm so nervous I was throwing up this morning."

"They're going to love you, dear."

"Oh God." I exhale heavily. "I hope so. It took me six damn interviews to get this job, and I had to move across the country for it." I screw up my face in fear. "Have I done the right thing, Mom?"

"Yes, love, this job is your dream, and besides, you needed to get away from Robbie. The distance from him will do you good."

I roll my eyes. "Mom, don't bring Robbie into it."

"Darling, you're dating a man who is unemployed and lives in his parents' garage. I don't understand what you see in him."

"He's just between jobs at the moment." I sigh.

"Then if he's got nothing going on here, why wouldn't he move to New York with you?"

"He doesn't like New York. It's too busy for him."

"Oh, Emily, can you hear the excuses you make for this man? If he loved you, he would be there supporting your dream, since he doesn't have any of his own."

I exhale heavily. I've been thinking these things myself, but no way in hell would I admit it to anyone.

"Are you calling me to stress me out about Robbie, or are you calling me to wish me luck?" I snap.

"I'm calling you to wish you luck. Good luck, darling. Go and show them what you're made of."

I jiggle on the spot nervously as I look at the towering building above me. "Thanks."

"I'll call you tonight for a full debrief."

"Okay." I smile. "I'm going to go in."

"Go get 'em, tiger." She hangs up.

I stare up at the building and at the fancy gold letters over the large double front doors.

MILES MEDIA

I exhale and drop my shoulders. "Right. You can do this."

This is the opportunity of all opportunities. Miles Media is the biggest conglomerate media empire in the United States and one of the largest in the world, with over two thousand staff based in New York alone. My fascination with journalism started in the eighth grade when I witnessed a car accident on my way home from school one day. Because I was the only witness, I had to give a statement to the police, and then when it turned out that the car was stolen, the local paper came and interviewed me. I felt like a rock star that day, and the shine never dulled. I've been to college to study journalism and done internships with the best companies in the United States. But it was Miles Media that I had my heart set on. Their stories are a cut above the rest; no other media company would do. I've applied for every position that has come up for three years and only recently got a callback. And even then, I went to six interviews before I was offered the job, and God, just don't let me screw this up.

I take out my security card and put the lanyard around my neck, and I glance down at my phone.

No missed calls. Robbie didn't even call me to wish me luck. *Ugh, men.*

I make my way to reception. The security guard at the front desk accepts my identification, and I am given a code to work the elevator. My heart is beating so fast as I get into the elevator with all the beautiful posh-looking people, and I push the button for the fortieth floor. I glance over at myself in the mirrored doors. I'm wearing a black pencil skirt that hangs to midcalf, sheer black stockings with patent leather high heels, and a cream long-sleeved silk blouse. I wanted to look professional and elegant. I'm not sure if I pulled it off, but here's hoping. I pull my hand through my thick dark ponytail as the elevator flies higher and higher. I take a side glance at the others in the elevator. The men are all in expensive suits, and the women are ultraprofessional and wearing full faces of makeup.

Damn it, I should have worn bright lipstick. I'll buy one on my lunch break. The doors open on the fortieth floor, and I stride out as if I don't have a fear in the world.

Faking confidence is my superpower, and today I'm totally faking it till I make it.

Or at least die trying.

"Hello." I smile at the kind-looking woman standing by reception. "I'm Emily Foster. I'm starting today."

She smiles broadly. "Hello, Emily, my name is Frances, and I am one of the floor managers." She steps over to me and shakes my hand. "Lovely to meet you."

Well, she seems nice.

"Come through, and I'll show you to your desk." She walks off, and I peer into the huge office space. The tables are grouped into lots of four or six with partitions separating them from the others. "As you know, each floor of this building is a different arm of the company," she says as she walks. "We have internationals and magazines from floor twenty down. Floors thirty to forty are news and current affairs, and above forty are television and cable."

I nod nervously.

"The two top levels of the building are senior management only, and your security card won't get you up there. It's customary for new employees to be taken on a guided tour of the building, and Lindsey from human resources will come and get you at two o'clock this afternoon."

"Okay, great." I smile as I feel my confidence seep out into the carpet. God, this is all so professional.

"Most people start on level four and work their way up the building, so congratulations for starting on level forty. That in itself is amazing." She smiles broadly.

"Thank you," I reply nervously.

She leads me over to a group of four desks by the window and pulls out a chair. "This is your desk."

"Oh." I feel the blood drain from my face. I've totally bitten off more than I can chew here. I fall into my seat as panic begins to rise in my stomach.

"Hello," a man says as he sits in the seat beside me. "I'm Aaron." He reaches over and shakes my hand with a broad smile. "You must be Emily."

"Hi, Aaron," I whisper, feeling totally inadequate.

"I'll leave you in Aaron's safe hands." Frances smiles.

"Thank you."

"Have a great day." She returns to reception.

And I stare at the computer on my desk as my heart begins to beat violently.

"Are you excited?" Aaron asks.

"Oh my God, I'm petrified," I whisper as I turn to him. "I've never done this job before. I usually find the stories with my group."

He smiles warmly. "Don't worry; we all felt the same when we started, but they wouldn't have given you the job if they didn't think you could do it."

I give him a lopsided smile. "I just don't want to let anyone down."

He reaches over and puts his hand on top of mine. "You won't. This team is great, and we help each other."

I glance down at his hand on mine.

"Oh." He pulls it away as he notices my discomfort. "I'm totally gay and way too touchy, apparently. Tell me if I get in your space. I have no sphere of reference."

I smile, grateful for his honesty. "Okay." I look around the office as people file in. "How long have you worked here?"

"Four years. I love it." He shivers his shoulders to accentuate his point. "Best job I've ever had. I moved from San Fran for it."

"I moved from California." I smile proudly.

"You here by yourself?" he asks.

"Yeah." I shrug. "I got a little one-bedroom apartment. I arrived on Friday."

"What did you do all weekend?" he asks.

"Freaked out about today."

He laughs. "Don't worry. We've all been there."

I look around at the two other empty chairs. "Who else do we work with?"

"Molly." He points to the chair behind me. "She doesn't start until nine thirty. She's a single mom and has to get her kids off to school first."

I smile; I like that.

"And Ava—she's just late because she probably went out last night partying."

35

I smile.

He rolls his eyes. "She's a deplorable party girl, and she's never at her desk—always finds somewhere she has to be."

"Hello," a girl says as she runs up the aisle and sits down in her chair. She's panting and holds out her hand. "I'm Ava."

I shake her hand and smile. "I'm Emily."

Ava is younger than me and very attractive, with a honey-colored bob and dramatic makeup. She's trendy and very New York.

"Open up your computer, Emily, and I'll show you through our programs," Aaron says.

"Okay," I reply as I concentrate on my task.

"Oh my God, Aaron," Ava says. "I met the hottest fucking guy last night."

"Here we go." Aaron sighs. "You meet the hottest fucking guy every night."

I find myself smiling as I listen to them.

"No, seriously, this time I mean it."

I glance over at Aaron, and he smirks at me and rolls his eyes as if he's heard it all before.

She gets to work, and Aaron goes through and explains the programs as I take notes. "At ten o'clock the stories will start coming in."

I listen intently.

"We, as reporters, go through them and all say yay or nay as to whether it's got legs and if we go and report on it."

I frown. "But how will I know that?"

"We just vote yes for stuff that interests us, I suppose," Ava says. "Obviously, news stories that are breaking are crucial, but it's the other content that they pay us for."

She reads an email. "For example, three coffee shops have closed down in one week within two blocks from each other." She rolls her eyes. "Honestly, who gives a fuck? This isn't news."

I giggle.

"Here's one." Aaron reads out, "A driver has been clocked traveling at one hundred fifty-five miles per hour, and he ran a police stop sign. He was involved in a hot pursuit and ended up crashing into parked cars in Brooklyn."

Ava nods. "Yeah, that's good."

"We'll go with that." He types something and puts the file into a saved folder.

"So how does this work?" I ask.

"We collect stories, and then we discuss collectively what each of us has done and put together a list of stories. You research your stories and have them in by four each day for the next day's news. Then we send them on to Hayden, and he sends them to editing. Obviously, if a good story comes in, it will take priority over everything else, and it will go to live news immediately."

I frown as I listen. "So we each get our own stories and leads sent to us?"

"Yes, by email. By others on this level."

I glance around at all the workers surrounding us.

"We keep our finger on the pulse of what sells and what news really is," Ava replies. "It's the coolest job ever."

I smile. Maybe I really can do this.

"Open your emails." Aaron reaches over and opens something for me on my computer, and then I watch as it keeps pinging.

"Those are all possible stories?" I frown.

"Yes." He throws me a playful wink. "Get reading, baby. They come in thick and fast."

I smile as excitement runs through me.

"Just make sure you get story details right. Nothing pisses management off more than incorrect names. You will get into huge trouble."

"Got it."

I've just gotten back from lunch when my phone rings. "Hi, Emily, this is Lindsey from human resources. I'll be up in about five minutes to get you," the kind voice says on the phone.

I wince. Oh, that's right—I have that damn building tour. "Okay, thank you." I hang up. "Oh no, I have to go on the office tour," I whisper to my colleagues.

"That's okay," Aaron replies as he continues reading his emails.

"I've got so many leads," I stammer. "I can't keep up."

"Don't worry. It's fine," he comforts me.

"What if I miss a really important story?"

"You won't—it's fine. I'll go through yours while you're gone."

"Really?"

"Of course it is. You aren't expected to know everything on day one."

"Oh no, you have to go to the top." Ava grimaces.

"What's the top?" I ask.

"Upper-management offices."

"They're not nice?"

"No, they're fucking horrible, and you have a good chance of being fired on the spot."

"What?"

"Oh, bullshit." Aaron rolls his eyes. "They just don't . . ." He screws up his face as he chooses his words. "They don't fluff. If something is going to be said, they just say it how it is. They don't take any shit from anyone."

"Who are they?" I whisper.

"Well, Mr. Miles won't be there. He never is. I think he's in London."

"Mr. Miles?" I ask as I feel my nerves dance.

"The CEO."

"Yes, I know who he is. I think everyone does. Although I've never seen a picture of him. It's him and his brothers, right?"

"Yes, it's the Miles family who owns everything. He and his three brothers."

"And they're all upstairs?" I whisper as I quickly take out the bright lipstick I bought at lunch and reapply. I need some courage here.

"Just don't say anything stupid up in the management levels," Ava says.

My eyes widen. "Like what? What do they consider stupid?" I'm really beginning to panic.

"Just keep your mouth shut, take the tour, and don't tell HR anything."

"Why not?"

"Because they're on speed dial to the management levels. This whole tour you're taking now is just so they can do a personality assessment on you in the two hours it takes them to show you around."

"Oh my God." I sigh.

"Hi, Emily, is it? I'm Lindsey."

I turn to see a beautiful blonde, and I stand immediately and put out my hand. "Hello."

She smiles at my coworkers. "Let's get started. We will go down to level one and work our way up."

I give my new work friends a nervous wave and follow her out of the office and into the elevator.

Here we go.

An hour and a half later

"And this is the gymnasium, for our staff's own personal use."

I look around at the expansive and swanky-looking gym on level sixty. "Wow."

"It's open from six in the morning until six thirty at night. It's busiest before work, obviously, but you can come here on your lunch break also. A lot of people take a late or early lunch so that it's not as busy when they come."

This place is ridiculous. A cafeteria on level two that is the entire floor, a movie theater, a gymnasium, a mailroom floor, a computer geek floor. Everything has been thought out with such care.

"Okay, let's get going." Lindsey smiles. "We will head up to the management floors now."

My stomach dances with nerves as we head back into the elevator.

She gets in and looks at the buttons. "Oh look, you're in luck."

I frown in question.

"Mr. Miles is here."

I fake a smile.

"I'll take you to meet him first."

Oh God.

Don't speak. Don't say anything stupid, I remind myself. I twist my fingers in front of me nervously as we ride to the top floor. The doors open, and I step out of the elevator and stop still.

What the hell?

White marble for as far as I can see, floor-to-ceiling glass, and luxurious white leather furnishings. "Hello, Sammia." Lindsey smiles as I look around in awe. This place is insane.

A beautiful woman looks up from her computer at reception, and she smiles warmly. "Hello, Lindsey."

"This is Emily. She's new and started on level forty today."

Sammia comes around and shakes my hand. "Lovely to meet you, Emily."

"Is Mr. Miles taking visitors?" Lindsey asks.

"He is." She smiles. "I'll just announce you."

Announce me . . . jeez.

Lindsey hunches her shoulders as if she's nervous too.

Sammia picks up the phone. "Mr. Miles, we have a new staff member to meet you in reception." She listens for a moment and smiles. "Yes, sir." She puts the phone down. "Just go in."

"This way, Emily." Lindsey directs me across a huge boardroom, and my heels click on the marble. Why don't Lindsey's shoes click?

Okay, buy rubber-soled shoes tomorrow.

We get to the end of the huge room and down another corridor, and my heels are clicking like I don't know what. They're even annoying me. I sound like a horse. I feel like taking them off and throwing them in the trash. *Just be quiet. I'm trying to appear professional here.*

We get to a set of black double doors, and Lindsey knocks as my heart pounds in my chest.

Just . . . don't say anything stupid.

"Come in," a deep voice calls.

Lindsey opens the doors, and I step into the office.

Familiar blue eyes rise to meet mine from behind the large mahogany desk, and I stop dead still.

What?

"Emily Foster, I would like to introduce you to Mr. Miles," Lindsey says.

I stare at him, unable to speak because there's no air in my lungs.

His eyebrow rises, and he sits back in his chair as he smirks. "Hello, Emily." His big eyes hold mine, the same beautiful deep-blue eyes that hypnotized me twelve months ago.

It's him.

41

Chapter 3

Oh my God.

He stands and walks around to my side of the desk and holds his hand out to shake mine. "Jameson Miles."

It's him, the layover guy who never asked for my number. I stare at him as my brain completely misfires.

I can't believe this. He's the fucking CEO?

"Emily, tell Mr. Miles all about yourself," Lindsey says, as if to prompt me to speak.

"Oh." I catch myself and shake his hand. "I'm Emily Foster."

His hand is strong and warm, and I'm instantly reminded how it felt on my skin. I pull my hand out of his grip as if he's given me an electric shock.

His mischievous eyes hold mine, and he keeps his face straight. "Welcome to Miles Media," he says calmly.

"Thanks," I croak. I look over at Lindsey. *Oh God, does she know I'm a dirty-talking whore bag who fucked our boss's boss's boss?*

"I'll take it from here, Lindsey. Emily will be out in a moment," Mr. Miles states.

Lindsey frowns and looks over at me. "I'll just—"

"Wait outside," he says as he dismisses her.

Shit.

"Yes, sir," she says as she scurries for the door. It closes behind her, and I drag my eyes back to him.

He's tall, with dark hair, and he's wearing the most perfectly fitted navy suit in the history of all suits. His blue eyes hold mine. "Hello, Emily."

I twist my fingers in front of myself nervously. "Hi."

He never asked for your number.

Screw him.

I tilt my chin to the ceiling as I act brave. I didn't want him to call me anyway.

His eyes blaze, and he rests his behind on his desk and crosses his feet in front of him. I glance down at his shoes. I remember those pretentious expensive shoes.

"Given any poor unsuspecting travel companions hickeys lately?" he asks.

Oh hell on a broomstick—he remembers. I feel my face flush with embarrassment. I can't believe I did that. *Shit, shit, shit.* "Yes, just last night, actually." I pause for effect. "On my flight here."

His jaw clenches, and he raises his eyebrow, unimpressed.

"So you're not Jim?" I ask.

"To some people I'm Jim."

"Women you pick up for one-night stands, you mean."

He crosses his arms in front of him as if annoyed. "What's with the attitude?"

"I don't have an attitude," I fire back.

He raises his eyebrow again, and I feel like slapping it down to his chin. I look around his over-the-top luxurious office. It's ridiculous, with a 360-degree view out over New York. It has a large lounge area with a fully stocked bar and leather stools lined up in front of it and a conference table area. I can see a hallway with a private bathroom, and then another few rooms are off that.

He runs his fingertips over his bottom lip as he assesses me, and I feel it all the way to my toes. *God, he's so gorgeous.* I've thought of him often over the last year.

"What are you doing in New York?" he asks.

"Working for Miles Media." A thought crosses my mind, and I frown as I remember something he said to me back then.

Welcome to the Miles-High Club . . .

Dear God, I thought he meant sex-in-a-plane club . . . he meant women who had slept with him.

Miles . . . *he's* the Miles . . . and there's a club?

Damn it, the hottest sex of my life was just an initiation into some sleazy bedpost club.

For the past twelve months, the night that we spent together was something special that I held dear. He awakened something inside me that I didn't even know existed, and now I find out that I'm one of many. My heart drops in disappointment, and I clench my jaw to stop myself from lashing out to try to hurt him back.

Bastard.

I've got to get out of here before I get myself fired on my first day.

"Nice to see you again." I fake a smile, and with my heart beating hard in my chest, I turn and walk out of his office and close the door behind me.

"All done?" Lindsey smiles.

"Yes." I nod.

We walk out through reception and into the elevator and begin to go back down to my level. "Don't feel rattled," Lindsey says softly.

I frown over at her in question.

"He's very abrasive and not good with people, but his mind is beyond incredible."

Like his dick.

"Oh, okay," I reply as I stare at the ground. "Good to know."

"Did he say anything to you?"

"No," I lie. "Just polite chitchat."

She smiles. "You should feel very privileged. Jameson Miles doesn't make polite chitchat with anyone."

"Oh." I frown. The door opens, and I scurry out to evade this conversation. "Thank you so much for showing me around."

"You're welcome, and if you have any human resource issues, please call me immediately."

"I will." I shake her hand. Does being initiated into the Miles dick-riding club classify as a human resource issue? "Thank you so much." I take off in the direction of my desk, and I discreetly grab my phone from my drawer. "Back in a moment." I head to the bathroom and bang the stall door open and lock it. Then in the privacy of the bathroom, I type into Google: *Jameson Miles.*

I close my eyes as I wait for the information to load. My heart is hammering in my chest. *Please don't be married . . . please don't be married.*

I've beat myself up over this for the last year, and it's played on my mind as to why he didn't even pretend to want my number. I felt like we had a connection, but there was something he didn't tell me. And for some reason, afterward, I got the feeling he was married . . . or in a relationship.

And that makes me a dirty ho. I've never been with a person who is in a committed relationship to someone else, and women who knowingly do that make me sick.

If I had known how much it was going to play on my mind, I wouldn't have gone near him that night.

Jameson Grant Miles is an American businessman and investor. Aged 37, Miles is the eldest son of media mogul George Miles Jr. and the grandson of George Miles Sr. In 2012, he inherited control of the family empire, Miles Media Holdings Ltd., as well as investments in television, film, and multiple other companies. He is the former executive chairman of Publishing and Consolidated Media Holdings, which predominantly owns media interests across a range of platforms, and also a former executive chairman of Netflix.

In May 2018, Miles's net worth was assessed as $5.50 billion, ranking him among the top 100 richest Americans, alongside his three brothers.

Oh hell. I read on.

Personal life.

Fiercely private, he is known for a penchant for beautiful women. He dated Claudia Mason from 2011 to 2015 and has had no known personal relationships since.

I put my hand on my chest and breathe out in relief. Thank God. I click on the link for Claudia Mason. Who is she? A barrage of images comes up, and I feel my confidence run down the drain.

Claudia Mason is an English businesswoman and fashion icon. Aged 34.

Mason is a British journalist. She is the editor-in-chief of the British edition of Vogue *and also the youngest editor in the history of British* Vogue. *She took the helm of* Vogue *in 2014. Mason is one of the country's most oft-quoted voices on fashion trends. In addition to her work with* Vogue, *Mason has written columns for Miles Media and has ten published books.*

Personal life.

Mason is the eldest of five children and is the daughter of French politician Marcel Angelo.

She dated and was engaged to media heir Jameson Miles from 2011 to 2015, but the relationship broke down and ended, which she cited was due to their individual workloads and commitments on different sides of the world. She is currently dating Edward Schneider, a solicitor who resides in London.

Engaged . . . they were engaged?

I exhale heavily and click out of my search in disgust. Of course he dated her.

Well, that's depressing. She's the damn editor of British *Vogue*. I can't compete with that shit. It took me three whole years to get a crappy job at Miles Media. I wash my hands and fix my hair in the mirror. Not that it matters anyway, I guess.

I have a boyfriend, and Jameson Miles is nothing to me. I storm back to my desk with a fire in my belly. I won't even see him. I fall into my seat.

"How was the tour?" Aaron asks.

"Yeah, good." I smile as I open my email.

"Did you go up to the top levels?"

"Uh-huh." I begin to glance through my five thousand emails that arrived in the two hours since I left. *Jeez, there's a lot of news around here.*

"What about the offices?" Aaron replies. "They're something else, right? All that white marble."

I roll my lips as I try to act casual. "Uh-huh."

"I didn't get to see the management offices when I started," Molly says. "He wasn't taking visitors that day."

I glance over at her.

"I went into his office, but he wasn't there," Aaron chimes in.

"Who? Jameson, you mean?" I pretend to be uninterested in this conversation.

"Yeah, did you see him at all?"

"Yep." I open an email. "I met him." *I fucked his brains out too.*

"Was he a rude pig?" Molly frowns. "Everyone is so scared of him."

"No, he seemed fine. I was in his office, and he seemed okay."

"You were in his office while he was there?" Aaron frowns.

"Uh-huh." I keep typing. *Please stop talking about him.*

47

"What are you guys doing tonight?" Molly asks. "The kids are with their dad, and I could do with pizza and beer. Screw the diet and the gym."

"Yeah, I'm in," Aaron replies.

"Really?" I smile. I can't believe they are asking me out on my first day.

"Yeah, why not? Do you have anything else going on?" Molly asks.

"Well, seeing as you two are the only people I know in New York, what else could I possibly have going on?" I shrug happily.

"Pizza and beer it is," Molly replies as she continues typing.

I begin to scroll back through my email list, and the name *Jameson Miles* pops up as a sender.

What?

I glance around guiltily and click to open it. It's probably a welcome email sent to everyone.

Emily,

You are required in my office at 8:00 a.m. tomorrow for a private meeting.

Go through security and tell them you are coming to see me. They will buzz you up to my floor.

Jameson Miles
CEO Miles Media
New York

"What the hell?" I whisper.
"What?" Molly asks.

"Nothing," I stammer as I minimize my screen. *Shit. What does he want? Just play dumb.*

I write back.

Dear Mr. Miles,

Would you like me to bring my team?

Emily

I tap my pen on the desk and look around nervously as I wait for his reply.

Emily,

No.

I do not want to see your team, nor do I want you to tell anybody about our scheduled meeting.

This particular meeting is of a private nature.

Jameson Miles
Miles Media
New York

My eyes widen. Oh my God . . . *private nature?* What the hell does that mean?

I pinch the bridge of my nose. I need pizza and beer too. Hurry up, five o'clock.

The bar is noisy and a hive of activity, and I can hardly wipe the goofy grin from my face as I look around at all the people who have just come from work. I'm sitting at a bench table with Molly and Aaron in a sports bar, and I'm feeling oh so New York.

It's a Monday night, and I'm out and about with what feels like a million cool people.

"All I'm saying," Molly says as she chews her pizza, "is that if you didn't see him all weekend, and he has no problem with that, there's an issue."

"Maybe he was just busy," Aaron scoffs.

"Maybe he's just lame," Molly huffs.

We're discussing Aaron's new boyfriend, and for some reason, I feel comfortable enough to make Aaron feel better about his situation because mine is worse. "Well, get this." I finish my mouthful. "You want to hear lame? I'm dating a guy I've crushed on since I was thirteen years old. A football star who was only interested in me after he injured himself. We had a few great months together, but then he dove into some kind of life crisis." I sip my beer. "He doesn't know what he wants to do outside of football. He's unemployed with no prospects. He lives in his parents' garage and just recently wrote his car off." I shake my head in disgust and pull my phone out of my bag. "He wouldn't move here with me because he doesn't like busy cities. He didn't call me this morning to wish me luck, and it's now"—I glance at my watch—"nine forty p.m., and he hasn't even bothered to call to see how my first day went."

They both groan in disgust. "What the fuck are you doing with him?" Aaron winces.

I sip my beer with an eye roll and shrug. "Who knows?"

They both chuckle.

"Well, all I want is some good sex." Molly sighs. "Every time I see someone I'm attracted to, I'm with the kids. So then I can't act on it."

I frown. "You wouldn't introduce anyone to your kids?"

"No. My God, they make their father's life hell with his new girlfriend."

Aaron laughs as if remembering something.

"What?" I ask.

Molly smirks. "My children are so fucking naughty you wouldn't even believe."

I giggle. "How old are they?"

"Mischa is thirteen, and Brad is fifteen," she replies. "They've decided between the two of them that they are going to make life a living hell for their father and me unless we get back together."

"How so?" I laugh.

"Brad has been suspended from school twice this year, and now Mischa is going off the rails too. A few weekends ago they each had a friend stay over at their father's while he and his girlfriend went out to dinner."

I frown as I listen.

"They got drunk from his bar and cut the crotches out of all of his girlfriend's underwear."

Aaron laughs, and my eyes widen in horror.

"And"—she sips her drink—"when their father asked them about it, they said that the underpants had rotted because her vagina was contaminated."

I burst out laughing. "No."

She shakes her head in disgust. "I wish I was joking."

Aaron throws his head back and laughs. "I fucking love your kids, man. That's a classic."

"No, it's a nightmare," she replies flatly.

"Why did you divorce him?" I ask.

"You know, I don't actually know." She thinks for a moment. "We just kind of lost our way. We were both working so hard, so we were always too tired for sex. We had two kids and a mortgage." She shrugs. "We never went on date nights or made an effort for each other. I don't have a precise moment that we knew it was over. We just kind of fell apart."

"That's sad." I sigh.

"He met someone else at work, and he talked to me about it. Nothing had happened at that stage, and he said he told me because he wanted to fight for us to get back what we once had."

"You didn't fight?" I ask.

"No," she says sadly. "And neither did he. We just kind of walked away from each other. It was all too hard at the time." She thinks for a moment. "I regret it now. He's a great man. And in hindsight, I think a lot of the problems we had just came from getting older. Sex drive is something you both need to work at, but we didn't realize that until it was too late." She smiles softly. "We're great friends now."

Hmm. We all fall silent.

"Lucky you've got those kids to cut up your competition's underwear." Aaron smiles.

We all laugh out loud. "Contaminated vagina. Where do they come up with this shit?"

I hold the black dress up against my body and stare at my reflection in the mirror. *Hmm.* I throw it and the coat hanger it's on onto the bed. I grab the gray skirt and jacket and hold it up to myself.

Maybe black?

Shit. What the hell do you wear when you want to be sexy without trying to look sexy? It's just now eleven o'clock, and I'm deciding what to wear to my meeting with Mr. Miles in the morning. What does he want to see me about anyway?

I think I'll go with the black dress. I lay it out on the chair. I pick up my patent leather pumps and put them on the floor under the dress. What earrings? *Hmm.* I twist my lips as I think.

Pearls. Yes, pearls don't scream *fuck me* like the gold ones do. Pearls are sensible working earrings.

Right.

I'll wash my hair and curl it in the morning. I look at my reflection and hold my hair up in a high ponytail. Yes . . . high ponytail. He likes high ponytails. *Stop it.*

I sit on the end of my bed and look around my little apartment. It's one bedroom and on the thirtieth floor—tiny and quaint. It is modern, though, and is in a nice building. It's different from what I'm used to; this New York–living thing is all so foreign, living alone and drinks and places to go on a Monday night. I pick up my phone and flick through my messages. My three best girlfriends all messaged me tonight to see how my day was. So did my mom. Robbie didn't.

Sadness sweeps over me. What's going on with us? Maybe I should call him. I am the one who left, after all. I dial his number, and it rings. Eventually, he picks up.

"Hey."

"Hi." I smile. "How are you?"

"Sleeping," he mutters. "What time is it?"

My face falls as I glance at my watch. "Sorry."

"Yeah, no matter. I'll call you tomorrow, babe."

My heart drops. "Okay." I pause. "Sorry to wake you."

"Bye." He hangs up.

I exhale heavily. "My first day at work went great; thank you for asking," I mutter dryly.

With a heavy heart and a stomach full of nerves, I crawl into bed, and I smile into the darkness as I remember my night with Jim.

I've thought of him many times when I'm alone at night. He was hands down the most amazing sexual experience of my life—not that I'll ever admit that to anyone, but I know it myself. I'm going to see him in the morning. I feel the nerves dance in my stomach. I wonder what he's going to say?

I sit at my desk and go through the folder, Emily Foster's file. I read through her details, school grades, references, and then her application letter.

Was this the job she was trying to interview for twelve months ago?

Buzz.

I press the intercom to security on the ground floor, and I glance up at the mirror on the wall and push the remote. It instantly turns into a television screen. "Yes."

"We have an Emily Foster here to see you, sir."

I catch sight of her, and I smile. There she is. "Send her up."

I watch as she is led through to the elevator with the guard, and he puts her into my elevator. I make my way out into reception, and soon the doors open, and she comes into view.

"Hello." I smirk.

"Hi," she whispers. She looks nervous.

I hold out my hand and gesture toward my office. "Please come through."

She walks in front of me, and my eyes drop to her backside. She's wearing a black fitted dress, sheer stockings, and high-heeled pumps, and her hair is in a bouncy ponytail . . . just ready to drag down to my . . . *stop it.*

"Take a seat," I say as I sit down at my desk.

She takes a seat and clutches her bag on her lap as her eyes find mine.

I swivel on my chair as I watch her. She's as gorgeous as I remember, and a potent sexual aura oozes out of her like a concealed weapon.

Long dark hair, brown eyes, and big fuckable lips. I've thought of her often—she was impossible to forget.

Nobody has ever ridden my cock the way she did, not before, not since. Not ever.

The hickey on my neck wasn't the only thing she branded me with that night.

"You wanted to see me?" she asks softly.

The sound of her voice has a physical effect on me. I remember her sex talk and what a turn-on it was to hear her sweet voice say such dirty things.

"Yes." I stare at her. "I did." Emily was the first woman I have been with in a long time who had no idea who I was. Strangely enough, I didn't need to be anyone that night.

Being Jim was enough.

"What about?"

I sit back in my chair, annoyed with her attitude. The majority of women gush over me—this one, not so much.

"What are you doing in New York?" I ask her to try to make polite conversation.

"You asked me that yesterday," she snaps. "Get to the point."

"I am asking you again now. Stop with the fucking attitude."

She narrows her eyes as if annoyed.

I sit forward in my seat. "What is your problem?" I sneer.

"You. You are my problem."

"Me?" I ask, affronted. "What did I do?"

"Do you have something work related to talk to me about or not, Jim?"

I glare at her. "You're very rude."

"You're very rich."

"And?"

She shrugs.

"What does that mean?" I snap.

55

"Nothing." She straightens her back. "If you don't have anything work related to talk to me about, I'll get going."

I clench my jaw as I stare at her; the air crackles between us. "Can I see you tonight?"

Her eyes hold mine. "No."

"Why not?"

"Because I'm a professional, and I have no intention of mixing business and pleasure."

I clench my jaw to stop myself from smirking. My interest in her is growing by the second. "What makes you so sure it would be a pleasure?"

"History has a way of repeating itself," she whispers as her dark eyes drop to my lips.

I get a vision of her naked and on top of me in my chair, and I inhale sharply as my cock begins to thump. "History will be kind to me, for I intend to write it," I say.

"Quoting Winston Churchill now, Mr. Miles?" she breathes.

I smirk, amused by her intelligence. "You must look at the facts because they look at you."

"I never worry about action, but only inaction," she fires back without hesitation.

"Exactly, so as a fellow Churchill tragic, I demand you have dinner with me tonight."

She smiles and stands. "I can't."

"Why not?"

"I'm washing my hair."

"Why would you want to wash it when you could be getting it dirty?"

She shrugs casually. "I'm just not interested in you. You're not my type."

I stare at her as her words roll around in my head. *Ouch.*

I purse my lips as my eyes hold hers. That's the first time I've ever been flat-out rejected. "Very well; your loss."

"Maybe." She turns to leave. "Nice to see you again, though. You must be very proud of your achievements."

I rise and open the door in a rush. She looks up at me, and I clench my hand at my side to stop myself from touching her. "Goodbye, Emily."

"Goodbye," she breathes as the air swirls between us. "Thanks for giving me a job." She smiles.

I nod once. *It's not the only job I have for you.*

She turns and walks out and into the elevator, and I slam the door and storm back into my office.

I'm not her type . . . since when?

I hold the remote up to the security television screen and turn it back on. "Get me the fortieth floor," I ask the voice control.

It flickers, and then a picture comes up with the fortieth floor. I watch as she steps out of the elevator. "Follow her."

The camera follows her as she walks up the aisle and then to her seat at her desk.

"Camera above that area," I command.

The screen flickers, and she comes into view. The office is empty, and she takes out her phone and begins to scroll. She crosses her legs, and I sit forward as her thigh becomes visible through the split. I watch her as arousal swirls between my legs.

So . . . fucking hot.

She's looking something up. "Zoom in," I command.

The camera zooms in, and I squint as I try to read what she's googling.

Jameson Miles.

I sit back and smile. *Bingo.*

Chapter 4

Emily

"What about this one?" Aaron smiles. "Hot firefighter rescues kitten from a drain."

I shrug. "I'll do that story for sure."

He smirks. "Me too."

"What are you guys doing over the weekend?" Molly asks as she works.

"Nothing," Aaron replies. "Hopefully seeing Paul."

"Me neither." I sigh.

Molly looks up. "I thought you were going home to see your boyfriend?"

I shrug. "Well, I was supposed to, but I've spoken to him for four minutes in total in ten days, and he hasn't called me once." I swivel on my chair as I consider my depressing situation.

"God, you need to dump him and move on to Ricardo."

I roll my eyes. Ricardo works on this floor, and for the last few days he's been loitering around my desk and making idle chitchat.

"He's into you," Molly mutters. "He's hanging around your desk like a fly."

"It's a shame." I smirk as I watch him talk to someone at their desk. "He's actually very good looking." Ricardo's Italian and has the whole tall, dark, and handsome thing perfected to a tee. Unfortunately, his personality isn't half as pretty as his face. He's either making fun of someone or talking about himself in the third person.

"Yuck." Aaron widens his eyes in disgust. "What would you even talk to him about?"

"You wouldn't talk to him—you'd stick a ball gag in and fuck him stupid," Ava says as she watches him. "I bet he's hung like a horse," she whispers.

We all burst out laughing. "What are you doing this weekend?" I ask Ava.

"She'll be chasing rich boys," Aaron says.

"Damn right."

My eyes flick to her. "What does that even mean?"

"I hang out at clubs where the men have money."

"Why?" I frown.

"I am not ending up with a broke loser."

My mouth falls open in horror. "So . . . you would marry a guy just for money?"

"No." She shrugs. "Maybe." She looks up. "Oh no, here he comes," she whispers.

Ricardo comes over and sits on the corner of my desk. The floor manager has gone home for the day, so he's not even bothering to pretend to work anymore.

"Hey there." He smiles.

"Hi," I reply flatly. *Please go away—you're embarrassing.*

"Ricardo wanted to come and check on his favorite coworker."

I stare at the stupid human being in front of me. "Why do you speak about yourself in the third person?" I ask.

Aaron snickers as he pretends not to listen.

"Ricardo wonders why you never come to his desk to see him."

"Emily likes to get her work done," I mutter flatly.

"Oh." He laughs as he points at me. "Ricardo likes your style, Emily."

I begin to work, and he stays sitting on the corner of my desk while he rambles, hardly coming up for air. Every now and then the four of us exchange looks, unable to believe what a tool this guy is.

From the corner of my eye I see the elevator doors open, and then I see somebody run back to their workstation. *Huh?* I look up to see Jameson Miles striding down the carpeted corridor toward my desk. His jaw is clenched, and he is glaring at Ricardo.

People are standing up in their cubicles to see who it is, and when they see him, they immediately drop into their chairs in fear.

What the hell is he doing here?

I watch in slow motion as he comes to a halt in front of my desk. Ricardo glances over and then nearly swallows his tongue and stands immediately. "Mr. Miles," he stammers. "Hello, sir."

"What are you doing?" Mr. Miles growls.

"I was training our new employee," he splutters. "This is Emily," he says, introducing me.

Aaron's eyes meet mine in horror.

"I am well aware of who Emily Foster is and how often you frequent this desk. This is your first and final warning," he growls. "Get back to work, and do not let me catch you here again."

The blood drains from Ricardo's face. "Yes, sir," he whispers.

Mr. Miles glares at him and clenches his jaw in anger. "Go. Now."

Ricardo practically runs back to his desk, and I stare at the gorgeous creature in front of me.

Gray suit, white shirt, paisley tie. He really is the epitome of suit porn.

"Emily, I need to see you in my office. Now," he snaps before he turns and strides back toward the elevator, not bothering to wait for my reply.

I swallow the lump in my throat as I stand.

Aaron's, Ava's, and Molly's eyes are wide with fear. "What the fuck?" Aaron mouths as he squeezes my hand in sympathy.

I exhale heavily and turn and follow the office god into the elevator as everyone watches. The doors close behind us.

Jameson glares at the doors, and I twist my fingers nervously in front of me as we fly up through the floors. *Oh man, he's going to fire me.* That stupid fucking Ricardo has gotten me into trouble. This is all his fault.

I wasn't even talking back to him . . . you know.

When we get to the top floor, the doors open, and once again he strides off. I hesitate. Does he expect me to run after him? I'm not a fucking puppy.

Who in the hell does this asshole think he is?

I fake a smile at his receptionist and storm in after him. He holds the office door open for me, and I brush past him. He closes the door and flicks the lock.

"What are you doing?" he snaps.

"Is that a trick question?" I hold my arms out wide. "I'm standing in your office. What does it look like?"

"I mean, why the hell are you openly flirting with that idiot from downstairs?" he demands.

My mouth falls open in horror. "I wasn't flirting."

"Bullshit. I saw it with my own fucking eyes."

"What?" I snap. "Don't tell me you dragged me all the way up here to chastise me about talking at my desk while I work."

"I am not paying you to get hit on, Emily," he growls.

I put my hands on my hips as fury begins to pump through my bloodstream. "Listen here, you." I hold my finger up. "Firstly, I'll get hit on by whomever I want."

He narrows his eyes and puts his hands on his hips, too, mirroring my stance.

"Secondly"—I put my second finger up—"as my boss, you do not get to comment on my dating life."

"Ha," he huffs as he rolls his eyes in disgust.

"Thirdly"—I hold three fingers up—"I'm new in town, and I have no friends, so if he's being nice, I'm not going to be rude, am I?"

"Not on my time," he growls.

"Did you really drag me all the way up here just to say that?" I frown.

"No," he barks. "I want to know why you won't go out with me."

My face falls. "Are you serious?" I whisper.

"Deadly."

The mood between us changes and turns from anger to something else.

"Because I can't risk losing my job if we don't work out."

He stares at me for a moment. "That job interview you were going for twelve months ago. Was it here?"

I pause for a moment. Now I'm going to sound like a loser. "Yes."

"How long have you been trying to get a job here?"

"Three years," I huff. "So forgive me if I don't want to throw it away for a one-night stand."

"Why would you think I would fire you?"

"Isn't that what CEOs do when they have finished with their secretaries? Throw them to the side?"

He frowns as he watches me. "I wouldn't know—I've never been attracted to someone I work with. And besides, I think this place is big enough that we could stay out of each other's way."

"You're still attracted to me?" I whisper.

"You know I am, and it's just dinner," he snaps. "Nobody would even know, and I most certainly wouldn't fire you in the morning."

"So . . ." I frown as I try to work out what the hell it is that he wants. "You would keep me a dirty little secret?"

He steps forward so that our faces are only an inch apart; our eyes are locked.

Energy begins to spark between us, and I feel my arousal sweep in. "Were you in a relationship when we spent the night together?" I ask.

"What makes you say that?"

"You never asked for my number."

He gives me a slow, sexy smile as he tucks a piece of my hair behind my ear. "Does everybody ask for your number, Emily?" His voice has dropped to a deep, sexy tone.

"Pretty much."

"I wasn't looking for anything back then, and I most definitely don't tell people I'm going to call them if I'm not." He dusts his thumb over my bottom lip as I stare up into his big blue eyes.

"Tonight," he whispers.

I smile softly as his breath tickles my skin. He really is quite . . .

"I'll pick you up. Dinner at my favorite Italian restaurant . . ." His voice trails off as if he's imagining something else.

Oh, that sounds good. I smile as he leans closer. His lips tenderly touch mine as he holds my jaw in his hand. My eyes close as my feet lift from the floor.

Robbie . . . what the hell am I doing?

Damn this man. What is this spell that he has over me that makes me do the most random things? Like one-night stands and forgetting I'm in a committed relationship . . . and breathing.

Oh my God. I have a boyfriend. Shit. "I'm so sorry if I gave you the wrong idea." I take a step back from him. "I have a boyfriend," I blurt out.

His face falls in horror. "What?"

"I know." I wince. "I . . . I . . ." I shake my head because I have no words that can get me out of this. "I have a boyfriend, and I can't go out with you."

"Dump him," he fires back.

"What?" I croak.

"You heard me. Dump him." He reaches for me.

I step back to create distance between us. "Are you crazy?"

"Maybe."

"I can't dump a boyfriend for one night of sex."

"Yes. You can."

"Jameson." I drag my hands through my hair. "Have you completely lost your mind?"

"Quite possibly." He hands me a business card. "Call me, and I'll come and get you."

JAMESON MILES
MILES MEDIA
212-639-8999

I stare at the card in my hand, my mind a clusterfuck of confusion. My eyes rise to meet his. I know what this is to him—it's just another one-night stand.

One night that could ruin every plan I've made for myself and jeopardize my career. I've worked too damn hard to get to

New York to throw it away now for one night with a player. It's the weirdest thing—I never picked him as a player when we were together, but the more I get to know him, the more I realize I never knew him at all.

The worst part about it is that I know Jameson Miles is the kind of drug that I don't need an addiction to.

The memory of our night together is bad enough.

"I'm sorry. I just can't." I turn to walk out of the office. My body screams for me to go back, and then I stop as a thought crosses my mind. I turn back toward him. "How did you know?"

He lifts his chin as my eyes search his.

I walk back toward him. "How did you know that Ricardo has been at my desk?"

I glance around the room and see nothing but a mirror on the wall. "Are there cameras in here?" I ask.

"Never mind."

"Oh, but I do," I sneer. "I think I have a right to know, if it concerns me."

He picks up a remote from his desk and pushes a button. "Give me level forty, please," he commands.

The mirror turns into a television screen. It rolls a few times, and then a vision of my office floor appears. I see Aaron and Molly and . . . my desk.

What the hell?

"You've been watching me?" I gasp. "Why?"

His dark eyes hold mine. "Because it turns me on." He grabs my hand and puts it over his crotch, and I can feel his rock-hard erection in his suit pants.

The air leaves my lungs as I stare up at him, and unable to help it, I wrap my hand around his hard length.

We stare at each other as our bodies' desires take over. "I just can't," I whisper.

His hand cups my face. "I want you."

"You don't always get what you want," I breathe.

"I do." His mouth drops to my neck, and in slow motion, he licks from my collarbone up my neck and then whispers in my ear, "Get rid of him."

Goose bumps shoot up my spine, and I step back, overwhelmed by the physical effect he has on me.

He grabs the erection in his pants and rearranges it as we stare at each other.

"I've got to get back to work," I breathe.

He glares at me, his face cold, and my chest rises and falls as I fight my arousal. It's taking every inch of my self-control not to jump on him, right here, right now.

He's so hard under that suit . . . such a waste.

No.

I turn and walk out, take the elevator, and before I know it, I'm back down to my floor. My heart is beating heavily in my chest, and I'm in complete and utter shock. That may just be the hottest thing that's ever happened to me.

I fall into my seat, visibly shaken.

"Oh my God," Aaron whispers.

Molly slides her seat over to me. "Holy shit, what happened?"

"I have no idea," I murmur as my eyes go to the ceiling. Where are the cameras?

I think back to what angle I saw on his screen, and I look in that direction and see it. A small black glass dome. I glare at it, and I know he's watching me.

I can feel his eyes on my skin. What's he thinking about as he watches me?

An unwelcome wave of excitement rushes through me as I imagine him up there, hard and watching me.

I feel like taking off my clothes and lying back on my desk and opening my legs to give him something to really look at. Can he hear what we're saying? Is there audio on that thing?

"What happened?" Aaron whispers.

"I can't talk now. There are cameras," I murmur with my head down. "But we need to have some seriously strong drinks after work."

"Jesus," Molly whispers as she turns back to her computer.

"Stupid fucking Ricardo," Ava huffs. "He's going to get us all fired. Why didn't he get hauled into the damn office?"

"I know." I open my email and stare at it for a moment as I try to calm myself down.

I know exactly why. Because Jameson Miles doesn't want to fuck Ricardo—he wants to fuck me.

I bite my bottom lip to keep my slutty smile from escaping onto my face.

New York is so fun.

It's five thirty, and we've just left work and are standing on the curb outside the Miles Media building while we decide where to go for dinner. It's the weirdest thing; it's as if along with this job, I was gifted three friends and unlimited options. Every night is Saturday night in New York.

We're all different ages, with different lifestyles, but somehow we get along famously. Ava has a date and isn't coming with us, but Aaron and Molly are by my side.

"What do you feel like eating?" Molly says as she scrolls through her phone.

"Something fattening and greasy. Paul hasn't called me." Aaron sighs. "I'm off him."

"Oh God, will you dump him already?" Molly huffs with an eye roll. "I swear he's seeing someone else on the side, and besides, he's nowhere near hot enough for you."

The front door of the building is opened by a man in a black suit, and the three of us turn. Jameson Miles walks out with another man. The two of them are deep in conversation and oblivious to anyone else.

"Who's that with him?" I whisper.

"That's one of his brothers, Tristan Miles. He's in charge of global acquisitions," Aaron whispers as his eyes stay glued to them. "I swear to God, these men are so fucking hot it's unbearable."

They have this charismatic air about them, their stances the epitome of power.

Everyone around them stops and stares.

Fitted expensive suits, handsome as all hell, cultured, and wealthy.

I swallow the lump in my throat as I watch in silence.

In slow motion, they walk out and get into the back of the waiting black limousine. The driver shuts the door behind them, and we watch as it drives away.

I turn to my new friends. "I really need to talk to somebody."

"About what?" Aaron frowns.

"Can you two keep a secret?" I whisper.

They exchange looks. "Yeah, of course we can."

"Let's get to the bar." I sigh as I link my arms through theirs and begin to drag them to cross the road. "You're not going to believe what I have to tell you."

Molly arrives with our drinks on a tray and drops into her seat. "So go. Did he give you a warning letter?"

I sip my margarita. "Hmm, this is good." I frown as I inspect the icy yellow fluid.

Aaron sips his. "Ew, I hate this bartender." He winces.

"Will you stop whining?" Molly snaps. "It's like hanging out with my fucking kids."

"This drink is too strong," he chokes. "I notice you didn't get one."

Molly's attention comes back to me. "Anyway, what's this secret?"

I stare at them. God, I don't even know if I should be saying anything to anyone, but I need someone to talk to.

"Promise me you won't say anything to anyone. Not even Ava," I ask.

"Yes." They both roll their eyes.

"Okay," I continue. "You know how I told you I have been trying to get a job at Miles Media for over three years?"

"Uh-huh."

"Well, just over twelve months ago I went to a wedding in London, and I was flying directly back to New York for an interview here."

Aaron frowns as he concentrates on my story.

"At the airport in London, this fruitcake man behind me in the line was having some kind of episode and started throwing my bag around."

They both stare at me, confused.

"Anyway, the security guard ushered me to the check-in counter and told the guy to look after me. I was given an upgrade to first class."

"How cool." Aaron smiles and raises his drink happily.

I brace myself for the next part of the story. "I was seated next to this man, and we began drinking champagne and . . ." I shrug. "The more we drank, the more inappropriate we got, and we began talking about our sex lives."

"Did you get kicked off the plane?" Aaron says, with wide eyes.

"No." I sip my drink. "Could have easily, though."

Aaron puts his hand to his chest in relief.

"Then there was a blizzard in New York, and we had to fly on to Boston for an overnight layover. This guy was like . . . ridiculously hot." I smile as I remember him. "He was so not my type, and I wasn't his, but somehow we ended up fucking like rabbits all night long. It was the best sex I've ever had in my life."

"I love this story." Molly smiles. "Go you."

"I never saw him again."

Her face falls. "He didn't call?"

"He never asked for my number."

"Ouch." Aaron winces.

"I know; so you can imagine my horror when I saw him at work this week."

"What?" they both gasp.

"Oh my God, it's fucking Ricardo, isn't it?" Aaron frowns as he takes a big mouthful of his drink. "I can't handle this story. Please don't tell me you fucked him, and he gave you an STD. I won't be able to cope."

"It was Jameson Miles."

Molly's eyes nearly bulge from her head. "What?"

"Are you fucking kidding me?" Aaron gasps and accidentally snorts his drink up his nose and has a coughing fit.

They both stare at me, wide eyed.

"When I went to his office on the tour, he asked to be left alone with me."

Molly shakes her head. "Is this real?"

I nod.

"I have no words for this story," she whispers.

"I do—oh my fucking God." Aaron hits her on the arm in excitement. "What happened?"

"He asked me out to dinner."

"What the actual fuck?" Molly cries really loud.

"Shh," I whisper as I look at the people around us. "Keep your voice down."

"Are you serious?" she whispers.

"I said no."

"What?" Aaron cries this time.

"Keep. Your. Voice. Down," I demand. "I can't go out with him. I have a boyfriend."

"Your boyfriend's a dick. You even said so yourself," Molly stammers.

"I know, but I'm not wired like that. I would never cheat on somebody."

Aaron shakes his head. "Jameson Miles could wire me any way he wanted to."

"Right?" Molly agrees. "What happened today?"

"He marched me up to his office and accused me of getting hit on in my working time."

Their mouths fall open in horror.

"And . . ." I pause. I probably shouldn't tell them we are being watched. I'll keep that one to myself. I dig out his card from my wallet and slide it across the table, and Molly picks it up and stares at it. "Even his name is hot." She reads the card out loud. "Jameson Miles. Miles Media. 212-639-8999."

"I told him he couldn't have everything he wanted, and he said he does, and then he licked my neck," I blurt out.

"He licked your neck?" Aaron shrieks. "Oh Lord have mercy." He picks up the menu and begins to fan his face. "Please tell me you're going out with him tonight."

"No." I shrug. "I can't, and besides, it's the fastest way I know how to get fired."

"No job is that good," Aaron snaps. "I wouldn't turn him down to be the fucking president."

We all giggle, and then my phone vibrates across the table.

"Oh . . . my fucking God," Molly whispers as she stares at my phone. "It's him."

"What?" I stammer as I look down at the number lighting up the screen.

She holds up the business card in her hands, and we compare them.

"The number calling you is fucking him."

My eyes widen. *Holy shit.*

Chapter 5

"Answer it, answer it," Aaron cries.

"What do I do?" I flap my arms around in a panic.

"Holy fuck. Answer it," Molly demands as she picks it up.

"Don't answer it," I stammer as I try to grab it from her hands. She holds it in the air and waves it around.

"Answer it, woman," she demands.

I snatch it from her and stare at it while it buzzes. "I'm not going to answer it."

Aaron snatches the phone from me and hits answer. "Hello," he says in a fake girl's voice, and then he passes it over to me.

"What the fuck?" I mouth.

"Hello, Emily," Jameson's velvety voice purrs.

My eyes widen as I look at my friends' awestruck faces. Aaron crosses himself as if he's in church and makes a praying gesture.

"Hello."

"Where are you?" he asks.

"In a bar." I glance around as I hold my hand over my other ear to try to hear him better. Shit, I'm not telling him where I am; I look like crap. I hold my breath as I listen.

"I want to see you."

I bite my bottom lip, and Molly hits me on the arm to snap me out of my nervous freeze. "I told you I have a boyfriend," I blurt out. "I can't see you."

"Holy fucking shit," Aaron mouths to Molly as he scrunches his hands in his hair.

"And I told you to get rid of him."

"Who do you think you are?" I stammer.

Molly and Aaron listen intently.

"Go outside. I can't hear you," he barks.

I stand and walk through the bar and outside onto the curb, and it falls silent.

"That's better," he says.

I glance up the street at the cabs all in a row. "What do you want, Jameson?"

"You know what I want."

"I have a boyfriend."

"And I told you what to do."

"It's not that simple."

"Yes, it is. Give me his number, and I'll save you the job."

I smirk at the audacity of this man. "You know, your arrogance is a turnoff."

That's a blatant lie—not even close.

"And you're a turn-on. I've been hard all day. Get over here, and put me out of my misery."

I hear my heartbeat in my ears. Is this really happening?

A drunk couple totter past me, and I have to move so they don't run into me. "Sorry," they call.

"I'm flying out to California in the morning," I blurt out.

"To see him?"

"Yes."

"He stayed behind?"

I scrunch my face up tight. *Damn it. Why did I say that?* "Yes."

"When you see him, I want you to do something for me."

"What's that?"

"Ask him if he feels like he might die if he doesn't get to touch you again."

I frown. "Why would I ask him that?" I whisper.

"Because there's another man who does." The phone clicks as he hangs up.

I frown as I stare at the phone in my hand as I feel tingles all the way to my toes.

Holy fucking shit.

I put my hand over my mouth; I can't believe this.

I stumble back into the bar to find my two friends bouncing in their chairs as they wait for my return. "What happened?" they all but scream.

I slump and put my hands in my hair. "He wanted me to go over to his place and put him out of his misery."

"Holy fucking shit," Aaron cries. "Can I have your autograph?"

"Are you going?" Molly stammers. "Please tell me you're going."

I shake my head. "No." I think for a moment. "He told me to ask my boyfriend if he felt like he would die if he didn't get to touch me again."

They frown as they listen.

"Because there is another man who does."

"What?" Molly screeches. "Oh holy hell, we need tequila." She gets up and disappears to the bar.

"He asked you to his place?" Aaron squeaks.

I nod.

"Do you know where he lives?"

"No."

"Park Avenue, overlooking Central Park."

"How do you know that?"

"Google. He used to live in the One57 Billionaire Building, but he moved out of there and into a building on Park Avenue. His apartment is worth something like fifty million."

"Fifty million," I gasp. "Are you serious? How could anything be worth fifty million dollars? That's just ridiculous."

He shrugs. "Beats me. Must have gold toilets or something."

I giggle as I get a vision of someone sitting on a gold toilet.

Molly sits back in her seat and hands me a shot of tequila. "Drink this, and then go and fuck him stupid."

"I'm not going," I snap.

"Well, what's the plan of attack?" she asks. "Are you playing hard to get?"

"No attack. I'm going home to see Robbie tomorrow." I exhale heavily. "I need to sort out our relationship, and hopefully he will come back with me."

Aaron rolls his eyes in disappointment. "Can't you at least be as excited about Jameson Miles as we are?"

"No. I'm not. And remember, not a word to anyone." I sip my drink. "I know exactly what will happen with Jameson Miles. I'll sleep with him once, and then he will move on to his next victim, and I'll be conveniently fired." I shake my head in disgust. "I've worked too damn hard to get this job, and this is the man who didn't even want my number the last time we slept together."

Aaron turns up his nose. "God, why are you so sensible?"

"I know, it totally sucks." I sigh.

Molly's phone rings. "Please let it be Jameson Miles looking for a backup plan," she huffs with an eye roll. "Hello."

She frowns as she listens. "Oh hello, Margaret. Yes, I remember who you are. You're Chanel's mother."

She smiles as she listens, and then her face falls. "What?" Her eyes widen. "Are you serious?" She pinches the bridge of her nose. "Yes." It sounds like she's unable to get a word in. "I can understand why you're upset."

She narrows her eyes and shakes her head at us. "I'm so sorry."

Aaron and I frown at each other. "What's happened?" I mouth.

"How explicit are we talking?" she asks. Her eyes widen. "Oh my God, I'm so sorry." She listens. "No, please, don't go to the principal. I appreciate you calling me first."

She closes her eyes as she listens. "Once again, my sincere apologies. Thank you. I'll handle it, yes. Goodbye."

"What?" I ask.

She puts her head in her hands. "Oh my God. That was Chanel's mother, the girl my son is crushing on. She went through Chanel's phone and found provocative messages between them."

I bite my lip to stop myself from smiling as I listen. "That's pretty normal in this day and age, isn't it?" I try to make her feel better. "I think they all do it."

"How old is this girl?" Aaron asks.

"Fifteen," Molly cries.

I giggle as I listen. God, I can't imagine what it's like to have a teenage son. She dials her ex-husband's number. "Hello," she snaps. "Go into your son's bedroom, and grab his phone, and throw the damn thing in the toilet. He is grounded for life."

She listens.

Aaron and I begin to giggle uncontrollably.

"Michael," she says as she inhales deeply to try to calm down. "I know he's been seeing her, and I know she probably likes it. He's fifteen years old," she whispers angrily. "Take his phone, or be prepared for me to come over and smash it." She hangs up in a rush and puts her head down on the table and pretends to bang it continually.

Aaron and I burst out laughing, and I put my hand on her back. "Do you want some more tequila, Moll?" I ask sweetly.

"Yes . . . I do. Make it a double," she snaps angrily.

I stand at the bar as I look over at the table, and Aaron has his hand over his mouth in uncontrollable giggles. I drop my head to hide my goofy smile.

This is hilarious . . . because it's not happening to me.

"Hey." I smile as Robbie opens his front door.

"Hey, you." He smiles as he wraps me in his arms. "This is a surprise."

"I know. I was missing you, so I flew home this morning for the night."

"Come in." He drags me into his converted garage.

I couldn't sleep last night. I was worried about my feelings, and I can't stop thinking about stupid Jameson Miles. I got up and went straight to the airport and caught the flight out. I look around Robbie's tiny studio apartment and at the empty pizza boxes and dirty glasses lying around. "What have you been doing?" I ask.

"Nothing much." He smiles; he lies on the bed and taps it beside him. I lie down, and he slides his hand up my top as he looks down at me.

"Did you go to any job interviews this week?" I ask.

"Nah, nothing suited me."

I frown. "Any job is a good job . . . isn't it?" I ask hopefully.

"I'm waiting for the right one." He kisses me softly.

I stare up at him as I feel his erection grow up against my leg. "Robbie, come back to New York with me. There are so many jobs there, and it would be a fresh start for you. We could discover the city together."

He snatches his hand away from my breast and pulls away from me. "Don't start your fucking shit. I told you I'm not moving to New York."

I sit up in a rush. "What's stopping you? You have no job here. What's holding you back? Explain it to me."

"I like living here. I don't pay rent, and my mother cooks all my food. I have a good deal here. Why would I leave?"

"You're twenty-five, Robbie."

"What's that supposed to mean?" he snaps.

"Don't you want to support yourself and experience something different?"

"No. I like it here."

"You need to grow up," I snap, and we both stand up.

"And you need to come back to fucking earth. The world doesn't revolve around you."

"I want to live in New York." I take his hand as I try to get through to him. "You should see New York, Robbie. You would love it there. It has this vibe like I've never felt anywhere else."

"New York is your dream, Emily, not mine. I'm never moving there."

Oh hell. We are worlds apart. "How are we supposed to be together from different sides of the country?" I ask softly.

He shrugs. "You should have thought of that before you applied for this stupid job."

"It's not a stupid job." I plead, "Don't you want to support me in my dream? Are you going to come and visit me at all?"

"I told you—I don't like cities."

"So what you're saying is, if I don't fly back to California, I won't see you at all."

He shrugs and sits down and picks up his PlayStation remote.

"Are you serious?" I snap as I begin to see red. "I flew all the way home to discuss our future, and you're going to play fucking *Fortnite*."

He rolls his eyes and starts the game. "Quit your nagging."

"Quit my nagging," I snap. "I don't want to live in your fucking parents' garage, Robbie."

"Don't, then."

"What is wrong with you?" I cry in outrage. "Why do you want to waste away here? You're twenty-five, Robbie. You need to grow up."

He rolls his eyes. "If you flew all the way back here to be a bitch, you needn't have bothered."

Steam shoots from my ears. "If I walk out that door, Robbie, we are over," I say.

His eyes rise to meet mine.

"I mean it," I whisper. "I want you in my life, but I won't sacrifice my happiness because you are too fucking lazy to get off your ass and make a future for yourself."

He clenches his jaw and goes back to his game. He begins to play.

I watch him through tears as I hear my angry heartbeat in my ears. "Robbie, please," I whisper. "Come with me."

He keeps his eyes on the screen as he begins to shoot people in his game. "Close the door on your way out." He puts his headphones on to block me out.

I get a lump in my throat as I finally see our relationship for what it really is.

A sham.

I take a long look around his room as he plays his game, and I know that this is it.

The defining moment where I decide what I'm worth. What I want from life.

I can't save him . . . if he doesn't want to be saved.

What I want is someone who wants to grow with me, and I don't even know what growth I want. But I can't be stagnant here in his parents' garage any longer.

I don't even know who he is anymore . . . but this isn't me.

The woman I want to be lives in New York and has the job of her dreams.

Sadness overwhelms me. I know what I have to do.

I walk over to him and take his headphones off. "I'm going."

He stares at me.

"You're better than this," I whisper.

He clenches his jaw.

"Robbie," I whisper. "You're much more than just a football star. You need to believe that."

His eyes search mine.

"Go and get some help." I look around his room. "It's going to be too late for us, but I want it for you."

He drops his head and stares at the floor. I take his hand in mine. "Come with me," I whisper. "Please, Robbie, pull out of this . . . if not for me, for yourself."

"I can't, Em."

My eyes fill with tears, and I bend and kiss him softly. I rub my fingers through his stubble and stare into his eyes. "Go and find whatever it is that makes you happy," I whisper.

"You too," he breathes sadly. I realize he doesn't even want to fight it; he knows this is for the best. I smile at the bittersweet moment, and I kiss him softly one last time, with tears rolling down my cheeks.

I get into my mother's car and stare at his house for an extended time.

That was much easier and much harder than I imagined.

I slowly start the car and pull out onto the road. I wipe my tears with my forearm as I feel a chapter of my life close.

I drive down the road and out of Robbie McIntyre's life. "Goodbye, Robbie," I whisper out loud. "When it was good, it was great."

Monday morning

"And what do you think would happen if you told the police of your suspicions?" I ask.

"Nothing. Nothing at all," the frail old woman replies. She has to be at least ninety. Her white hair is in perfect finger waves, and her dress is a pretty shade of mauve. "They're useless."

I dutifully scribble down her reply on my notepad. I'm out in the field today, following up my own lead. There has been a string of satanic graffiti on the fronts of houses lately, and this particular woman's house has been done three times. Fed up with the lack of support from the police department, she contacted Miles Media, and I was the lucky one who picked up the phone.

"So . . . tell me when this all began," I ask.

"Back in November." She pauses as she tries to remember. "November sixteenth was the first time. A huge mural of the devil himself."

"Right." I look up from my notes. "What did it look like?"

"Evil." She gets a faraway look in her eye. "Pure evil, so life-like, with huge fangs and blood dripping everywhere."

"It must have been terrifying for you."

"It was. That was the night when a jewelry store got robbed around the corner, so I remember it well."

"Oh." I frown. She didn't mention this before. "Do you think it's related?"

She stares at me blankly.

"The graffiti and the robbery, I mean," I clarify.

"Don't know." She pauses for a moment and then contorts her face as if in pain. "I've never thought of that before, but it's all making sense now. The police are in on this conspiracy." She begins to pace. "Yes, yes, that's it." She taps her hand on the top of her head as she walks back and forth.

Hmm. There's something off here. Is this woman of sound mind? "What did you do when you found the graffiti on your house?"

"I called the police, and they told me that they don't have time to come out for graffiti but to take a picture of it and email it to them."

"And you did that?"

"Yes."

"What happened then?"

"My son got my house acid washed and removed it, but three nights later it happened again. But this time it was an image of someone getting murdered. A woman had been stabbed. The graffiti was so intricate that it looked like a painting."

"Oh." I continue to take notes. "What did you do this time?"

"I went down to the police station and demanded someone come and look at my house. My neighbor had his house vandalized too."

"Okay." I scribble down her story. "What's your neighbor's name?"

"Robert Day Daniels."

I glance up from my notes, surprised by his name. "His name is Robert Day Daniels?"

"Or is it Daniel Day Roberts?" Her voice trails off as she thinks. "Hmm."

I stare at her as I wait for her to decide which it is.

"I forgot his name." She scrubs her hands in her hair as if about to launch into a panic.

"That's okay. I'll just write Robert Day Daniels for the moment, and then we'll come back to it a little later."

"Yes, okay." She smiles, pleased that I'm not pushing her for an exact name.

"What was drawn on his house?" I ask.

"One of those horrible devil stars."

"I see. Tell me, what did the police do this time?"

"Nothing. They didn't even come out here."

"They're very busy," I reassure her as I write. "Tell me about the last time it happened."

"The entire house was painted red."

I glance up in surprise. "The entire house was red?"

"The whole street."

Uneasiness sweeps over me. "That is weird." I frown.

She leans in close so that only I can hear her. "Do you think it's the devil?" she whispers.

"What?" I smile. "No, it's probably just kids acting up," I say, trying to reassure her. "Have you told anyone else about this?"

"No, only Miles Media. I want you to publish this story so that the police will actually pay some attention. I'm getting scared that it's something more sinister."

I take her hand in mine. "Yes, I think we have enough to go forward with the story."

"Oh, thank you, dear." She holds my hand tightly.

"Is there anything else you can think of that may be relevant?" I ask.

"Just that I'm living in fear every night that the devil is coming back. My neighbors said to go and speak to them too."

"Okay, great." I hand her my card. "If you think of anything else, please call me."

"Yes, I will." She clutches the card.

I go down the street and interview seven more people, and the stories all correlate. I definitely have enough evidence to go forward. I go back to the office and type the story up and hand it in to Hayden. It feels good breaking news.

I sit at my desk and stare at my computer screen. It's four o'clock on Monday, and I'm in a funk. Since I got back to New York late last night, I've had a bad case of the guilts. Even though I knew that Robbie and I were reaching our expiration date, I kind of feel like I sped it up and didn't let it run its course. But then, on the other hand, we'd been stagnant for months, and if I took this job knowing he wasn't coming with me . . . I think I subconsciously knew we were close to the end.

"The god is here," Aaron whispers.

I glance up. "Who?"

"Tristan Miles," he whispers.

I spy over the screening above my desk as he talks to the manager of the floor, Rebecca.

He's wearing a pin-striped navy suit, his brown wavy hair is in just-fucked perfection, and he has this dreamy smile on his face as he talks. He has the whitest teeth I've ever seen and huge dimples.

"She's giggling like a schoolgirl." Aaron frowns.

"He's never on this level," Molly says.

"What do you reckon he's doing here?" Aaron whispers as his eyes stay glued to the fine specimen.

"His job," I reply flatly. "He does work here, you know."

The more I think about it, the more I know I've romanticized this whole Jameson Miles thing. He doesn't like me—he's just horny, and there's a big difference. He's probably had sex with five women since Friday night when I spoke to him. I haven't heard from him since, and I don't want to either.

I didn't leave Robbie because Jameson told me to; I left Robbie because he'd stopped putting in any effort. If Jameson knows we broke up, he's going to assume it's because I want to sleep with him . . . and I don't.

I really don't. Stupid men.

I'm not telling my coworkers that we broke up. I don't want to make a fanfare of it. I want to take my time to get my head around it.

Tristan Miles says something, and Rebecca laughs. Then he disappears into the elevator, and we all get back to work.

I struggle with my umbrella as I trudge down the pavement in the rain. New York isn't as dreamy in the wet. I grab the *Gazette* while I'm waiting for the lights to change and stuff it in my bag. I'll read this while I wait for my coffee. My phone rings.

"Hello, Emily Foster speaking," I answer as I power walk among the crowd.

"Hello, Emily," a familiar voice says.

I frown, unable to place who it is. "Who's speaking, please?"

"This is Marjorie. We spoke yesterday."

Oh shit—the graffiti lady. "Oh yes, hello, Marjorie. It's a bad line, and I couldn't hear you properly," I lie.

"It's Danny Rupert," she replies.

"I'm sorry?" I frown.

"My neighbor's name is Danny Rupert. I couldn't remember it yesterday."

I screw up my face and cringe. Oh God. I hope it hasn't gone to print. I completely forgot to go back to it. Panic begins to swirl in my stomach.

Shit.

"I think the story has already gone to print, Marjorie. I'm so sorry I didn't recheck it with you."

"Oh, that's okay, dear. It doesn't matter—no harm done. I felt foolish being unable to remember, and I wanted to call you."

My stomach rolls. It does matter—you don't get names wrong in a story. Reporting 101.

Fuck.

I puff air into my cheeks as disappointment in myself runs through me. Damn it. This is not a little mistake; it's a major fuckup. "Thanks for the call, Marjorie. I'll call you when I get into the office and let you know when it's running." With any luck it won't be until tomorrow, and I will have time to change it.

I hang up and internally kick myself. *Damn it. Focus.*

I walk into the café opposite the Miles Media building and order my coffee. I drag the paper out of my bag and slam it onto the table.

I am not going to hold on to this job with sloppy mistakes like that. I'm so annoyed at myself.

I flick through the paper, and then something catches my eye.

Satanic Graffiti in New York

A spate of bizarre graffiti attacks on houses in the West Village has the residents running scared. Marjorie Bishop's house has been graffitied three times, and the police are refusing to take action. Another resident, Robert Day Daniels, has been suffering too.

I frown as I read the story. *What?*

Marjorie said she didn't tell anyone about this other than me. I read it again and again. It quotes my story almost word for word, and each time I get more confused.

Did she tell another reporter the same wrong name? I take out my phone and dial her number, and she answers on the first ring. "Hello, Marjorie, this is Emily Foster."

"Oh hello, dear; that was quick."

"Marjorie, did you speak to anyone else from another paper about this graffiti story?"

"No, dear."

"You haven't told anyone?" I frown.

"Not a soul. The street and I made a collective decision that we only wanted Miles Media to report on it. That way we knew the police would have to listen."

I begin to hear my heartbeat in my ears. What the hell is going on?

"Coffee for Emily," the cashier calls.

"Thank you." I take my coffee and head back out into the rain, confused as all hell.

It's one o'clock, and I'm on my lunch break. I arrive at the top floor and walk through to reception. "Hello." I smile nervously. "I'm here to see Mr. Miles. It's an urgent matter."

I've been racking my brain all day, and the only theory I can come up with isn't pretty. I need to talk to Jameson.

The blonde receptionist smiles. "Just a moment, please. Your name is?"

"Emily Foster."

She pushes the intercom. "Mr. Miles, I have an Emily Foster here to see you."

"Send her in," his velvety voice purrs without hesitation.

I feel my stomach dip with nerves, and I follow her out into the corridor and across the marble. Damn it, I still haven't bought rubber-soled shoes yet. I try to tiptoe so I don't click as I walk. "Just knock on the end door."

Holy shit. My heart begins to pump, and I force a smile. "Thank you."

She disappears up the hall, and I close my eyes as I stand in front of the door, bracing myself. *Okay, here goes.*

Knock, knock, knock.

"Come in," I hear Jameson call. I scrunch my eyes shut as nerves dance deep in my stomach.

I open the door, and there he sits in a navy suit. With his white shirt, dark hair, and piercing blue eyes, he looks like God's gift to women. Maybe he is. "Hello, Emily," he whispers as his sexy eyes hold mine.

"Hello."

Jameson stands and stares at me. Our eyes are locked, and the air swirls between us. "Please, take a seat."

I fall into the chair, and he sits behind his desk and leans back in his chair; his eyes don't leave me.

"I wanted to see you about something," I say as I glance at the glass of scotch beside him. I don't know what kind of work has scotch involved, but where's my glass?

I could do with a drink or ten right now.

He sits back and smirks as if amused.

"Umm." I pause and swallow the sand in my throat. "So something has happened, and I know I could get into trouble for it, but I feel like you need to know," I blurt out in a rush.

"Such as?"

"I got a name wrong in a story."

Jameson's unimpressed eyes hold mine.

"But it's the weirdest thing," I stammer. "Today the *Gazette* has published the same story . . . with my error in it."

He frowns. "What?"

"Look, I don't know, and I could be totally wrong, and I don't know why I'm even telling you this, but I think . . ." I pause.

"You think what?" he snaps.

"I just know for certain that the *Gazette* didn't get that story themselves, and they most definitely couldn't make the same mistake as I have. The old lady in the story contacted me directly because she would only talk to Miles Media." I put the *Gazette* down on the desk in front of him, and he reads it and stares at me for a moment as if processing my words.

"Are you sure?"

"Positive. I got the name wrong." I point to the name where my mistake was made. "This here is my error."

Jameson brushes his thumb back and forth over his bottom lip as he stares at the paper before him, deep in thought. "Thank you. I'll discuss this with Tristan and get back to you."

"Okay." I stand. "I'm sorry for making the error. It was unprofessional, and it won't happen again." My eyes go to Jameson, and I wait for him to say something. Is that it?

"Goodbye, Emily," he says flatly.

Oh, he's dismissing me. "Goodbye." I turn, feeling dejected, and make my way downstairs. I don't know whether I just did the right thing by telling him my theory. Maybe it will only work against me.

It's four o'clock, and I'm drinking my afternoon coffee. My phone rings, and I answer it. "Hello."

"Hello, Emily, this is Sammia. Mr. Miles would like to see you in his office, please."

I frown. "Now?"

"Yes, please."

"Okay. I'm on my way up."

Ten minutes later, I knock on Jameson's door. "Come in," he calls.

I walk in and find him sitting behind his large desk. His face breaks into a sexy smile as his eyes find mine. "Hello."

My stomach dances with nerves. "Hi."

"Have you had a good day?" he asks, and in slow motion I watch as his tongue swipes over his bottom lip. He's different this afternoon. He has a playful air about him.

"You wanted to see me?" I ask.

"Yes, I've spoken to Tristan, and we have a special project that we would like you to work on," he says as he leans back in his chair.

"You do?"

"Yes. We want you to write a story to publish."

I swallow the lump in my throat. "Okay." I shrug. "What's the story on?"

Jameson narrows his eyes as he thinks. "I was thinking . . . something along the lines of lovebites."

I frown in confusion. "Love bites?"

Amusement flashes across his face as if he's trying to keep it straight. "Lovebites, one word. Plural."

I stare at him for a moment in confusion. I don't get it.

Oh my God. He's talking about the hickey I gave him. Of all the nerve. Trust him to bring that up.

I tilt my chin to the sky in defiance. "I think I'm better equipped to write a story on premature ejaculation. That way you could help me with it." I smile sweetly.

Jameson's eyes dance with delight. "Is that so?"

"Yes," I reply straight faced. "News stories are so much better when they have evidence to back them up."

Amusement crosses his face as he sips his scotch. I have no idea what's going through that head of his this afternoon. Maybe he's had too many scotches. We stare at each other, and I want to blurt out, "Did you ever think of me?" But I can't because this is work, and I'm acting uninterested. Actually, let me rephrase that. I'm not interested—I'm slightly fascinated. Huge difference.

"How was your weekend?" he asks.

"Fine."

His eyebrow rises. "Just fine?"

I nod. "Uh-huh." I don't want to tell him that I broke up with Robbie, but then I don't want to lie to him either.

"You got back Sunday night?"

"Yes."

His eyes hold mine, and I know he wants to ask about Robbie and me but is holding his tongue.

"How was your weekend?" I ask.

"Great," he replies as his eyes drop to my lips. "I had a great weekend."

I frown. Does *great* mean just generally great, or does *great* mean "I had great hot sex with a gorgeous, great woman all weekend"?

Stop it.

"Sorry about that," Tristan says as he breezes into the room. He smiles warmly and shakes my hand. "I'm Tristan." He's slightly younger than Jameson, and his hair is a lighter brown and has a curl to it. His eyes are big and brown. He's very different from Jameson but has that same power thing going on.

"I'm Emily."

His eyes hold mine. "Hello, Emily." He and Jameson make eye contact, and at that moment, I know that he knows Jameson and my history together. I swallow the nervous lump in my throat.

Why would he have told his brother about me?

Tristan glances at Jameson's scotch. "What time is it? Has happy hour started?"

"Four thirty, and yes," Jameson replies.

Tristan goes to the bar and pours himself a glass of the amber liquid. He holds a glass up. "Would you like a drink, Emily?"

"No thanks. I'm working," I reply nervously.

Amusement crosses Jameson's face as he lifts his drink to his lips.

Okay, what the hell is that look? Is it a condescending smirk or nearly a smile? I can't read this man at all.

Jameson sits still and stares at me. Our eyes are locked, and the air swirls between us.

"You wanted to see me?" I ask. I really don't know what kind of meeting has scotch involved. Maybe I should have had a glass. *God, no. Remember what you did last time you got drunk with this man. You tried to suck all the blood out of him.*

"As we just discussed, we have a special project we would like you to work on," Jameson says.

I nod as I look between them.

"Yes. In light of what you told me this morning, we want you to write a story for us to publish."

I swallow the lump in my throat. "Okay." I look between them. "What's the story on?"

"Name a subject." His tongue slips out and runs across his bottom lip, and I feel it all the way to my toes. "We have a secret project coming up, and I wanted you to be involved, but I need to know if you can report on a subject."

"You know I can. I've worked for regional papers for five years as a reporter."

"This is strictly off the record," Tristan says. "You cannot tell a soul. It's imperative."

"I won't," I say as I look between them.

"For some time, we have thought that somebody on your floor is selling our stories to our competitors so that they are breaking before us. What you told us this morning all but confirms it."

I frown. "How do you know?"

"Trust me; we know," Jameson replies. "Our stocks are falling and so is our credibility. It needs to stop."

I frown as I listen.

"We want you to make up a fake news story and submit it through the normal channels, and we will see if it turns up in our competitor's papers."

I stare at him as I try to get my brain to keep up. "What would I write about?"

"Something worth selling. It doesn't have to be real. The faker the better—then it's more easily traceable."

"Who do you think it is?" I ask as excitement runs through me. This is my chance. If I do well here, I can prove myself as a valuable employee. Imagine if I cracked the case. I bite my bottom lip to hide my smile. I need to act as if exciting things like this happen to me every day.

"We have no idea, but we know it's not you."

"How do you know that?"

"Because it began before you started," Jameson says as he stands and goes to the bar.

"Okay." I think for a moment. "I could do that." I look between them. "When do you want the story by?"

"Tomorrow afternoon, if possible."

"Okay."

A voice comes through the intercom. "Tristan, you have London on line two."

He stands and pushes the button. "Give me a moment to get back to my office."

"Okay," the receptionist answers.

"Sorry, I have to take this call. We are settling today on a new company. We'll talk more tomorrow afternoon," he says.

"Sure." I smile. Oh, I like him. He's friendlier than his brother.

He shakes my hand. "Remember, not a word to anyone. I would hate to have to fire you." He gives me a playful wink, but something tells me he's not joking.

I frown. *What the hell?* "Okay."

"I look forward to reading your story," he says. He turns and walks out of the office and closes the door behind him.

I turn to Jameson. His eyes are dark, and he's holding his glass of scotch. He sips it in slow motion, and I smile nervously as my heart begins to race.

He raises his eyebrow and sips his scotch again. The electricity in the air between us is palpable.

"I should get back to my desk," I whisper.

His eyes stay fixed on me as if he wants to say something, but he remains silent.

"Is there anything else you wanted, sir?" I whisper as I stand.

He puts his drink down on the desk and walks toward me. "Yes, actually. There is."

He stops in front of me so that our faces are only an inch apart, and I stare up at him.

His close proximity steals my breath, and like a wave in the ocean, arousal swims between us. "Can you feel that?" he breathes.

I nod because it's undeniable.

"I'm so sexually attracted to you that it's insane," he whispers. "From the first moment I saw you on that plane."

I stare at him as I get a vision of him throwing me across his desk.

He trails his index finger down my face, over the center of my chest between my breasts, and then lower to my stomach, and then he skims it over my pubic bone before resting his hand on my hip. "I have a request."

"Yes." I close my eyes as I feel myself melt under his touch.

He leans forward so that his lips are almost touching my ear. His breath tickles and sends goose bumps down my spine. "I want you to wear your gray skirt tomorrow, the one with the split."

I frown as I listen to his whispered words.

"Your white silk blouse, and the lace bra that you wear underneath it."

Holy shit . . .

"No stockings." His hand grips my hip bone, and I clench my sex.

He licks my ear. "I want you to wear your hair in a ponytail so I can wrap it around my hand."

I get a vision of him wrapping my ponytail around his hand, and I nearly combust.

This man is a god.

I stare up at him. "Anything else?" I breathe.

"Yes." His eyes darken, and he reaches up and rubs his pointer finger over my bottom lip. "Tonight, I want you to take your vibrator." His voice is deep and hushed and doing things to my insides that I didn't know were possible.

My eyes widen as he slightly parts my lips with his finger. Then he puts it in my mouth, and I find myself sucking it. His

96

eyes darken as he watches me, and a slow, sexy smile crosses his face.

"I want you to fuck yourself. Long . . . deep and slow."

Oh . . . Lord have mercy.

"Why would I do that?" I breathe.

"Because I know it will be my face that you will see when you come."

He bends and licks up my neck, and then he bites my ear, and my legs nearly buckle underneath me. "Do your homework, and you will be well rewarded," he whispers in my ear before tenderly kissing my neck with an open mouth.

I'm like putty in his hands. I can't even pretend to fight this . . . whatever *this* is.

He dusts his lips across mine but then steps back, and my body jerks at his withdrawal. I pant as I stare at him.

"Do your homework, Emily. I'll see you tomorrow."

I stare at him for a moment; he's dismissing me.

I frown as he turns and goes back to sit at his desk as if nothing ever happened.

He picks up his scotch and sips it as his eyes hold mine. He slides a security key across the desk. "This will get you to this floor."

Huh.

What in the hell was that?

I snatch the key and leave his office in a fluster. I get into the elevator with my heart hammering.

For fuck's sake. I need to find some self-control, and I need to find it quick.

Because he has it all.

Chapter 6

I sit in the café across the road from the Miles Media building. I told myself I came here to get some takeout for dinner. But the truth is, I want to see him leave. I want to see his face, to see if it's as flushed as mine. I'm so close to orgasming in public; it's not even funny. How can one finger through clothes arouse me so much? This man turns me into a puddle, a wet, soppy, pliable puddle. I have absolutely no resistance when he touches me.

For twelve months I've dreamed about Jim, the funny, carefree man I spent the night with. And now that I've met another version of him, I'm not sure that I like him. I mean, he's hot, hotter than hot. Blazing fucking inferno.

Who is Jameson Miles?

I sit on the bench seat by the window and stare across the street, and then I see the limousine arrive and pull into the parking bay.

I sit up. My stomach flips, and I hold my breath as I watch the door open. In slow motion he walks out; he's like a rock star, and everyone turns to watch him.

Mr. Orgasmic.

I watch as he gets into the back of the limousine and the driver closes the door behind him, and then it slowly pulls away.

I watch it all the way up the street as it disappears, and I feel a wave of disappointment roll over me.

I wonder what he's doing tonight. It's late, nearly six thirty, and the Miles Media building is emptied out for the day. I can't believe I waited around to get a glimpse of him leaving . . . what a loser. I guess I may as well order something to eat here. I'm only going to go and eat alone at home anyway. I pick up the menu and scan the choices, and then the front doors of Miles Media open again, and Tristan walks out. I frown as I watch him. He's with a woman; she's blonde and beautiful and wearing a gray woolen fitted dress and high-heeled short black boots. She has a trendy vibe about her, and her hair is in a bouncy ponytail. She says something, and he laughs out loud. They walk around the corner but are still in my view, and he puts his hand on her behind and leans in and kisses her.

Who is she?

He then takes her hand in his, and they disappear up the street together.

Does she work in the building? I would have thought they had some no-dating-the-staff kind of rule. Maybe not?

Maybe it's a free-for-all, and they're fucking their way through the floors?

Am I the only girl he's flirting with? Does he summon anyone else up to his office?

I close my eyes in disgust.

Stop it.

God, I need to get a grip.

I go through my wardrobe and take out my clothes for tomorrow. It's late, and I've been working on that story that they want. I hope it's all right. My preparation is different this time. What should I wear tomorrow? Do I do as I was told?

I lay out the clothes Jameson told me to wear, and I stare at them on my bed.

The gray skirt with the split, the white silk shirt. How does he know that I wear a white lace bra with this shirt? How does he even know about this outfit?

He watches me.

A sick thrill runs through me. Fuck, this guy is playing with my head.

I'm walking around, a raging mass of hormones, and he hardly touches me.

Imagine if he did.

I think back to this afternoon and the way his finger traced my body and then how he put it in my mouth and I sucked on it.

His words come back to me. *I want you to fuck yourself. Long . . . deep and slow.*

I close my eyes as arousal begins to heat my blood. He wants me to think of him while I come.

I go to my bedside and take out my vibrator, and I hold it in my hand and look at it.

"It's a very cold substitute, Mr. Miles," I whisper into the silence. I have a good mind to call him and tell him to come over and get the job done in person.

But of course I won't. I turn off the light and crawl under the covers, and my hand brushes across my naked breast.

I close my eyes and open my legs and imagine Jameson Miles is here with me.

"Do you guys want to get some dinner after work?" I ask Molly and Aaron.

"Yeah, all right. Something healthy, though," Molly replies as she types. "I'm never going to get laid if I don't start working on this fat ass." She types some more. "I have to be done by eight, though. I have to pick up the kids."

"Yeah, okay." Aaron sighs. "Sounds good."

"I have training this afternoon," I reply as I try to sound casual.

They both look up from their work. "Where?"

"In the management offices."

"Oh my God." Molly smirks. "Did he say anything?"

I drop my head. I glance up at the cameras. "I'll tell you tonight."

"God, I live for these stories," Aaron whispers. "Please tell me you fucked him on his desk?"

I giggle as I finalize what I'm doing. "No, don't be stupid." I grab my manila folder with my fake news story. "I'll see you guys later."

They both look up at me and smirk. "Good luck."

In five minutes, I find myself on the top floor with a ferociously beating heart. I decided not to wear what he told me to wear; that's just way too eager.

What makes him think he can tell me what to wear, anyway?

Sammia smiles when she sees me. "Mr. Miles, you have Emily Foster here to see you."

"Send her in," his velvety voice replies.

I walk through the marble hall on my tiptoes as I make another mental note to buy rubber-soled shoes. How do I keep forgetting to do this? I knock on his door.

"Come in," he calls.

I open the door and find him sitting at his desk on the phone; his eyes find mine.

"Hello, Emily," he mouths.

"Hi." I smile as I clutch my folder.

"Please take a seat." He gestures to a chair and holds up his finger. "One minute," he mouths.

I smile and nod as I sit down.

"I understand that, Richard. Yes, I know." He listens. "I don't care if she's hardworking. She broke protocol, and there are consequences."

I frown. What the hell? Who's he talking to?

"Richard," he snaps. "You will fire her this afternoon, or I will. And we both know who's going to make it less painful."

He rolls his eyes.

"Tristan is aware, yes," he snaps. "But as the CEO I have the control. You have two hours to escort Lara Aspin from the building, or I'll come down myself." He hangs up angrily.

I stare at him, wide eyed. What did she do?

He bites his bottom lip angrily as his eyes hold mine.

"I've got the story you requested," I murmur.

"Good." He takes the folder from me and rolls his chair back as he opens it and begins reading.

He's different today, angry. But maybe it's just that call he came off from.

He inhales deeply and flicks the pages, clearly frustrated.

"Is it okay?"

He raises his eyebrows as if unimpressed.

I frown.

"A seismic weather event is hardly breaking news, is it?"

"Well, what do you want me to write about?" I stammer. "I can't name a person or place or anything because it's fake news. I don't want to get us sued."

"I am well aware of what it is, Ms. Foster," he snaps.

"What's wrong with you today?" I whisper.

He flicks the pages as he reads. "Nothing." He reads on. "This won't do. I'll write it myself."

I frown. "I spent four hours on that last night."

He looks up from the papers, and I wither under his glare.

"Well, what do you want me to write about, then?" I ask.

"Anything but fucking weather." He closes the folder as if disgusted and places it on the table.

He pushes the intercom. "Tristan, come in here, please."

"Yep."

I shrivel in my chair a little. God, he's mean when he's angry.

Tristan comes into the office, and Jameson exhales heavily. "Ms. Foster has written her story." He gestures to the folder.

"Good." Tristan smiles, and he picks it up and begins to read.

"A seismic weather event won't do," Jameson barks.

Tristan twists his lips as he reads on. "It's very good, though," he comments.

Hmm, I'm totally crushing on the wrong brother . . . my one is an asshole.

"Thank you." I fake a smile. "With all due respect, Jameson," I state, "if we name this weather event and hype it up as coming in the next four months and that it's going to cause extensive damage, it will have legs. No names to trace, people, or places. I don't see how I could have written a story about something else without jeopardizing our integrity."

"We are not here to prove our integrity," he growls. "We are trying to withhold it."

I sit back in my chair, annoyed.

"I want a story on an FBI murder case." He narrows his eyes as he thinks. "Make up a fake murder and name and a fake investigation and how close they are to closing it."

My anger bubbles. "If you knew what you wanted me to write, why didn't you say that yesterday?" I snap. "You told me to do what I wanted, and I spent four hours writing that for you."

Tristan rolls his lips to hide his smirk. "I have things to do. Let me know what story we're going with," he says as he walks toward the door. "Thanks, Emily. Great work." He closes the door behind him.

I glare at the asshole in front of me. "So what do you want me to do?"

His cold eyes rise to meet mine. "I told you what I wanted you to do yesterday, but you didn't do that . . . did you?"

I frown. Wait, what's he talking about now? I'm confused.

He doesn't have to be so damn rude. I snatch the folder from the table. "All right," I snap. "I'll write a fake story about a fake murder of a fake CEO by a fake new employee."

He glares at me.

"With a fake ax."

"Well . . . ," he says with a sneer, "just make sure she has a fucking gray skirt on."

My mouth falls open; he's pissed that I didn't do what he asked.

The nerve of this jerk.

"No, she doesn't wear gray skirts on demand. She's naked because she's just had wild sex with her hot boyfriend right before she chops off that spoiled-brat CEO's dick."

He narrows his eyes in contempt.

I stand. "You will have your story by five. I'll email it over."

"No, you'll deliver it up here in person."

"With all due respect, Mr. Miles," I say as I smile sweetly, "I don't feel like seeing you again today. I'll deliver it to Tristan."

"Deliver it to Tristan, and see what happens," he barks.

I turn and storm out of the office with red steam shooting out of my ears.

The man's a fucking pig.

It's five thirty, and I sit at my desk as I type the last word of my fake story. I hate to admit it, but this one is better. My coworkers have gone to the bar, and I'm meeting them there. I'm supposed to be taking it up to his office, but I'm not.

Screw him.

I hit send to email it over, and I turn off my computer and pack up my desk.

My phone rings, and the letter *J* lights up the screen. I saved his initial so I'd know if he calls me. I pick up my phone and hit decline, and then I smile sweetly at the camera, knowing full well he's watching me.

I did not just break up with one selfish asshole to go out with another.

He can kiss my ass. A text comes through.

Answer your fucking phone.

I glare at the text and write back.

I have nothing to say to you.
I've finished work for the day.
You have your story.
Good luck with it.

A reply bounces back.

This is a personal call.

I roll my eyes in disgust and reply.

Find someone else in a gray skirt to suck your dick
on demand. I'm not interested in the position.

I put my phone on silent and then into my bag and continue to pack up my desk.

I take the elevator down to the foyer, and as I walk through, a security guard is on the phone. "Excuse me, miss," he calls.

"Yes."

"I've been instructed to tell you to wait here."

Shit. He's on his way down. "Um, no, I can't. I'm sorry. Apologize for me," I stammer as I brush past him and out through the front doors. I run around the corner, and then when I'm out of sight of the security guard, I run across the street and duck into the café I was in yesterday afternoon so I can see.

What does he want?

I take a seat in the café by the window, and then I see Jameson come out the front doors in a rush and then look up and down the street. He takes out his phone and calls someone. My phone starts to vibrate in my bag.

Shit. I'm going to totally screw up this opportunity and get myself fired.

Is that why that other girl got fired today? Was she sleeping with him, and things turned bad? I watch him look up and down the street and dial the number again. I let it ring.

He's openly furious. The front doors of the building open, and Tristan comes out. Jameson says something to him, and Tristan laughs.

What did he say?

I watch with my heart beating hard as they both look up and down the street, and then the limousine pulls in. He calls me again, and I close my eyes. *Stop calling me.*

They finally get into the limo, and I watch as it pulls away. I drag my hand down my face in despair.

His temper and my temper are a bad combination.

We are officially a bad idea.

"What do you mean?" Molly frowns. "I'm confused."

"It's all just one big mess." I sigh.

"I went home to California, and it turns out that Robbie didn't actually give a crap, so I ended it. But I didn't tell Jameson that because I don't want him to think that it was because of him."

"Yeah, I get that." She frowns. "But why is Jameson being such an asshole now?"

"Because she didn't wear the gray skirt," Aaron interrupts. "Don't you listen?"

"But why?" she gasps. "That's ridiculous."

"I know," I snap.

"It's not about the skirt," Aaron replies as he chews. "It's a power thing. He wants her to do as he asks."

I frown as I listen. "You think?"

"I still don't get it." Molly frowns.

"It's symbolic to him. He wants her to submit."

"Well, I'm not," I huff. "Honestly, the man is fucking stupid if he thinks that I will."

Molly rolls her eyes. "Oh God, if he asked me to wear a skirt made of kidneys, I would," she huffs as she stares into space. "I would even kill fifty men to get the said kidneys."

Aaron chuckles. "Right? Me too. There isn't actually anything that he couldn't ask me to do." He holds his hands in the air. "I would do it all."

I roll my eyes, and we all think for a moment.

"You know what I would do if I were you?" Molly says.

"What?"

"I would wear the gray skirt tomorrow, and I would ignore the fuck out of him."

I stare at her.

"Make the bastard weep."

"Yeah." Aaron smiles broadly. "Flirt your ass off in that gray skirt."

I smirk as the idea rolls around in my head. "You know, guys . . . that's not actually a bad idea."

I hold my glass up in the air as I smile at my two friends. "To Operation Flirty Office Slut." Molly smiles as she clinks her glass with mine.

I smirk as I stare at her. "Game on."

I march into the office like a rock star.

No stockings . . . check.

White lace bra . . . check.

White silk shirt . . . check.

High ponytail . . . check.

Gray skirt with split . . . check, check, double check.

"Good morning." I smile at my friends as I arrive at my desk.

Their eyes come to me, and they smirk as they see I'm wearing the requested outfit. Aaron gives me a wink and turns back to his computer.

"Does anybody want coffee?" I ask.

"Yes, please," they both reply.

I walk into the kitchen, and Ricardo follows me in. "Hey, chickie, I've been waiting for you."

I smile an over-the-top fake smile. God . . . can't I have someone better to fake flirt with than this guy? "Hi," I reply excitedly. "How are you?"

"I'm good." He smiles at my enthusiasm. "Listen, I'm so sorry I got you into trouble the other day."

I smile and pull my hand through my ponytail. "That's okay. Come and see me later, though, won't you?"

His eyes light up. "Okay, it's a deal."

I walk back to my desk and take a seat with our three coffees, and I open my emails and get to work. Jameson called me six times last night, and I don't know why.

I'm not sure if he wanted to apologize or fight . . . but I'm not giving him the satisfaction of answering his call so he can do either.

I'm going to have a good day, and I'm not going to think about Jameson Miles once.

It's three o'clock, and Operation Flirty Office Slut is in full swing. I've smiled and laughed with every loser in the building today. I'm not sure if he's even watching, but I'm about to up the ante. I'm on my way up to see Tristan about the story I wrote.

The elevator doors open, and I smile sweetly at the receptionist.

"Hello, I'm here to see Tristan."

"Sure, just a moment." She frowns as she tries to remember my name.

"It's Emily Foster."

"That's right. I'm sorry." She calls through. "Tristan, I have Emily Foster here to see you."

"Okay, send her in," he replies happily.

"Just go through to the main conference room, but instead of turning left to go to Jameson's office, turn right, and go down the corridor on the other side of the building."

"Thank you." I follow her directions and head down to the other end of the building. I frown; there are four office doors. I hesitate. Which door did she say?

I walk down the corridor, and a door is open. I see Jameson is in there, talking to a man. "Sorry to bother you. Is Tristan's office down here?" I ask.

Jameson's face falls as he sees me.

"Next door," the other man replies.

I smile sweetly. "Thank you." I head over and knock on Tristan's door.

"Come in," he calls, and I walk in and close the door behind me.

"Hello." I smile.

"Hi, Emily." He smiles warmly as he gestures to the chair in front of his desk. "Please take a seat."

As I sit down, I come to the realization that Tristan doesn't make me nervous at all; I wish his brother didn't.

"I just was wondering if you had time to look at the story I wrote?"

"I did, yes, and I loved it. Were you happy with it?"

"Yeah, I think it was better. I wasn't sure what you wanted me to do with it next."

He frowns. "We'll need to submit it as if it has come to you. Did you talk to Jameson?"

"Umm."

The office door opens, and Jameson marches in. "Hello."

"Speak of the devil." Tristan smiles.

"Hello," I reply as I turn my attention back to Tristan. It's hard not to stare at Jameson when he's in a room; he dominates any space.

This playing hard to get is harder to do than it looks.

"Emily is here to talk about the story she wrote."

"I see." He stares at me, and I feel the magnetic pull to him as it begins to surround me.

"Was it okay?" I ask.

"It was." His eyes hold mine. "It was very good."

"Are we just going to submit it now as if it has come to her as news?" Tristan asks.

Jameson's eyes stay fixed on mine. "Yes, I think so."

My eyes flick between the two men. "Okay. I'll submit it and let you know what happens."

Jameson's eyes hold mine. "I have something I need you to add with it. It's on my computer. Come with me, and I'll get it now."

My nerves tingle. "Okay," I reply as I stand.

Jameson holds his hand out. "Ladies first."

I turn to Tristan. "Thank you. See you later."

Tristan smiles broadly. "Goodbye. Have a nice afternoon."

I walk to Jameson's office, and I can feel the heat of his stare on my behind.

Just play it cool . . . no flirting . . . no touching. Just play it cool.

I am here to prick tease the bastard . . . nothing more and nothing less. We get to his office, and he opens the door. I walk past him, and then he closes it and flicks the lock.

I turn to him as he steps toward me in slow motion. His face comes to within an inch of mine.

Our eyes search each other's, and without a word said, he grabs my ponytail and wraps it around his hand and pulls my head back to his face.

"Don't fight with me," he breathes, then leans down and licks my lips.

"Don't be an asshole," I whisper.

He bends and runs his hand up my bare leg as he holds my hair in his hand. His tongue licks up the length of my neck, which is stretched out for him, as his hand grabs my behind.

"Tell me he's gone," he whispers in my ear as he kisses it softly.

Ah . . . this is not how the plan went in my head. I'm supposed to be rejecting him right about now.

Abort mission . . .

"He's gone," I breathe.

His lips take mine, and his tongue slides effortlessly through my mouth as my senses awaken.

His hand grinds me onto his waiting erection as our kiss turns frantic. He pushes me up against the wall and tears my skirt up and slips his thick fingers underneath my panties. His dark eyes hold mine. "Tonight, we fuck."

Chapter 7

"Jameson," I whisper. "Will you behave?" I pull my skirt down over my hips.

He smiles into my neck and pulls me closer; his lips brush against mine as he takes my face in his hands. The kiss is slow, long, and deliberate, and I find my feet floating in the air.

"Dinner?" he breathes.

"Hmm." I smile against him as he holds my face. There's no mistaking that kiss. It's tempting, sensual, and a promise of sexual satisfaction.

"What time will I pick you up?"

"That depends."

"On what?"

"On whether you think you can tell me what to wear and what to do."

He smiles softly, and I feel my heart skip a beat; he hasn't smiled at me like that since the first night we met. "Forgive me," he whispers as he leans in and kisses me again. "I simply wanted you to wear my favorite outfit so I could admire you in it." His lips drop to my neck as if he's unable to stop himself. "I didn't mean to offend."

"Do you have to be so abrasive with me?" I whisper as his teeth skim my jawline.

"Abrasive is who I am."

"The man I met was funny and carefree."

He smiles down at me as he brushes the hair back from my forehead. "Our meeting was a luxury that I've never been afforded."

"How so?"

"I had the gift of anonymity."

Our lips touch, and I rub my fingers through his stubble.

"Why are you so different here?" I whisper.

He pulls out of my grip and walks over to his desk. "I am who I have to be, Emily. Funny and carefree can't successfully run an empire."

I stare at him as I think for a moment. "Okay, then I guess I'll have to decline dinner."

"Why is that?"

"Because I want to spend a night with Jim."

His eyes hold mine.

"Jameson Miles the CEO doesn't interest me. I couldn't care less about your money or your power."

He stares at me for an extended time as if processing my words.

I walk over and kiss him softly. "Tell Jim to pick me up at seven," I whisper as I run my tongue through his lips. "I'm aching for him."

Tenderness crosses his face. "I'll see what I can do."

I walk back down to my floor and take a seat at my desk.

"How did it go?" Aaron whispers as he types. "Did you make him beg?"

"God, I'm totally crap at playing hard to get." I sigh.

Molly smirks. "Aren't we all?"

I open my computer.

"Well?" Aaron whispers as he stops working. "Tell us."

"We're having dinner tonight," I reply as I try to sound casual.

"Oh my God," Molly whispers in excitement. "What the hell are you wearing?"

"I don't know." I frown. "Something insanely hot."

I hold my hand over my heart as I try to will it to slow down, and I glance at the clock on the wall—6:55 p.m.

He'll be here any minute.

I shake my hands around and pace back and forth. "Just be cool . . . don't sleep with him. Whatever you do, don't be easy," I remind myself out loud.

I walk back to the mirror in the bathroom and reapply my lipstick. "Get to know each other, and then make an informed decision based on his personality and not how much he turns you on." I smirk at the ridiculous girl talking to her reflection. If his dick wasn't so perfect, I wouldn't be thinking about it at all, then . . . would I?

My phone buzzes. "Hello," I answer as my heart races.

"I'm downstairs," his deep, velvety voice purrs. "What number are you?"

"I'll come down now. See you soon." I walk back to the full-length mirror and take one last look. I'm wearing a black fitted dress that hangs to just below my knees. It has spaghetti straps and a low back. It goes with my black stilettos and matching clutch. My long dark hair is set in big Hollywood curls and pinned back on one side. I've gone all out with my makeup and have smoky gray eyes and glossy red lips.

And of course, I'm waxed to within an inch of my life . . . *just in case.*

I take the elevator, and when I walk out through the foyer, I see him through the glass front doors of my building. He's wearing a navy sports coat and blue jeans with a white T-shirt. He looks like he's stepped straight out of a magazine.

My breath catches at the sight of him, and I smile as he turns toward me.

"Hi." He smiles.

"Hi."

His eyes roam down the length of my body as he takes my hand in his. "You look beautiful."

"Thank you." I smile bashfully.

We stare at each other . . . and it's there again. The electric current that runs between us whenever we're alone. "What do you want to do?" he asks as his eyes drop to my lips.

I smile. Jim's here—Jameson wouldn't ask me what I wanted to do. "Didn't you mention Italian?"

He leans in and kisses me, with just the right amount of suction to raise my feet from the floor. My arms go around his neck, and we stand in the street and stare at each other. "You really do turn me on, Emily Foster," he breathes.

I smile as I pull my fingers through his dark hair. "Did you come all the way across town to make out with me on the street?" I ask innocently.

"No." He smirks. "But now that I'm here, it's the only thing I want to do."

We kiss again, and it's slow and tender, and I feel my arousal fly in like a 747.

His hard length makes an appearance up against my stomach, and I smile broadly.

"What?"

"Is he coming to dinner?" I ask.

He chuckles. "Well, he does seem to want to hang around whenever you are near."

"*Hanging* isn't a word that I would use to describe that thing."

His eyes sparkle with a certain something, and he takes my hand in his. "Let's go this way."

"We're walking?" I ask in surprise.

"I got dropped off. They'll pick us up later. We'll catch a cab from here to the restaurant."

"Okay."

We walk around the corner, and he hails a cab, and we climb into the back of it. "Waverly Place, please."

"Okay." The driver pulls out into the traffic.

"How long have you lived in New York?" I ask.

"My whole life."

"Your parents live here?" I frown. I can't imagine growing up in a city like this.

"Yes, although I went to school elsewhere."

"Where did you go to school?"

"Many places—finished in Aspen."

I stare at him. *What the hell?* "You went to school alone in Aspen?"

"No, I always had my brothers with me." He picks my hand up and kisses the back of it with a soft smile.

I stare at him. We come from completely different worlds. I can't even fathom his upbringing.

"What's that look?" he asks.

"I wasn't even allowed to have a sleepover at my friend's place."

"Independence has always been encouraged in my family."

I smile as I think of something.

"What?"

"If you've been living on your own since you were . . . ?" I pause as I wait for his answer.

"Twelve."

"You should have the emotional intelligence of a ninety-year-old. Is that right?"

He throws his head back and laughs out loud. "*Should* being the operative word." His eyes dance with delight. "And what would your emotional intelligence be at?"

"Hmm." I frown as I think. "Emotionally I think I would be about age thirty."

"Physically?" He smirks.

"Oh God, eighteen." I laugh. "I'm not very experienced at all."

His eyes hold mine, and I feel the burn from his gaze.

"What would your physical experience be at?" I whisper.

"I'm more of a show than tell kind of person." He gives me a slow, sexy smile. "Happy to give you a demonstration, though."

I giggle as the cab pulls to a stop. "I bet you are." We climb out of the cab, and two minutes later Jameson pulls me by the hand into a restaurant named Babbo. It kind of looks like a mini English pub from the outside, all quaint and cute, but when we walk through the door, it's a lot bigger than it seems. The space is dark and moody, and gold light fixtures add to the ambience. Fresh flowers are in giant vases everywhere, and it feels super romantic.

"Hello, Mr. Miles." The man at the desk smiles. "Your table is this way, sir." Jameson takes my hand and leads me through to the corner of the restaurant; the waiter pulls out my chair.

"Thank you."

"Would you like something to drink to start?"

"Yes." Jameson peruses the wine menu. "Red?" he asks me.

"Whatever." I shrug with a nervous smile.

"We'll have a bottle of Henschke."

"Yes, sir; which one?"

"Hill of Roses, please," he replies as he closes the menu. The waiter disappears, leaving us alone.

"I'm guessing that you know your wine?" I ask.

He pours us both a glass of water. "I only go to restaurants that stock the wine I like. So yes, I suppose I know wine."

"Ah. I see." I smirk. "One of those."

He smiles. "Perhaps."

Our eyes linger on each other's faces for a moment.

"I can't believe you're the frigging CEO."

He chuckles and rests his face on his hand. "I thought you wanted a date with Jim tonight?"

"I did . . . I mean, I do."

"Well, why are we talking about CEOs?"

I smile softly. "I don't know."

The waiter returns and opens the bottle of wine and pours a little in a glass. Jameson tastes it. "That's fine." The waiter fills our glasses and disappears.

Jameson holds his glass up, and I softly clink it with mine and take a sip and taste the rich, velvety flavor. "Hmm." I nod. "I'm impressed."

"I have excellent taste." He smiles before falling serious again. "In all things."

I smile bashfully; he's talking about me.

"Tell me about last weekend," he asks.

"Not much to tell."

"You broke up with him?"

"It was a long time coming."

"You weren't happy?"

"No. Not for a long time."

"What's his name? What does he do?"

"I'm not telling you his name," I snap. "He's a businessman—successful and handsome," I lie.

He sips his wine as he watches me, and I know he has something else on his mind.

"What?" I ask.

"Did you ever think about me?"

"Yes." I smile softly. "Did you ever think about me?"

"I did, actually." His eyes hold mine.

"What did you think about?"

A slow, sexy smile crosses his face.

"What?"

"You don't want to know."

"No, I do." I smile. "Tell me."

"I was thinking that you were probably the hottest sex I'd ever had." His eyes drop to my lips.

The air crackles between us.

"And even now, every time I'm in a room with you, it's as if my body takes on a need of its own."

Time stops as we stare at each other.

He sips his wine in slow motion. "When I look at you . . . I have one thing on my mind," he murmurs. "I can't help it. It's almost primal."

Primal.

"It's getting damn hard to control," he whispers darkly.

Damn, this man is something else, but every warning signal is telling me to run away as fast as I can. If he can affect me the way he did after one night . . . what could two nights do?

Our eyes are locked, and arousal heats my blood. Suddenly I don't want to play hard to get; I don't care if we don't know each other. I don't care about the risks. He has something that I need . . . and damn it, I'm taking it without questions.

"We should order," I whisper.

He opens the menu with a sense of urgency. "What do you want?"

"Whatever's the quickest."

An hour later, he pulls me up the sidewalk by the hand. "My car is parked around here." He turns and takes me into his arms and aggressively kisses me, and I smile against his lips. The way we laughed and talked over dinner tonight reminded me of the Jim I remember, the man on the plane who was interested in everything about me and my life. As if he felt it, too, we nearly made out in the middle of a crowded restaurant. He's not wrong; this attraction is insane.

"Hurry," I whisper against his lips.

It's one thing to go out to dinner with a gorgeous man—it's another to imagine yourself under the table, sucking his dick the entire time.

I don't know if it's that he told me that I was the best sex he's ever had, but . . . damn it, I want to blow his frigging mind. I'm desperate to get him naked. I want to be that girl he turned me into in Boston again. I've missed her.

We turn the corner, and I see the big black limousine parked by the curb. I stop still.

"What?" He frowns.

"The limo is here?"

"Yes. So?"

I stare at him for an extended moment.

He rolls his eyes and opens the back door. "Get in."

I climb in, and within two seconds, he's in the car and has me straddled over his lap with my dress up around my waist. The security screen is up, providing us with privacy. His cock is hard, and he grabs my hip bones and guides my sex back and forth over him as we kiss. His hands are on my behind and then trailing up and down my back as my body takes on a rhythm of its own.

His eyes are dark, and his fingers dip into my panties, and he slides them through my flesh. "Fuck," he whispers. "I could blow just by feeling this beautiful, hot pussy."

I begin to rock down on him with force, searching for a deeper connection, and his jaw hangs slack as he stares up at me. I don't know what the hell kind of nympho pills someone slipped into my drink at dinner, but I find myself on the floor between his legs, and I unzip his jeans with force.

He hisses as I push him back into his seat and spread his legs aggressively.

Our eyes lock, and I lick the end of him and taste the pre-ejaculate as it oozes from his head. He cups my face, and I take him deep down my throat as he clenches. "Fuck," he growls in a whisper as his stomach contracts. "Fucking hell, Emily."

I begin to fist him hard, and he lurches underneath me. He's going to come.

I want him to come hard, quick . . . and unbridled. I need to own him tonight.

Pleasing him makes me feel good about myself, and this new version of Emily is someone I like. I want to keep her.

"Emily," he growls as he grabs a handful of my hair. "We're home." He pushes the lock down on the door just before his driver tries to open it.

I scramble to the seat, and he zips his jeans up as we both pant, gasping for air.

What the hell? This man makes me an animal.

He turns to me and smirks as he fixes my hair. "Let's just get to the apartment, shall we?" He kisses me tenderly; his lips linger over mine as we stare at each other.

"It's good to see you again, Emily Foster," he whispers.

I lick my lips as I climb back over to straddle him. "It's good to taste you again, Jameson Miles." I rock my sex over him, and he grabs my hip bones and holds me still.

"Stop," he commands. "Stop now."

I put my lips up to his ear. "I want you to blow your load in your car," I whisper before biting him. "Fuck me right here."

"Jesus Christ." He pushes me off and opens the door in one swift movement, and the driver drops his head as he pretends not to know what we were doing in there.

"Thank you," Jameson says as he pulls me out and marches into the building.

We get into the elevator, and the attendant stares straight ahead. I'm panting, dripping wet, and my sex is throbbing.

I'm a hot mess.

Jameson's eyes are dark as he stares straight ahead at the closed doors.

God, I need him.

The doors open, and he pulls me out by the hand. Our lips are locked, and he walks me into his apartment backward. "Isn't this how we got into the room last time?" I smile as he lifts me.

"Similar."

He puts me down, and I look around, and my heart drops. "What the hell, Jim?" I whisper through shock.

"What?" He frowns.

"This is your house?" I ask as my eyes scan the room.

His lips drop to my neck as he licks and sucks down my collarbone; he's completely preoccupied.

The apartment is huge and modern, with floor-to-ceiling windows and the lights of New York twinkling everywhere I look. Lamps are strategically placed to give a warm feeling. I've never been anywhere so beautiful . . . or foreign.

The floors are a light timber parquetry, and luxurious velvet and leather furnishings fill the space. The living room has a fireplace with a huge gilded mirror hanging over it and a beautiful antique rug.

"Stop looking at the apartment, and look at me." He grabs my face and drags it back to his.

I stare at him.

"What?" he murmurs.

"This apartment."

"What about it?"

"You come from a different world than me," I whisper.

"Who cares?" His eyes hold mine. "I want you, and you want me. What else is there?"

Our kiss turns desperate as he slams me up against the wall and tears my dress from my body in one quick movement. I push his jacket over his shoulders and grab his T-shirt and lift it off and then unzip his jeans, and he kicks them to the side.

We stare at each other, both in our underwear, both panting, both craving a deeper connection.

It's like Christmas morning . . . only better.

Next thing I know, I'm being dragged through his apartment and thrown onto the bed. He tears my underwear from my body. His hungry gaze drops down the length of my body as he drinks me in.

And there it is—the heat that this man creates with his stare could light up the earth. The way he looks at me is something I've never forgotten.

He lifts my legs and puts them around his waist and then begins to slide his thick cock through my swollen flesh.

A sexy smile crosses his face as he looks down at me. "I remember now."

"You remember what?"

"What the *F* stands for in your initials."

"What's that?"

"Fuck bunny."

I burst out laughing. "I'd forgotten about that."

"How could you forget anything? Every detail from that night is burned into my brain." He hands me a condom. "Put it on me."

My lips softly kiss his dick before I follow his instruction. So bossy.

"Like what?" I whisper up at him. I lie down, and he crawls back over me.

"Like the way you looked at me, the way you tasted under my tongue." His lips take mine, and our kiss deepens. "I remember how every muscle deep inside you felt when your body rippled around mine."

I smile up at him in wonder as I run my fingers through his stubble. *Please don't be any more gorgeous. I won't be able to deal with you at all.*

"But it was the way you kissed me that I remember the most."

My eyes search his. "How did I kiss you?"

"Like you'd been waiting your whole life to kiss me."

He slides in deep, and my heart constricts. I bring my legs higher. "Maybe I had."

We stare at each other, his body inside mine, and even though I know that this is just sex and that it means nothing, it feels intimate and special . . . more than it should.

Stop it. Stop overthinking this.

"Are you going to keep jabbering on, or are you going to fuck me?" I tease to lighten the moment.

He chuckles and pulls out and slams into me, knocking the air from my lungs. I cry out.

Oh . . . dear God. I think I just woke the devil.

He pumps me with his knees spread wide, harder and harder, and with every slam he lifts my legs a little higher and a little wider.

He holds himself still and then circles deep inside me. My head tips back to the sky as I lose all coherent thought. "Oh God," I whimper as his teeth graze my neck. "That's so good." He keeps doing the delicious movement as his thumb circles over my clitoris. My body begins to shudder, and he grabs my face and brings it to his.

Our eyes lock as my body arches and writhes beneath him.

"Look at me while you come on my cock," he commands as he straightens his arms and puts my legs over his shoulders. The change in position deepens him inside of me, and I convulse as he slams into me. His body begins to take mine at piston pace, and I grip his arms as I stare up at him.

"Fuck yeah," he growls. "Fuck . . . fuck . . ." He tips his head back and cries out as I feel the telling jerk as he comes deep inside me.

We're wet with perspiration, and he bends and tenderly takes my lips with his.

My heart races out of control as I stare at the ceiling, gasping for air. His head is in my neck, his lips trailing along my collarbone.

What the fuck was that? That wasn't sex—that was an apocalyptic event.

I'm ruined.

I wake in the darkness; the glow of the New York city lights illuminates through the room. It's late—or early. About four in the morning, I think. We didn't shut the drapes before going to sleep.

What a night.

We devoured each other until we had nothing left.

I stare at him as he lies flat on his back in an exhausted sleep. I don't know what we are to each other, but I do know that he's my sexual soul mate. Is that even a thing? Our bodies are like animals with each other; neither of us could get enough.

The thirst just couldn't be quenched. If he were to wake up now, I would be instantly aroused, as I know he would be.

He's right, *this is primal.*

I'm thirsty, so I climb out of bed and throw on his robe and make my way out to the kitchen in search of water. We left the lamps on, so the rooms are partially lit. I don't even remember getting to the bedroom.

I find a glass and pour myself some water from the fridge, and as I look around, my heart drops. What the hell kind of kitchen is this? It's like a restaurant.

I walk back out to the living room and stare out over the city way down below.

My eyes roam over the apartment, and my heart flutters. This is real money.

Stupid money.

My entire apartment would fit into his bedroom alone. What does a place like this cost? Our clothes are strewn all over the floor, and I pick them up and fold them and put them onto the coffee table. I see something light up on the floor.

I frown and bend to pick up Jameson's phone. It must have fallen out of his pocket as we were undressing. The screen lights up as a message comes through, and the name *Chloe* flashes on the screen.

Where are you?
Did your meeting go late?

I stare at the phone. *What the fuck?*
Who's Chloe?

127

I wake to the sound of my alarm, and I smile as I stretch; I'm sated and sleepy.

Relaxed for the first time in a long time.

What a night . . . what a woman.

I reach for Emily and frown when I realize she's not in bed with me. She must be in the bathroom. I doze for another twenty minutes, and eventually when she doesn't return, I get up. "Emily?" I call as I walk into the bathroom.

It's empty.

I walk out into the living area. "Emily?" I call.

Silence.

"Where is she?" I look around to see my clothes folded on the coffee table and notice that hers . . . are gone.

"Emily?" I call as I do a 360 of my apartment. "Emily?"

I clench my jaw as my anger begins to escalate. I dial her number as a shade of red clouds my vision. I hear my furious heartbeat in my ears as adrenaline fills my bloodstream.

"Hello," she answers.

"Where the fuck are you?" I sneer.

Chapter 8

Jameson

"I had to go," she stammers.

"Why?"

"I needed to be at work early."

"You didn't think to wake me?" I snap. "You piss me off."

"Don't start your righteous shit with me. I'll leave when I fucking want to." The phone goes dead.

I inhale sharply; nobody hangs up on me.

Nobody.

I clench my jaw and throw my phone onto the couch. This woman is fucking infuriating.

I walk into my office, open my laptop, and log in to my security footage. I take a seat as I wait for it to load. An image of my front door comes up, and I hit rewind and watch as it goes back in fast-forward. I catch sight of her leaving, and I stop the film. What time was it?

It was 3:58 a.m. She had to go to work early? Bullshit.

She waited for me to fall asleep and then immediately left. I sit back in my chair as my anger escalates.

"I don't know what the fuck you're playing at, Emily Foster, but I won't have it. If you're with me, you're with me. And you'll do as I fucking say."

I slam my computer shut and storm upstairs.

She's looking for a fight. She just found one.

An hour later, I walk through the foyer of my building and out to my car. "Good morning, Mr. Miles." Alan smiles as he opens the door of my limo.

"Morning," I say as I get in.

The usual pile of newspapers is on the seat, along with my coffee, and I begin my morning ritual. It takes us forty minutes to drive the thirteen miles to my building, so I use this time to keep track of our competitors. I flick through the pile and pick up the *Gazette*, our closest competitor, and I scan the front page.

"Their formatting is appalling," I mutter under my breath as I flick it open. I read page one and two, and then I get to page three.

Breaking News

The NYPD has closed in on a top-secret investigation.

The murder was originally attributed to a man police had nicknamed Stoneface, who has been linked to more than 85 burglaries in Brooklyn, New York.

But with DNA evidence, investigators now believe the crimes were committed by the same suspect that has been called the Red Ribbon Killer in other parts of the state.

"With this filing, we have officially linked Stoneface to an individual known as the Red Ribbon Killer," said Matthew Price, Brooklyn County district attorney.

Stoneface, an auto mechanic, is wanted after police tracked him down by matching his DNA with a genealogy website.

He has been accused of killing 5 and raping 45 people in what police are describing as a premeditated crime spree.

He was nicknamed the Red Ribbon Killer because the victims had a red ribbon tied around their neck after they were murdered.

Police have tracked his whereabouts, and an arrest is expected today.

"Fuck." It's Emily's story, just worded differently. I take out my phone and call Tristan as my blood pressure rises to boiling point.

"Hey," he answers.

"Page three of the *Gazette*," I snap.

"You're joking?"

"Nope."

"Fucking hell." He sighs. "See you soon."

I hang up, and my phone vibrates. The name *Chloe* lights up the screen; I hit decline.

I sip my coffee and stare out the window as contempt drips from my every pore. It's one thing to be deceived, but to be sold out by one of our own staff members is a whole new level of betrayal.

When I get my hands on whoever is responsible for this, there will be fucking hell to pay.

Half an hour later, I walk into my office and find three of my favorite people inside. My brothers.

"Hello." I smirk. "Jesus, you've both got uglier since I last saw you. I didn't think it was possible."

They chuckle, and we hug. I miss my brothers. Their role in the company requires them to live in the UK; they work out of the London office. I only get to see them once a month when I travel over there, Tristan the same. Although he gets to stay longer, so he gets more time with them.

I slap the *Gazette* onto my desk. "What the hell is this?"

"Fucking hell," Tristan whispers as they all take a seat around the board table.

"What's going on?" Elliot snaps. "I don't believe this."

I exhale heavily. "We got a new staff member, Emily Foster."

Tristan smirks, and I roll my eyes. "And?" Christopher interrupts.

"She ran a story on her second day and wasn't sure of the name of the suspect, so she made one up on the spot and planned on changing it when she got back to the office."

They frown as they listen.

"Only she forgot."

"Jesus." Elliot rolls his eyes. "Useless."

"No," Tristan says. "Diabolical. The exact same story ran in the *Gazette* the next day . . . with the bogus name."

Elliot and Christopher frown as they listen.

"How do you know this?" Christopher asks.

"I know the reporter. We met a while ago." I pause, not wanting to elaborate.

"You know who she is?" Tristan smirks.

"Who?" Elliot's eyes flick between us.

"Remember ages ago Jay got a motherfucking huge hickey?"

Their faces fall. "No."

Elliot pinches the bridge of his nose. "Please . . . don't tell me." He laughs out loud. "What did you call it? Stopover shame."

"I had to wear a fucking turtleneck for two weeks." I sigh in disgust.

"Remember the black-tie dinner for Mom's charity?" Tristan throws his head back and laughs. "And you had the hugest hickey anyone had ever seen." He chuckles at the memory. "And you had to hide from Mom all night and wear cover-up on your neck. That was fucking hilarious, man."

"Mortifying." I shiver as I think back. "Anyway, back to the story." I glare at Tristan for bringing it up. "Emily—that's her name—unbeknownst to me got a job here. She started three weeks ago, and then this mishap with the name happened. She came to me with suspicions that something fishy was going on. A fake name that she made up on the spot was no coincidence." I look around at my brothers. "Our stories are being sold on the black market."

"For fuck's sake," Elliot snaps.

"Our share prices are dropping because we are no longer breaking news."

Elliot shakes his head in disgust.

"Because the reporters that we are paying for are working for our competition," Tristan snaps.

"We tested the theory this week. We got Emily to write a bogus story and submit it through the regular channels, and look." I hit the paper with the backs of my fingers. "Here it is, page three of the *Gazette*."

They all stare at the paper in front of us, deep in thought.

"So . . . what do we do?"

"Firing everyone works for me," I snap.

"No, we have to do this properly. There are a hundred people on that floor. Not to mention IT and the mailroom."

The boys break into chatter as they discuss our options.

I push my intercom. "Can we get Richard from legal up here, please?"

"Yes, sir."

"Should Emily write another story so we can track it more closely?" Elliot asks.

"No," I snap. "I don't want her involved again. I don't want her up here at all."

Tristan smirks.

"I'm going to wipe that stupid smirk off your face in a minute," I snap.

"Scared she's going to give you another hickey?" Elliot jokes. "Must have some pretty good suction going on."

They all laugh.

I glare at him. "Cut the shit. I'm not in the fucking mood for this today."

There is a knock on the door. "Come in," I call. Richard comes into view. "Please take a seat."

"How can I help you?" He smiles.

"We have reason to believe that someone on the news floor is selling our stories to a competitor. How do we legally handle this?"

Richard frowns as he looks between us. "Are you sure?"

"Yes."

"Well." He exhales as he thinks. "You would hire a corporate investigation firm."

"What do they do?" I ask.

"They are business-centric and can involve verifying the legitimacy of a business partner or deal, looking into loss or theft of proprietary information, identifying the potential of a damaged reputation, things like that."

"No," I say as I stand. "I don't want a stranger in here sniffing around. What if the story breaks? It will do more damage to our reputation."

"With all due respect, Jameson, I don't see how you have any other choice," Richard says.

"Do you know any?" Tristan asks.

"No. But I can find out who to use."

"I don't like it."

"They're professionals. They deal with things like this all the time. You won't even know they are in the building," Richard continues.

"How does it work?"

"They usually come in undercover, act as one of the workers while they watch and trace."

I roll my eyes in disgust. "How ridiculous. This isn't a fucking *MacGyver* episode."

I stare at my brothers, and I know I've been forced into a corner. There is no other way around this, and I know I must concede. "Fine."

Emily
An hour earlier

I power walk up the street among the crowd. I'll never get used to these busy New York sidewalks no matter how long I live here. I'm exhausted. I was up half the night having sex, and I haven't been back to sleep since I left Jameson's at four o'clock. God, what a nightmare this whole situation is. And who the fuck is Chloe?

I order my iced coffee, and as I wait, I buy the *Gazette* at the newsstand. I'll read it at lunch. I wonder if they have any jobs available. I'm probably going to need one soon. With a heavy heart, my mind goes to Jameson. Damn it, why does something always have to go wrong with the men I like? If only he were just a normal guy—with a normal shitty apartment and a shitty car and no women texting him—he would be perfect. In every way.

I get a vision of us last night as we made love and kissed for hours, and sadness sweeps over me.

I hate that we connect so deeply on a physical level.

It's just sex, you idiot. Bone-shattering, awesome, toe-curling sex.

I imagine Jameson Miles would have that with every woman he's with. He's that kind of guy with that kind of a dick.

Ugh. I take my coffee and make the depressing walk to the office. I'm not thinking about him today, and I'm most definitely not telling him that I know about Chloe.

Whoever Chloe is.

All I know is that if she's texting him with where-are-you messages in the middle of the night, something's going on, and he's all hers. She can have him.

I may be a lot of things, but a man stealer I'm not.

Douchebag. How dare he use me for sex? The bitter taste of betrayal lines my mouth; I can act brave all I want, but the truth is I'm upset. Last night was perfect—more than perfect—and then he had to go and wreck it.

I thought I spent the night with Jim, but instead I got the sleazebag Jameson Miles version. How didn't I see it?

I trudge into the building and up to my floor, and I fall into my seat in disgust. "Hi," I say.

"Hey." Aaron spins on his chair toward me. "How did it go?"

I glance up at the camera above. Is he watching? "Good," I lie. "I'll tell you about it tonight. We are drinking."

"Drinking?"

"Everything we see."

His face falls. "Oh . . . it went that kind of good."

"Precisely," I mutter flatly.

"What's going on around here today?" Aaron whispers.

"What do you mean?" I look up from my computer.

"Tristan is buzzing around, and Jameson has been down to the floor already."

"What time is it?" I glance at my watch. "It's only eight forty-five. They are never down here at this hour, if at all."

"I know."

"Hmm." I watch Tristan as he talks to the floor manager, and he seems to have a stern face on. "Do you think something's wrong?" I ask.

"I don't know. Did you piss Mr. J off last night?"

I smirk.

137

"Maybe he's upstairs throwing a tantrum."

"I'm probably about to get fired." I smile happily as I open my computer. Good, I hope he's pissed.

Two hours later, I glance up and see two men I haven't seen before. "Who are they?" I whisper.

Molly looks up, and her face falls. "Oh Lord have mercy . . . thank you, God."

"Huh?" I frown.

"That's Elliot and Christopher Miles. They've flown in from the UK. Must be a board meeting or something going on this week."

My eyes widen. "Jameson's brothers?"

She smiles dreamily as she watches them. "Uh-huh." She looks over to Aaron, who is also openly staring. "I call Elliot."

"Good, because I call Christopher," he whispers right back.

"Can you please set us up on a brother date?" she whispers.

"Yes, and we need to swing," Aaron replies. "Because I want all four. I can't choose."

"Can you imagine?" Molly murmurs. "Makes me blush just thinking of it." She fans her face with her manila folder as her eyes stay glued to the brothers. "Imagine all of them in bed together . . . taking turns with your body."

I roll my eyes in disgust. "The Miles brothers are overrated, if you ask me."

They're not, though. I'm lying through my teeth. All with dark hair, tall, and built . . . square jaws in their designer playboy suits. Everything about the four of them screams power and gorgeousness. *Assholes.*

Jameson hasn't been to see me today. I haven't heard from him, and if the truth be known, he's probably upstairs making out on his office couch with Chloe as we speak.

Ugh. I'm off all men. How could I have been so stupid?

4:30 p.m.

"Oh my God, did you see the story in the *Gazette*?" Molly says.

"No, what?"

"The Red Ribbon Killer. I don't even feel safe on the subway tonight."

My eyes flick to her. "What?"

"Yeah, it's one of their lead stories today. I was reading it online just now."

"Are you kidding me?" I click onto their website and search for the story, and sure enough, the story comes up, almost word for word . . . my words.

I put my hand over my mouth in horror as I read it.

Oh my God. That's why they're all here today; they're in damage control.

I stare at the story on my computer. It's there in black and white, but I can't actually believe it. I look at all the people in the office acting calm and professional. Who is it?

Thieving bastard.

"I've got to go and see someone. Back in a minute." I practically run to the elevator and take it to the top floor. Why didn't he say anything to me?

"Hello," I say as I brush through reception.

"Excuse me, Emily," the receptionist calls. "He's not taking visitors right now."

"Whatever." I storm through to Jameson's office, and I knock on the door.

"Yes?" he barks.

I open the door to find him sitting behind his large desk; blue eyes rise to meet mine. "What is it?" he asks coldly.

I walk in and close the door behind me. "I saw the story."

"And?"

"Well . . . why didn't you tell me? It was my story. I thought you would have at least told me."

"Ms. Foster." He clenches his jaw as if I'm a huge annoyance. "I don't have time to play your juvenile games."

"What does that mean?"

"It means I'm very busy." He goes back to typing.

I stare at him for a moment. *What?*

"Close the door on your way out, please."

The fucking nerve of this man. He sleeps with me while he's seeing someone else and then has the audacity to treat me like this. Something snaps deep inside me. "Who the hell do you think you are?"

"Here we go," he mutters under his breath.

"What?" I cry. "Here we go? Are you fucking serious?"

He rests his chin on his hand as he glares at me.

"What was last night? Huh?" I cry. Alarm bells start screaming around me. This is the worst thing I could possibly do, but I've lost all control. "You're seeing someone else?" I stammer. "Who's Chloe, Jameson?"

His eyebrow rises, and he stands and walks toward the door. "Out."

"What?" I snap in disbelief. "You're kicking me out?"

"What I'm doing is being professional. I suggest you do the same thing." He stands over me.

"You know what?" I whisper up at him through tears of rage. "You can go fuck yourself."

He glares at me. "Not that it's any of your business, but Chloe is my masseuse. I had an appointment with her last night that I wasn't home for. Those text messages came through hours after she sent them."

I stare at him as my heart hammers in my chest.

"Do not check my fucking phone ever again." He sneers as he turns his back on me and goes and sits back at his desk.

I stare at him through tears. I feel . . . used. "I thought we had something."

"So did I." His cold eyes hold mine. "But you fucked that up this morning when you left like a two-year-old." He turns back to his computer.

"Do you sleep with your masseuse?"

His eyes come to mine. "That is none of your business. Now get out."

Chapter 9

I storm out of his office and down the hall, and I fall into the ladies' room. I burst into the stall, sit down, and put my head into my hands.

Embarrassment fills me. I just completely lost control and made a fool of myself. *You stupid fucking idiot.*

My heartbeat sounds through my body, and I'm so angry right now that I can't even see straight. His words come back to me: *But you fucked that up this morning when you left like a two-year-old.*

God.

Angry tears stream down my face, and I wipe them away as quickly as they appear.

Stop crying, you baby. I'm not even upset—I'm angry. Now I have to get off this floor without anyone seeing me.

Why *am* I fucking crying?

I know why. Because I'm sleep deprived, and I deserve to be treated better, that's why. The fucking asshole. Who the hell does he think he is?

The longer I'm in here, the worse it is. I wash my face, dry my eyes, and drop my shoulders as I steel myself to walk past reception.

I'm fine, fine . . . totally fine. Jameson Miles does not have the power to affect me at all. I open the bathroom door and walk out, and Tristan comes around the corner. His face falls when he sees me. "Emily?" He frowns. "Are you all right?"

"Yes, of course." I storm past him.

"He's had a bad day," he calls after me, and my eyes fill with tears anew.

Yeah, well . . . so have I.

"Where have you been?" Molly asks on my arrival back to my desk.

"I went and saw Ricardo," I lie.

"So where do you want to go tonight?"

"Oh." I wince. I can't think of anything worse. "I'm sorry, guys. I'm going to bail. I need to sleep."

"But we want to hear all the juicy details."

"Oh." My heart sinks. I don't want them to know that I'm the world's biggest loser. "We didn't meet up last night. He pulled out."

"What?" Aaron frowns.

"Whatever. I don't care." I shrug, acting casual. I wish I hadn't told them anything at all about him now.

"Yeah, that's okay. I need to save money anyway." Aaron sighs as he packs up his computer.

"You coming?" Molly asks.

"I'm just going to finish this up." I open my computer back up. The last thing I want to do is give the bastard a reason to fire me. I finish my task, and finally, an hour later, I close my computer and head downstairs.

I walk through the front doors and glance up to see the black limo parked at the curb.

Shit.

I look around nervously. Is he in there? Damn it, I don't want to see him. I power walk across the street to the safe haven of the café. I order a drink and take a seat at the window.

Great. I drag my hand down my face. Seriously, what next? This is the last thing I need.

"Here you go." The waiter smiles as he puts my iced tea down in front of me.

"Thank you." I watch the driver across the road as he leans on the limo, and I think back to the other night when I was on my knees, and he tried to open the door, and it was locked. I wonder how long he's worked for him, how much he's seen. I watch as he answers the phone and then gets in the car and drives off.

Huh? Was Jameson already inside the car? Why did he drive off? *That's weird . . .*

The front doors of the building open, and a group of men walk out. *Shit, it's them.* I pick up the menu and cover my face as I peer through the window and across the street.

Tristan, Elliot, Christopher, and Jameson . . . and the blonde girl who was with Tristan the other night. She's super trendy, and her work clothes look like they belong in a modeling shoot. The boys look so similar. Elliot is the most like Jameson, with dark hair and piercing blue eyes. Then Tristan and Christopher look alike, lighter hair with a curl. They're talking as they walk, and Jameson says something with a straight face, and they all laugh out loud.

What did he say?

They walk around the corner. Elliot puts his hand affectionately on Jameson's back as they cross the road while deep in conversation. I watch them walk up the street and then into a cocktail bar.

I pinch the bridge of my nose and close my eyes with a huge sad sigh.

Ugh, I just want this day to be over.

It's amazing what a weekend and some sleep can do for a girl. I march into the building on Monday like the most powerful woman on earth. "Good morning." The security guard smiles as I walk through the security screen.

"Morning." I smile. "Lovely day, isn't it?"

"Sure is." He winks as I walk past him.

To hell with Jameson Miles.

So what? We had sex. So what? It was great. But guess what? I don't care.

I'm not letting him dull my New York shine. I moved here to start a new and exciting life, and to be honest, the first three weeks have been pretty amazing . . . well, except last week. But I'm scratching that from the record, so it doesn't actually count.

I'm moving onward and upward, and twelve months from now I'll probably look back at this and laugh.

I make it to my floor to find Ava and her friend Renee talking by the elevator. "Hi, girls."

"Hi." Ava smiles. "How are you?"

"Good. Great, actually. What are you guys up to?"

"We're discussing where we want to go this weekend."

"Oh."

"Hey, you should come clubbing with us," she offers.

"Really?"

"Yeah, for sure. We have a blast."

"You know what? I'd love to." I smile.

"Awesome." She takes her phone out of her pocket and puts my number in. "We usually meet up about eight or nine on Saturday night."

"For dinner first?" I ask.

"No." She smirks. "We eat mac and cheese before we go out and then buy hella expensive drinks. Priorities."

I laugh. "Okay, sounds good."

I make my way to my desk and find Aaron already working. "Hi."

"Hi." He says sadly.

"What's wrong?" I frown as I take my seat.

"I got stood up again last night." He sighs. "I'm just getting sick of this, you know?"

"Have you talked to him?" I ask.

"No, he's always working or got things going on or a legitimate excuse. Maybe I'm looking for problems that aren't there."

"Maybe," I reply. "Anyway, you'll be glad to know that I'm in a much better mood today."

"Really?" He smirks. "What's your secret?"

"Sleep," I reply. "And I'm even going to start going to the gym on level three next week. Want to come with me?"

"Maybe." He thinks about it.

"We could become superhot fitness freaks."

He chuckles. "Yeah, okay. Are you high?"

"I had such a shitty day on Friday, and I'm determined to change my mind-set."

"Good for you."

Molly arrives and puts her bag onto the desk with a bang. "Anybody want a kid?"

I giggle. "What now?"

"Ugh." She flops into her chair. "So you know how Brad got caught messaging that girl. I took his phone from him because his father wouldn't do it," she snaps.

"Yeah."

"Well, he was angry, but he wasn't that pissed off, you know?"

"What do you mean?"

"Well, he wasn't hassling me for his phone back all the time like normal, and he wanted to go to bed really early last night."

I frown as I listen.

"I felt like something was off, so I checked the hiding spot to see if his phone was still there, and it was. Then I had this strange thought to check the SIM."

Aaron chuckles, already knowing where this story is going.

"The little shit had taken the SIM out and put it into an old phone."

"Oh, crap."

"I barge into his bedroom, and sure enough, he is on his phone, and it is hidden under the covers. I snatch it off him and lock myself in the bathroom while I go through it. He's banging the door down, so I know there is something on there that he doesn't want me to see."

My eyes widen as I listen.

"Get this," she sneers. "Pure little Chanel has been sending him nudes too."

I frown.

"This fifteen-year-old little girl is built like a fucking *Penthouse* Pet."

We chuckle.

"Oh, it gets worse," she continues. "While I'm looking through his phone, a new message comes through from her."

"What was it?"

"I got a Brazilian like you wanted. You like?"

My mouth falls open.

"Can you believe that message?"

Unable to help it, I burst out laughing.

"I would find this funny, too, if it weren't my child," she whispers.

"Then Brad had a complete meltdown and told me that if I call Chanel's parents, I'm effectively committing social suicide for him as his whole reputation will be ruined and that he's never going to school again." She hits her computer keyboard with a hard bang.

"That's true," Aaron replies. "You can't call her mother."

"So it's all right for her to call me, but I can't call her?" she stammers.

"I don't know," I whisper. "I probably wouldn't call her mother either."

"Well, what would you do?" she asks.

"I'd buy him a box of condoms, that's what I'd do."

She stares at me, wide eyed.

"Because imagine if he got her pregnant," I add.

"Oh my God." She drags her hand down her face. "I can't deal with boys. They are so stupid."

"The amount of testosterone in a male teenager is ridiculous," Aaron replies casually. "I was jerking off four times a day when I was fifteen."

Molly and I wince.

"Four times a day?" I stammer.

"Don't girls do that?" He frowns in surprise.

"No," we both gasp.

"Men are gross." I fake a shiver in disgust.

The phone on my desk rings. "Hello," I answer.

"Hello, Emily, this is Sammia, Mr. Miles's PA."

What does she want? "Hi."

"Mr. Miles asked me to let you know that you have a meeting in his office in an hour."

"I'm very busy today. Can you tell Mr. Miles that, unfortunately, I won't be able to make it?"

"He told me that your attendance is mandatory, and he's already spoken to your manager to get clearance."

I roll my eyes. *Stupid twat.* "Fine. I'll be there. Thank you."

Knock, knock. I tentatively knock on Jameson's door.

"Come in," his strong voice calls.

My stomach flips with nerves, and I open the door. Jameson sits alone at his desk. His eyes rise to meet mine.

"You wanted to see me?"

"Yes, please take a seat."

I drop to the chair as I clasp my hands together with white-knuckle force.

His eyes hold mine. "How are you?"

"Good, thanks." I drop my eyes to the desk. I'm not looking at those beautiful blue eyes. He's like the snake from *The Jungle Book*—one look in those hypnotic suckers, and your panties drop to the floor.

"Look at me, please," he commands.

"What do you want, Jameson?" I snap. "I don't have time for your games."

"I want you to look at me."

I drag my eyes to his.

"Why don't you want to look at me?"

I stare at him for a moment. "Because I just find your face really . . . punchable."

He smirks and leans back in his chair, clearly amused. "Is that so?"

"Yeah, it is." I look around his office. "Can we talk about work?"

"Later. Right now I would like to talk about your tantrum on Friday."

"I wouldn't."

"She's my masseuse."

"Like you said, it's none of my business." I glare at him, my resting bitch face in full swing.

"I was going to call you last night."

Now it's my turn to be amused. "Don't waste your time. I wouldn't have answered."

He runs his thumbnail back and forth over his bottom lip as he watches me, as if fascinated. "Why are you so snarky?"

"I'm not snarky. I'm just not about to put up with shit from an entitled asshole. You may be a CEO here, but . . ."

He sits back and raises his chin as if angered. "Finish what you wanted to say."

"No. I'm good." I clench my teeth together to stop myself from elaborating.

"I may be the CEO here . . . but what?" he demands as he swivels on his chair.

"I wasn't angry with you on Friday. I left in the middle of the night because I was confused . . . about a lot of things. I was going to talk to you when I was thinking clearly because I didn't want to be a drama queen."

Our eyes are locked.

"And then I came to your office, and you treated me like a two-bit whore that you ejaculated in the night before."

He clenches his jaw.

"I'm nobody's whore, Jameson, least of all yours. No job is worth my self-respect."

The air crackles between us.

"So excuse me if the privilege of sucking your golden CEO dick doesn't excite me any longer."

He rubs his thumbnail back and forth over his bottom lip as his eyes hold mine.

"Were you on the debating team, Ms. Foster?"

"What does that have to do with anything?" I snap, annoyed.

"You make a good argument." He licks his bottom lip as he tries to hide his amusement. "Impressive."

I roll my eyes. *Sarcastic asshole.* God, he infuriates me so bad. I get an image of myself diving over the desk and punching him in the nose as hard as I can. It would wipe that smug smirk off his stupid face. I'm not even joking; his face really *is* punchable.

"Please," I mutter under my breath.

"Please what?"

"Please stop insulting my intelligence. Run your meeting so I can get back to work. You're wasting my time."

Knock, knock.

"Come in," Jameson calls.

Tristan puts his head around the door and looks between us. "Are we on?"

I get the feeling that Jameson told them to give us ten minutes alone before they joined us. "Yes, come in," he replies coolly as he rearranges some papers on his desk.

They all pile into the office, and I straighten in my chair. These four men together are an extreme sucker punch. Gorgeous overload.

"Hello." Tristan smiles. "Emily, this is Elliot and Christopher, our brothers." I stand and shake both of their hands.

"Hello." Elliot and Christopher smile.

"Hi."

"Please be seated," Jameson commands. "Tristan, you can do the honors, please."

"Okay. So as per our meeting on Friday, we have recruited a private corporate investigator to work on your floor and get to the bottom of this mess."

"Okay." I look between them.

"What we want you to do is keep sending in bogus stories."

I frown. "Why?"

"Because if there are a lot of stories going through that are bogus, it will be easier for us to trace."

I sit back in my seat, annoyed.

"And as you can see—" Tristan continues.

Jameson holds his hand up. "Stop there." He turns his attention to me. "What is it, Emily?"

I stare at him.

"What did you want to say, then?"

My eyes flick between the four men. "With all due respect, Mr. Miles, I didn't apply for my dream job to do bogus stories."

"Fair point," he snaps as he rubs his thumb over his fingertips.

"What's going to happen when this is all over?" I ask.

"You will return to your normal duties."

"I would like that in writing, please," I snap.

Elliot smirks and drops his head.

Jameson's eyes hold mine. "Very well." He turns his attention back to Tristan. "Please continue."

"The investigator will be starting next week on Monday, and Emily, we would like you to be his eyes on the floor."

I frown. "I don't really want to get involved in all this."

"You involved yourself the moment you stepped through my office door," Jameson replies.

I drop my head. *God.*

"Emily, if you could give us a few bogus stories to start with next Monday, that would be great."

"Okay, what would you like me to write about?"

Jameson's eyes meet mine. "The first story I would like to be about a fake prostitution racket."

I frown in question.

"Call the ringleader a two-bit whore."

The fucking nerve of this man. "Okay." I smile sweetly. "I have enough material to work with on that one."

"Good." Tristan smiles. "Work on those stories, and we will touch base next Monday afternoon."

"Yes, okay," I reply as I stand and walk toward the door. "Sounds good."

"Emily, I'd like to see you for a moment, please," Jameson replies calmly.

I stop on the spot. *Seriously?*

The boys file out of the office. "Bye, Emily," they call.

"Bye."

The door closes behind them, and Jameson stands and walks up behind me.

I can feel the heat from his body. The power he emanates is like nothing I've ever felt.

He takes my ponytail in his hand and wraps it around his knuckles three times and pulls my head to the side to give him access to my neck. In slow motion, he licks from my collarbone to my jaw with his thick, strong tongue. His lips go to my ear. "I didn't get to taste you yet."

I close my eyes as arousal runs through my blood like a river rapid. Goose bumps scatter up my spine.

I turn to him, and he takes my hand and puts it over his large erection in his pants.

Electricity zaps between us, and our eyes are locked. My breathing becomes ragged.

"Can I see you tonight?" he breathes.

I squeeze his dick as my sex clenches in appreciation.

"No, Jameson, you can't." I turn and walk out of his office with my heart hammering in my chest.

I get into the elevator as my body screams for me to go back. Every molecule in my body wants that man.

But he's just an asshole . . . and I'm just another groupie.

It's not going to happen.

It's Saturday night, and we are lined up to get into Sky Bar. I'm with Ava and Renee, and this is our third club. It's nearly midnight. I'm having the best time ever. We have laughed and danced and prick teased every stupid man in New York.

"Why are we waiting here in line again?" I frown. "What was wrong with the last place?"

"Nothing. This place is better, but it doesn't heat up until eleven."

"Oh." I shrug. Gosh, I know nothing about New York night-life. The doorman removes the red rope blocking the door and ushers us in, and my breath catches.

Wow, this bar is way up on the fiftieth floor and has a huge balcony overlooking the city lights. There's a dance floor and numerous cocktail bars, and the girls are right—the men here are another caliber.

I glance down at myself nervously; I hope I look all right. My long dark hair is down, and I'm wearing a cream-colored fitted dress. It has long sleeves and a plunging neckline. I splurged and bought myself a new dress for tonight; I wanted to look nice.

It's paying off; I've never gotten so much male attention in my life. Amazing what a tight dress and a little cleavage can do for a girl.

We order drinks and go and find a space to stand as I look around in awe. I've never been in such a cool nightclub before. "This place is insane." I smile at the girls.

"Right?" Ava smiles. "The men here are off the hook."

"And filthy rich," Renee adds.

"Who cares about rich?" I smirk as I sip my drink.

"Me," they both reply in unison.

"If you're going to be with a guy, he may as well be wealthy, if you ask me. Fuck being with a poor bastard. I'm poor, and opposites most definitely attract," says Ava.

I laugh as I listen to them.

"So who do we have here tonight?" Ava says as she looks around the club.

"What do you mean?" I ask as I watch her eyes scan the room.

"This place is a huge celebrity hangout."

"Really?" I frown as I look around. "I wouldn't even know any celebrities."

Over the next hour, we dance and laugh, and Ava explains to me in great detail about who is who. Apparently, the men are all very impressive. None take my fancy, though.

A gorgeous man comes up through the crowd and puts his hands on my thighs. "Do you want to dance?" he asks. He's blond and big and totally in my space, but the way he looks, I think I can deal with it.

"Yes, she does," Ava stammers as she stares at the god in front of us.

He grabs my hand and drags me to the dance floor, and I give my friends a scared wave with my fingertips as my eyes widen.

Ava blows me a kiss and jiggles on the spot in excitement.

"What's your name?" he asks as he wraps his arms around me.

I put my hands on his shoulders as I stare up at him. "Emily. What's yours?"

"Rocco."

I smile up at him. What a weird name. Gosh, I feel tipsy. I need to stop drinking.

"This is your first time here?" he says, as if he already knows the answer.

"How do you know that?" I smirk.

"I would have noticed you if you were here before."

I smile bashfully.

His hands roam down to my behind, and I lift them back to my waist. "You're very forward, Rocco."

"I know what I want when I see it."

I smile as he leans in and puts his lips to my ear.

"I want you," he breathes.

Chapter 10

"Hmm, not bad," Christopher murmurs as an attractive redhead walks past us.

We both watch her as she saunters over to the bar. She's wearing a tight black dress, and she has a perfectly rounded ass. I scrunch my nose up in distaste. "Average."

"She is not average." His eyes drop to her behind and stay firmly fixed. "Far from it, actually."

"Not doing it for me." I sigh against my glass as I look around the crowded club. It's a rarity that a woman catches my attention these days, with the exception of Little Miss Snarky. I can't get enough of her . . . even if she is completely unmanageable.

Our exchange in my office on Monday runs through my mind, and I exhale heavily.

She's so fucking difficult.

It would help if I could keep my mouth shut when I see her. For some reason, she has me blurting out demands and grabbing her by the hair; it's as if my body takes on a need of its own and completely leaves my brain out of the equation.

Every time Emily leaves my office in a huff, I kick myself for handling her the wrong way.

I know women; I know how they think, and I can usually get them to do whatever I want. Her . . . not so much.

Christopher licks his lips as he watches the redhead. "I'm going in." He strides across the club and says something to her as she stands at the bar, and in slow motion, she smiles up at him.

I smirk and sip my drink as I watch him in action. He loves women—all women. It seems to be a family trait; we're all wired the same way.

Something's changed for me lately, though. My appetite for variety has waned. Something's off, and I can't quite put my finger on it. I glance over to Tristan and Elliot as they talk to two girls in the lounge. The women are being all animated and laughing on cue at everything that comes out of the boys' mouths.

Bimbos.

I sip my drink as I look around the room. "Hey," Tristan says as he comes to stand beside me. "Look who's here."

"Who?" I mutter, uninterested.

"Cream-colored dress, hair down, and looking absolutely fucking sensational."

I frown as I look over to where he is gesturing.

It's her. Emily is here.

A broad smile crosses my face. "Well, well. The night just got interesting."

Tristan chuckles. "That's if you don't kill each other first." He slaps me on the back. "I'm going to the bar."

"Yeah, okay." She's with two women I've never seen before, although they do look vaguely familiar; they might be from work. They're talking and laughing. Emily is wearing a tight cream-colored dress with long sleeves and a plunging neckline. I can see every curve on her delicious body, and my cock swells in appreciation. Her hair is down, and she pulls it over to one side as she talks, and I see the curve of her bare neck; my stomach clenches in excitement.

Fuck . . . she's hot.

I've never had such an intense physical reaction to a woman like this before. I just can't get enough of her body. The more I have her, the more I want her. If only she didn't have the snarkiest damn attitude I've ever seen.

Maybe that's the appeal?

Most women fall at my feet; she seems determined to push me away. *Hmm.* That's something to think about. If the truth be known, I should stay away from her. She works for me, she's a firecracker, and who knows what she will do if we fight again. I smirk. I already know that we will fight again— the writing is on the wall. She has a way of pissing me off like no other.

A song comes on that she obviously likes, and she starts to dance on the spot. Her ass slowly moves to the tantric beat, and I stand and stare, transfixed by the goddess in front of me.

She has no idea how fucking sexy she is.

"New York sour," Tristan says as he hands me my drink.

"Thanks." I take it from him.

"You know, the way you're looking at her is illegal in some countries, right?"

I watch her hips roll, and I imagine them over me doing the same thing. I inhale sharply as my arousal starts to thump between my legs. "Have you ever been so physically attracted to someone that you lose the ability to think around them?"

"No. Thank fuck," Tristan replies as he watches her dance. "Although with that ass, I can imagine—"

"Don't even fucking look at her ass, or I will sit you on yours," I say, cutting him off.

He chuckles. "Look at you getting all territorial." He sips his drink as mischief fills his face. "She did want to report to me with that story, you know."

I look at him flatly. "And you report to me, fucker. Go near her, and you will fucking die."

He throws his head back and laughs out loud.

A blond man walks over to her and says something, and she smiles up at him.

"Oh, look out," Tristan teases. "Competition is on the horizon."

I watch as uneasiness begins to swirl.

His hands go to her thighs, and I clench my jaw. I sip my drink as I watch.

He says something, and she laughs out loud before he takes her hand and leads her to the dance floor.

Are you fucking kidding me?

Tristan turns and laughs when he sees my face. "Well, this is about to get interesting."

The blond slides his hands down to her behind, and she lifts his hands back to her waist.

I watch as the sky turns red. *Get your fucking hands off her.* He says something, and she laughs out loud.

I swallow the lump in my throat.

So this is what she's here for, is it? To pick up a man. Fury begins to fill me.

"Looks like your territory is about to be stolen." Tristan smirks.

"Shut the fuck up, Tris, before I knock you out," I snap as my eyes stay glued to them.

The blond leans down and kisses her neck. Something inside me snaps, and before I know what I'm doing, I'm on the dance floor beside them.

"Fuck off," I growl.

Emily turns to me, and her face instantly drops. "Jameson," she stammers.

My arm goes around her waist, and I pull her from his grip. "She's here with me."

Emily

Oh my God, what the hell is Jameson doing here? I step back from the blond god, and he grabs me and pulls me back toward him. "Don't," he snaps.

"Don't you," Jameson growls. He pulls me out of the guy's arms and holds me against his chest. "I said she's with me," he repeats.

The guy stares at me, and I nod softly. I don't want any trouble, and I just want this guy to disappear. "I'm with him," I whisper.

With one last look between Jameson and me, he turns and storms off toward the bar. I turn my attention to Jameson Miles, the infuriating prick, and I pull out of his arms. "What do you think you're doing?"

"What do you think you're fucking doing?" he growls.

"Don't you swear at me."

"You came here to pick up a man?"

I put my hands on my hips in outrage. "I came here to dance. What are you doing here?"

"I'm here with my brothers."

"So go back to your brothers and ruin their fun," I huff. I go to turn, and he grabs my arms and pulls me to the side of the dance floor and pushes me up against the wall.

His body covers mine, and I can feel his hard erection up against my stomach. We stare at each other, and instantly the air between us changes.

"Don't," I whisper up at him.

"Don't what?"

"Hypnotize me with that magical dick."

He gives me a cheeky wink. "You've got that the wrong way around, baby. I'm the only one who's hypnotized around here," he whispers as he leans down toward me. His tongue slowly slides through my lips. He kisses me again, with just the right amount of suction, and my knees begin to buckle beneath me.

Dear God . . . the man can kiss.

"Jameson," I breathe against him. "We shouldn't." His hands roam up and down my body, and God, he feels so good.

"Don't fight me on this," he murmurs as he grinds me up against the wall with his hips.

"I can't."

"You can, and you will. Why would you deny your body what it so desperately needs from me?"

Oh God, he's so right. My body does need his body . . . hard. So fucking hard.

Our kiss turns desperate, and my hands go to his hair. I know this is crazy, but I want him . . . all of him, and not just his body.

For a long time, we kiss like we're the only two people left on earth. Hidden up against the wall, his body grinding on mine. Two bodies chasing their own pleasure in the darkness.

"I need you," he murmurs against my lips.

I pant as his open mouth drops to my neck. God . . . the way he touches me is just so . . . "Jameson."

"Now." He pins me to the wall, and I feel his cock pulse.

Jesus, he's close. He does need me.

"My place," he pants against my lips.

"My place," I fire back.

"No, my place," he demands.

I pull back to look at his face. "It's my place or nothing. Take it or leave it."

He clenches his jaw; it's obvious he hates losing a fight . . . any fight. "Fine." He grabs my hand. "This way."

"No." I pull my hand out of his grip. "I don't want anyone to see us."

He frowns in question.

"You're my boss," I remind him. "I'm here with work friends."

He rolls his eyes. "Fine. Go and say goodbye, and I'll wait for you downstairs. You have two minutes before I come up and drag you out." He gives me a long, lingering kiss, and I turn, and he swats me on the behind.

Adrenaline courses through my veins as I walk over to my friends.

He's here. I'm going with him. *It's on.*

Excitement fills me, and I try to act casual.

"Hey, where's the god?" Renee asks.

"Oh." I frown. "He was a dick," I lie.

Ava rolls her eyes. "Typical. Men who look that good can't be blessed with brains too."

I smirk. I know someone who was blessed with both, but I'll just keep that under my hat. I look over and see Jameson walking toward the elevator, and he gives me the hurry-up look. I smile; the pull to him is strong.

"Guys, I'm going to go."

"What?" Their faces fall. "Why? The night is young."

"I know. I've had such a great time, but my feet are killing me. These stupid new shoes are hell on earth. Next weekend I'll make it up to you. I promise. I'll just jump in a cab downstairs."

"Okay." They roll their eyes and kiss me on the cheek.

"Text me when you get home," Ava says.

"I will." I smile, grateful that they aren't bothered at all. "Thanks for asking me to come."

Two guys walk up to us, and the girls both smile broadly. I take that as my out. "See you," I call as I walk toward the elevator.

"Bye," they call.

I jump in the elevator. "Where to?" the attendant asks.

163

"Ground floor." He pushes the button, and we make our descent. My heart is hammering in my chest. Jameson Miles makes me nervous as all hell. I can't remember when a man made me this excited to get him alone.

Act cool . . . just act cool.

The elevator doors open, and I walk out and look around. Where is he?

I continue through the foyer and peer out to the busy street; I can't see him. *What the hell? Did he leave without me?*

"Lose something?" a deep voice asks from behind me.

I turn to see Jameson leaning up against the wall, and my heart somersaults in my chest. I walk over, and he takes me in his arms. "I did, actually." I smile up at him.

We kiss softly, and it's different from how we normally kiss; it's tender and sweet, as if he's been waiting to get me alone too.

"Let's go home," he whispers.

I smile. That sounds so good. "Okay." We walk out the front, and he hails a cab. Ten minutes later, we pull up in front of my apartment.

"Thank you," I say as I climb out. I turn and hand Jameson twenty dollars, and he shakes his head as if annoyed.

"I've got it," he says.

He climbs out, and we walk through the foyer, hand in hand, as he remains silent.

"Where are the doormen?" he asks as he looks around.

"There are no doormen."

"There's no security in this building?" He frowns in surprise.

"There's security." I point to the intercom on the wall. "Nobody can get up without being let in."

He frowns as he assesses it. "Any fucker could walk in here."

"You are said fucker tonight." I smirk.

He chuckles as he wraps his arms around me. "That I am."

164

We ride to my floor and walk down the corridor; my heart is beating so fast. This is different from the other times we've been together. Normally we're so blinded with arousal that we don't even remember walking through the front door. I open the door and lead him into my apartment, and I hold my breath as his eyes scan the space.

My apartment is tiny—it would literally fit into his bedroom.

"It's nice," he says.

I giggle. "You're a terrible liar."

He chuckles and takes me into his arms. "Anywhere with you is good."

Our eyes lock, and something changes between us. The anger and animosity between us has been replaced with tenderness.

The man I met in Boston is here.

"Are you hungry?" I ask. "We could get some Uber Eats. Caramel cheesecake."

"What the fuck? You don't actually get Uber Eats, do you?" he asks, horrified.

"All the time." I shrug.

"Are you serious?" he stammers. "You actually give strangers access to your food?"

"They're delivery drivers. Why wouldn't I?"

"They see a meal for one. Put some Rohypnol into your food, wait for half an hour until they know you've eaten it and are unconscious, and then come back, break in, and take advantage of your body." He dusts his hands in front of him. "Boom, easiest crime in history."

My face falls. "What?" God, I've never thought of that.

"True story," he says as he walks around my apartment. "If I were a rapist, that's what I would do."

"I don't know whether to be impressed or terrified by your evil thought process."

He turns back to me, and his face softens. "Impressed—let's go with impressed."

I giggle as he takes me into his arms. "Okay," I murmur. "Impressed it is. Why have you been so cranky with me this week?" I ask softly as I run my fingers through his dark hair.

"Because you're fighting with me," he whispers. "I don't like it." His lips take mine, and his tongue swipes softly through my lips.

"I'm not fighting now."

"And look how fucking beautiful you are," he says tenderly as he cups my face in his hands.

Our kiss deepens, and I want him naked. In my bed and naked. I slide his shirt off over his head and unzip his pants; his lips stay locked on mine as if he's unable to drag them away.

His chest is broad with a scattering of dark hair, and his stomach is ripped . . . but it's his dick that's a standout.

The man's hung like a horse. I don't know if this thing even goes down. I most definitely have never seen it soft.

"You need to get on my bed on your back now," I whisper as my eyes drop down his delicious naked body.

He smiles broadly. "That's the best thing you've ever said to me." He drags me through the apartment by my hand and into my bedroom; in one quick movement, he's unzipped my dress, and then he slowly slides it down.

He holds my hand as I step out of it, and his eyes drop hungrily down my body. "You are so fucking beautiful, Emily."

My heart swells at the way he is looking at me.

He lays me down and spreads my legs and slowly strokes himself as he stares down. I writhe as I wait for his touch. His lips take my nipple into his mouth, and my back arches off the bed. His fingers slide through the lips of my sex. He hisses in approval as he feels how wet I am. My breath quivers on the inhale. He's just so . . .

Jameson Miles knows how to touch a woman.

Everything is magnified, to the point where even his blazing stare could make me orgasm.

His lips make a delicious trail down my body, and he kisses my inner thighs with his open mouth. My hands go to the back of his head. His hands hold my legs wide open, and his thick, strong tongue swipes through me.

My back arches in pleasure as my head tips back to the ceiling. "Oh God."

He licks me, slowly at first, and then as if he's unable to control himself, he begins to really eat me. His stubble burns my sex as my body begins to ride his face. "Oh . . . so good," I whimper.

He lifts my legs to sit over his shoulders, and the change in position has my body trembling with need.

"Oh God," I whimper as my hands fist in his hair.

"Come. I want to taste you," he moans into me.

I convulse and shudder deep inside my body as I cling to him. He laps me up like I'm his last supper. He pulls back and unwraps a condom and passes it to me; I slide it on him with a soft kiss to his cock.

With his eyes locked on mine, he lifts my legs around his waist and in one strong movement slides deep into my sex.

We stare at each other as the air is knocked from our lungs.

"So fucking good," he whispers as our eyes search each other.

He pulls out and then slowly slides back in. My mouth hangs slack at the feeling of his possession.

Nobody fucks me like Jameson Miles . . . *nobody*.

I can try to deny this emotional attachment all I want, but the physical . . . I just can't.

He circles deep inside and then slams back in. I cry out as the air is knocked from my lungs. Then he's riding me—deep, punishing hits—and my bed is hitting the wall so hard it may knock it down.

"Fuck, fuck, fuck," he moans into my neck.

He lifts one of my legs, and I can't hold it any longer. My body contracts around his, and he hisses as he comes with me.

We cling to each other as we pant, and I smile up against his cheek as euphoria runs through my blood.

Jameson Miles is my new drug.

And I am his crack whore.

I wake to the gentle breathing beside me, and I roll over and smile. Jameson is flat on his back and asleep. We had an incredible night.

The tender, witty guy was back . . . with no sight of the asshole CEO.

I lean up onto my elbow as I watch him. His dark hair hangs over his forehead, his big red lips are slightly open, and his eyelashes flutter as he sleeps. He has one arm behind his head, and the other is splayed on his stomach.

He's beautiful—everything about him physically is beautiful. Last night I got a little peek that maybe he's as beautiful on the inside as well. *Stop it.*

You're getting clingy and attached.

Jameson is not the kind of man you get attached to.

He inhales deeply as he wakes, and slowly his eyes open and focus on me. "Hey, beautiful," he whispers in a husky voice as he cups my face in his hand.

I smile and lean over and kiss him. "Good morning, Jameson."

"Call me Jay."

I frown in question.

"My friends call me Jay."

"So we're friends?"

He pulls me over his body onto his chest. "No, you're my fuck bunny."

I smile as I kiss his chest beneath me.

"What's planned for today?" he asks.

"Nothing."

He frowns as if trying to focus his eyes, and he pinches the bridge of his nose. "I'll get my driver to pick us up, and I'll make us some breakfast at my place."

I lean up onto my elbow and look down at him. "What's wrong with here? I've got breakfast things you can cook."

"Nothing. I just feel more comfortable at my place. We will hang there today."

"I'm more comfortable here, Jameson," I reply, slightly annoyed.

"What?" He winces. "How could you be?"

I sit up, affronted. "What's that supposed to mean?" I snap.

He rolls his eyes. "Here we go a-fucking-gain."

"What's that supposed to mean?"

"You asked that question twice," he replies dryly. "Do you have to argue about every fucking thing that we do?"

"I'm not arguing. I'm just saying I want to stay here today. Your apartment may be fancy, but it doesn't impress me."

He stares at me for a moment.

"And for the record, I don't argue about everything. I was annoyed that your masseuse is on personal terms to message you the way she did."

He rolls his eyes and puts the back of his forearm over them. "Here we go."

"Will you stop saying that?" I snap as I get out of bed and put on my robe. "I was just lying here thinking how gorgeous you are, and then you go and open your big mouth and ruin the whole thing."

"I'm thinking the same thing," he snaps as he gets out of bed. "And stop going on about Chloe—it's not a relationship."

I stop still. What the hell does he mean by that? "What do you mean, it's not a relationship? Do you and she have sex?"

He bends and picks up his jeans, ignoring me.

"Jameson." I put my hands on my hips as I watch him.

He pulls his jeans on and zips them up. "Sometimes."

"You have sex with her?" I gasp.

"I have a standing appointment on Tuesdays and Thursdays. She doesn't come for sex, but sometimes it just happens. She's touching me, I'm oiled up . . . it just happens."

My mouth falls open. "Did you have sex with her this last week? Since you've been with me?"

He rolls his eyes.

"Stop rolling your fucking eyes at me," I snap.

"No. I didn't have sex with her this week."

"Did you have your regular two massages?"

"Yes."

"So you had someone else's hands all over your body?" I fume.

"Like you did last night on the dance floor. Stop looking for a fucking fight, Emily. You are pissing me off."

"Well, you're pissing me off. Get out."

"I'm already fucking leaving," he barks.

"Go and have a massage today, you big sleazebag."

He shakes his head in disgust. "You know what? You're perfect for this fake news job. This drama thing is right up your alley." He throws his shirt over his head and then sits on the bed to put his shoes on.

Rage fills me, and I pick up one of his shoes and throw it to the other side of the room.

"So tough," he huffs.

I narrow my eyes as fury boils in my blood. "Yeah, like your Chloe's vagina. How many clients does she fuck each week?"

"She isn't my Chloe."

"You know what? Make her your Chloe, because I have no intention of taking her sloppy seconds."

"What's that supposed to mean?"

"It means that you sleep with me and only me, or you get out of my life."

He puts his hands on his hips in outrage. "I'm not looking for a relationship."

"Good. There's my answer. Get out."

"You know what? This little Dr. Jekyll and Mr. Hyde thing you've got going on here is a real turnoff."

"And your overshared dick isn't?" I shriek. "You're an insult to my intelligence, Jameson. Go home to your fancy apartment in your fancy car and have sex with whoever you want." I wrap my robe around me in disgust. "I'm too good for you anyway."

He glares at me. "Why are you such a fucking bitch?"

"Because you're a self-centered asshole. Get the hell out!" I scream. I pick up a pillow and throw it at him.

He brushes past me in a rush. "Nobody treats me as bad as you do, Emily!" he yells as he storms toward the door.

"Because you pay them!" I screech. "Good thing you've got lots of money, Jameson. You're going to need it. Nobody would put up with your shit for free."

He turns and glares at me. "That's a low blow."

I fake a smile. "Have a nice life, asshole." I turn and walk into my bathroom and lock the door.

Screw him.

Chapter 11

I turn the spoon upside down, put it into my mouth, and suck the Nutella from it as I stare at the television.

It's four in the afternoon, I'm still in my pajamas, and I've had a shitty day. After I woke up in a dream lying next to the most gorgeous man on the planet, Jameson Miles the asshole CEO decided to make an appearance and ruined everything.

To be honest, I'm regretting not going to his place for breakfast, but then, on the other hand, I'm glad I didn't because I wouldn't have found out about Chloe, his masseuse.

They fuck.

I hate that it bothers me. I hate that I can feel myself getting attached to him when he clearly isn't feeling the same.

I dig into my jar of Nutella again. The smooth chocolate melts on my tongue, offering a momentary distraction.

I stare at the television in a daze, a horror movie. My favorite rom-com category is scratched from the viewing repertoire. My mind goes back to the first time I met Jameson, when he told me that he didn't believe rom-coms were true.

Maybe he was on to something? Maybe I'm just a romantic fool?

Does he have feelings for Chloe? Who cares? He's an asshole.

I need to cut this out. Stop thinking about him. He's a self-absorbed player who sleeps with whoever he wants, whenever he wants. I look around my shitty apartment, and sadness fills me. If he liked me, it wouldn't matter where we were—he would want to spend time with me regardless. But he couldn't get out of here quick enough.

My mind goes over our fight this morning.

"Nobody treats me as bad as you do, Emily."

"Because you pay them. Good thing you've got lots of money, Jameson. You're going to need it. Nobody would put up with your shit for free."

"That's a low blow."

Did I go too far? Was it a low blow? Probably, but what does he expect? And I can't believe that nobody treats him as badly as I do. If he treats other women the way he treats me, surely they wouldn't put up with it? Nobody is that stupid . . . are they?

"I'm not looking for a relationship."

I punch the pillow on my lap in disgust. Six words have never made me feel so cheap.

Monday morning, I ride in the elevator to the top floor. We scheduled this meeting last week so that I could meet the private investigator, but it's the last thing I want to do now.

I want to forget Jameson Miles, forget I ever met beautiful Jim . . . or Jay, or whatever the heck I'm supposed to call him. I've come to the realization that they're a package deal, and unfortunately, I can't have Jim without Jameson, even though it's only Jim I want. So I'm doing what's best for me. I'm cutting ties; I'm not falling into the pattern of sleeping with Jameson without strings in the hope that I get a glimpse of Jim every now and then.

It would be easy . . . too easy.

But I already know my poor heart couldn't take it. I'm not wired for casual sex.

It's just not who I am.

I'm going to be professional and try to concentrate on my job. If I didn't have to see him, it would be so much easier, but it is what it is. I need to learn to deal with it. He's not going anywhere, and I really want this job.

Damn it, Emily, why do you always take the hard way? Why do you always fall for the wrong guy? The last man had no motivation, and this man has too much. Both men didn't care enough to go the extra mile for me. Maybe my expectations are too high from my book boyfriends in my romance novels—maybe Jameson was right on that one. But damn it, I want the fucking fairy tale for once.

The elevator door opens, and I walk out and through reception. "Good morning, Emily," Sammia says.

"Morning." I smile.

"Just go through to his office."

"Thanks." I walk down the corridor and knock on his door.

"Come in," his deep voice calls.

I close my eyes and brace myself. I drop my shoulders and open the door. I stop on the spot. *Shit.*

The room is full of men.

"Come in," Jameson says, devoid of emotion. "Take a seat."

"Thanks." I drop nervously into the seat near the end of the large rectangular table.

Jameson sits at the head, and Tristan, Elliot, Christopher, and an older man are on Jameson's left. Then there are another six men I have never seen before.

Jameson's eyes hold mine. "This is Emily Foster," he introduces me.

"Hello," the men all say.

I smile awkwardly as I look around the table.

"Emily, this is my father, George." He gestures to the older man.

"Hello," I whisper nervously.

"Hello, dear." He smiles warmly; he's in his sixties and looks like an older version of Jameson and Elliot. Gorgeous and distinguished with those piercing blue eyes.

"This is Martin and Gerrard, Max and Barry," Jameson says as he points around the table. "And on the end are Calvin and Jake."

"Hello." I force a smile. I'll never remember all these names.

"This is the corporate investigation team," Jameson continues. "Jake will be the eyes on the floor, and the other five men will be assessing the data that's collected."

I watch him as he talks, devoid of emotion, and my heart cracks a little. He's completely unrattled by me . . . *by us*.

There is no *us*.

"Okay." I smile as I look around at the team. "Nice to meet you all."

"We are going to hit the ground running this morning," he continues. "Emily, you are going to show Jake around, and then you will be reporting directly to Tristan in regards to the stories you are putting forward."

My heart drops, and I nod. My eyes go to Tristan, and he smiles warmly.

He knows why I've been designated to him. I feel like throwing myself on the floor and having a crying tantrum. "Thank you. That's great," I lie.

For the next fifteen minutes, I sit in my chair and stare at the CEO as he runs through the day's events with a controlled detachment. He's assertive, hard, and fiercely intelligent, and the room hangs on to his every word.

And he fucks his masseuse on Tuesdays and Thursdays.

I don't know how I got myself into this messed-up situation, but it has to end.

Well . . . it's already ended, so I don't need to bother anyway.

"Thank you; that wraps it up. I would like a report on my desk at four thirty every afternoon," he tells the men from the investigation company.

"Yes, sir," they reply as everyone stands. I wait at the back, unsure whether to leave or not.

"Emily, just a minute, please," Jameson asks.

My heart flips. "Yes."

"Can you take Jake down to your floor under the guise that he's new and that you two are going through a training program together?"

My eyes search his.

He stares at me blankly, cold as ice.

"Sure." I turn to Jake and smile. "Are you ready now?"

"Show me the way," Jake says playfully. "After you."

I turn and walk out of the office with my heart dripping into my high-heeled pumps. Well, that's the end of that.

He's done. I wish I were. I'll get there—I always do.

I sit in the café at the bench seat by the window and stare at the limo waiting outside Miles Media from across the street. It's been a long week, and today was especially flat.

It's Thursday, massage day.

I get a vision of Jameson oiled up on the table and another woman roaming her hands over his body; my stomach clenches as I picture it so clearly. My mind's playing evil games with me and showing me the worst reality-porn scenario in history.

Jim . . . being touched by another woman.

Is she dressed while she massages him? Do they talk? Do they laugh like we do?

I need to stop this; it's so destructive. I want a man who doesn't even exist.

The driver opens the front door of the building, and I watch in slow motion as Jameson Miles walks out, navy suit, perfect posture, dark hair . . . emanating power.

Everyone stops what they are doing and watches him get into the back of the limo. His driver shuts the door, and it slowly pulls out and disappears down the street.

I stare back at my ham-and-cheese toasted sandwich in front of me, my dinner. Deflation fills me. I just lost my appetite.

It's three o'clock on Friday, and I stare at the bogus story in front of me. Ha . . . what a joke. I moved all the way to New York to make up fake news for a twat and his twat media company . . . and his twat brothers.

I hit the keys on my computer with force. Twat, twat . . . fucking twat.

So much for my years of university study. My parents must be so proud. When they offered me the chance to do this, I thought it was going to be exciting and a chance to prove my worth. Maybe not?

"Down the end," I hear someone say. I glance up to see a man with a big brown paper bag.

"Uber Eats for Emily Foster."

"What?" I look around, embarrassed. "I didn't order anything."

He reads the docket. "It says here that . . ." He pauses as he reads and frowns as if confused. "It says here that this Uber Eats delivery is quality controlled and safe for human consumption."

I stare at him and take the bag from his hands.

He squints as he continues to read the docket. "This doesn't make sense . . ."

"What doesn't?"

"Sugar to sweeten you up."

I open the bag to find a huge passion fruit cheesecake in its entirety, and I look up at the camera and smirk. Is he kidding?

"Who sent this?" I ask.

"It says here, the sender is a Mr. Nice Guy."

I stare at him deadpan. "Mr. Nice Guy?"

"Yeah, weird, huh?"

"Thank you." I try my hardest not to smile. I know he's watching.

Molly and Aaron peer into the bag. "Score," Aaron screeches. "I'll get the plates." He takes off to our staff kitchen.

"Thank God for cheesecake," Molly sings in excitement.

Okay . . . he's made the first move. What do I do?

I take out my phone and text him.

Dear Mr. Nice Guy
Thank you.
Although, I should have you know
I'm already sweet enough.

I hit send and wait. A reply bounces back.

**I have no doubt. Can I take you out to dinner
tonight?**

I sit back in my chair, surprised by his request. This is a no-win situation. He wants a fuck buddy to join his harem, and I want him all to myself. I write back.

**I think we both said all we needed to on Sunday
morning.**

God . . . why can't he just be normal? A reply bounces back.

I have a proposal for you.

I stare at the message but don't reply. A proposal? What, does he want me to be his new masseuse?

I feel my anger bubble at the mere thought of her. Ten minutes later, another text comes in.

Hear me out, please.

Please. He said please. *Ugh, okay.* I reply.

Fine.

I wait.

I'll pick you up at seven.

"Here you go," Aaron says as he passes me a plate with the biggest slice of cheesecake I've ever seen. He passes Molly hers and then takes a seat with his.

"This is fucking delicious," Molly mumbles with her mouth full.

Aaron moans in appreciation. "Oh my fuck, foodgasm."

I take a bite as I concentrate hard on not smiling too hard—just in case he's watching.

Well played, Mr. Miles . . . well played.

Sometimes you just know in your gut that you shouldn't be doing something. The outcome is already written in the stars, and sometimes you should just be stronger and say no. But what if you can't?

I can't physically bring myself not to go tonight. The masochist in me wants to see him. The same masochist wants him to take me and throw me onto his fancy bed and fuck me till I forget my own name. It's been a long and lonely week. But I have to stay strong tonight. If I cave in now, the last week has been for nothing.

And I still stand by what I said on Sunday. I am too good for him with the way he is at the moment, and I won't share, and money means nothing to me at all.

He needs to step up or step away.

The security buzzer sounds, and my stomach dances in excitement. "Hello."

"Uber Eats." I hear his velvety voice.

I smile broadly. "What have you got for me?"

"Italian sausage."

"Hmm," I tease. "Are you going to drug my sausage and take advantage of my body after I fall unconscious?"

"Undoubtedly."

I smile and push the button to let him up, and then I begin to pace as I wave my arms around in the air.

180

Play it cool . . . play it cool . . . play it cool.

Knock, knock. I open the door in a rush, and there he stands, gray shirt and black jeans . . . blazing blue eyes. A slow, sexy smile crosses his face. "Hello."

"Hi," I whisper as I stare at the beautiful specimen in front of me. I just want to throw myself at him, the pull to him unbearable.

He leans down and kisses my cheek as he walks past me into my apartment.

"Are you ready?" he asks.

"Uh-huh." I grab my purse and wrap.

His eyes drop down my body in my black dress. "You look lovely."

"Thanks," I breathe.

"Let's go." He holds his arm out, and I link mine with his.

We take the elevator in awkward silence. He is pensive, and I'm just nervous as all hell.

Playing cool, calm, and collected is terrifying, and I remind myself not to drink too much tonight. We walk out the front of the building, and the limo is parked at the curb.

He opens the door, and I climb in. Memories of the first time I was in this back seat accost me, and the phrase *dirty ho* rolls around in my head.

I slide in, and he gets in beside me, and then he picks up my hand and takes it in his and rests them on his lap. Okay . . . he's touchy. What does that mean?

I don't know what to say or where this sits in my playing-hard-to-get act, but the warmth of his touch is so comforting that I let him. The limo drives through the city, and I stare out the window as a million thoughts run through my head.

Tonight is important; we either have to come to some sort of understanding or cut our losses. We can't keep fighting over nothing like we do.

The car comes to a stop, and the driver opens the door. I climb out, and Jameson takes my hand and leads me into a fancy restaurant, Lucino's.

"Booking for Miles," he says as he holds my hand tightly in his.

"This way, sir." The waiter smiles as he leads us through the restaurant to a cozy little table in the corner. He pulls out my chair, and I take a seat.

Jameson sits opposite me; the restaurant is dark, with candles flickering on the tables and fairy lights hanging from the ceiling. It's very romantic.

Don't get excited. It's probably just a coincidence.

"Can I get you something to drink?" the waiter asks.

"Yes, we'll have a bottle of S Salon please." He closes the menu and hands it over.

I stare at him. *Here we go again.*

The waiter disappears, and Jameson's big blue eyes come to mine. He takes my hand over the table again. "Hello." He smiles softly, as if finally relaxing.

Drop arguing about the drinks. It doesn't fucking matter who orders the drinks. "Hi." I smile.

He dusts his thumb over the back of my knuckles as his eyes search mine. "How are you?"

"Good."

Oh, his touch makes me weak. I just want to blurt out that I'm lying and that I've had a shit week and he's the king of Twatsville.

We stare at each other across the table. It's as if both of us don't want to speak in case we break out into all-out war. "What's this proposal, Jameson?"

He sits back, seemingly annoyed at my tone.

I grip his hand. "And I'm not giving you attitude. I just want to know what you're thinking," I say softly. "Stop being on the defensive with me."

He relaxes a little, and the waiter returns with the bottle of champagne and opens it. He pours a little into the champagne flute, and Jameson tastes it. "That's fine." The waiter then fills our glasses and leaves us alone.

"I've been thinking about what you said last weekend."

"And?"

He sips his drink. "I canceled my massages this week."

I smirk as my eyes hold his; I stay silent.

"The thing is with me . . ." His voice trails off.

I wait for him to speak, and when he doesn't, I squeeze his hand in mine for reassurance.

"I'm married to my job, Em."

I frown.

"When I said I wasn't looking for a relationship, I didn't mean . . ." He shrugs as if lost for words.

"You didn't mean what?"

"I didn't mean that I don't want to see you. I meant that I am a workaholic, and I know that very few women can deal with how much I work."

"Jameson, I don't care about how hard you work. I just don't want to be one of many."

He frowns. "Meaning what?"

"I'm not wired for one-night stands, Jameson. It's not who I am. But I'm not looking for a deep and meaningful relationship either. You've misunderstood me."

"What do you want, then?"

"I want to have a friendship with a man and know I'm the only person he's sleeping with."

He listens.

"And I most definitely don't want to share you with a fucking masseuse."

He rolls his eyes.

"And I don't want you to roll your fucking eyes at me."

He clenches his jaw, unimpressed. "Watch your tone," he warns.

"See that?" I say.

"What?"

"This defensive shit. It has to stop between us. We can't keep fighting over every little thing like we do."

"You're just as bad," he fires back.

"I know, and I'm trying to stop it. Just now I held my tongue because you ordered my drink without asking what I wanted."

"I'm used to being in control, Emily," he snaps.

"So am I. That won't change."

His eyes search mine, and he rearranges the napkin on his lap as if he's thinking.

"I'm not asking you to be my boyfriend, Jameson," I whisper. "That's not what this is about. We have a great sexual connection, and I want it. I feel like I have to have it . . . but I can't, not if I know you have it with other women. I need to be the only one."

"Fine, I won't sleep with anyone else," he snaps in exasperation.

"And?" I ask.

He rolls his eyes. "And you can order the fucking drinks."

Chapter 12

I giggle. "This isn't about the stupid drinks, Jameson."

"What is it about, then, for Christ's sake? Speak English."

"I want you to drop being defensive with me."

"I'm not."

"Yes, you are," I whisper as I hold his hand in mine.

"So are you."

"I know I am, because I feel like you will walk all over me if I'm not."

His brow furrows. "I would never walk all over you."

"Not purposely."

He clenches his jaw, and I know that's exactly how it is.

"I just want the guy I met on the plane. The one who let himself go."

His eyes hold mine. "I don't know how to be that guy all the time, Em. It's a very small part of my personality."

"Then just save that small part for me," I breathe.

A soft smile crosses his face as he watches me, and he sips his drink. "What was so good about that guy on the plane, anyway?"

"He made me laugh." I smile as I remember. "And he gave me the best sex of my life."

"Of your entire life?"

"Uh-huh."

He smiles, pleased with himself.

"So do we have a deal?" I ask.

"Let me get this straight—you want to have friends with benefits but only with each other?"

"Yes."

"What happens when I'm at work all the time or away and you're out and . . ." His voice trails off.

"Then I'll call you and tell you I need you."

His eyes hold mine.

"And you'll talk me through it over the phone, or I'll wait till you come home."

He rubs his thumbnail over his bottom lip as he listens, as if fascinated.

"I don't want to have sex with anyone else, Jameson. I'm not that kind of girl. You are the only one-night stand I've ever had."

He squeezes my hand, pleased with that answer.

"I've had sex with four people in my whole life, and you're one of them."

He leans onto his hand and smiles dreamily at me.

"What?"

"Do you know how often I think about fucking you?"

I giggle, surprised by that statement. "How often?"

"All the time. I'm like a starstruck eighteen-year-old."

"You wouldn't know it."

"Why?"

"You acted like you hated me all week. You can be so cold when you want to be."

He sits up in his chair and straightens his back. "I don't like to be challenged for the sake of it, Emily. You fought with me last weekend just to prove a point. It angered me."

"No. I fought with you last weekend because I wanted to spend the day at my apartment, and you just assumed that your place was better than mine. Your money doesn't impress me, Jameson. I don't care for your fancy apartment. Mine is just as good."

He rolls his eyes. "Are we going to fight now about why we fought?"

I smile. He's right; this is ridiculous. "No. No more fighting." I pick up his hand and cup it around my face. "We're going to have dinner, and then we're going to go back to your place, and then I'm going to ride your cock . . . just the way you like it," I whisper.

He inhales sharply as his eyes flicker with excitement. "You fucking turn me on."

I put his thumb into my mouth and suck it in slow motion, our eyes locked. "As your dedicated fuck bunny, Mr. Miles, I take my job very seriously," I whisper darkly. "Your wish is my command, sir."

He gives me a slow, sexy smile. "Now you're talking."

Two hours later

Lathered with a sheen of perspiration, I rock forward onto his cock. Jameson is sitting with his back against his headboard. One hand is on my hip, the other cupping my breast.

He's so big that I can feel every inch of him deep inside my body. He took me hard and fast the first time, me on my knees and him behind me. I watched us in the mirror. Every muscle in his torso contracted as he pumped me, and his dark eyes held mine.

It was the hottest thing I've ever seen.

His hand has a strong grip on my hip bone as he rocks me back and forward with force. Our eyes are locked, and this is one of those moments where neither of us speaks—it's perfect without words.

He grabs a handful of my hair and drags me down to him; his lips take mine, and we kiss. His tongue is sliding into my mouth at just the right angle.

"Legs up," he whispers as he lifts my knees to a squatting position.

My face falters.

"What?"

"Be careful."

"I won't hurt you—you know that." He kisses me again with just the right amount of suction; my body knows who's in control here. Jameson Miles may have given me control of drink ordering, but it's glaringly obvious he will never give me control in the bedroom.

Not that I want him to; what he does is sheer perfection.

He begins to lift me, slowly and carefully at first, and we go at a controlled speed. He looks up at me in awe.

"Oh," I moan. "So . . . good," I whimper.

His eyes roll back in his head as he lifts me higher and slams me down harder. My hands are on his broad shoulders, and I feel the muscles contract beneath me.

He begins to moan as he slams me onto his body, the look on his face one of sheer ecstasy.

I tip my head back as a freight train of an orgasm comes shuddering deep within me.

"Oh fuck," he cries out as he holds himself deep inside me. I feel the telling jerk as his body empties itself in mine.

His eyes search mine, and in slow motion, he reaches up and cups my face and brings my lips down to his.

We kiss, and it's slow, tender, and intimate—nothing like the detached version we talked about.

He's right here with me. I know he is.

"You are so fucking beautiful," he murmurs against my lips as he pulls me close.

I lie down on his chest and smile against his skin as his arms wrap around me. I can feel his heart beating hard against mine, and I feel so safe and cherished.

I know this is supposed to be friends with benefits. But it's not . . . it's more.

What kind of more I just don't know.

I feel a hand on my behind, and it gives me a sturdy pat. "Come on."

I screw up my face and roll toward him. "What?"

"Up you get."

"Huh?" I stretch and open my eyes. The drapes are pulled, and sunshine is beaming through the huge windows. I look around, half-asleep. "What time is it?"

"It's eight. Get up. We're going for a run around Central Park."

"Who is?" I frown. He's in a towel and freshly showered.

"Me and you."

I scratch my head in confusion. "You had a shower to go for a run?"

"I smelled like sex." He smirks as he leans down and kisses me on the lips.

I wrap my arms around him and hold him down.

He pulls from my grip. "Come on."

"I have no stuff here. What shoes would I wear?"

"What size are you?"

"Eight."

"Hmm." He puts his hands on his hips and thinks. "Well, you can wear some of mine."

"I'll fall over and break my neck, Jameson."

"Hmm, okay." He disappears into the walk-in closet and comes out in black Nike shorts and a blue Nike T-shirt.

I smirk when I see him.

"What?"

"Are you sponsored by Nike today or something?"

He looks down at himself and smiles. "No, it just happens to be comfortable."

"Like this bed." I smile sleepily as I snuggle back under the covers.

He sits down to put his shoes on, and I watch him for a moment. "So how does this work?" I ask.

"How does what work?"

"Well . . ." I pause as I try to articulate what I want to say without sounding needy. "I've never done this casual thing before." I shrug shyly. "How do we navigate this? When do we see each other?"

"Well . . ." He bends to tie his shoe. "We just play it by ear, I guess."

I frown. But what if he didn't call? I'd be waiting all week. Oh, I don't like the sound of that. "I think I would prefer set days."

He frowns. "How many days?"

I shrug. Shit, did that sound clingy? I'll play it down. "One day a week."

"I want to see you more than once a week," he scoffs.

"You do?"

He smiles, knowing exactly what I'm doing. He stands and then leans down and kisses me. "Yes, three times a week."

I try to hide my smile. "What days?"

"Do we have to have set days?"

"I kind of do."

"Why?"

I shrug as I twist the blanket between my fingers, embarrassed by my neediness.

He puts his finger under my chin and brings my face to his. "Why, Emily?"

"Because I hate waiting around, and then we know not to plan anything else on our days."

"Okay." He puts his hands on his hips. "When do you want to see me?"

"Maybe twice through the week and once on weekends." I hesitate as I watch for his cues. "But only a few hours each time, of course."

"No."

Shit. I'm going too far with my demands here.

"Two full nights through the week and one full night and half a day on the weekend."

I smile. "Half a day."

"Yes, starting today. I want my half day this morning."

"Today? Why today?"

"I'm going to go for a run while you go back to sleep. Then I'm coming home, and we are going to shower, and then I'm making you breakfast."

I smile softly. That sounds really good.

"And then we're going to come back to bed, and I'm going to fuck you stupid again to get me through another few days without you." He cups my face in his hand. "Okay?" he asks.

He's really quite swoony when he's being nice. I nod as I try to control my goofy smile.

He closes the drapes and then lays me back down and tucks me in and kisses me softly on my temple. "Go back to sleep, sweetheart," he whispers.

I close my eyes and smile into my pillow, and I hear him leave the apartment.

I roll onto my back and look up at the fancy ceiling.

The man's a god.

I doze for the next hour and wake as Jameson walks into the bedroom. He's wet with perspiration and breathing heavily, and I sit up on my elbows as I watch him. "Where the hell did you run to, Antarctica?"

He chuckles and shakes his head, still out of breath.

"You must really run hard, huh?"

He nods as he puts his hands on his hips. "The harder I run, the better the effects."

"Effects on what?" I frown.

"My stress levels." He disappears into the bathroom and turns the shower on.

Oh, this is news. He has stress issues? Well, I guess he would. His workload is huge, after all.

"Are you getting in?" he calls.

"Yes," I call as I amble in. He's in the shower, and the water is running over his head. His breathing is slowly returning to normal. I get in, and he wraps me in his arms and kisses me softly.

"Good morning," I whisper.

"Good morning, my Em." His lips dust mine.

I smile goofily up at him.

"What?"

"I like it when you call me that."

"You do?" He smiles.

"Your princess Em." I bat my eyelashes to prove my point.

He chuckles as he picks up the soap and begins to wash me. "I have no doubt that underneath all that snarky Ms. Foster act is a pure sweetheart."

"I haven't been snarky once," I gasp.

He smiles down at me as he tucks a piece of hair behind my ear. "And look how beautiful you are."

I giggle and lean against his chest. He washes my back, my shoulders, my breasts, and then down my legs. I watch him as he concentrates on his task. Then he moves down to my sex, and his eyes come to mine while he touches me there.

Our eyes are locked, but this doesn't feel sexual. It feels intimate.

I stare into his big blue eyes, and I swear this isn't the same man who runs Miles Media. The man with me now is sweet and tender. Everything Jameson Miles is not.

"Let me wash you." I take the soap from him and lather my hands together and roam them over his broad chest and muscular shoulders and biceps, then down his rippled abs to his groin, and I clench my insides while I wash him there. He leans down and kisses my temple softly, as if knowing I'm holding myself back from pouncing on him. We need to stop having sex all the time; it's getting ridiculous.

The sexual attraction is so strong that neither of us can get our fill of each other.

"You've turned me into a complete sex maniac," I whisper.

He smiles down at me as his lips dust mine. "I think you already suffered that affliction before we met—if our first night was anything to go by."

"I've never been like this before."

"Like what?"

"You bring something out in me that no other man has." My eyes search his. "You're different from anyone I've ever been with."

The water falls over us, and I don't know why I just told him that. I can feel myself getting attached, and I don't know how to stop blurting things out. I'm going to ruin everything.

Stop talking, fool.

He takes my face in his hands and kisses me. His tongue swipes through my open mouth, and it's deep, erotic, tender, and goddamn . . . so fucking perfect that I can't even deal. "I'm taking you back to bed," he murmurs darkly.

"Please," I whimper.

We get out, and he dries us both and then leads me back to bed and lays me down and spreads my legs open.

I watch as he rolls a condom on and lies down on top of me. We stare at each other as he holds himself up on his elbows, and his body finds that place between my legs. I grab his behind, but he stops me from pulling him in.

"I want it slow," he breathes.

Oh God, my insides begin to ripple in excitement. "I want you."

His lips take mine, and our kiss becomes frantic as his body slides in slow and deep. My back arches off the bed in pleasure at his possession.

I moan loudly, and his eyes roll back in pleasure.

For twenty minutes, we slowly appreciate each other's bodies; he's gentle and loving and so, so deep inside me. His open mouth roams from my collarbone, up my neck, and across my jaw to my lips.

"Fuck, Emily," he whispers. "You turn me inside out, baby."

If I could reply, I would, but I'm too busy in making-love heaven here.

Being fucked hard by Jameson Miles is hot as hell, but being made love to by Jameson Miles is life changing. *I'll never be the same.*

Where the hell does a girl go after sex like this?

It builds inside me, and I begin to quiver, but instead of getting harder like he normally does, he stops still. "Take it," he whispers.

"What?"

"Stay still, and take it from me. Clench your orgasm in."

My eyes search his. *Holy mother fuck.* I can't deal with how hot this man is.

"Fuck me," he whispers. "Don't move a muscle, except for here." He flexes his dick, and I feel it deep inside. "I want you to show me, just me . . . how you feel."

"Oh God," I moan.

"Come on," he coaches.

I clench, and he smiles darkly. "Harder."

I clench again, and his lip curls in excitement. "That's it, baby." His eyes close in ecstasy. "Milk me, and show me who it belongs to."

Something snaps inside me when I hear him say that his cock belongs to me. I bring my legs up and wrap them around his waist and begin to clench in a rhythm.

He hisses in approval.

"So . . . good," I whisper as we stare at each other. "So . . . fucking good."

To the outside world it would look like we are just cuddling as we lie perfectly still, but inside, every wall I've ever built up is being demolished, clench by clench.

He begins to moan, and it sounds too good—I can't hold it. I clench as hard as I can, and we both cry out as an orgasm tears between us.

And then he kisses me, and it's sweet and tender, and I feel emotion run between us.

I hold him close, cheek to cheek, as I hang on to him for dear life.

"You're so fucking perfect, Emily," he whispers.

I run my fingers through his stubble. "It's you who's perfect." I kiss him softly. "You should stop it immediately."

"Why is that?" He smiles.

"I think I may be addicted."

He chuckles and rolls onto his back and pulls me over him. "No, I want you addicted."

I laugh. "Why would you want me addicted?"

"Because I am, and I don't want to be in this alone." His eyes search mine, and I feel my heart free-fall from my chest.

"You're not in this alone, Jay."

"Good." He kisses my temple as he seems to relax.

We lie together in a tangled mess, and he dozes back to sleep. My mind begins to go into overdrive.

I have feelings for him—I know I do. In just two days, I've developed feelings for him. How is this going to end?

I'm totally screwed.

An hour later, I wake to the smell of bacon cooking, and I smile up at the ceiling. I don't know what this alternate universe is, but I like it. I throw on a robe I found hanging in the bathroom and make my way out into the living area. I turn the corner and see a glass wall with a view over New York and Central Park. Over-the-top wealth and luxury hit me in the face, and I stop still on the spot. I can't get my head around the fact that this is all his.

This money is *his* money.

My eyes roam over the beautiful floors, gorgeous rugs and furnishings, then to the fireplace and up to the huge gilded mirror above it. I've never even seen an apartment like this in a magazine, let alone been in one. I feel so out of place.

"Hey, there you are." He smiles as he comes around the corner and sees me.

I give him a lopsided smile.

He frowns as he sees my face. "What's wrong?"

I twist my hands in front of me nervously. "Your apartment freaks me out."

"Why?"

I shrug, embarrassed by my slummy standards. "It's so fancy. I feel like I don't belong here."

He takes me in his arms. "What does that mean?"

I shrug.

"Is that why you didn't want to come here last weekend?"

I nod. "Yes."

"Explain to me why?"

"When I'm here, I'm reminded of how much we don't have in common."

"And that bothers you?"

I nod shyly.

He frowns, as if trying to understand. "You're the first woman who's ever had a problem with my money."

"It's a turnoff to me."

"Turnoff?" he splutters.

"I would prefer you to be poor, actually." I smile, knowing how ridiculous that sounds.

He chuckles. "Well, that makes one of us." He leads me into the kitchen, and I see a breakfast of bacon and eggs on sourdough bread with a side of avocado.

"Yum." I smile as I take a seat.

"I'll have you know that I'm an excellent breakfast chef." He sits down beside me, looking very pleased with himself.

My smile fades, and I pick up my knife and fork. *That's because he cooks so many breakfasts.*

Stop it.

I take my first mouthful. I wonder how many women have sat here just like this and eaten his cooking after having amazing sex all night.

For Christ's sake, stop it.

"What are you doing today?" I ask to take my mind off my negative thoughts.

"Playing golf with my brothers this afternoon, and then I'll probably have dinner with them and my parents. They go back to London this week sometime." He sips his coffee. "You?"

I smile as I imagine the four of them playing golf. "I have to food shop. I'll go for a walk and then write some bogus news stories."

He stops eating. "You don't have to work on the weekend, you know."

"I know. I just like to be ahead of schedule in case something comes up."

He nods and goes back to his breakfast. "Are you going out tonight?" he asks casually.

I'm not, but I don't want him to think I'm at home pining over him. "Yes, I am."

His eyes come to me, and his jaw ticks as if he's angered. "Where are you going?"

"Out to dinner with Molly and Aaron."

"Who's Aaron?"

"My friend I work with, the one who sits next to me. He's gay."

"Oh." He cuts into his toast, mollified for the moment.

I watch him for a moment as he eats in silence. "Would it bother you if I were going clubbing?"

He sips his coffee, stalling for his answer. "Well, if your performance from last weekend is anything to go by, yes, it would."

I smile softly.

"What?"

"Nothing." I shrug; I like that it bothers him.

He rubs his hand up my bare thigh and leans over to kiss my cheek. "I'm not sharing you. I don't want you dancing with anybody."

I smile and rub my hands through his stubble as I look into his big blue eyes. "Good, then I won't."

An hour later, the limo pulls up in front of my apartment.

Jameson picks up my hand and kisses the back of it as his eyes hold mine. "Until Tuesday."

I smile softly at the beautiful man in front of me. "Until Tuesday."

I kiss him softly on the lips. The driver opens the car door, and I walk up to the front door of my building and turn and wave. The car waits for me to go inside and then pulls out slowly and drives down the street.

I exhale heavily as I anticipate spending the rest of my weekend alone.

Damn it, Tuesday is so far away.

I lie in a state of deep relaxation on my couch. Rebelling against Jameson, I did in fact order Uber Eats for one, and yes, I put the chain on my door, just in case.

My phone dances across the table, and the name *Aaron* lights up the screen.

"Hello." I smirk. Damn, this man makes me laugh.

"Oh . . . my fuck," he stammers. "I just hacked Paul's email, and he's meeting a guy at a club tonight."

I sit up. "What?"

"Yes, and it gets worse."

"How can it possibly?"

"He's been on Grindr."

"Oh my God, are you kidding me?" I gasp. "He's on Grindr?"

"Yes, get dressed. We are going down there to bust a move."

"What?" I shriek.

"You heard me. Put on something sexy. I'll be there in half an hour."

"But . . ."

The phone clicks as he hangs up. *Oh shit. Damn it, I don't want to go out tonight.*

My phone rings again, and the name *Molly* lights up the screen.

"I know," I answer, knowing that Aaron would have called her too.

"He's on fucking Grindr?" she shrieks.

"I know."

"You do me a favor. Tonight when you see Paul's pencil dick, you grind it to a pulp with your fucking shoe."

I giggle. "I'm hoping not to see it, Moll."

"I can't believe this shit," she snaps in outrage.

"I know."

"Aaron is way too good for him."

"I know. Are you coming on our bust-a-move mission?"

"I can't. I've got the kids. Wear a GoPro strapped to your head so I can see what happens."

"Can't you drop the kids with their dad?" I ask. "This is an emergency."

"No. He's on a date with a whore bag."

I giggle again. "Honestly, so much shit going on around here."

"I know," she snaps. "Okay, I'm calling you every hour. Answer your phone." She hangs up.

An hour later, Aaron leads me through the nightclub by the hand as he scans the club. It's small and dark, and the music is the dance-club type. The beat is tantric.

"Do you see him?" I call.

"Nope." He narrows his eyes as he looks around.

"What are you going to do if you do see him?" I ask.

"End it."

"Why don't you just end it anyway?" I frown.

"I need proof."

"The email is the proof, Aaron," I huff.

"I knew he was up to something," he fumes. "That fucking asshole has spent the last week in my bed, and he's trolling Grindr for sex."

"Were you in a relationship, like full-on?"

"No, he said he didn't want a boyfriend but that he wanted to have sex with me only."

I frown. That sounds very familiar. "So you've been monogamous with him all along?"

"Of course I have. I don't fuck around."

I scrunch up my nose in disgust. "Honestly, kick this douche to the curb."

"I will. As soon as I find him."

I roll my eyes and feel my phone vibrate in my bag. I dig it out. "Hello, Molly."

"What's happening?"

"We can't find him," I reply as I look around.

"Go and sit in the corner out of view, and wait for them to get there. Don't stand where they can see you."

"Oh, right." I put my hand over the phone. "Molly says we should sit somewhere out of sight so he doesn't see us."

Aaron points at me. "Great idea." He grabs me by the hand and leads us over to a booth. "I'll sit here. You go and get drinks," he snaps as he slides into the seat.

I roll my eyes. "Are your kids really fucking home?" I snap to Molly. "How did I get stuck with this job?"

She laughs. "I'll call back in an hour." Then she hangs up.

"What do you want to drink?" I ask.

"A pink flamingo."

I look at him deadpan. "That is the gayest drink I ever heard of."

"Because I'm gay." He widens his eyes in exasperation; he's in no mood for my jokes tonight. "Just get it."

I giggle and head to the bar to wait in line.

"Hey, Foster," I hear a man's voice call from behind. I turn and see Jake from the investigation team.

"Oh, hi." I smile. "What are you doing here?"

He holds up his drink. "Drinking."

"Obviously." I smirk.

His eyes scan up and down my body in my black dress. "Wow, you look hot."

I smile bashfully. This is awkward. "Thanks."

"Want to come dance?"

"Um." I frown. *Oh God.* "No, thanks anyway. I'm here with Aaron."

"Oh, where is he?" He looks around.

Oh shit, now I've done it. "He's in a booth at the back."

"I'll go say hi." He disappears off in that direction.

Oh great. Now we are going to have to act normal, when all we want to do is Paul-hate and spy.

202

I get our drinks and head back to the table and find Aaron and Jake deep in conversation about work.

Hmm. I wonder. Does he think Aaron's involved and is milking him for information? I sip my drink as they talk, and I do an internal assessment of him. He's actually quite good looking, with sandy hair, a square jaw, and dimples, and he has a great laugh. I've never noticed him before because whenever Jameson is in the same room, all men pale in comparison.

"I'm going to get a drink and come back and sit with you guys," he says as he stands. "You want one, Foster?"

"No thanks." I fake a smile.

"You, Az?"

"No, I'm good," Aaron replies.

He disappears to the bar.

"Oh my God," Aaron scoffs. "I didn't come here to talk about work, and what's with the fucking nicknames? He's not my friend."

"I know, right?" I roll my eyes.

"Why did you tell him where I was?"

"I don't know," I stammer. "He put me on the spot."

"Ugh, great. Now we have to sit with this wanker."

"Can we just go?" I whisper. "This whole fucking night is a disaster."

"No. We are staying here until the lights come on."

I put my head into my hands, and my phone rings. "Hello, Molly," I snap, annoyed that she's avoided this hell. "Nothing's fucking happened yet."

Monday morning, 10:00 a.m.

My phone on my desk rings. "Hello, Emily," Sammia says. "Mr. Miles would like to see you in his office right away, please."

Excitement runs through me. "Okay, I'll come now."

I fix my hair and reapply my lipstick and practically run to the elevator. I hope he's missed me and is making an excuse to see me. I get to the top floor and stride through the foyer. "Hello, Sammia."

"Hi, Emily. Just go through."

"Thank you."

I can walk on the marble today, because I finally bought those new shoes with the rubber soles. Not a click in sight. I knock on his door.

"Come in," his deep voice purrs.

I open the door, and my face drops. Jake is sitting in front of Jameson's desk. "Hello." I smile.

What's he doing here? *Buzz off. This is my time with him.*

Jake turns to me, and his face lights up. "Hey, Foster."

Jameson's eyes hold Jake's. "You two seem very chummy."

"Oh, we went clubbing together on Saturday night, didn't we, Foz?" He smiles happily.

Jameson's eyes come back to me, and his jaw ticks in anger.

Holy fuck.

Chapter 13

"Oh," I stammer in a fluster. "We ran into each other, that's all."

Jameson raises an eyebrow, unimpressed.

"Oh, don't be shy, Foster. We get along famously," Jake the imbecile says.

I feel the blood drain from my face. *Just shut the hell up, would you?*

I turn back to Jameson, hoping to change the subject. "You wanted to see me, sir?"

"Yes." His eyes float over to Jake. "I want to know what leads you have, Mr. Peters."

"Call me Jake," he says.

Jameson glares at him but remains silent. *Oh man. This is uncomfortable.* I grip my notepad with white-knuckle force. Why did he have to say we went out together?

We did not go out together. I feel my face begin to perspire.

"Get to the point," Jameson snaps.

"Well, I'm chasing a few leads, nothing concrete yet. It's very early days."

"Early days?" Jameson repeats. "Are you aware, Mr. Peters, of the importance of a swift resolution on this matter?"

"Yes, sir, but—"

"No buts," he growls. "Our stocks dropped by four million dollars today. Every damn day they drop by that much." He slams his hand on the table, making us both jump. "Do not tell me it's early days," he bellows.

Jake and I wither in our chairs. I've never seen Jameson this angry. He *is* stressed.

I wonder if he went for a run this morning. I'm guessing not.

"Mr. Miles," I interrupt.

Jameson puts his hand up to silence me. "Emily, I want four stories this week."

"Yes, sir."

"They need to be sharp, relevant, and, most importantly, traceable."

I nod. "Okay."

"You can go," Jameson snaps. "That is all."

I frown as my eyes flick between him and Jake. Who's he talking to? "Me?" I point to my chest.

"Yes, you," he snaps. "Who else would I be talking to?"

I feel anger flutter in my stomach. "Fine." I pick up my notepad and stand.

"I want the stories by four o'clock each day."

"Very well," I call as I walk toward the door.

"Send Tristan in," he snaps.

I'm not your damn secretary. I open the door and fake a smile. "Sure," I say through gritted teeth as I close the door behind me.

Damn rude pig. Who the heck does he think he is? I close my eyes in pity for Jake. He's going to get eaten alive in there.

Jameson Miles is fucking mean when he's stressed. I see why he runs—probably keeps him out of jail. Who knows what would happen if he didn't exercise?

I walk out to the reception area and then through to the other side of the building, and I knock on Tristan's door.

"Come in," he calls.

I smile when I hear how much he sounds like his brother. I open the door. "Jameson asked me to . . ." I pause as I try to make it sound nicer than how it came out.

"He wants to see me?" Tristan smirks.

"Yes."

He stands. "Everything okay?" he asks casually as we begin to walk back to reception.

"He's . . ." I shrug as I try to think of a description. "Agitated."

"Hmm." He frowns as if concerned. "He has a lot going on, but you already know that."

"Yes." I smile as my eyes hold his. Does he know?

He winks as he walks down the corridor toward Jameson's office. "Catch you later."

What was that wink? Was that code for "I know you fuck him"? Does he know we are back together?

Shit.

The receptionist isn't at her desk, and I glance down the hallway toward Jameson's office. *Damn it, what's going on in there?*

The door opens. *Shit, I don't want them to see me.* I duck behind the reception desk, and then I hear Jameson's sharp voice as he says something, and I wince. Jake storms past and gets into the elevator and hits the button with force.

The doors close, and my eyes widen as I peer out from behind the desk. What the hell did he just say?

I inhale deeply through my nose as I try to calm myself down.

"For God's sake, Jameson," Tristan snaps. "Tone it down. The poor bastard is doing the best he can."

"Bullshit. He's useless. He's been here a week and hasn't a fucking clue what's going on. He's more interested in chasing the damn girls around downstairs." I go to the bar and pour myself a scotch and then walk over to the window and stare at the city below.

"It's ten o'clock," Tristan says dryly as he watches me.

"So?" I snap as I sip the scotch and feel the warmth of it roll down my throat.

"And the *damn girl downstairs* wouldn't happen to be Emily Foster, would it?"

"Don't fucking start." I roll my eyes. I'm fucking livid that she went out with him on the weekend. "Have you got the management report?" I snap to change the subject.

"No, it's in my office." He heads for the door. "I'll go get it." He disappears as I stare out over New York.

"Hi." I hear a soft voice from behind me.

I sigh as my gaze stays out the window. "Go back to work, Emily."

"Are you all right?" she says as she walks toward me.

"I'm fine." I clench my jaw to stop myself from looking at her.

She walks over and takes my scotch from me and goes to the sink and pours it down the drain.

"What the hell are you doing?" I frown.

She smiles up at me and slides her hands under my suit jacket and around my waist. "Looking after my man."

"Don't tip my fucking drink out."

"Then don't drink because you're stressed. You're playing with fire, Jameson."

"You're not my mother."

She smiles sexily and goes up onto her toes and kisses me softly.

I glare at her. "I'm furious at you."

"I know." She kisses me again. "I wasn't going out, and then we had to spy on Aaron's boyfriend because he was meeting someone there from Grindr. And Jake turned up and wouldn't stop talking to us. He's so annoying."

I glare at her.

She smiles and snuggles into my chest. "I missed you this weekend."

I feel myself relax for the first time since I dropped her off at home on Saturday.

"Don't miss me, Em." I sigh.

"I can't help it." She kisses my lips, totally oblivious to anything I'm saying. "If you're stressed, you go down to the gym, or you come and get me. What about karate? I hear that's amazing."

I roll my eyes. "Doing karate and turning into the fucking Kung Fu Panda will not relieve my stress, Emily. It's laughable that you think that it would."

"Okay, well, hell, go for a run. I don't want you day drinking."

I snap my arm around her waist, unable to control myself any longer. "And I told you I don't want you out with other men. Especially him."

She runs her fingers through my stubble as she smiles softly. "You're my only man," she whispers up at me. "It's you that I'm thinking about."

I feel my anger slowly leave me as we kiss.

"I need you tonight," she says softly.

God, I need her too. *No, stick to the rules.* "It's not Tuesday."

"I don't care."

"Do you have to disobey me on every single thing, Ms. Foster?"

"Just you wait to see how naughty I'm going to be tonight, Mr. Miles," she breathes as I pull her against me to feel my erection.

"Ahem." A voice sounds at the door, and we both look up, startled.

Emily jumps back from me. "Tristan," she splutters. "I was just . . ." Her eyes flick between him and me. "I mean, I . . ."

Tristan chuckles. "Do you want me to leave?"

"No," she stammers. "I'm leaving." She practically runs for the door. "Ah, um, goodbye."

I smirk as I watch her face turn a deep crimson. Tristan already knows—we tell each other everything. "Goodbye, Ms. Foster. I shall send the car for you at seven."

She nods in embarrassment and scurries from the office, and I smile after her.

Tristan's eyes hold mine for a moment. "She's good for you."

"That's debatable."

Emily

I smile broadly at the closed elevator doors in front of me. It worked. I wanted to calm him down, and it worked. He's a mirror. If I'm calm, he's calm.

Maybe if I'm honest, he'll be honest, and I don't know what that means for my little hard-to-get act, but I guess I'll find out soon enough. He didn't seem annoyed when I told him I missed him—he actually seemed relieved. Or maybe that's just wishful thinking on my part. I get back to my floor, and my eyes scan the room as I walk back to my desk.

Somebody working here, alongside me, is a thief. They're stealing from the Miles family; the company's value is plummeting, and my Jay is stressed beyond belief.

I wish I could talk to Molly and Aaron about this. I'm sure if we brainstormed together, we could come up with more than Jake has.

I can't; I gave them my word I wouldn't tell a soul. I take a seat back at my desk.

"How did it go?" Aaron asks.

"Fine," I lie.

"It's blatantly obvious that Mr. Miles has a thing for you." Molly smirks.

"Why is it?" I ask.

"We never got this kind of specialized training program." Her eyes flick to Aaron. "Did we?"

"Nope," he replies as his eyes stay glued to his computer. "Please tell me you are secretly going up there to suck his dick."

I smirk but stay silent.

Molly's eyes come to me in question. "Are you?"

I shrug. I can't lie to them; I just won't elaborate.

"What the fuck?" Aaron whispers as he rolls his chair over to mine; Molly, too, rolls her chair over next to mine. "You have seen him?"

"Possibly."

"What the fuck?" Molly whispers. "When?"

"A few times, but Friday night was the last time I saw him."

Aaron does a cross over his chest and pretends to pray. "Thank you, Jesus."

"But don't say anything," I whisper. "It's just very casual, nothing to get excited about yet."

Molly's eyes widen in exasperation. "Are you kidding me? Screwing Jameson Miles is something to get excited about, woman. Have you seen him?"

I smile broadly at their over-the-top reactions. "I'm just playing it cool, but I am going up there for a project with Tristan and not to see Jay." That's not lying—it is true . . . ish.

Aaron puts his hand over his chest. "Oh hell, she calls him Jay. Be still my beating heart."

"Kill me now." Molly sighs dreamily. "Have you been to his apartment?"

"Uh-huh, and he spent the night at mine."

Their eyes widen. "He came to your house?" Aaron shrieks.

"Shh," I whisper as I look at the people around us. "Keep it down, and you can't tell a soul. Especially not Ava—you know what she's like."

"Oh God, can you imagine?" Molly rolls her eyes. "She'll be your new bestie if she knows you are with him. She'll be stuck to you like glue if there's a chance she will get to his brothers."

"Well, she can't have Tristan." I tut as I turn on my computer. "He's way too nice for her." I shrug. "He's taken, anyway, I think."

We begin to work, and Aaron's phone rings. "It's Paul," he stammers in a panic.

"Decline," I say without looking up.

"But I want to see what he has to say." He picks up the phone, and Molly snatches it from him and hits decline.

"He says 'fuck me on Grindr' to the whole world. Will you stop being pathetic? Kick this asshole to the curb," she snaps.

Aaron's shoulders slump sadly.

I rub his back in sympathy. "It will get easier, babe."

"Yeah, when we set fire to his sleazy ball sack," Molly whispers angrily.

I giggle. "Set fire to his sleazy ball sack—you speak with such articulation, Moll."

"I know, right? This is why I'm a reporter." She stands. "I'm going to make us coffee. You both want one?"

"Uh-huh."

Aaron blows out a deflated breath. "Can you find us some cake too? Surely it's somebody's birthday around here."

Molly looks around. "Yep, where's that Uber guy when we need him?" Her eyes come to me. "Oh my God, was that cheesecake last week sent from Jameson?"

I smile broadly.

Aaron puts his head down and pretends to hit it on the desk. "He even sends cheesecakes. The man is a for real fucking god."

Buzz goes my door buzzer. "Hello." I smile.

"Hello, Ms. Foster. This is Alan, Mr. Miles's driver."

My face falls. "Oh. Is everything all right?"

"Yes, Mr. Miles asked me to collect you and take you to his apartment. He's been delayed on a conference call and will be joining you shortly."

"Oh, okay. I'm on my way." I grab my overnight bag that I packed, and with one last look around my apartment, I head downstairs.

I walk out onto the curb to see the driver in his customary black suit standing next to the limo. "Hello," I say nervously as I approach him.

"Hello."

"I'm Emily." I hold out my hand, embarrassed that I haven't introduced myself before now.

"I'm Alan." He smiles warmly as we shake hands. "Are you ready?"

"Yes." He opens the door, and I climb into the back of the car. He closes the door, and we drive through the New York night. This doesn't seem real—me sitting in the back of a limo being driven to Jameson's apartment by his driver.

We get to his building, and he stops in the pull-up area and opens the door. "I'll take you up." He goes to take my bag from me.

"It's okay. I've got it. Thank you anyway."

He frowns. I see his disappointment.

"Unless you want to carry it," I splutter.

"Thank you." He smiles as he takes it from me. "I would prefer to."

Jeez. He got offended that I wanted to carry my own bag. What is this alternate universe?

We get into the swanky elevator, and the attendant already knows what floor to take me to. He must know Alan.

I hold my breath, nervous as we ride in silence. We get to the floor, and I tentatively follow Alan as he opens the door.

"Mr. Miles shouldn't be long. He's still at the office. His call is going longer than he expected."

"Thank you." I smile.

"Can I get you anything else?"

"No, all good."

With a courteous nod, he closes the door and leaves me alone. I turn to see the lamps strategically on, creating a breathtaking canvas to the view. The twinkling lights over New York are nothing short of spectacular. I take my phone out and snap some pictures. I couldn't be such a fangirl when he is here.

I walk into the bedroom and put my bag into the empty walk-in closet, and then I walk into his. Suits and business shirts are strategically lined up, and there are rows and rows of expensive polished shoes.

I run my hand over the sleeves of the suits as I look around. I open the top drawer of the dresser, and I smile at his over-the-top organization. His ties are all rolled and displayed as if this is a luxury men's boutique. Watches . . . I count them. Ten expensive watches are lined up. And then I see something rolled up next to his watches. My heart stops when I see the initials.

E.F.

My scarf.

He kept it.

Not only did he keep it, but it's also with his special things. I pick it up and hold it in my hands as I stare at it. My eyes close, and I inhale deeply; the faint smell of my perfume still lingers.

I didn't imagine it back then. He was right there with me. I smile broadly and put the scarf back where it was and carefully close the drawer.

I don't know what to do with this information, but I'm pretty damn pleased with my find. My heart is racing.

He kept it.

I walk through the apartment as I look around. I run my hand over the heavy marble countertops in the kitchen and smile at the sheer luxury of the place.

I wonder if he has eaten.

I open the fridge, but it's surprisingly sparse. There is chicken and a few ingredients. I open the pantry and find some other things. I glance at the wine fridge and frown—it's full.

Of course it is.

How often does Mr. Miles have a liquid dinner?

Hmm, I need to get a grip on this stress of his.

I pour myself a glass of wine, take out the ingredients, and look through the cupboards to find the pots and pans and chopping boards and knives. I search Spotify on my phone and put on some chill music.

I begin to chop the chicken with a huge goofy smile on my face.

He kept my scarf.

Forty-five minutes later, I hear the front door open. "Em?" he calls.

"In the kitchen."

"Hmm . . . something smells good." He kisses me and wraps his arms around me from behind. "What are you cooking?"

"Fuck bunny stew."

He laughs loudly, and it's a beautiful sound. It does things to my insides. "Does your mother know you're a cannibal?" He kisses my cheek from behind.

I giggle as I stir the pot. "No, and don't tell her."

"You didn't need to cook. I would have taken you out." He pours himself a glass of wine.

"It's Monday." I frown.

"And?" He sips his wine.

"You don't go out to dinner on a school night."

"I go out every night."

"What?" I frown. "You eat out every night?"

"Yeah, of course. Why?"

My mouth falls open, and I put my hand on my hip. "Jameson Miles, you have more money than sense. How do you relax if you go out to dinner every night?"

"I sit in a restaurant and eat." He shrugs. "It's really quite easy."

I roll my eyes in disgust as I keep stirring. "Are you hungry?"

"Starving." He takes me in his arms and stares down at me. "Did you really miss me over the weekend?"

I go up onto my toes and kiss his big beautiful lips. "I did, actually."

He holds me tight.

"This is where you tell me that you missed me too," I mutter dryly into his shoulder.

"I don't miss people."

"Ugh," I huff as I pull out of his arms and go back to stirring the dinner. "Can you go out of the room so I can drug your food now?" I ask. "I plan on robbing your place."

He chuckles. "Only if you promise to take advantage of my body while I'm sleeping."

I giggle. "Deal."

I dish up our dinner, and we take seats at the kitchen counter. I hold my breath as he takes his first bite. "Hmm, delicious," he hums.

I smile proudly.

"A fuck bunny who cooks." He smirks around a forkful of food.

"I love to cook. It's my hobby."

He frowns and watches me for a moment. "I've never met anyone quite like you, Emily."

"Why?"

"I don't know. I can't put my finger on it. You're very . . ." He pauses as he thinks of the right word. "Unaffected."

"Unaffected by what?" I smirk as I eat.

He shrugs. "New York."

"You've never had a girlfriend who cooked for you before?"

"I've only ever had one serious relationship, and she was a workaholic like me." He shrugs. "We would both get home too late from work. Eating out was easier."

I sip my wine as I stare at him. I would love to blurt out a million questions about her . . . but I won't. I'll play it cool.

He moves to get his wine, and he winces.

"What's wrong?"

"My back's tight." He stands and twists his upper body to stretch. "Somebody insisted on me firing my masseuse."

"Oh, her," I scoff. "Don't ruin my night. I'll find you a new masseuse tomorrow."

He stretches some more. "Please do."

"Why does your back get so tight?"

He sits back down. "When I get wound up, my back tightens."

"What else happens when you get wound up?"

He chews his food as if contemplating his answer. "My temper gets the best of me."

I smile broadly.

"What?" He smirks.

"All this time I thought you were an asshole, when really you were just stressed out?"

He chuckles. "And what's your excuse for being a bitch?"

I sip my wine. "Nothing. I really am just a bitch."

He holds his glass up to clink it with mine. His eyes have a tender glow to them.

"Thank you for dinner. It's delicious." He leans over and kisses me. "Like you."

I remember something. "Oh, and you will be pleased to know, I brought my workout gear so I can come running in the morning."

"You did?" he asks in surprise.

"Uh-huh."

"I run fast."

"Good, because I walk slow."

A few hours later we both laugh out loud into the darkness.

"You did not," he says.

I giggle. "Uh-huh." It's late, and we are lying in bed, facing each other, and talking after making love.

"What on earth?" He rubs his hand up over my stomach and then breast as he listens. His face is alight with mischief. "How?"

"Well . . ." I think for a moment. "It was my first car, and I'd only had it a week. I was driving with my friend, and the day was as hot as hell. We were on our way to buy some cheap jeans from a market, and the temperature gauge started overheating."

He smiles as he listens.

"We pulled into a service station, and I called my dad, and he told me to put oil in it." I shrug. "But we didn't know where the oil went, so we assumed it went in the little hole that you measure it from."

"The dipstick?" he gasps in disbelief. "How on earth did you get it in there?"

I laugh. This is the most ridiculous story I ever heard of. "We borrowed a funnel and then poured it in, and it overflowed everywhere." I shake my head as I remember it as clear as day. "We thought it was fine and started driving, and then oil we'd spilled on the engine caught on fire."

His eyes widen. "What happened?"

"My beloved five-hundred-dollar car that I saved up for a year for was frigging totaled in just one week; that's what happened."

We both laugh and then eventually fall silent.

I lean onto my elbow as I look over at the gorgeous naked man beside me. "You must have done something stupid in your life, Jameson Miles."

He smiles softly over at me in the darkness. "Yeah. I have."

"What?" I smirk.

He reaches over and cups my face in his hand, and his thumb dusts over my bottom lip. "I never asked for your number."

Chapter 14

"Will you hurry up, woman?" Jameson calls from his running position up in front.

I'm panting for dear life as I try to keep up. *Oh hell, he's trying to kill me.*

"What's the rush?"

He turns around and runs back to me.

I frown as I watch him. "God, you're so perky and energetic in the morning."

He laughs and sprints off as I keep shuffling along. I watch him do a loop so that he can still see me, and then he sprints back.

"How do you run so fast?"

He jogs backward in front of me as we talk. "Well, what I do is I imagine someone is chasing me with an ax." He's hardly even out of breath.

"What?" I frown. "Are you kidding me?"

He shakes his head with a cheeky grin.

"Your relaxation tool is to imagine someone is chasing you with a fucking ax."

He laughs as he jogs backward. "It works. I run much faster that way."

"This is all making sense now," I puff. "The puzzle is falling into place here."

"What puzzle?"

"Your back is tight because your masseuse continually puts it out so she can fuck you again."

He grins.

"Your relaxation exercise is to be chased by an ax murderer."

He laughs.

"And you go out seven nights a week. No wonder you're stressed out, you crazy bastard."

He pulls me to him by my T-shirt and kisses me on the lips. "Lucky I have you to fuck me calm, then, isn't it?"

"Damn straight," I pant. We need to stop talking. I can't run and talk at the same time. What kind of Olympic athlete does he think I am?

"What exercise would you recommend I do? For relaxing, I mean," he asks as he falls in to jog beside me slowly.

I think for a moment. "Aqua aerobics."

"Ha." He laughs. "I'm not that old."

"You're pretty old," I pant.

"Do you want to race me?"

"No."

"Why not?"

"Because that murderer has his ax in my lungs, and I'm about to die at any second. I hope you know resuscitation."

He chuckles. "Wimp." He takes off at high speed, and I shuffle along and smile as I watch him loop Central Park as he always keeps me in sight.

Jameson Miles is extremely fit . . . and extremely hot.

And luckily for me, I'm his fuck bunny.

I stand in the foyer as I wait for Ava and Molly. We're just going on our lunch break, and Molly is talking to one of the security guards. I think she's a little sweet on him.

"You coming out this weekend?" Ava asks.

"Um, I'm not sure what I'm doing yet. I might be going home." Jeez, I don't really want to go out with her again. She's only interested in men if they have money. That's just so left field for me that I can't deal with it.

One of the elevators opens, and Tristan steps out and then Jameson. They have two other men with them. Wearing a navy suit and a crisp white shirt, he is the epitome of gorgeous man. Dark hair, square jaw, and those piercing blue eyes. It's hard to believe that just six hours ago, he was deep inside my body in the shower. He took me twice when we got home from our run this morning. The man's an animal. His dick is out of this world.

I've died and gone to CEO heaven.

"Oh my God," Ava whispers. "Look who's coming."

Jameson is deep in conversation with the men as the four of them stride through the crowded foyer. Everyone stops and stares. I stand still as he walks past, and at the last moment he glances up and catches sight of me. His step falters, and I give him a subtle shake of my head. I don't want anyone to know about us. He nods once as if in understanding and keeps walking as he falls back into his conversation. We watch as they leave through the front doors and disappear up the street.

They must be going out for lunch.

"Seriously, where do we find men like the Miles brothers?" Ava sighs.

"Right?" I watch the street they disappeared up.

"One of these days," she whispers. "One of these days."

I wonder if Jameson had a long and boozy lunch, and more importantly, did he bring back cake? It's getting to that time of the day where my mind is fixed firmly on something sweet to have with my coffee. "Hi, Emily, have you got your stories we are running with tomorrow?" Hayden asks.

I smile up at him. *Hmm.* "I didn't think they were due until four, and it's only three."

Hayden is the person who I turn the news in to, and he then passes them on to the next stage.

"I know, but I like to get a head start," he says casually.

Head start on what? Is he the one selling the stories? Is that why he wants them early, so he can get them off to the highest bidder?

"They're not ready yet."

"Okay, cool." He smiles. "Email them over as soon as you get them sorted."

My eyes hold his. "Sure."

I watch him walk back to his desk and fall into conversation with the person who sits next to him.

I'm watching you, asshole.

I look around the office with renewed determination. *I'm watching all of you. Every single one.*

It's just now four, and I email Jameson.

> Hi,
>
> I booked you a massage with a physio. They will be at your place at seven. Hope this suits your plans.

FB

xoxoxo

A few moments later, a reply bounces back.

Dear FB,

Please define "they."

J
xx

I roll my eyes. I knew this was coming.

Dear Mr. J,

They . . . aka . . . male physiotherapist professional, nonsexual-act-performing masseuse. Specializes in back treatment and hella expensive.

FB
xoxoxo

I wait for a few moments, and a reply bounces back.

FB,

Fine, can you let them into my apartment, please? I'll have Alan pick you up at six thirty. I'll meet you there, maybe fifteen minutes late.

J

xox

I smile broadly as hope blooms in my chest. I write back.

Are we seeing each other tonight?

He replies.

Yes. I'm away for the week next week, therefore, I'm taking next week's meetings too.
See you tonight.

Jay

xox

I probably should play a little hard to get and pretend I have something going on . . . but I just don't have it in me. I email back.

Jay,

I'll make dinner. What do you want?

FB

xoxo

A reply bounces back.

The only thing I want to eat tonight is you.
Now get back to work before I bend you over
your desk.

I smirk as I feel my face flush, and I click out of my emails. He is undoubtedly the hottest man on earth.

I feel like a master chef in Jameson's fancy kitchen. It's just now seven, and I turn the gas on and lift the pot of water onto it. I like having dinner ready for him. I know he's never had it, so it feels special to do it for him.

The security buzzer sounds, and I look around. *Shit. Where's the intercom?*

I see a phone and screen near the front door. I pick up. "Hello?"

"Hello, this is Matthew, the physio. I'm here for a massage therapy session."

I smile as I stare at the screen. Matthew is good looking, has the whole Scandinavian thing going on. "Come up." I push the button and release the door for him, and he disappears into the elevator. Moments later, he knocks on the door. "Hello." I smile.

"Hi." He walks in wearing a white uniform and carrying a fold-up massage bed.

Wow . . . Matthew is really hot. Maybe I should get a massage too?

"Where do you want me to set up?" he asks.

"Umm." I frown as I look around. Where do I want him to set up? "Just hang on a minute." I walk down the hallway and peer into the rooms. There's a room at the end with a treadmill and weight bench. "Just down here at the end, please."

He saunters down with his sexy walk and begins to set up. Suddenly I'm reminded that this is the exact scenario that Jameson had with Chloe . . . only they really did have sex. My stomach rolls at the thought.

Stop it.

"I'll be out here if you need me." I walk nervously back out into the kitchen. Shit, is it safe to leave him down there alone? Should I be watching him or something?

I peer back down the hall to make sure he doesn't come out of that room and snoop around. Oh, damn it, what's the protocol with strangers in a place like this?

The front door clicks, and Jameson comes into view. "Hello," he says flatly.

I smile. "Hi." I wrap my arms around him. "How's my man?"

"Fine." He brushes past me in a rush.

Oh. I frown. That's not the greeting I was hoping for.

"Is he here yet?"

"Yes, in the room down at the end."

"I'll just have a quick shower. Can you tell him I'll be five minutes, please?"

"Sure."

He disappears into the bedroom, and I walk back down the hall. "Jameson is just taking a quick shower. He will only be a few minutes."

"Okay, thanks." Matthew smiles.

I walk back out into the kitchen and stir the vegetables I have cooking. Maybe I should have stayed at my place tonight. He didn't seem too pleased to see me.

Ten minutes later warm hands come around my waist from behind, and Jameson's lips find my temple. "Hey, babe," he whispers softly.

228

I turn to find him with a white towel around his waist. "Everything all right?"

"Yeah, I'm just really tired." He exhales heavily. "The last thing I feel like is a fucking massage," he whispers as he holds his cheek to mine.

"You'll feel much better after it," I say. "Massage, dinner, and bed."

He rolls his eyes and trudges up the hall.

I smile as I listen. Every time Jameson inhales, he gives a slight snore. I'm sitting on the couch in my pajamas watching a movie, and he's lying with his head on my lap, fast asleep.

This feels strangely . . . normal.

He wasn't joking when he said he was tired. He's more than tired—he's exhausted.

I think it's more mental exhaustion than physical, and I can't imagine what he deals with at work every day. He's had the pressure of running Miles Media from such a young age. Even in his youth, he would have been coached for this role. But Jameson Miles the CEO is a mere mortal, and I feel a protective urge roll over me.

I mindlessly run my fingers through his hair and enjoy this close time with him.

I don't imagine many people see him so relaxed. "Jay," I whisper softly.

He frowns in his sleep.

"Jay, bedtime, baby," I whisper.

He inhales as he stretches and blinks, as if not knowing where he is.

I run my fingers through his hair. "Bedtime." I smile softly.

I get up and turn off the lights and the television, and then he takes my hand and leads me down the hall to his bedroom. He brushes his teeth and gets into bed.

A few moments later, once I'm ready, I climb into bed beside him, and he pulls me into his arms. "Good night, sweetheart," he whispers as he kisses my forehead. We lie cheek to cheek. There's a closeness between us that I haven't felt before.

"Good night." I snuggle against his chest.

This night has been nonsexual . . . and normal . . . and weirdly intimate.

I may be addicted.

I wake to the feeling of strong hands holding my inner thighs apart. Jameson's head is between my legs, and his thick tongue swipes through my sex. My head throws back, and my hands go to the back of his head. My body is pumping with arousal, so I know he's been at it awhile. "Oh God," I moan. "Good morning, Jay."

He turns his head and kisses my inner thigh. "Morning."

He bites my clitoris, and I close my eyes. *Good God.* He's awake now and in all his glory. He continues to suck as waves of pleasure start to pulse through me. He pushes three thick fingers aggressively into my sex, and I wince. This is Jameson's specialty—finger fucking me with such force that I orgasm before we even have sex.

I've never been with a man who can pleasure me in so many different ways.

He begins to ride me, his whole hand centered on the task. My legs are back to the mattress, and God. "Oh God . . . so good," I breathe. The sound of my wet arousal echoes through the silent room as he works me.

This man is insane. Ten minutes ago I was dead asleep.

He bends and nips my clitoris, and I convulse as I come in a rush. My body lurches forward, and he pushes me back down. "Shh," he whispers as he calms me. "Again," he chants as his eyes hold mine.

"No." I sit up in a rush and grab his shoulder and pull him up over me. We kiss as we fall back to the mattress, and my leg wraps around his waist.

Hell, what a way to wake up.

Our kiss turns frantic, and I feel his cock nudge my opening, and then he pauses.

"It's okay. I'm on the pill," I breathe as I hold his face to mine.

He closes his eyes for a split second, and then, as if unable to relax without a condom, he drags himself off me and goes to the bedside. I watch as he tears one open and rolls it on.

Then he's back on me. He slides home deep in one swift movement. I cry out as my sex begins to spasm around his thick muscle. "Hold it," he growls.

Fuck . . . how are you supposed to hold it? Like that's a thing.

He looks down at me. His olive skin has a sheen of perspiration, his blue eyes are beaming, and I smile in wonder at the perfect specimen in front of me . . . inside me.

He widens his legs and goes up onto his knees and then lifts my legs in front of him by my ankles and begins to pump me—thick, heavy hits—and his jaw hangs slack as he watches the place our bodies meet.

I can see every muscle in his torso contract as he pushes forward. Goddamn . . . watching Jameson Miles fuck is the world's best porn. He picks up the pace, and his body goes into overdrive. I scrunch the blankets beneath me as I feel myself build.

The sound of our bodies slapping together echoes through the room. His eyes close in ecstasy, and he moans as his body really goes to town. "I'm close," I whimper.

"Hold it," he barks as he pumps.

"Jameson."

He grabs my legs and puts them to one side and together, and his eyes flicker with arousal as his pumps become slow and measured.

Oh . . . my man likes it tight.

I clench down, and his head throws back. I clench again, and he can't hold it. He holds himself deep, and I feel the telling jerk as he comes deep inside my body. He empties himself, and then, knowing I can't come in that position, rises over me and kisses me as we fall tender.

This is what I love . . . this is my favorite kind of sex with him. Gentle, tender lovemaking. He holds himself up onto his elbows and kisses me as his body gives me exactly what I need.

Him . . . I need all of him.

Our eyes are locked as something so beautiful runs between us. His kiss is tender, but it's the look in his eyes that's turning me inside out.

We're falling for each other.

This is not casual sex; this isn't even sex. This is the ultimate lovemaking.

"Jay," I pant as my eyes search his.

"I know, baby," he whispers. I grip his shoulders, and he holds himself deep, and my body contracts around his.

His lips take mine, and our kiss is slow and unhurried and everything I've never had.

He slowly finishes me and then drops to the mattress beside me and rolls me to face him.

We look at each other, and I'm overwhelmed with a feeling of closeness.

I stare at his beautiful face, and I smile softly. "I feel like—"

"Don't." He cuts me off.

"What?" I frown.

"Don't ruin this."

I'm at a loss by what he means. "How would I ruin this?"

"Don't fall in love with me, Emily."

What the hell? I stare at him. "Why not?"

"Because we're not like that. Get that through your head. Right now." He gets up in a rush and walks into the bathroom and closes the door. It shuts with a sharp snap.

I roll onto my back and stare at the ceiling. I was going to say that I felt like that was the best alarm clock of all time.

Love was just an afterthought.

Chapter 15

I get out of bed and storm into the bathroom. I find him under the shower.

"For the record, Jameson," I snap, "I was going to tell you that you should wake me up like that every day."

He narrows his eyes in anger.

"It seems to me that the only person who's thinking about love around here is you."

He rolls his eyes as he soaps his groin.

His eye-rolling infuriates me. "So don't turn this around and push me away because you are falling in love with me!" I don't know what to say next, so I storm out. I grab my bag and head down to one of the other bathrooms to shower. I'm not getting in with him. *Stupid jerk.*

Half an hour later, I walk out into the kitchen to see Mr. Miles the CEO—gray suit, white shirt, and cranky controlled persona firmly back in place. "Are you ready?"

"Ah." I look around. "I'll just get my things." I go into the bedroom and glance at myself in the mirror. I'm wearing his favorite outfit today, and he didn't even notice. *Well . . . poof to him.*

Damn control freak is pissing me off.

I walk back out with my overnight bag over my shoulder. "Let's go."

His brow furrows when he sees what I'm carrying. "What are you doing with that bag? Just get it later."

"I'll take it to work with me. That's fine." My eyes hold his. "I have a lot going on this week."

His jaw clenches as he glares at me. "Good." He turns and walks out, and I smirk.

I let you have the control for the last few days, Mr. Miles, but don't misjudge my submission as a weakness.

I will not beg for any man to love me, CEO billionaire with blue eyes or not.

Don't wreck it.

I know I told him I want friends with benefits . . . but the rules have changed.

For me, anyway.

We get into the elevator, and I stare straight ahead. I can feel the animosity oozing out of him. Part of me hates that I'm letting him get worked up before he even starts for the day, but screw it. I can't spend my life tiptoeing around his stress levels.

We walk out through the foyer, and the limo is parked and waiting. Alan is standing next to the door.

"Hello, Alan." I smile as we approach as if I don't have a care in the world.

Alan smiles and nods in acknowledgment.

Jameson stays silent. He holds his hand out for me to get in first. I climb in and shuffle over the seat, and Jameson gets in beside me.

A folded newspaper sits on the seat, and I pick it up and begin to read.

Jameson stares at me, and I know it's his paper. Well, too bad—I got it first. For ten minutes, I read in silence. There is none of my fake news today. *Hmm.* I wonder if this has a correlation to me not having it to Hayden by four yesterday. I think about it for a moment. I'm going to test this theory today. I'll have a story to him by three and see what happens.

"What are you doing tonight?" he asks.

"I'm going out with Ava," I lie as I pass the paper to him.

"I told you I didn't want you going clubbing with her."

I smile. The nerve of this control freak. "What I do when I'm not with you is none of your business, Jameson."

"So now you're going to be all dramatic?"

I roll my eyes. "Will you just stop."

"Stop what?"

My eyes hold his. "I'm not in love with you. So . . . you can stop worrying that I am. I enjoy your company, but you obviously have a hang-up about someone caring for you and mistake it for love." I roll my eyes. "It's all a bit too hard, to be honest."

His jaw clenches, and I know he's fuming on the inside. "What does that mean?"

"What?" I ask.

"That it's too hard."

"It means go and find someone else not to fall in love with you." I shrug. "I'm fine with that."

"You're fine with that?" he whispers angrily. "So if I went and had sex with someone else tonight, you'd be fine with that?"

I frown as I stare at him. What the hell is going on in that head of his? I drag my hand down my face. "Jameson, for fuck's sake. What do you want from me?"

"I don't know," he snaps.

"Fine." I blow out a deep breath. "Let's leave it at that, then."

"What does that mean?"

"My God," I snap in exasperation. "For a smart man, you're being really stupid. I can't help you work out what you want from me, Jameson."

He stares at me.

"One minute you're telling me not to ruin it by falling in love with you, and the next minute you're telling me you don't want me going out without you."

He sits back in his seat, affronted.

"I want a close friend to have sex with. We talked about this. It seems to me that the only person breaking the rules here is you. Why are you even thinking about love?"

"Don't turn this on me," he whispers angrily.

"All right, then," I snap. "Can you look me in the eye and tell me that you have no feelings for me?"

He rolls his eyes in disgust.

"Can you?"

"Of course I can."

I look him straight in the eye. "Do it, then."

"What?"

"Tell me that you don't have feelings for me. Tell me you have never thought of me once over the last year and that you never kept my scarf."

He narrows his eyes in anger.

"Like I thought," I huff as I turn my attention back out the window.

"I wondered how long it would be until that snarky bitch reared her ugly head," he mutters under his breath.

"Ha," I huff. "At least that bitch knows what she wants."

"And what's that?" he sneers.

"A man; that's what she wants—one who isn't afraid of his feelings."

"Go to hell," he whispers. "Just stop talking. You're stressing me the fuck out with all your shit. If I wanted a psychiatrist, I would date one."

I smirk as I look out the window. "We're not dating, Jameson. We're just fucking. Get it right."

"You go out with Ava trolling for men tonight, and we won't even be doing that."

"Excuse me?" I snap as my anger starts to simmer. "You can't tell me what to do."

His eyes hold mine. "I can. And I just did."

"Jameson." I pause as I try to think of a calm and intelligent reply. "I would never sleep with someone behind your back—you know that. But you can't tell me where I'm allowed to go. Even if you loved me, which you don't, I wouldn't allow you to dictate what I can do."

"I mean it."

"Go to hell." The car pulls up around the corner at my spot where I get out, and I open the door in a rush.

"I'll see you tonight," he snaps as I climb out.

I lean back into the car. "Yeah, wait for me. I'll be there when hell freezes over." I slam the door in a rush.

The limo pulls out and slowly drives down the road toward the Miles Media building, and I inhale to try to calm my furiously beating heart.

Stupid fucking jerk.

"Wonder what this is about?" Molly frowns as she reads the news from her computer.

"What what's about?" I reply as I type.

"It says here that Miles Media is having crisis meetings today with shareholders and that more meetings are scheduled in London next week."

My heart drops; Jameson's going to London next week. "What?"

She turns her computer screen to face me, and I read the financial reviews story on the Miles Media stock prices slump. I lean my face onto my hand as I read on.

God . . . what a nightmare. I look over and see Jake laughing with one of the girls in her cubicle as if he doesn't have a care in the world. What is that stupid idiot doing? Is he even investigating the damn case at all?

Ugh, honestly, I think he's the wrong man for the job. No investigating seems to be getting done, although I'm sure he has the phone numbers of every single girl on the floor. Should I tell him my thoughts about Hayden? No, it's only a hunch with no real evidence. I'm testing the theory today.

Screw this. I'll have to find out who's doing this myself. It's obvious Jake has no frigging idea.

From the corner of my eye, I see people scurry back to their desks, and I glance up to see Jameson and Tristan walking through the floor. Tristan smiles and talks to people as he walks along. Jameson stays solemn, in all his cranky gorgeousness.

His back is ramrod straight, and his face is so damn kissable it hurts.

You're angry with him . . . remember, fool? Look away, look away.

I go back to my computer, but then I see out of the corner of my eye the familiar gray suit. I look up to find Jameson standing next to my desk. "Hello, Mr. Miles." I fake a smile.

His eyes hold mine. "Hello."

"Can I help you, sir?"

"Where is Jake?" he says through gritted teeth.

"Jake would be flirting somewhere in the office," I say quietly. "Look for a good-looking woman, and you will find him." I point in the direction of Jake with my pen.

Jameson inhales sharply as he glares over at Jake as he talks to a blonde, completely unaware that he is being watched. Jameson's eyes flick to Tristan, and they both give a subtle shake of their heads.

"Tristan, I was wondering if I can see you for a few moments at some point this afternoon, please?" I ask.

"Yes, of course. Come up in half an hour."

Jameson's eyes stay fixed on me for a beat longer than necessary, as if he's waiting for me to say something. I smile warmly as I hide my anger. Maybe he's right, and I really am a bitch. "Bye."

"Goodbye," he says as he turns and walks over toward Jake.

I smile as I watch the moment Jake sees him coming and how fast he jumps up from the corner of that desk. Jameson says something to him, and then I watch as Jake is marched to the elevator.

I hope they fire him. He's definitely not worried about the enormity of this case.

Forty minutes later, I knock on Tristan's door. "Come in," he calls.

"Hello." I smile.

"Hi, Emily." He gestures to his desk. "Come take a seat."

I sit down. "I just wanted to keep you updated on something that happened yesterday that felt out of the ordinary."

"Great, okay." He holds his pen in his hands. "What is it?"

"Hayden came and asked me for my stories early."

He frowns as he listens.

"It felt weird that he needed them early. So . . . I lied and said they weren't ready yet."

"And?"

"And there was no fake news today."

He narrows his eyes.

"I don't know if I'm grasping at straws, but it kind of felt like the fake news stories only go to print if they are in by a certain time."

"Interesting. That's great work." He thinks for a moment. "Hold the story back today so we can test the theory, and I will start to dig up some info on Hayden. Good work."

I stand.

"Is everything all right?" he asks.

"Yes, why?"

His eyes hold mine for a beat, and I know that Jameson has said something about our fight this morning. "Just checking."

"Everything's great."

"Good."

"See you later." I bounce out of the office like I don't have a care in the world.

It's late Friday night, and I stare at the television, my mind in a blurred haze. I haven't heard from Jameson since our fight on Wednesday morning. I've seen him in passing at work, but that's all.

Maybe that's it—maybe I won't see him again.

On Wednesday, the romantic in me was convinced he had real feelings for me and that he would come back begging. On Thursday, I decided that the man has deep emotional flaws if he couldn't see he had feelings for me.

Today . . . I wonder if I meant anything at all. Maybe I've looked at the whole thing through rose-colored glasses? All along he's given me signs, and like a fool, I've ignored every one of them.

He leaves for London on Monday, I think—not that I would know if his plans have changed.

My mind goes back to the flight where we met, and now that I know the life that he leads . . . I can see it all so clearly.

He didn't ask for my number because he didn't want anything—he even said that was the reason why. But I never thought that he actually meant he didn't want anything. I thought there was an ulterior motive and that was just the lie he used to cover it. Maybe some people are just wired never to want more. Or maybe he just hasn't met the right person yet.

So many maybes.

My door buzzes, and I frown and get up and push the button. "Hello."

"Hey." The voice is distorted.

"Who is it?"

"It's me," he pants.

"Jameson?"

"You expecting someone else?" he says, obviously annoyed.

I smile, buzz him in, and run into the bedroom to take off my ragged nightdress that has hot chocolate spilled down the front of it. I flap my arms around in a panic and grab a towel off the rack. I wrap it around my chest as if I just got out of the shower. It's a lot better than a soiled nightdress with dancing teddy bears on it. Why my grandma thinks dancing teddies is something I need, I'll never know.

A knock sounds at the door, and I open it in a rush. And there he stands. Piercing blue eyes greet me. He's wet with perspiration and panting.

My face falls. "Did you run all the way here?"

He nods. He has a melancholy feeling oozing out of him.

"Are you all right?" I ask.

He shrugs, and his eyes search mine.

"Jay," I whisper as my heart melts. I take him in my arms and hold him tight. He clings to me as if his life depends on it.

We stand in each other's arms for a long time; no words are needed. At this moment, he needs me.

"Did the ax murderer chase you here?" I whisper up against his cheek.

He smiles and grips me tighter. "Maybe."

"I paid him to do that."

"Witch." He smirks.

"Come on, let's get you in the shower." I take his hand and lead him into the bathroom and turn on the shower and take his shirt off over his head.

His eyes darken, and I slowly slide his track pants down his legs.

"I've had the worst few days," he murmurs.

I nod as I slide his briefs down his legs. "I know, baby. This work nightmare will be over soon."

"It has nothing to do with work."

"What's it got to do with?"

His eyes hold mine, and he swallows the lump in his throat. "You."

I smile softly as my heart free-falls from my chest. "You missed me?"

He nods as if he's feeling stupid.

I kiss him and hold his face in my hands. "I missed you, too, you big dope."

"But you said—"

"Don't worry about what that snarky bitch said. She's off her chops. Pay her no attention."

He smirks as his hands drop to my behind. "Off her chops? What the hell does that even mean, Emily?"

I giggle. "When snarky bitches go crazy, they go off their chops."

He chuckles and holds me close and inhales deeply into my hair as if he's relieved.

"I don't know what's going on between us, Jay." I hesitate as I try to articulate what I want to say. "But you can depend on me. Don't be scared of us. Because I'm not."

"You should be," he fires back.

"Why would I be scared of someone who makes me feel the way you make me feel?"

His face softens, and he dusts my bottom lip with his thumb. "It's been a long few days without you."

I smile softly. I love him when he's like this. "Get in the shower, and wash away the last week, and stay with me."

His kiss deepens, and I feel his erection begin to grow up against my stomach. He pulls off the towel and leads me into the shower by the hand and pushes me up against the wall.

We kiss like we've been starved of each other. My man Jim is back . . . and I feel like we just jumped over some invisible hurdle between us.

What exactly that is I just don't know, but I feel if I can bring Jim to me for long enough for things to become real between us, maybe I can help Jameson get some kind of work-life balance.

Monday morning

Jay holds me tight in his arms as we say our goodbyes. He goes to London for a week today. He has meetings all week. We've had the most amazing weekend. We stayed here at my apartment the entire time. I've cooked for us, we've made love and watched movies, and we even went for a run. Not a cranky CEO in sight. We went back to his place last night to pack his bag, and even then, we came back here to my house to sleep. I feel that when he's here at my house, he's able to detach from being Jameson Miles the CEO and just be a regular man . . . my man. He can forget who he is for a while and what is expected of him.

The dynamic has shifted between us.

I don't know how to stop it, but I'm falling for him.

I can feel myself slipping under the water, his water . . . the beautiful spell of Jameson Miles.

"No layovers, okay?" I whisper.

He smiles as we kiss.

"No talking to girls who get upgraded."

He grabs my behind. "Stop talking, wench."

I grip him tighter. "Oh. I hate the thought of a week without you."

He kisses me again but remains silent.

"Will you say something?" I whisper. "Say something sweet to put me out of my misery."

His eyes come to mine as he cups my face. "I packed your scarf in my luggage."

I smile softly.

"It's nothing new. I've taken it on every trip I've been on . . . since we met."

A wave of unexpected emotion overwhelms me, and my eyes fill with tears. I blink them away in the hope he doesn't see. "You have?" I whisper.

He nods and kisses me as he holds my face, and it's tender and perfect and God, I just want to blurt out that maybe I really do love him for real now.

But I won't, because then I will ruin it.

Whatever *this* is.

I lie in bed and aimlessly scroll through Instagram, but my mind is anything but on my feed. Jameson is my focus. I've missed him this week, but I know he's missed me too. Even with all his meetings and stress over there, he has kept in constant touch.

Hopefully when he gets back, we can decipher what's really going on here. My phone rings, and the letter *J* lights up my screen.

"Hello." I smile.

"Hey there," his deep velvety voice purrs down the line.

"How's my man?"

"Good, busy. How are you?"

"Lonely."

We've spoken every day since he's been gone . . . twice a day, actually.

He chuckles. "You didn't look too lonely last night in that Skype session."

I feel my face flush. We've been sexting each other every night, and last night I may have given him a little vibrator show. The look on his face was one of pure pleasure. I clench my sex just thinking about the way he was pulling himself as he watched me.

God . . . deviants.

"What's going on today, sweetheart?" he asks.

My stomach flips every time he calls me that; it will never grow old. "Working." I try not to talk about work with him. I want to keep our relationship as separated as I can. "What are you up to?"

"I'm just about to go out to dinner with Elliot. He's introducing me to some girl he's met."

"Really?" I smile. "Has he fallen in love?"

"God, no. He falls in lust every week, though."

I giggle.

"Are you going out tonight?"

I roll my eyes. "No, Jay; relax, will you?"

God, he's frigging traumatized from that night I was dancing with the blond god.

"It's hard to relax when I know how gorgeous you are on the other side of the world all alone."

246

"Well, in four more days you'll be back." I glance at my watch. "I've got to go. I'm going to miss my bus."

"Okay. I'll let you go. Have a nice day, babe." He sighs.

"You too," I whisper.

He lingers on the line.

Even on the other side of the world, he has an effect on me. He's waiting for me to tell him I'm missing him . . . he always does.

"I'm missing you." I smile.

"Me too."

"I'll speak to you tonight."

"Okay. Bye."

Molly and I've just been out for dinner, and she's driving me home. Her phone rings through the Bluetooth in her car. The name *Michael* lights up the screen. "Hello," she answers.

"Oh my God, Molly. I need your help."

"What's wrong?" she stammers as she slows the car down.

Michael is her ex-husband; my eyes widen as I listen.

"I took something, and now I'm driving, and I just passed out, and my car hit a guardrail."

"What?" she cries as she pulls the car over to the side.

"I feel so dizzy."

"Holy shit, tell me where you are!"

"I'm on the interstate near the garage we get gas from."

"Okay, I'm on my way." She does a U-turn and starts speeding in the other direction.

She's driving like a bat out of hell, and I hold on for dear life. "Do you know mouth to mouth?" I ask.

"No." She shrugs. "Maybe a little bit. Can you google passing out for me?"

I start to google. "Should we just call an ambulance?"

"Maybe." She looks between me and the road; she calls him back.

"Hello," he says in a meek voice.

"Are you okay?"

"Yes."

"Should I call an ambulance?"

"No," he snaps. "Just get here."

Five minutes later we pull up behind his parked car, and we can see him slumped in the front seat. We both get out to run up to the car.

"Thank God you're here," he splutters when he sees her. Then he sees me, and his face falls.

"It's all right. This is Emily," she says. "What happened?"

He points at her and me. "Do not tell a soul."

"What?"

He gets out of the car, and we both look down. He has a huge erection.

"What the fuck?" Molly gasps.

"I have a Tinder date tonight, so I took a Viagra, but it didn't seem to work, so I took another two."

I put my hands over my mouth in horror.

Molly's eyes widen. "You took three Viagra?"

He nods, his erection nearly splitting his pants.

"You are the stupidest fucking man I've ever known."

"Without a doubt." He winces. He goes to move and then gets dizzy and has to hold on to the car for balance.

"Get in the car," she demands. "I'm taking you to the ER."

"What?" he stammers. "No."

"You have no blood left in your body, you stupid fuck!" she cries.

He puts his head into his hands, and I want to burst out laughing so hard. I bite my lip to stop myself as I look between the two of them.

"What's the ER going to do?" he cries.

"Other than laugh at the middle-aged man with a Tinder erection, nothing. Get in the damn car."

He goes to walk and then falls to the ground, and we both run to pick him up and put him in the front of Molly's car. I climb in the back.

Molly's eyes flick to him as he lies back on the seat in pain, and I stay silent, unsure what to say. I'll catch a cab home from the ER. I don't want to be in the way.

Molly shakes her head as she drives. "So . . . let me get this straight, Michael. You're going out with Madam Whorebag tonight, and you go to all this trouble to satisfy whoever she is in bed?"

He looks over at her and clenches his jaw as if he knows what's coming next.

"You couldn't even be bothered to have sex with me at all, Michael!" she screams. "How the hell do you think that makes me feel?"

"Because you didn't fucking like it," he fires back.

"Because I got two fucking pumps."

My eyes widen. *Oh jeez.* I so don't want to be here right now. I slump into my seat to try to hide.

"Why do you think I have to take this shit? Huh?" he yells. "Because I knew what a fucking disappointment I was to you."

Molly's eyes widen in rage. "You were never a disappointment. You were fucking lazy and didn't care."

"I did so care!" he screams. "Losing you is the biggest regret of my life."

I put my head into my hands. I wonder if they would notice if I dived out of the moving car.

Molly glares at him, and the car coasts to one side of the highway. I wince. "Eyes on the road, Moll," I whisper. She straightens the car.

"So why didn't you call her to come and get you tonight, huh?"

"Because I wouldn't tell her anything about me." He sighs as he leans his head onto his hand, clearly upset.

"Why not?" she yells.

"Because she's not you!"

The car falls silent, and my eyes fill with tears. He still loves her.

Oh . . . this is so sad.

Moments later we pull into the hospital and help him out of the car and into the reception room, and Molly goes up to the desk. "My husband needs to see somebody, please."

"What's the problem?" the nurse asks.

She drops her shoulders as she steels herself to say it out loud. "I accidentally gave him too much Viagra."

Michael takes her hand in a silent thank-you, and I smile softly.

She's covering for him to save him the embarrassment.

"Oh." The nurse's face falls, and she gets a wheelchair. With Molly walking beside him, he is wheeled down the corridor.

I take a seat and inhale deeply as my faith in the human race is restored.

I learned a lesson tonight—love comes in all shapes and sizes.

I tap the whiteboard in front of me as I stand and go through our discussion topics. "This projection here is based on the current climate. However, that may change when the election goes through."

Buzz. My phone dances across the table, and I look up at the men sitting around the board table. *Damn it, just let it ring out.* Elliot glances down at my phone at the same time to see the caller ID.

FB.

But I want to hear her voice; two minutes won't hurt. "I have to take this call. Elliot, can you go through the advertising strategy for next month, please, while I do?"

"Sure thing." Elliot stands and takes over, and I answer the call and leave the room and head into Christopher's office next door.

"Hello."

"Hi." Emily's happy voice beams down the phone line.

"Hi." I find myself smiling stupidly as I stand at the window overlooking London.

"Did I interrupt anything?" she asks.

I smirk. *Only a meeting with twelve management staff.* "No, not at all."

"I called to tell you I bought new sneakers."

I smile. "You did?"

"Uh-huh, they're motorized, so I will be whipping your ass on park runs from here on in. Just thought I should warn you."

God . . . she's so refreshingly normal. When has a woman ever called me to tell me she bought new sneakers? "I highly doubt that."

"Oh hell, you won't believe what happened last night," she continues. "Molly's ex-husband took two Viagra, maybe three, and passed out while he was driving because he had no blood left in his body because it was all in his dick, so we had to take him to the ER."

I laugh out loud. "What the hell? Is that a thing?"

"Yes, it's a thing. Who knew?"

I widen my eyes. *Jesus.* "I'll have to stop taking it, then," I tease.

She laughs. "No, it's okay. I completely know what to do now. Passing out is well worth it. You stay on that shit—we just need to tourniquet it. I've got us covered."

We both laugh and then fall silent.

"Three days," I murmur.

"Three days," she repeats.

God, I've never been so anxious to get home in my life.

"What are you doing now?" I ask.

"I'm about to put a face mask on and take a bath with cut-up cucumber over my eyes. You're missing out on a real visual sensation over here."

"No doubt." I smile. This woman is so naturally beautiful. She doesn't try to be something she's not. I love that about her.

I love a lot of things about her . . .

"So you've added cucumbers to your beauty regimen now?" I ask.

"Yeah, it's supposed to make you less puffy."

I smile broadly. "Cucumbers are good for a lot of things. Maybe it should be added to our sexual regimen as well."

She bursts out laughing. "You're a sicko, Mr. Miles."

"So you keep telling me."

"I'll let you go."

I smirk as I look out the window. "Goodbye, Emily."

"Goodbye, Jay," she whispers. The phone goes dead, and I head back into the boardroom and take a seat.

Christopher is now talking about something, and I take my seat next to Elliot.

He leans over and whispers, "You have Zuckerberg on speed dial now?"

"Huh?" I frown.

"FB . . . that stands for Facebook, right?"

I frown and then realize he's talking about the call from Emily.

FB stands for fuck bunny, not Facebook. I smirk, and then I pinch the bridge of my nose as my chuckle breaks through.

"What's so funny?" Elliot whispers.

"Zuckerberg bought motorized sneakers."

Elliot rolls his eyes. "It wouldn't surprise me. That guy's fucking crazy."

I catch a cab with a thousand thoughts running through my mind. There's so much history between the two of us. I'm on my way to see my ex, who was supposed to be the love of my life.

It's been a long time since I've seen Claudia. She was in the States the last time I was in London. Both being workaholics has always worked against us—time together is precious.

I knock on the door and exhale; my nerves are thumping heavily. The door opens in a rush, and her beautiful face comes into view. She smiles broadly and wraps her arms around my neck.

"Thank God you're here," she whispers into my neck. "I've missed you."

Chapter 16

"Hello." I smile as she leads me into her house by the hand. Her touch is warm . . . familiar. "How are you?" I ask.

"Good now that you're here." She takes me in her arms, and I smile down at her. There's a bond between us that can never be broken. Realizing what I'm doing, I pull out of her arms and stand back. Being in her arms wasn't on today's agenda.

Her face falls before she quickly recovers. "Any news on the sabotage?"

"No, none yet."

She watches me for a moment, and her knowing eyes hold mine. "You have something on your mind. What is it?"

"I've met someone."

"Don't." She turns her back to me and walks to the kitchen and puts the kettle on.

"I couldn't help it." I walk up behind her and put my hand out to touch her and then recoil it. I take a safe step back.

"Don't tell me you couldn't help it when we both know you can."

"The pull to her is strong."

"Physical pull?" she asks flatly.

I roll my lips as I watch her; she's going to go postal any moment. "At first, yes. I thought it was just physical."

Her eyes come to mine. "How long ago did you meet her?"

"Twelve months."

Her face screws up in fury. "You've been seeing someone for twelve months?"

"No," I snap. "I met her on a flight a year ago, we spent a night together on a layover, and I've recently run into her again."

"Big deal, Jameson. You've slept with a lot of women while we've been on this break," she fires back angrily.

"This one's different, Claudia," I say softly.

She rolls her eyes in disgust and turns her back to me once again.

"I've thought of her"—I pause, unsure how much to share—"a lot since we met, and then it was as if I . . ." My voice trails off, and I stare at her back as I wait for her reply.

"As if you what?" she eventually asks.

"It was as if I willed her back into my life."

She turns sharply. "Meaning what?"

"She'd been on my mind a lot . . . and then she showed up in my office."

She rolls her eyes, unimpressed. "Of course she would—you're Jameson Miles."

"She had no idea who I was when we met. I gave her a fake name."

"So why are you here, Jameson?" she demands.

I swallow the lump of regret in my throat. "I'm here to end it with you."

"Don't you." She points at me. "Don't you dare throw away everything we've worked so hard to keep together." Her eyes fill with tears.

"Claud." I sigh softly. "We're no good together. We're both workaholics, we live on other sides of the world, and unless one of us loses our job, that's never going to change. I can't be anywhere but New York."

"What if I moved back?" she offers.

"And give up your dream job?" I sigh. "I wouldn't let you do that for me. I know how hard you've worked for this job."

She stares at me, and I take her in my arms. "You need to fall in love with someone who can support you in your role."

"I have," she whispers as she clings to me.

I close my eyes as I kiss her temple. "Two people who are wired the same way can't be in a forever relationship. We need to be with opposites, Claud." I squeeze her a bit tighter. "Two workaholics will never work. We're both too focused and too stressed out to properly look after one another."

She stares at me, and I know that deep down, she knows I'm right. Her eyes well with tears. "What happened to our five-year plan?" she whispers.

"It was good in theory, but come on. We both knew when we made the break that there was a big chance we wouldn't make it through to the other side."

"I'll move back," she pleads.

My eyes hold hers, and I know there's no easy way to say this. "It's too late. I have feelings for Emily. It's her that I want now."

Her face screws up in anger. "Emily, is it?" she sneers.

I clench my jaw as I watch her.

"Who is she? What does she do?"

"She's just a normal girl from the suburbs."

She rolls her eyes in disgust. "You . . . with a normal girl? Ha, what a joke. I suppose she cooks and cleans and fusses over you and sucks your dick on command, does she?"

I inhale to hold my anger deeply. "She's good for me."

"I'm good for you," she fires back.

"As a work colleague or employee, yes—as a mate . . . not so much."

Her eyes fill with tears anew.

"I'm not good for you." I shrug. "I'm so busy that I can't be there for you either. You deserve to be doted on, but I can't do that from New York, Claud; you know I can't. There is no way around this situation. Our lives are traveling on different paths. Two CEOs can't hold their careers and nurture a relationship from different sides of the world. It's an impossible task." I pause as I try to articulate what I'm saying. "Until I met her . . . I didn't realize what we were both missing out on. Both me and you."

Her eyes hold mine.

"I wish it were you telling me you'd met someone, so then I wouldn't be saying this. I love you, and you're the last person I want to hurt. I would much rather you hurt me."

She walks over and drops to the couch as she processes the information.

I stay silent as I watch her.

"So what now?" she asks.

"I'm going home to move her into my apartment."

Her face falls. "What?"

"And I will be announcing our relationship."

She drops her head in sadness. "What's the rush?"

"You know me—I'm all or nothing."

She screws up her face in tears. "Are you going to marry her?"

I stay silent.

"You asked me to marry you four weeks after we met. Are you . . ." Her voice trails off in hurt.

I clench my jaw to stop myself from saying something I'll regret. She drops her head, and I watch as she cries for a moment. I have to leave before she gets angry. "I'm going."

Her haunted eyes come to mine. "I love you," she whispers.

I smile sadly and take her in my arms. "I love you too." We hold each other for an extended time. "Be happy," I whisper into her hair.

"How could I possibly be happy without you, Jameson?" she whispers. "Don't go."

"I have to."

I pull out of her arms, and without another word I turn and walk out of Claudia's terrace house. I get into the back of my waiting car and stare solemnly out the window as it pulls away.

"Goodbye, Claudia," I whisper as the scenery zooms by. "Fly high, baby." I get a lump in my throat for all the good times we shared. "You deserve the best."

I sprint the last block. It's four in the morning, and I'm running in New York.

I love this city at night; it has a peace that daylight doesn't deliver.

Last night at the airport I had my fill of scotch and slept the entire flight home, and now I'm a ball of energy. My flight landed at two o'clock, too late to go to Emily's . . . not that it's stopped me from running here.

I pant as I approach her building, and I stare up at it and go to the intercom. My finger hovers over her button. My chest rises and falls as I hesitate.

It's four o'clock, and she has to work tomorrow.

Don't be selfish.

Fuck, I can't help it with her—I am selfish. I want her around the clock.

I walk out onto the street and stand at the gutter with my hands on my hips as I struggle for breath. Spits of rain begin to splatter, and I look up at the sky.

I love running in the rain. It starts to really come down, and I turn back and look up at Emily's building. I count the floors until I get to her windows.

I imagine her sleeping in her bed with her long dark hair splayed across her pillow, her beautiful curvy body curled up like she does, and eyes that could talk me into anything.

Tomorrow . . . well, today now.

I smile up at her window as the rain really comes down, and I turn and begin the long run home.

Tomorrow I start fresh with Emily Foster.

Emily

I walk through the security check with a spring in my step. Jameson got home last night. I get to see him today. I'm so excited that I even got up early and curled my hair, and I'm wearing my gray skirt in full swing.

A week has never felt so long. I take the elevator up to my floor and sit at my desk.

"Hey," Aaron says over his coffee cup.

"Hi there." I smile.

"What's that look?" He smirks.

"Jameson's home."

"How do you know?"

"Well, I hope he's home. He called me from the airport, and he was all boozy, so I'm hoping he made it onto the plane."

I look over to see Hayden at the photocopying machine area. He's talking to a group of girls. "How well do you know Hayden?" I ask.

"Hmm." He thinks for a moment. "Not that well. Molly knows him from her old job."

"Where was that?" I ask as I turn my computer on.

"They worked at the *Gazette* together."

My eyes flick to him. "Molly worked at the *Gazette*?"

"Yeah, for years. Miles Media headhunted her."

Shit. A sinister thought crosses my mind. *No, not Molly. Don't be stupid. It couldn't be. Don't even think that.*

Tristan and I tested the theory over the last week, and every time I gave Hayden a story before four o'clock, it was printed in the *Gazette* the next day. There's definitely a correlation somewhere. Whether it's Hayden or above him, we're trying to find out.

I really like Tristan; he's funny and intelligent and a lot softer around the edges than his brother.

"What happened with Paul last night?" I ask.

"He turned up." He looks at me sheepishly.

"Oh God," I mutter dryly. "Don't tell me you slept with him."

He hits the keys on his computer with force. "Yep. I can't resist that fucking asshole."

"Did you have it out with him yet?"

"No. I want to catch him in the act."

"So why are you still fucking him?" I snap. "For God's sake, Aaron, don't be used."

"For the record, I'm using him." He rolls his eyes as he sips his coffee.

"Nobody's dick is that good," I huff.

"Except his." He sighs sadly.

"Ugh." I wince. "Leave me alone with the asshole for five minutes with a carving knife. I'll get it for you to take away."

He laughs, and my phone rings. "Hello."

"Hi, Emily, this is Sammia."

"Oh, hi." Excitement runs through me.

"Mr. Miles would like to see you in his office right away, please."

A huge smile splits my face. "On my way." I hang up and stand.

"Where are you going?"

"Oh, more training," I lie.

"Jesus, you'll be more qualified than anyone on this floor soon."

"I know." I smile. "Back soon." I take the elevator up to the top floor, and the doors open. I can hardly keep a straight face.

He's here.

261

I want to run.

"Good morning, Emily." Sammia smiles. "Just go through."

"Morning. Okay, thanks." I walk through and down to Jameson's office, and I knock on the door.

"Come in," his deep velvety voice calls.

I open the door, and his eyes come to me with the best "come fuck me" look I've ever seen. My breath catches. Standing by the window in his navy suit and crisp white shirt, he is the ultimate male specimen. I forgot how gorgeous he is.

He gives me a slow, sexy smile. "Hello."

"Hi," I breathe. I have to stop myself from running to him.

The air crackles between us, and he walks to me and takes my face in his hands and kisses me, all suction and a little tongue. I feel my legs go weak at the knees.

"I've missed my girl," he murmurs against my lips.

I smile, and he wraps my ponytail around his hand three times and pulls my head back aggressively. His thick tongue goes to my collarbone and licks up to my neck. "Have you missed me?" he asks as his teeth nip my neck. I wince as arousal runs through my blood like a river rapid. Jesus, the CEO is back in all his glory.

"God, yes," I breathe.

He kisses me again, and the door opens. "Hey," Tristan's voice calls before he stops instantly.

"Not now, Tristan," Jameson says without letting my ponytail go. His dark eyes stay fixed on mine.

My heart races at the way he's looking at me. He's different . . . more intense.

"Sorry," Tristan says before the door closes.

He kisses me again, my head held back just as he wants me. "I want to make a go of this."

"Of what?" I breathe.

"Of us."

"I thought we were?" I frown.

"No. We were fucking before. Now I want you."

He bites my neck, and I whimper.

"I want all of you." His hand grabs my behind, and he pulls me against his waiting hard cock.

Oh jeez . . . welcome home.

I kiss his big lips. "Okay."

He holds my face in his hands and stares down at me as the air leaves my lungs. "Tonight. My place," he breathes.

I smile softly as my sex begins to throb in anticipation. "Yes."

"Do you want to go out for dinner?"

"No, I want to cook. Do you have groceries?"

His brow furrows. "I'll get Alan to pick something up."

"No." I frown. "I want to go to the grocery store."

His hands roam up and down my body as if he doesn't know where to start. "Take the limo."

I screw up my face. "I'm not going to the grocery store in a limo."

He grabs my hand and places it over the huge erection in his suit pants, and I grab it as his eyes flicker in arousal. "I need you," he breathes as he bites my bottom lip.

"Oh God, me too." I pull out of his grip as I pant. "I have to get back to work."

God . . . it would be so easy to stay here and fuck the boss instead.

"I'll have Alan deliver the car to you. You use it from now on."

"The car?" I frown. *He has a car?*

"Just use it as your own." His hands grind me onto his body. He's completely preoccupied with arousal.

"I only need it to do groceries just today. Don't bother Alan. I can get it from your apartment."

"Our apartment." He bites my neck as he really begins to eat me. Goose bumps scatter all over my body.

"Huh?"

"You'll be moving in with me."

"What?" I pull out of his arms as my arousal fog temporarily lifts. "What did you say?"

His dark eyes dance with delight. "If I'm doing this, I'm fucking doing this."

I stare at him. *What the hell?*

"I don't do things by half, Emily. If you're with me, you're with me."

"Jameson," I whisper. "Have you gone crazy?"

"I have meetings scheduled back to back all day, or I would be bending you over my desk right now." He turns me around and slaps me on the behind. "Now get back to work before I do it."

I pant as I stare at the door. A visual of me lying across his desk with my legs open swirls through my head. How am I supposed to string two thoughts together after he says that?

"Yes, sir." I begin to walk to the door.

"Oh, and Emily," he calls in his commanding voice.

I turn.

"I will be announcing today that we are in a relationship."

I frown as I stare at him. Confusion swirls around in my head. "Why?"

"Because I hate speculation." He pauses as his eyes hold mine. "And I want everyone to know that you're mine."

I stare at him. *Huh?*

His.

I have no words . . . rendered completely speechless. "Oh." I stare at him. "Okay?" I turn and walk toward the foyer. "Goodbye," I mutter, distracted.

Either Jameson Miles has gone completely crazy, or I am in a parallel universe.

Two hours later, I sit and stare at my computer. I was too freaked out to talk about this morning's *Twilight Zone* encounter in Jameson's office when I returned. It's taken me this long to get my head around what he said.

I've come to the conclusion that he's obviously jet lagged to holy hell and is suffering some kind of delusion. My phone dances across my desk, and my favorite letter appears.

J.

I smile as I answer. "Hello, Mr. Miles."

"How's my girl?" his sexy voice purrs down the line.

"Are you feeling all right?" I frown.

"I'm feeling great. Why?"

"You just seem very . . ." I pause as I think of the right word. "Odd."

He laughs his deep velvety laugh, and I feel it all the way to my bones. "I don't feel odd."

"You're acting odd."

"I'm just calling to tell you that we have a dinner tomorrow night."

"What dinner?"

"The Media Awards," he replies calmly.

"The Media Awards," I repeat.

"Yes, that's what I said."

I look around at my two work friends, who are completely oblivious to the crazy shit that's coming out of my running partner's mouth. "Where is it?"

"Here in New York. My entire family will be there. You'll get to meet everyone."

My eyes widen in horror. "Well, what's the dress code?"

"Black tie."

I feel the blood drain from my face. "I don't have any evening dresses here," I stammer. I don't have any at home either, but he doesn't need to know that.

"That's okay. I'll have some things delivered home tonight, and you can pick what you want to wear."

I scratch my head in confusion. "I'll just come to the next one," I say. "I'll wait at home in bed for you. The Media Awards aren't really my jam."

"Emily," he says calmly.

"Yes."

"You are coming with me."

"Jay," I whisper as I feel nerves rise in my throat.

"I'll see you tonight. I'll be a little late as I have a conference call. Alan is going to meet you out the side entrance at five with the keys to the car and the apartment."

"Okay." I puff air into my cheeks. "See you then."

I hang up and put my head into my hands.

"What?" Molly asks.

"Jameson has gone insane."

"Why?"

"He wants me to go to some awards dinner with his entire family tomorrow night."

Aaron's and Molly's eyes widen. "What?"

"And he gave me his car to use, but I don't even know where a grocery store is in New York."

"Oh, you would go to the one on Fifth."

"Well, how do I get there?" I frown.

"It's on my way. I can go with you if you want, and I'll get on the subway from there."

"Are you sure?"

"Yeah, I haven't got the kids this week anyway. It's not like I'm doing anything."

It's five in the afternoon, and we have just finished work. "Where did he say it would be?" Molly asks as she links her arm through mine as we exit the Miles Media building through the front doors.

"Around here to the side exit."

"What are you going to cook?" she asks.

"Hmm, rib eye with a mushroom sauce, honey carrots, and broccolini."

"Hmm, yum. Lucky bastard. Wish someone was coming over to cook that shit for me."

"True." We turn the corner and look up and both stop dead on the spot. "What the fuck?" I whisper.

Alan is standing next to what looks like a time machine, and my eyes widen in horror.

Black, low slung, and the sportiest looking car I've ever seen. The mag wheels alone probably cost more than an average car.

Alan smiles warmly. "Hello, Emily."

I look at the car and then at the people walking past as they stare at it. "Hi."

He passes me the key and then a card. "This is for the car, and this is your new key to the apartment."

I stare at them in my hand. "This is the car?" I whisper as the blood drains from my face.

He chuckles at my reaction.

Molly puts her hands over her mouth and begins to laugh nervously, reminding me that she's here. "This is Molly, my friend," I introduce her.

"Hello." She smiles.

"Mr. Miles asked me to make a time with you to move your things out of your apartment."

My eyes nearly pop from their sockets. "What?"

"Would Saturday morning suit you? I can arrange a packing service."

My eyes flick to Molly as she stares wide eyed at me. Okay, what the actual fuck is going on here? "I'll get back to you on that," I reply.

He smiles kindly. "Okay." He opens the car door. "So you know how to drive a manual, obviously."

"Can you just hold on a minute." I hold my finger up. "Just a minute."

I turn my back on them and dial Jameson's number.

"Hello," his sexy voice purrs.

"What the hell kind of car is this?" I whisper.

"A Bugatti."

"What's that?" I whisper as I turn back and look at it.

"A Bugatti Veyron. It's a limited edition."

"I can't drive this," I whisper angrily.

"Why not?"

"Well." I look around in a fluster. "I'm not a very good driver, Jameson. I'm going to crash this thing for sure."

He laughs, and it's deep and velvety and makes me smile.

"I assure you, Emily, anyone can drive this car. It practically drives itself. Relax. You'll be fine."

"When you said you had a car, I thought you meant you had a Toyota . . . like a normal person," I stammer. "What if I crash it?"

"As long as you're not injured, I don't care."

"Jameson," I whisper.

"Babe, I'm in a staff meeting right now with twenty people sitting here. Get what you need, and I'll meet you at home," he says calmly.

"Oh my God," I cry as I get an image of all his staff listening. "Goodbye." I hang up in a rush.

I come back to Alan and Molly, and they both wait for me to say something. "It seems Jameson has gone completely crazy," I whisper as I stare at the time machine.

Alan chuckles, and Molly stares at the car in disbelief.

"I thought it would be a Toyota." I wince.

Alan smiles and opens the driver's side door. "Mr. Miles doesn't do Toyota, Emily."

I get in, and Molly sits in the passenger seat.

"Where are you going?" Alan asks.

"Vegas." Molly laughs. "We're going to Vegas. How much is this car worth, Alan?"

"It came in at around two million dollars, I think."

"Holy fuck," Molly shrieks. "Get in, Alan; we really are going to fucking Vegas."

I put my head down on the steering wheel and burst out laughing. "This is unbelievable."

"You'll be fine." Alan laughs as he leans in and starts the car. It purrs like a kitten. "Blinker, brake, reverse." He points to all the dials and knobs. "Take it slow. It flies." He closes the door, and I put the blinker on.

I slowly take off into the traffic to the sound of Molly screaming and laughing in excitement, and as soon as I get out of sight of Alan, I burst out laughing too. "What the fuck is going on?" I cry.

Two hours later, I pull into the underground parking lot of Jameson's building. I know why he takes the damn limo—finding a parking spot in this city is insane. In the end, I made Molly sit in the car in the parking lot and wait for me while I grabbed what I needed, and then I drove her home. I was petrified someone was going to steal it. Alan is waiting, and he guides me into the garage, where I park.

"Thank you." I smile as I get the groceries out of the trunk. "This is a poser car," I stammer.

He smirks as he takes the bags from me, and we begin walking to the elevator.

"Did you lock the car, Emily?" he reminds me.

"Oh yeah." I turn and hold the remote up, and it blips as it locks. I giggle. "Oops."

We get into the elevator, and he stays silent and looking straight ahead.

"How long have you worked for Jameson?" I ask.

"Ten years."

"Oh." I frown. "That's a long time."

He smiles. "Yes, he's very good to me."

We get to the top, and Alan opens the door and walks in and puts the groceries on the counter. "Do you need anything?" he asks. "Mr. Miles is still in his meeting. He will be at least another half an hour."

My eyes hold his, and I want to ask him a million questions about the enigmatic Mr. Miles. "Do you speak to him often throughout the day?" I ask.

"No." He smiles at the suggestion. "I am in constant contact with his PA."

"Oh."

"His masseuse is expected here at seven." He glances at his watch. "Would you like me to wait for her?"

"Her?" I frown.

"Oh." He corrects himself. "It's a him now, isn't it?"

Something tells me that Alan knows a lot more about Mr. Miles than he makes out.

"No, I'm fine. I'll let him in." I fake a smile. "Thank you." I show him to the door.

"Call me if you need anything." He smiles.

"Okay, thanks."

I walk back to the kitchen and begin to put the groceries away, and the doorbell chimes. "Hello," I say as I push the intercom.

"Hello, I'm here for the massage."

"Come up."

I open the door and wait for him to arrive. "Hello." He smiles. "Same room as last time?"

"Yes, please."

He takes off down the hallway to set up.

The door clicks open, and Jameson comes into view. Every time I see him in a suit, I am reminded of exactly who he is. Power personified.

"Hello." He smiles as he takes me into his arms.

"Hi." His lips dust mine, and I melt into his touch. "Your car is ridiculous." I smile.

He chuckles as he takes my jaw in his hand; then he kisses me deeper, and my hands go around his broad neck.

The intercom sounds again.

"For God's sake, this place is like an airport," I whisper, annoyed that my kiss is being interrupted.

"Oh, that's the stylists with your dresses," he says.

"Your masseuse is set up in the end room."

He kisses me again. "Let them in, and choose what you want."

"Jay," I whisper as my eyes search his. This change in him is confusing me.

"Get a few." He grabs my behind. "I'm going to take a quick shower." He disappears up the hall, and I open the front door.

My face falls when I see the two gorgeous women pushing a huge garment rack of gorgeous dresses. "Hello." One is tall with long dark hair, and the other is blonde and beautiful. Both have that trendy, confident vibe.

"Hello, Mr. Miles ordered some dresses," the blonde says. "I'm Celeste, and this is Saba."

"Yes, please come in," I whisper, embarrassed. "I'm Emily." We shake hands.

God, don't tell me they are going to watch me try this shit on? How mortifying. "Just in here." I show them to the living area, and they start to unpack shoes and accessories as I watch awkwardly. This seems all very over the top.

"Back in a moment." I smile.

I turn and take off up to the bedroom, and I burst into the bathroom to find Jay washing under the shower. "What the hell is going on?" I whisper in a panic.

"What?" He frowns, totally oblivious.

"Two *Penthouse* Pets are out there with a load of dresses that are way too exotic for me, and I'm driving around in a fucking space machine, and you're saying I'm moving in, and I'm freaking the fucking hell out, Jameson," I blurt out in a rush.

He smirks as he turns the taps off. "Just go out there, and pick what you like, Emily. Don't overthink this."

"Don't overthink this," I whisper. "It's overthunk already."

"*Overthunk* isn't a word," he says casually as he dries himself.

"Oh my God," I stammer in a fluster at his lack of care, and I storm back out to the stylists. "Sorry," I say as I stand next to the rack of clothes. I twist my fingers nervously in front of me.

"Tell me about your style." The blonde smiles. "What makes you pop?"

I stare at her. Oh jeez. What the fuck is this bullshit? "Umm." I look at the dresses on the rack.

"What makes you come alive and feel sexy?" the brunette gushes. "When are you living your best life?"

Oh, Jesus . . . not this. "I'll just"—I gesture to the rack of clothes—"see what I like."

I begin to flick through the dresses. Wow . . . they're all beautiful.

"Anything you like, sweetheart?" I hear Jameson's deep voice purr from behind me.

I turn to see him with a white towel around his waist. His hair is wet, and his tanned muscles are bulging. He looks fucking edible.

The two bimbos' eyes bulge from their sockets. "Hello, Mr. Miles," they both stammer as their eyes drop down his body.

"Hello." He smiles sexily.

I look at him deadpan. Is he for real? "I'm not sure. I like everything," I snap as I turn back to the rack.

In a fucking towel . . . what next?

Ugh.

He comes behind me and puts one hand on my hip as he goes through the rack. "We'll take this one, this one . . . this one." He scans the rest of the rack. "And all of these from here on."

"Yes, sir," they both gush.

His eyes go over the shoes and lingerie they have laid out on the coffee table.

"We'll take all of the lingerie and whatever shoes Emily chooses." His eyes come to me, and he smiles and leans in and kisses me. "Done."

The two women hold their breath as they watch.

His hand drops to my behind, and he gives me a firm squeeze. "Nice to meet you, girls," he says before he saunters up the hall for his massage.

I turn back to the girls as they watch him disappear in awe.

Good grief.

I think I just met the real Jameson Miles . . . in all his glory.

Chapter 17

I stir the mushroom sauce with my mind in overdrive.

Jameson's different . . . I'm talking *Twilight Zone* different. I'm not sure if it's a good thing or the beginning of the end for us. Just when I get used to his old weirdness, he ups the ante.

The masseuse has just left, and he's in the shower again as he washes the oil off. I'm not going in there because we will end up having sex, and dinner is nearly ready . . . and I want to talk to him without my arousal high clouding my brain cells.

It happens a lot with him.

He walks back out in his towel, and his eyes find me across the room. He gives me a slow, sexy smile.

"Can you not walk around in a towel when we have visitors, please?" I snap.

He smirks.

"Those two ditzy shoppers are at home going to town on their vibrators at this very moment as they picture you in that white towel." I roll my eyes. "Living their"—I hold my fingers up to accentuate my point—"best life."

He chuckles as he takes me in his arms. "Jealous?"

"Yes, I am, actually. I don't like other women looking at you. It makes me stabby," I snap as I stir the sauce. "Cut it out with the sexy smiling around other women too."

His lips come to my neck as he holds me from behind, and I can feel his erection up against my behind. "Let's go to bed."

"No, you're eating first." I point to the kitchen counter. "Sit."

His eyes dance in delight, and he does as he's told. I place his dinner in front of him. "Hmm, looks good." He smiles.

I sit beside him and watch him for a moment as he eats. "Why did you ask Alan to move my stuff in here?"

He chews his steak. "Because I want you to move in."

"Since when? We haven't discussed this at all."

"Yes, we have." He swallows his food. "We talked about it this morning."

"When?" I frown.

"When I told you that I wanted to do this, and you said me too."

I stare at him, my mind a clusterfuck of confusion. "Jameson, *doing this* is in my mind holding hands in public and dating. Maybe meeting each other's families."

He frowns as he watches me.

"What's with the sudden change? Last week you got angry with me for falling in love with you. I couldn't even look at you after sex without you getting upset with me."

He sips his wine, obviously annoyed. "You said you didn't love me. Are you saying that now you do?"

"That's not the point. You know what I mean."

"I want us to make a go of it." He shrugs. "So today I moved forward with my plans."

"Plans?" I frown. "I'm not a business transaction, Jameson. You don't move forward with your plans without talking to me first. They aren't just your plans, you know."

He clenches his jaw, unimpressed, as his eyes hold mine.

"There are two people in this relationship, Jay, and me loving you does not mean you get to take me over."

"I know that," he snaps. "So you do love me now? Make up your mind, woman."

"Stop changing the subject. Do you understand what I'm saying to you?"

"Yes, Emily." He sighs as if he's getting lectured by the school principal.

"I just don't know why you've had this sudden change of heart." I shrug. "It's peculiar."

"My heart hasn't changed at all. My situation has."

"What does that mean?" I frown.

He exhales heavily. "I went and saw Claudia in London."

Oh no, his ex. I'm not supposed to know that. I had better play dumb. "Who's Claudia?"

"My ex."

I frown as I try my hardest to hold my tongue. *Act calm, act calm.*

"I broke it off with her."

My eyes widen in horror. "What the hell?" I snap. "You were still with her?"

"No, but we had promised each other that we wouldn't date anyone else seriously."

I begin to break into a cold sweat as I try to hold it together. "Why?"

"Because we planned on getting back together in a few years."

I knew it; I knew it back then that something was off. Damn it, why didn't I see the writing on the wall? I pick up my wineglass and drain it as I stare at him. Jeez, this is news. *Bad news.*

"I told her I have strong feelings for you."

"You did?" I frown as a tiny piece of hope blooms in my chest.

He smiles and tucks a piece of hair behind my ear. "I did."

"What else did you say?" I ask calmly. I want to blurt out a million questions about the two of them.

"That it was over between us."

"Did you love her?"

"Yes." He pauses for a moment as if contemplating that statement. "In my own way, I did. In hindsight, I realize that our relationship was never normal. Not like ours is anyway."

I stare at him, lost for words. Grateful that he's finally being honest and yet terrified that their union was so strong that it withstood an open relationship. There's no way in hell I could ever do that. "You think our relationship is normal?" I ask.

He smiles and leans in and kisses me softly. "Don't you?"

"No. To me our relationship is exciting and wonderful and exotic." I stare at him. "Normal gets boring very quick, Jameson."

"I told her that I want to build a future with you."

Okay, that sounds a bit better. I smirk as I try to hold in a smile.

"I also told her that I've had feelings for you since the day we met and that you are the only woman I want to be with from here on in."

A broad, goofy smile does break through this time. "Did you tell her I had motorized sneakers?" I whisper.

He chuckles, and his eyes twinkle with something special as he cups my face in his hand. "I did."

"What does this mean, Jay?" My eyes search his. "For us."

"It means that I'm all yours." He shrugs. "If you want me."

What? *All mine?*

I blink . . . in shock. "Have you been holding yourself back from me all this time?"

"I have, and I can't do it any longer."

"What does this mean . . . for us?"

"It means I want you to move in, and we go full steam ahead from here."

"What's the rush?" I frown. "Can't we ease into it?"

He leans in and kisses me softly; his big blue eyes hold mine. "I don't do things in halves, Emily."

"Meaning?" I whisper.

"Meaning that my woman is my world."

I stare at him as the air leaves my lungs.

"I work hard . . . but I love harder."

My heartbeat sounds through my ears. Is this really happening?

"I'm in love with you, Emily Foster." He leans in and kisses me slowly. His tongue swipes through my open lips with such emotion that I get a lump in my throat. "I can't help it. I tried to stop it, and I couldn't. I think I've loved you since our first night together in Boston. You stayed with me. I fought it, and still, I couldn't forget you. I've been carrying your scarf around like a lovesick fool for more than a year."

I stare at him.

"So please forgive me if I want to go full steam ahead. This is not a snap decision. It's been coming for a long time, and now that I'm in a position to act on it, I don't want to waste any more time. I want you with me. By my side."

I stare at him while my brain catches up. *What the . . . ?*
Holy shit.

He picks up his knife and fork. "Now I'm going to eat this beautiful dinner that you've made for me, and then I'm going to take you to bed and make you forget everything that I said to you about not falling for me, and then, hopefully, you can show me that you have some kind of resemblance of feelings for me too."

I smile as my heart swells.

"Okay?" he asks before he takes a mouthful of food.

"Okay." I sip my wine with a shaky hand. I look down at my dinner and smirk.

Mushroom sauce . . . my new love potion.

Abracadabra.

Jameson Miles just blew my fucking mind.

I roll over and put my hand out, and I frown. Jameson isn't in bed beside me. I glance over at the clock: 3:33 a.m. Where is he?

I get out of bed and walk down the hall in search of my man. The kitchen light is on.

Hmm, but no Jay.

I walk down to the other end of the apartment and see the light coming from his office, and I tiptoe up the hall.

Jameson is sitting at his desk; his thumbnail rubs back and forth over his bottom lip as he stares at the computer screen as it lights up the room.

I stand silently at the door as I watch him. He's frowning, deep in concentration.

What's waking him up in the middle of the night? What's he worried about?

For five minutes, I watch him in silence. I can feel the worry oozing out of him. Finally, I can take it no more. "Hey," I whisper.

He glances up, startled. "Hello, sweetheart." He smiles softly.

I walk over and look over his shoulder at the screen. It displays a graph with a red line that gradually declines.

Stock Value: Miles Media.

Shit.

I climb onto his lap and kiss his lips softly. "You can't sleep?"

He runs his hand down my naked back. "I'm fine."

279

But he's not fine—his company's value is plummeting. How many millions did his family lose today? "Any news?" I whisper as I stare at the graph in front of me.

"On?"

"The case?"

He shakes his head. His jaw ticks in anger as his eyes go back to the graph.

He's like a raging ball of anxiety; I can almost feel his pain. I need to make him forget this for the moment. I kiss his neck, and he smiles as I softly nip down to his collarbone.

I drop to the floor between his legs, and he looks down at me as he runs his hand through my hair. Emotion runs between us, electricity I can't explain.

"I missed you when you were away," I whisper as I slowly slide his boxers off.

He smiles softly as I kiss his dick. It flexes in approval. "I missed my man," I whisper as I take him in my mouth. "My body missed you." I need to make him forget where he is, who he is. This stress has to leave. Now I want to be that spontaneous woman he met twelve months ago, the one who blew his mind.

He inhales sharply and spreads his legs, granting me access.

Our eyes are locked as I suck on the most private part of his body, the one that nobody gets to see. He's thick and hard, and I can see every vein on his engorged length. I lick up his length and then flick my tongue over his end, and I can almost hear the arousal as it runs through his body like a river rapid.

"Fuck my mouth," I whisper as I watch him.

His eyes darken.

"Take my hair in your hands, and fuck my mouth," I murmur around him.

His eyes dance with fire, and he grabs my hair in both hands and surges forward.

I'm blessed with a burst of preejaculate, and I close my eyes and moan.

He begins to slide his cock deep down my throat, and I hum around him. What must I look like, on my hands and knees, naked, under my boyfriend's desk? My own arousal takes shape, and I spread my legs, and he moans as he begins to really pump. I take him in my hand, and my fist follows my mouth as I begin to work him hard.

He needs it hard.

I can see every muscle contract in his stomach as he clenches, and I push his legs open farther and take his balls in my hand.

"Fuck," he moans.

"Come," I whisper. "Blow. I want to drink you down."

His eyes roll back in his head, and he really lets me have it.

I smile around him. I love it when I bring him undone like this. It's like I hover up in the air and watch with a special detachment.

An audience of one—the best porn on the planet.

His stomach contracts, and I smile as he shoots down my throat. I concentrate on not gagging. It's hard with a cock this big, but when he opens his eyes, they're blazing . . . and all my fears are laid to rest.

This is what I love. I love loving Jameson with the unbridled passion that he brings out in me. I've never been this woman before, but with him . . . it's natural. As if he was the missing link in my sexuality. We've already had sex once earlier tonight, and that time was intimate and loving. Nothing like this, but just as important.

I keep working him, emptying his beautiful body until he drags me up to him and spreads me over his lap.

His lips take mine, and he moans as he tastes himself in my mouth.

I pull back to look at him, the air between us electric, and our eyes lock.

"I love you," I whisper.

He smiles, and then his lips crash to mine. Our kiss is desperate, and he stands and carries me down the hall back to bed as I cling to him.

Our attachment is deep.

So deep.

For the first time in my life, I feel like I'm home.

I sit and watch Hayden walk across the street toward the café we are in. He's carrying a briefcase. Why would he need his briefcase on his lunch break? This guy is suspicious as all hell.

"How long have you known Hayden, Moll?" I ask her.

Aaron sips his drink through his straw as he listens and watches Hayden.

The three of us are at our favorite lunch spot and sitting at the bench by the window.

She gives me a lopsided twist of her lips. "About eight years, I think."

"Aaron said that you used to work with him at your old job."

"Yeah." She chews her toasted sandwich as she watches him. "He worked at the *Gazette* with me."

My attention goes back to watching him. "You know, I think he's up to something."

"Wouldn't surprise me." She wipes her mouth with her napkin.

"Why do you say that?" I ask.

"He was fired from the *Gazette*."

"What for?" Aaron frowns.

"I don't know for certain, but the word on the street was that he was involved in a phone-tap scandal."

"What?"

"Apparently." She rolls her eyes. "And this is complete speculation, but he was caught tapping one of his coworkers' phones and stealing her leads."

My eyes widen. "Really? Who?"

"A girl named Keeley May."

"Oh yes, the redhead," remarks Aaron. "She's fucking hot."

Molly's and my eyes go to him. "Since when do you think girls are hot?" Molly asks.

"I'm gay, not blind. I can appreciate a fine female form," he huffs.

We both roll our eyes.

"Why do you think he's up to something?" Molly asks.

God, can I tell them? No . . . I have to run it past Tristan first. I can't break their trust in me. "I told him one of my stories the other day, and I saw that he submitted it as his own," I lie.

Molly narrows her eyes. "Fucking snake."

"I have no proof, of course," I add. "I was just wondering about his character, that's all."

"From what I know of him," she says dryly, "I wouldn't trust him as far as I could throw him."

"Like Paul," Aaron sneers.

"Oh God, what happened now?" I ask.

"Nothing." He sighs. "He's just an asshole, that's all."

Molly rolls her eyes in disgust. "You know what, Aaron, stop playing the fucking victim here. You know he's sleeping around, and you're still sleeping with him. It's one thing to be deceived, but to willingly go back for more when you know exactly what is going on is just plain pathetic."

He rolls his eyes. "You don't have to be such a bitch about it."

"Yeah, I do. You're acting like a damsel in distress. You don't have kids with him. You don't have a mortgage. You don't work with him. The break would be easy. Tell him to fuck off and move on," she scoffs. "Breakups are hard. Staying with an asshole is harder."

"Speaking of moving on—Jameson asked me to move in with him," I say to change the subject.

Aaron snorts his drink, and it goes up his nose. "What the hell?"

"Apparently." I shrug.

Aaron frowns. "What's with the turnabout?"

"He went and saw Claudia, his ex, while he was in London."

"Did he fuck her?" Aaron asks as he chews his straw.

"No, Aaron, fucking other people isn't normal behavior," Molly snaps. "Get that through your thick head. Your view on reality is seriously distorted."

"Fuck, you're a real bitch today, you know that?" Aaron snaps.

"Well, that communal dick of your boyfriend's is pissing me off," she scoffs.

Aaron and I roll our eyes. Molly is especially testy today.

"He said that he and Claudia had planned on getting back together, but he told her he wanted a future with me. He ended it."

"Holy shit," Aaron whispers.

"He told me he loves me."

"What the fuck?" Molly cries. "Are you serious?"

"But . . ." I shrug.

"But what?" Aaron whispers. "There should be no *buts* anywhere in this story."

"It's all so fast. What's the rush, you know?" I shrug. "I'm scared he's just stressed."

They both continue to listen.

"He told me that he's had feelings since we first met, and it's been coming for a long time."

"That could be true." Molly frowns.

"It could be." I sip my coffee. "It could also be in his takeover strategy."

"What takeover strategy?" Molly frowns.

"Jameson Miles gets what he wants," I reply. "If he's decided he wants me—"

"Which he has," Aaron interrupts.

"He will make it happen. I don't know." I shrug. "It just all seems too good to be true, and the whole Claudia situation has freaked me out a little. Can I really believe that Claudia and he will just break off all communication now?"

Molly rolls her eyes. "Here we go. Have you two idiots been sniffing ink cartridges today?" She screws up her napkin with force. "Stop being a fucking negative bitch. If he didn't tell you he loved you, that would have been a problem. Now that he has, he has an ulterior motive." She throws her hands up in disgust. "Will you two come back to Earth?" She gets up. "We have to get back." She storms out, and Aaron and I watch her cross the street.

"She needs a good deep dicking," Aaron mutters. "She's in full bitch mode."

I giggle as I watch her walk into the building. "You could be right."

I stare at my reflection in the mirror and exhale heavily. I turn and check my behind. I'm wearing a gold Chanel dress that Jameson picked off the rack yesterday. My long dark hair is set into large curls and pinned behind one ear, and my makeup is glamorous with glossy red lips.

I'm nervous as all hell. This is the first time I've ever been anywhere formal with him as his date . . . and of course, his whole family is going to be there to witness it.

Could be a complete disaster.

Just don't spill anything on your dress or drink too much champagne and be embarrassing, I remind myself.

God, I couldn't cope.

The worst thing is, because I'm so nervous, I want to power drink.

"Are you nearly ready, my fuck bunny?" Jameson calls. He appears around the door and gives me a slow, sexy smile as his eyes drop down the length of my body. "Jesus, you look beautiful."

I brush my hands nervously over my thighs. "Is this okay?"

"Perfect." He takes me in his arms and kisses my cheek. "I don't like those red lips, though."

"Oh." My face falls.

"I can't kiss you without wearing the evidence."

I smile as he holds me. Something has changed between us again today.

Another day, another dynamic.

I feel so close to him. Something about all that honesty yesterday tore down my defenses against him. Molly is completely right, and I am looking for the negative in this, but I can't help it; I fear my heart may be in dire danger.

If he leaves me . . . how would I cope?

I've been hurt before, and although I know that Jameson is in a completely different league than my past relationships, the prospect is terrifying.

This one will hurt . . . deeply.

He's wearing a black tuxedo and a bow tie; his eyes are a brilliant blue, and his dark hair frames his beautiful face.

I've never had a man terrify me the way that Jameson Miles does. He's everything I never knew I needed.

He takes my hand in his. "Do you have everything?"

"Uh-huh." I put my hand over my heart to try to will it to slow down.

"What's wrong?" he says softly.

"I'm nervous."

He smiles sexily. "You'll be fine."

"Don't let me drink too much, okay?"

"Okay." He smirks as we walk to the door.

"And if you see me drinking too much, take my glass from me."

He frowns.

"Honestly, Jay, I go from a level four to a ten in two mouthfuls."

He smirks and then, thinking on that statement further, throws his head back and laughs out loud. "Not a truer word has ever been spoken."

I drop my mouth open in fake horror. "I'm not talking about head, Jameson."

"I am." He kisses my hand. "And for the record, you went from a ten to a twenty."

I smirk, and he bends and kisses my neck and then my shoulder and then my breast through my dress.

"The sooner we go, the sooner we can leave." He runs his hand down my behind and gives me a sharp slap.

Half an hour later, the limo pulls into the parking bay, and I look around at all the beautiful people in black tie. As my nerves begin to kick me hard, Jameson picks up my hand and kisses the back of it, oblivious to my inner turmoil.

What will I say to his mother? His father? Oh hell . . . why did I come?

Alan opens the door, and Jameson climbs out and then takes my hand and helps me. His hand tenderly goes to my lower back. "Thank you," he says to Alan.

"Thank you." I smile.

Jameson takes my hand, and we walk up toward the large front doors. A few people do a double take as they see us, and people are staring. I hold my breath as he leads me through the crowd. "Hello, Jameson," someone says.

He nods politely but doesn't stop to chat. We walk in through the double doors, and he leads me straight to a table up at the front. It's round with a white linen tablecloth and silver cutlery all lined up, and beautiful white flowers and candles sit in the center.

Crap, what's the eating order of the cutlery? I need to go to the bathroom and google this shit. Jameson's father is sitting at the table along with an older woman. She has dark hair that sits in a perfect bob. She's very attractive and wearing a glamorous black evening dress with long sleeves.

"Mom, Dad, this is Emily." He presents me proudly. "These are my parents, Elizabeth and George."

"Hello, dear." His mother stands and kisses both my cheeks and holds me at arm's length as she inspects me. "Well, aren't you something special." She smiles warmly.

Oh, she's nice. I smile awkwardly, and his father pulls me from his mother and kisses my cheek. "Hello, Emily. I didn't get a chance to talk with you properly the other day. Lovely to meet you."

"Yes, you too," I whisper.

Jameson pulls out my chair, and I sit down as my heart races in my chest. I can feel my face flushing, and I silently die a little. *Don't go red now, stupid.* I get an image of a beetroot face sitting next to Mr. Gorgeous here. Jameson pours me a glass of champagne and passes it over.

"Thank you," I whisper as I take it from him. My eyes hold his in a silent "help me" signal.

He gives me a sexy wink and slings his arm around the back of my chair. "Where's Tris?" he asks casually as he looks around the room.

"On his way," his father replies.

I look around at all the people filling the ballroom. The who's who are here—not that I remember any of their names. I'm only going on what Molly and Aaron prepped me with today. Two of the managers I've seen upstairs on the top floor arrive with their dates. "Hello." They all shake hands, and then the men frown when they see me.

"Have you met Emily, my girlfriend?" Jameson asks them.

"Oh yes." They smile in an over-the-top way. "Hello, Emily," the four of them splutter before shaking my hand and sitting down at our table.

Jameson sits next to me, and his father is on the other side of him, then his mother, then the other four. Two seats are to my left—must be for Tristan.

"Hello," Tristan says happily from behind me. I turn and see that the blonde woman is with him.

"Hello," everyone calls.

"Emily, this is Melina," Tristan introduces me.

"Hello." I shake her hand.

"Hello." She smiles as she takes a seat beside me and looks around the table. "I just couldn't decide what to wear tonight. How is everyone?"

The table instantly falls into chatter.

She's confident and beautiful, and she looks like a high-fashion model rather than a . . . what does she do again?

I glance over to see Jameson and his father subtly roll their eyes at each other. *Hmm, what's that about?*

Tristan begins to talk to a man at the table next to us and laughs out loud. He really is very friendly.

Melina takes out her phone and pulls a duck mouth and takes a selfie. She leans toward me. "Get in," she says. "I'll tag you."

I pull out of her grip and lean away. "No thank you." I smile. "I don't do social media."

"What?" she gasps as she looks me up and down in disgust. "Why on earth not? What's wrong with you?"

Okay . . . this woman's a rude pig.

"I don't like social media, that's all." I shrug.

"What's not to like?" She keeps taking her own photo.

I stare at her deadpan. "A misrepresentation of society with unrealistic images that portray a fake lifestyle with impossible ideals," I reply as I sip my wine. *Don't piss me off, bitch.*

Jameson smirks as he stares straight ahead. His finger circles on my bare shoulder.

"Oh God." She rolls her eyes and takes another selfie.

I glance over, and Jameson's mother smirks and winks at me.

I can hear my heartbeat in my ears. *God, cut out the snarky bitch act, Emily,* I remind myself. Just be nice *for once.*

Jameson and his father fall into conversation, and I sit quietly. The waiter comes over and goes to refill my glass. "No thank you." I smile.

Melina talks to the other people at the table; she's laughing loudly and loves attention. She's not at all the type of woman I thought Tristan would go for.

"Emily, you must come and visit us in the Hamptons," Jameson's mother says.

"Thank you." I smile. "That would be lovely." I should try to make conversation. "Do you go on weekends?" I ask.

"We live there mostly now," she says. "We still have our apartments here, of course, but the change of pace is lovely."

"Oh." I smile. How many apartments do they have here? Jeez, they really are from a different world. "Sounds great."

"Jameson said you are from California?" she asks.

"Yes." I fake a smile. He told them about me? "I've only been here a month."

"And what do you think of New York?"

"I love it." I smile. "It's amazing."

Jameson's hand sits on my shoulder for moral support while he talks to his father.

"Jameson told us that you met each other more than twelve months ago," Elizabeth continues.

"Yes." I fake a smile. *Oh dear God.* What did he tell them about how we met? Please don't let it be the truth, that we sat next to each other on a boozy flight and flirted like sex-starved fools and then had wild layover sex for twelve hours while I tried to suck every last drop of blood from his neck. I pick up my wine and tip my head back and kick Jameson's foot.

Help me, fucker.

He smiles as if he already knows what's going on in my head.

Tristan finally takes a seat, and Melina leans over and kisses him. "Let's go mingle."

He frowns as he takes his first sip of scotch. "No, babe. I'm staying here. Knock yourself out."

Melina waves at a woman on the other side of the room and stands. "Back in a moment." She smiles to the table as she practically runs to the woman and air kisses her two cheeks. "Darling," she cries, and they fake gush over each other.

My eyes find Jameson's, and he rolls his lips in amusement. It's as if he can read my mind.

She's a twit.

Jameson's jaw tilts skyward, and his tongue runs across his teeth as if he's angered. I follow his line of sight and see a group of men and women arriving at a table across from us. My eyes flick to his father and mother as they look on as well.

"Who are they?" I whisper.

"The Ferrara family."

I frown in question.

"They own the *Gazette* and Ferrara Media."

My eyes widen. "Oh." I go back to watching them as they all sit around the table. Three sons and a mother and father, Italian by the looks of it. Gorgeous-looking people . . . all dark hair and brown eyes. Only one son has a date; the other two are alone. The eldest son looks over and smiles when he sees us. He waves and dips his head. Jameson dips his head back in a polite but cold gesture.

"Who's that?" I whisper.

"Gabriel Ferrara," Jameson replies as he sips his drink. Contempt drips from his every pore. "The CEO."

My eyes widen. I can tell that there is no love lost between the two families.

CEO versus CEO.

"Emily?" a woman's voice gasps from behind us.

We all turn to see a woman. I know her. "Athena." I laugh as I stand. Athena is in her sixties and a woman of the world. I adore her.

"Oh my God," she gasps as she pulls me into an embrace. "Jameson Miles, how on earth do you know Emily Foster?"

He chuckles.

"Emily has been my intern every college holiday for three years." Athena laughs.

George looks on as if impressed.

"She wouldn't move here for my company." She smiles as she rubs my arm.

"What do you mean?" George asks.

"Best damn reporter I ever had," Athena replies. "I've offered her a job every year, but she always turned me down, stating that Miles Media would be the only reason she would move to New York."

I smile awkwardly. *Please shut up. I'm trying to play it cool here.*

"Is that so?" George smiles over at me. "Well, she's found her place at Miles Media."

Athena looks down at Jameson's hand as it rests on my lap. "I can see that." She smiles down at me. "Emily, come, I have someone I want you to meet." She glances at Jameson. "Can I steal her for a moment, please?"

"Of course." He kisses my hand before he lets me go. His eyes linger on my face, and I smile softly.

This man is just so . . .

Athena pulls me over to the other side of the room. "Oh my God," she splutters as we weave between the tables. "You're dating Jameson Miles."

"Yes." I laugh.

"He's the most delicious man on the planet." She turns back and smiles at me. "And the crankiest." I giggle as she drags me to the bar to a group of women and men who are all standing around. "Lauren, look who's here! Emily Foster."

"Oh my God." Lauren laughs as she hugs me. Lauren and I were interns together in our second year. Lauren went on to work with them. "What are you doing here?" She smiles excitedly.

"I've moved to New York now. I work for Miles Media."

"Really?"

I laugh. "Yes."

"Oh my God, we have to catch up."

"Yes." It would be so nice to have a friend here that I don't work with. "Make sure we get each other's numbers."

I glance around, and everyone has a drink. "I'm just going to get another champagne."

Someone grabs my elbow from behind, and I turn. I'm taken aback. It's the tall Italian man, the CEO of the *Gazette*.

"Hello." He smiles sexily down at me.

"Hi."

"Who are you?" he asks.

I frown, and my eyes flick back to my table. Jameson is talking to Tristan. "Emily," I reply nervously.

He picks up my hand and kisses the back of it. "My name is Gabriel Ferrara."

"Oh."

"And I like to take over all things owned by Jameson Miles."

My eyes widen.

His dark eyes drop to my lips. "Women included."

Chapter 18

"Excuse me?" I frown as I snatch my hand from his grip. "What did you say?"

He smiles sexily. "I was merely stating that you are gorgeous. Don't be alarmed."

"Well, don't," I snap.

He smiles as he sips his drink, clearly amused by my response. "Who are you?"

"Someone whose intelligence is insulted by your audacity. Goodbye, Mr. Ferrara. Go away." I turn my back to him and take my place at the bar.

His lips come to my ear from behind. "Lovely to meet you, Emily. We will meet again. I'll make sure of it." His breath prickles my neck, and traitorous goose bumps scatter up my arms.

"Don't bother," I sneer, annoyed by my physical reaction to him.

My heart is hammering. No wonder poor Jameson is stressed to the max. He's dealing with complete and utter snakes here.

Good grief, I'm completely rattled.

I get my drink and go back to talking to Lauren, although my mind is anywhere but on our conversation.

That fucking asshole Gabriel is sabotaging Jameson's company and is openly making a play for his women.

Woman.

I feel outraged on his behalf, and I want to march over and tell Jameson what just happened, but then I don't want to stress him out. But maybe that's exactly what Gabriel wants—an open war.

Shit . . . this is hectic.

From my place by the bar, I watch as person after person goes and strategically says hello to the Miles family at their table, as if wanting to be acknowledged by them. Tristan is all smiles and happy, and Jameson and his father are polite. It's blatantly obvious to me that they are not at all seduced or fooled by the fake greetings and well wishes.

After the longest conversation in history, I make my way back to Jameson. I sit beside him, and he takes my hand in his and puts it on his thigh.

"Do you like these people here?" I whisper.

His eyes hold mine. "I like the people at this table."

I look around nervously.

"What's wrong?" he asks, sensing that something is off.

"Nothing," I whisper as I lean in and kiss him softly on the lips. "I don't particularly like any of these people."

"Me neither, and as long as you like me, that's all that matters," he murmurs.

I smile over at my beautiful man and lean up to whisper in his ear, "I more than like you."

He squeezes my hand in his. "Two hours, and we can go," he whispers.

"Good."

Dinner has been served, we are on to dessert, and the award ceremony is about to take place.

The lights are dimmed, and the stage is lit up by a spotlight as they go through the categories. They must start with the smaller awards first.

Jameson sits and stares at the stage as he holds my hand on his large muscular thigh. He's completely expressionless, and I have no idea what he's thinking.

He does it so well, keeps his emotions completely under control. Tristan is laughing and talking about the categories with the other managers sitting at the table. He's completely relaxed and having a good night.

How are two brothers so different?

Tristan is open and jovial, and Jameson is closed and hard . . . at least to the outside world.

Although, knowing what Tristan's role is in the company—acquisitions—he has to be hard on some level. Perhaps even harder than the rest of them because he takes over companies and dissolves them. I think on it for a moment as I stare at Jameson. No, that's impossible—nobody could be harder than Jameson. My eyes flick to his father, who wears the same steely face as he watches the stage . . . perhaps George is.

I think back to Jameson's childhood and how he went to boarding school overseas with his brothers. How do you learn to be soft and nurturing when you're in a cold school environment? I wonder if that is why he's all or nothing with me.

Does he have to give himself permission to feel before he can physically do it?

It would make sense. I mean, since he told me he wants me, we've moved forward in leaps and bounds. Every touch I feel him let me in a little more. Is it because he can finally verbalize things now?

I exhale heavily as I clap for an award. My mind is far from here. I'm fixed on the complex man I've fallen for, as I try to unravel his inner demons.

Maybe Jay needs to talk about the company. Maybe he needs someone he doesn't have to pretend with that he has everything under control.

He's the CEO of Miles Media. The family is looking to him for guidance. Waiting for him to rectify the situation.

Of course he's stressed.

The reporter in me wants to deal with this situation, find the leak, and fight our way back to the top.

The lover in me wants to steal my Jay away and take him to an island in the Bahamas and let him live a peaceful, relaxed lifestyle . . . where the only thing he has to worry about is pushing his children on a swing.

His children.

I feel my chest constrict as I get a peep into the future with Jameson.

Will his children bear this stress? Will they be able to feel their father's worry through his touch?

They'd have to—I know I do.

God, I need to wind him down so that he can deal with all of this crap. How do I do that? I think for a moment and clap on cue as another award is announced.

He needs to get out of New York. Yes, that's it. A weekend away. Somewhere crazy different. I smile as the idea takes shape in my mind.

"And now for the major award for the night," the MC announces. "The Diamond Award for exceptional media coverage goes to . . ."

The drum rolls.

He opens the envelope and smiles with a shake of his head. "Well, well . . . it seems we have a changing of the guard."

The crowd falls silent.

"Ferrara Media."

The crowd applauds, and the Ferrara table erupts into cheers. Jameson clenches his jaw and sips his drink.

"Fuck," Tristan mutters under his breath.

Our table stays silent as we watch Gabriel Ferrara take the stage to accept the award. He holds it up in the air, and the people in the crowd all laugh and cheer, and he takes the microphone.

"Thank you." He looks around the room. "It means a lot. Commiserations to Miles Media, who have won this award consecutively for the last sixteen years." He blows a cheeky kiss to Jameson and then waves down to our table.

Jameson glares at him. His tongue runs across his teeth as sheer contempt drips from his every pore.

"I think it is safe to say"—Gabriel smiles sarcastically—"that in the last twelve months we have led the market with our cutting-edge news delivery." He holds up his finger. "We are now the number one media empire in the world."

The crowd claps and cheers.

He holds the trophy in the air.

The Ferrara table goes wild.

"You've got to be joking," I scoff, unable to help it.

The Miles family glares at Gabriel as he stands on stage . . . and I can feel their anger because I have it too. I can feel it growing inside me like a pulsing disease.

It's one thing to lose your crown, but to have it taken by a thief who's stealing your work is a completely different ball game.

Gabriel bows and then takes a seat back at his table. He kisses the trophy as the photographers snap away. This win will be headlining tomorrow's news stories across the country.

Fury and silence sweep around our table. Nobody says a word.

I stare at him across the room and want to wipe that sleazy smile off his gorgeous face.

And I will.

Prepare yourself, Mr. Gabriel Ferrara. I'm taking you down.

I gasp for breath as I watch Jameson lap me in Central Park. It's six o'clock, and the sun is just rising. He's running particularly fast today . . . and I'm letting him.

I get it now; his responsibility is not something he can just switch off at the end of the day. I feel it for him too now. Last night, however infuriating it was, taught me a valuable lesson on his competitors.

They have no morals and no fear, and that makes them very dangerous players indeed.

Jameson turns and sprints back to me. He's always careful he keeps me in his sight.

He was quiet when we came home last night, deep in thought. We had a shower and made love, and then he finally relaxed a little. I made us a snack, and we lay on the couch in each other's arms and watched a movie for a while. We went to bed late, but we needed the time together to wind down.

Neither of us brought up the award ceremony. We didn't speak of it at all—there's nothing to say.

It is what it is. No amount of conversation can take away the fact that Ferrara Media has been rewarded for being deceitful. It's eating me alive; I can only imagine what it's doing to Jameson.

He comes to a stop in front of me, panting heavily. "You're especially slow this morning," he teases.

"You're especially fast today. That ax must be big."

He chuckles as he leans in to kiss me. "Fucking huge." We turn and begin the slow jog back home. "I'll organize Alan for the weekend to get your things?" he says as he runs.

"About that . . ."

"Yes?" he pants, still exhausted from his sprinting.

"I have a proposal for you."

He stops running. "Such as?"

I turn and take his hands in mine. "I'll move in with you on one condition."

"What?" He stares at me as if already annoyed by my bartering.

"I'll move in with you if we can get out of New York on the weekends."

"What?"

"Well, not every weekend." I shrug. "But enough that we can relax."

"New York is my home. I am relaxed. What are you talking about, woman?"

I smile and start jogging again.

He catches up with me. "What?"

"It's impossible to relax here, Jay. This city is hectic. The energy of this place could be seen from space. Sirens sound all night, cars and traffic and millions of people all buzzing at a million miles an hour."

He watches me as he listens.

"We don't have to go far out of the city. I've already booked a surprise trip away for us this weekend."

"Since when?"

"Since yesterday." I'm totally lying through my teeth here, but whatever. "Think about it. We live in your apartment through the week and work hard. Then on the weekends, we completely switch off. No phones, no internet. Just us."

"What?" He frowns. "That's impossible. I need to be online at all times, Emily."

"No," I pant as we run. "What you need is to recharge so that you can be the best CEO you can be. A tired, stressed-out version of you won't be half as switched on."

We run until we hit the street, and then we look both ways as we wait to cross.

"And besides," I pant, "this way I get the best of both worlds."

"What do you mean?"

"Well, I'm utterly in love with my Jim, the man I met on the plane."

He listens.

"And I'm learning to love the stressed-out CEO who takes over his body sometimes."

Jameson smiles as he runs, finally putting the pieces together.

"This way . . ." I pant. *God, why do I insist on talking as I run?* "This way I get to spend time with both of my men."

He grabs my hand and pulls me back to him; his lips take mine as he clutches my face in his hands. His tongue swipes through my lips, and his kiss is electric with just the right amount of suction. We kiss again and again, and my hands go to his hips. What must we look like, making out on the street corner?

My eyes search his. "Do we have a deal?" I whisper. "Am I moving in?"

He trails his fingers down my face. "I guess we can come to some kind of weekend arrangement."

I smile.

"Only because both of your men love to fuck you." He grabs my hips and bounces them off his.

I giggle against his lips as he holds my head to his. "You're a sex maniac, Miles," I whisper.

He grabs my behind once more, and a car horn sounds. "Get a room," a man calls.

We both laugh and begin to run across the street. I smile over at him as we run.

"What?" He smirks.

"Nothing." I slap his behind. "Race you home." I take off.

"I could beat you with my legs tied." He laughs from behind. "In fact, if I beat you, I am tying you up."

"Not if I tie you up first," I call as I sprint. I giggle as I hear his footsteps behind me. Now there's an incentive to run fast.

Knock, knock. I tap on Tristan's door.

"Come in," his deep voice calls.

I peek around the door. Tristan is sitting at his desk. "Come in, Em." He smiles.

Em.

I smile and take a seat at his desk. I've decided that I'm keeping Tristan completely up to date . . . with everything. He loves Jameson, and he will decipher what Jay needs to know and what he doesn't.

His eyes hold mine with a tender glow. "You were a hit with our parents last night."

I smile. "Really?"

"My mother was gushing about you this morning." He smiles as he holds his pen in his hand and swivels on his chair.

"I just wanted to keep you updated on a few things."

He frowns. "Okay."

"I'm going to keep my relationship with Jameson completely unrelated to work. I feel he needs a break from it."

"I agree. He does."

"So, therefore, there are a few things that I wanted to discuss with you."

"Great. Fire away."

"Well, you know how we've been suspicious of Hayden?"

"Yes." He frowns.

"I found out from Molly—and this is just rumors—that Hayden was fired from the *Gazette* for a phone-tapping scandal."

He sits forward in his seat. "Like what?"

303

"Apparently—and honestly, I have no idea if this is true, but Molly said it was what circulated at the time—he was tapping Keely May's phone and stealing her stories."

"What?" he snaps. "Are you fucking kidding me?"

"No."

He smiles broadly. "This is excellent. This gives me enough ammunition."

"To do what?"

"To get a search on his computers. We haven't tapped him yet."

I smile proudly. "Hopefully this will help us."

"Good work, Em." He swivels on his chair and makes a note.

I watch him for a moment. "There was also something else."

His eyes rise.

"I haven't said anything to Jameson, but Gabriel Ferrara made a pass at me last night."

His face falls. "He did what?" he snaps.

"Don't get excited," I stammer.

"What did he say?"

I frown as I think back. "I was at the bar, and he asked me who I was. I thought he was just being nice, and I replied Emily."

Tristan frowns as he listens.

"Then he picked up my hand and kissed the back of it and said, 'My name is Gabriel Ferrara, and I like to take over all things owned by Jameson Miles.'"

Tristan's eyes widen.

"Then he said, 'Women included.'"

"What the fuck?" Tristan snaps. "Are you fucking serious?" He stands in a rush.

"But I don't know if I read it the wrong way or . . . ," I stammer. "I don't want to be making more of this than it is, but I felt that it was really quite off."

Tristan's eyes blaze with anger. "What did you say?"

"I told him he was insulting my intelligence and to go away." I curl my lip in disgust. "He makes my skin crawl."

"Fucking hell." Tristan sighs as he turns and puts his hands into his suit pockets and stares out the window, deep in thought.

"I didn't say anything to Jameson because I feel like that's exactly what Gabriel wanted me to do."

Tristan's jaw ticks in anger. "He wants to start a war."

"That's what it felt like . . . there could be no other explanation," I whisper.

"He's trying to rattle him by attacking him on a personal basis."

"Yes." I sigh as my heart bleeds for my Jay. "I worried about whether I should say anything to you all night."

Tristan's eyes come to me. "Don't tell Jameson."

"Okay."

"Let's keep this between us."

I exhale heavily.

"I'm concerned about Jameson," he says. "He's about to fucking crack."

"I know; I'm going to try to get him out of the city for the weekends and get him offline. I'm doing all I can to keep him calm."

"Good idea." He nods, still deep in thought. "If you had told him about Gabriel, he would be over there strangling the fucker right now."

I pinch the bridge of my nose. "I know."

"You did the right thing." He smiles. "Thank you for telling me."

My eyes hold his. "I hate not telling Jameson, but I feel like I need to protect him from this. Gabriel is just trying to rattle him."

"My thoughts exactly," he agrees. "Thanks, I'll get on this now. Can you do me a favor and try to find out as much about Hayden's personal life as you can? Where he hangs out, partner, that kind of thing."

"Okay, I'm on it." I stand and leave his office and walk over to Jameson's office, and I knock on the door.

"Come in," his deep, velvety voice calls.

I open the door to see my beautiful man sitting behind his desk. He smiles warmly when he sees me and pats his lap.

I lock the door and sit on his lap and take his lips with mine. "Hello, boss."

He runs his hand up my thigh. His mouth goes to my neck, and I smile, and then I see it.

A half-empty glass of scotch sitting on his desk. I glance at my watch.

"It's eleven o'clock, Jameson."

He rolls his eyes and pushes me off his lap. "I needed something to take the edge off. Don't fucking start, Emily."

"Okay," I whisper. "Are you okay?"

"I'm fine," he snaps as he turns back to his desk.

"Three days until our weekend away," I whisper.

His phone rings, and he glances at the screen. "Can't come soon enough. I have to take this. See you tonight."

I kiss him softly, and then he answers the call. His voice instantly turns to the authoritative tone he uses with everyone else.

I stand at the door and watch him as he listens. He mindlessly picks up the scotch and sips it before he talks.

My heart drops.

Many a stressed-out CEO has been found in the bottom of a Blue Label scotch bottle.

Please, not mine . . .

I look around guiltily and then back down to my phone, and I put into the search bar "budget weekends away."

"God," I sigh. "Where can I take him?"

"Are you still going on about that?" Aaron asks.

Molly slides her chair to look over my shoulder.

"I want to take him somewhere that money can't buy." I twist my lips as I think. "It has to be something really special."

Aaron chuckles. "Your *special* and Jameson Miles's *special* may be a little different."

"The thing is, when he's at my apartment, he detaches from who he is. I want him to realize that we don't need to live in a swanky apartment to be happy."

"You're fucking crazy." Molly sighs. "What I wouldn't give to live in his swanky apartment. Anybody would be happy as a pig in mud there. When are you inviting us over, bitch?"

"Right?" Aaron laughs.

"Hmm." I narrow my eyes as I think.

"What about camping?" Molly says.

My eyes flick to her. "Oh, but we don't have a tent or anything, and I won't have time to buy it."

"I've got it all. You can borrow ours. Michael and the kids go camping all the time."

I stare at her for a moment. "Do you reckon he's ever gone camping before?"

"Umm . . . that would be a definite *no*." Aaron widens his eyes to accentuate his point. "Nobody goes camping of their own free will."

Excitement fills me. "Really? Could we borrow your things? You wouldn't mind?"

"Not at all. Take it. Michael and the kids are going to Dallas on Friday to see his parents for a week. They won't be using it."

"Maybe." I smile as the idea takes shape in my head. "But the car," I say, thinking out loud.

"Take Michael's pickup truck, Bessie. Give him the full *Swamp People* experience."

"Really?" I smirk as I imagine Jameson in a pickup.

"Yeah, it's a total piece of shit, but it's reliable."

Aaron shakes his head in disgust. "Are you trying to scare him away on purpose?"

"No, I'm trying to bring him back to earth." I smile as excitement sweeps through me.

"He'll land with a thud; that's for sure." Aaron smirks.

I laugh as I begin to google campgrounds. "This is going to be so much fun."

On Friday afternoon, I drive into the underground parking lot of Jameson's building with a huge smile on my face. I've laughed all the way here from Molly's house. I've called Jay and told him to be waiting near the door for me to collect him.

I drive around the corner, and I see him standing there waiting with Alan and our bags. He sees me, and his face drops.

I honk the horn and bounce in the seat and pull Bessie the pickup truck up beside him.

His face horrified, he comes to me, and I roll down the window. "Going my way?" I ask.

"What the fuck is this?" he gasps.

"This is Bessie." I smile proudly.

Alan puts his hand over his mouth to stop himself from laughing out loud.

"What?" Jameson frowns as he looks at the huge, beat-up light-blue truck. His eyes come back to me.

"Get in, Miles." I smile and wiggle my eyebrows. "I'm taking you camping."

Chapter 19

He stares at me, lost for words.

Alan drops his head as his chuckle breaks through.

Jameson stares at me . . . horrified.

I laugh out loud at the look on his face. I put the pickup into park and jump out and start throwing our bags into the back.

"You can't be serious," Jameson stammers.

"Deadly."

His eyes scan the beat-up old truck. "This car isn't even roadworthy."

"It's not a car—it's a truck." I smile as I slam the back shut. "Her name is Bessie."

Jameson puts his hands on his hips. His eyes glance to Alan, who is laughing out loud.

"This isn't fucking funny, Alan," he snaps. "I don't camp, Emily. Surely you would know this. What on God's earth would make you think of this cockamamie idea? This is not relaxing me in the slightest. I can feel my blood pressure skyrocketing by the second."

Alan drops his head and really begins to laugh. "Forgive me, boss man, but this is the funniest thing I've ever seen. Can I take a photo for Tris?" he asks.

"Absolutely not," Jameson huffs. "Shut up, or I'll make you come with us."

Alan bites his bottom lip to stop the giggles.

"Why would we need to take this . . ." He pauses as he finds the right word. "Hunk of junk?"

"Because we're going off the grid."

"Emily Foster, this isn't off the grid. This is a recipe for instantaneous death."

I slump in the seat and pull a whiny face. "You promised. It's three days, Jameson, and then I'll come back and move in."

He puts his hands on his hips and rolls his eyes, and he knows I've got him. He did promise.

I toot the horn, and he comes around to the driver's side and opens the door.

"What are you doing?" I frown.

"Driving."

"Do you know how to drive a column shift?"

"A what?" He frowns.

I point to the gear stick on the steering wheel.

His face screws up. "Is this even legal to have on the road?"

I laugh. "Yes."

"Then get out. I'm driving." He pulls me from the car, and I jump around to the passenger side and climb in.

He gets in and goes through the gears with a look of sheer concentration on his face.

Alan and I giggle at each other as we wait for him to work it out.

"Okay, I've got this," replies Jameson Miles, the control freak.

"Let's go," I sing. "Toot the horn for Alan."

Jameson looks over at me deadpan, and I do a "toot the horn" signal that I used to do to passing trucks when I was a child.

"Emily, I don't know what that means, but it's a surefire way to get thrown in the trunk."

Alan bursts out laughing again, and I bounce in the seat in excitement. "Bye, Alan," I call. He waves.

Jameson stops and calls to Alan through the open window. "Have your phone on. We're going to need you to pick us up from the side of the road in approximately seventeen miles when we break down."

Alan and I laugh again, and as Alan waves, Jameson bunny hops the pickup out of the parking lot.

We get to the security gates, and he's too high and can't swipe his card. "Fuck this piece of junk," he mutters under his breath as he puts the car in park and gets out to open the gates. He swipes his card, and the gates slowly open. He jumps back in and revs the truck, and it bunny hops up the driveway to the sound of gears crunching.

"Fuck." He winces. "Who owns this piece of shit, anyway?" he asks as we pull out into the New York traffic.

"Michael, Molly's husband."

His eyes flick to me. "Isn't that the fucking idiot who OD'd on Viagra, and you had to take him to the emergency room?"

"That's him." I smile.

"Figures," he mutters as he drives. "Okay, where are we going?"

I pull up my maps on my phone. "Okay . . . we need to get on the interstate."

He looks at me in question.

"We're going to High Point State Park, New Jersey."

"What?" He frowns. "What in the hell is there?"

"Me." I smile as I lean over and kiss the side of his face. "Nothing but me."

He smiles as he keeps his eyes on the road and slides his hand over to my thigh and gives it a squeeze. "Lucky you're my favorite thing, then, isn't it?"

A huge beaming smile is plastered across my face. He's actually doing this.

"It sure is." I lean over and begin to kiss him all over his cheek.

He scrunches his face up. "Stop. It's hard enough to drive Bitchy as it is."

"Her name is Bessie, not Bitchy."

He smirks. "We'll see if she gets us home in one piece, shall we?"

Two hours later, we see the sign into High Point State Park. There's a dirt road, and Jameson looks over at me in question. "Is this it?"

I shrug, suddenly feeling a little nervous. "Uh-huh." I look around. "I think so."

I really need this weekend to work out; I want us to have fun and relax. Deep down I know that if Jay doesn't get a handle on his stress from work, I may lose him anyway. His temper is not something I could live with long term.

We turn off the main road and drive down the track. We both fall silent as we follow the trail. I study the map on my phone. "It says here to go right to the end of this road and then turn right."

"Okay," he replies as the truck bounces around on the rough road. His eyes glance over to me. "Are you sure it's down here?"

I shrug. "That's what it says here."

The trees are tall and are blocking out the last of the sun.

"I saw a documentary made here once," Jameson says as he concentrates on the road.

"What was that?"

"*The Blair Witch Project*," he mutters dryly.

I get the giggles as we go farther and farther into the forest. What the hell was I thinking? This is freaking even me out.

We pass a campsite on the left as we go down the hill. There's a small tent, and two teenage boys are sitting at an open campfire. I watch them as we pass. "They look like they're having fun." I smile.

"They're about to go into the tent and take turns fucking each other," he mutters. "Only logical explanation as to why they would come out here."

I smirk. "Will you stop being so pessimistic? It's three nights, and we get to be alone without anyone around."

He nods and then frowns as he thinks of something. "Where are the bathrooms?" His eyes flick to me. "We have our own bathroom, right?"

"Well . . ." I pause.

"Well, what?" he snaps. "I am not fucking staying anywhere without a bathroom, Emily."

"There are bathrooms." I turn the phone map around as I try to locate where they are from our tent. "Ah yes, here they are. Just a short trek."

"A trek?" His eyes flick anxiously to me. "Define *trek*."

Oh man, it's a long trek, but I won't tell him that just yet. He's likely to turn around. "It's close—don't worry," I lie.

We get to the bottom of the hill, and the road goes into a fork. A lake is straight ahead, and the sunlight is just beginning to fade. I smile in excitement. "Turn right." He carefully turns right, and we go along a little bit. "Should be just up here."

"Where?" He frowns.

313

"Just park anywhere."

"What do you mean?" His eyes come over to me.

"We just set up where we want."

"What, like"—he screws up his face as he looks around—"on the dirt?"

I laugh. "Were you expecting oak parquetry floor?"

He rolls his eyes and parks the truck, and I get out and walk up and down the water's edge. "What are you doing?" he asks.

"Looking for a good spot to set up. It needs to be high and flat."

"Why high?" he asks as he starts to look around.

"In case it rains."

His eyes come to me in horror. "Don't even say that."

"Quick, we have to get a move on."

"Why?"

"It's getting dark. We're running out of sunlight."

He looks up at the sky. "Do we have lighting?"

"We have a flashlight and two of those little headlight things that strap on our heads."

"Good grief," he snaps as he begins to throw the things out of the back with urgency. "I'm not wearing a fucking strap-on headlight in this stupid man-versus-wild experiment. It's bad enough when I can see."

I laugh as I grab the tent in its bag and begin to unpack it. I hand him the broom. "Sweep the dirt."

He looks at me, completely lost. "What?"

"Sweep the dirt—clear a patch for us. No sticks or anything can be under the tent."

"Sweep the dirt," he repeats.

"Yes, Jameson. Hurry up, or you will be doing it in the dark."

"Jesus Christ . . . now I've heard it all," he mutters as he begins to sweep a patch of dirt to clear it. "Who sweeps fucking dirt?"

"Campers." I smirk as I open the instructions, and then my face falls. The instructions look like they're to build a nuclear reactor. Oh jeez, Molly said it was easy to put up.

Okay . . . whatever. It will be fine. I inwardly begin to panic. *We are not going home.*

I spread the tent out, and I hear a slap. "Ow."

I keep concentrating as I get the poles out of their bag.

I hear another slap. "What the hell?" he cries.

"What?"

"These bugs are from Jurassic Park." He swings his arms around to get them off him. "No bugs are this big."

I go back to my instructions. *Okay, so it says here that this pole goes into this . . .*

"Ahh," he cries as he slaps his arm. "I'm getting fucking malaria over here, Emily."

I roll my eyes. "Stop being a baby." I put the pole into the correct place. "Can you grab the corner and stretch it out, please?"

He swings his arms around and goes and gets the corner of the tent and stretches it out. The sun is just setting. "Step back a little farther," I say.

He slaps his legs. "Fuck off," he whispers as he swings his arms around, trying to swat whatever it is he's swatting.

"Step back farther."

He walks backward and trips over a rock and falls into a bush. "Ah," he cries.

"Oh." I burst out laughing and run to help him up.

"What kind of fucking lunatic does this for fun?" he splutters as he climbs out of the bush.

"We do." I laugh.

"This isn't fun, Emily," he huffs as he brushes the dirt off him. "This is a living hell in a hydroponic mutated-bug breeding zone." Something bites him again, and he slaps his neck. "Fuck off," he whispers to the bug.

"For God's sake, get the bug spray, princess. It's in the bag of supplies in the truck."

"We have bug spray?" He looks at me deadpan. "Now you fucking tell me, after I've lost four pints of blood already."

He storms to the truck, and I hear the spray can go . . . and go . . . and go . . . and go.

"Are you saving any for me?" I call.

"This is man versus wild, and every man is for himself. Don't you watch *Survivor*? I'm voting you off the island tonight," he calls before launching into a coughing attack and waving the air in front of him. "What the hell is in this stuff, anyway?"

"Poison." I widen my eyes. "To kill the bugs."

He storms back over. "Hurry up with the tent," he demands. "What's taking so long?"

"You put it up if you're so perfect," I snap.

"Fine." He snatches the directions from me and stares at them for a moment as his eyes flick to the outstretched tent. He turns the paper around and twists his head. "Well, this all makes perfect sense now."

"It does?" I frown. "I couldn't work it out at all."

"This isn't directions to put up a tent—this is a map for an escape from Alcatraz."

I burst out laughing.

"What's funny?" he barks. "Nothing about this situation is funny, Emily."

He turns the page and then turns it again and then again. We both frown as we stare at it. "Okay, I see now."

"You do?" I ask hopefully.

"No. I don't. We find a hotel."

"Jameson," I plead. "I wanted to do something with you that you've never done with an ex-girlfriend. I just wanted us to do this first together. Will you just humor me, please?"

He exhales heavily.

I take his hands in mine. "I know this isn't what you're used to, but I wanted to take you out of your comfort zone. I really want to do this—it's important to me. This is how uncomfortable I feel in your fancy apartment."

"Not possible." His eyes hold mine, and then he exhales in defeat. "Fine." He begins to study the directions again; the light is fading, and he's squinting to see.

I go to the supply box and take out the two headlights and put one on his head and then my own. I switch them on.

He looks up at me deadpan.

I put my hand over my mouth as I get the giggles, and he continues reading the directions.

"Okay, it says the poles are in a separate bag," he says.

"Got them."

"And we need to peg out the corners."

"Already done it." I rub my hand down his back and onto his behind. He swats me away.

"We need to put the poles in the end and hoist them up."

"Okay." I lean up to kiss him.

"Emily." He looks at me, and the flashlight strapped to his forehead shines in my eyes. "I smell like a toxic dumping ground of bug poison, and I have never felt so unsexy in my entire life. I wouldn't be surprised if my dick has been poisoned off like a weed."

I burst out laughing. "You could never be unsexy to me, and your dick is more of a tree than a weed."

He raises his eyebrow, unimpressed.

I get the uncontrollable giggles. He really does look ridiculous. I want to take a photo for Alan, but I know he would go postal. He's teetering on the edge here.

"Okay, let's just get in and do it, and then we can pump up the bed." I smile.

His face falls. "We have to pump up a bed?"

"No. You have to blow it up with your mouth," I tease.

He throws the directions in the air. "That's it—I'm out."

I burst out laughing. "No, you don't. I'm only teasing. We have a pump."

He puts his hand on his hips and stares at me for a moment.

"Jameson." I smile softly. "This weekend is symbolic in our relationship. You're expecting me to give up everything I know to live in a world that's completely foreign to me."

He stares at me.

"I'm just asking you for three days." I bounce on the spot. "Please. Can you just do this . . . for me?"

He pinches the bridge of his nose, and I know I've nearly got him. I lean up and kiss his big lips. "I'll make it up to you. I promise."

"Fine," he snaps as he bends and picks the directions up and begins to reread them. "Get me the longest pole."

Two hours later, the tent is finally up. The bed is ready, and I put out two fold-up chairs. "Come sit with me." I smile as I open a bottle of red wine.

He sits down beside me, and I pass him his glass. I brought two wineglasses. I knew if I tried to make him drink out of a plastic cup, it would have been all over.

He sits in his cheap fold-up chair and takes his glass from me, and I smile and raise mine to him. "To a successful escape from Alcatraz."

He smirks and takes a sip and looks around at the darkness. "Okay, so what do we do now?"

"This is it."

"This is it?" He frowns.

"Yeah . . . you just sit here."

"And do what?"

"Relax."

"Oh." He looks around at the dark forest and sips his wine, and I bite my bottom lip to stop myself from laughing. It's completely dark now, and the forest is beginning to come alive with animals. Echoes can be heard in the distance.

He's in complete freak-out mode inside and holding it in. He tips his head back and drains his glass and holds it out for an immediate refill.

"What are you doing?"

"I'm getting plastered so I don't remember getting eaten by a bear." He shakes his head. "It's the only way."

I laugh. "This is completely safe, Jameson."

He widens his eyes. "That's what Daniel said right before he went missing."

"Who's Daniel?"

"*Blair Witch* Daniel . . . ever watched it?" he mutters dryly as he looks around.

"No." I smirk.

"Probably best you don't." He looks around at the forest. "Hauntingly familiar."

I laugh as I get up. "I'm going to the bathroom."

"What?" He stands in a rush. "Where's that?"

"Up the trail."

His face falls. "You can't walk up there alone. It's dangerous."

"No. I'm not. You're coming with me."

"What?" He frowns.

"Come on, Jay."

"No, we are not leaving the campsite. I don't want to be walking around."

I smile as I look down at the lake. The moonlight is dancing across the water. "All right." I stand and take my shirt off and then slide my panties down.

"What are you doing?"

"I'm going skinny-dipping."

"What?" His eyes flick to the black water. "No . . . no you're not. I forbid it."

I take off my bra and throw it over his head, and he snatches it away.

"Emily."

I kick my panties off.

"Have you gone completely fucking crazy?" he whispers.

"Maybe."

He looks around. "Anybody could be watching."

I smile and run to the water's edge. "You coming in, chicken?" I wade thigh high into the water.

"Are you fucking insane?" he cries from the water's edge.

I splash water his way. "Get in, yellowbelly."

He runs his hands through his hair in a complete panic. "Emily, this is not safe."

"This is a lot safer than New York, Jay. Come on . . . live a little."

He looks left, and then he looks right as he clenches his hands at his sides.

"Jay, come on, baby." I smile as I lower myself into the water. "I'll protect you."

He closes his eyes. He wants to come in—I know he does.

"Come on." I laugh as I swim. "The water is beautiful."

With a shake of his head, he takes his shirt off and throws it to the side. I laugh as I float on my back. He begins to wade into the water.

"Take your shorts off."

"No way in hell am I offering my dick as live bait for a fucking eel," he barks.

He wades to me and takes me into his arms. The water is cold and fresh, and I wrap my arms around his neck.

The moonlight is beaming off the water, and he smiles as he kisses me gently. "You're crazy, Emily Foster."

"And I love you." I smile up at him. This does feel crazy . . . crazy good.

"You better." His lips dust mine.

I wrap my legs around his waist as I feel my arousal wake from its slumber. Our kiss turns passionate. "I think we need to christen the lake," I whisper up at him.

"You're a complete sex maniac."

I smile as I kiss him and pull his shorts down a little. "We've already established this. Now fuck me, Lake Boy, before your wiener gets eaten, and I don't mean by me."

He smirks against my lips as he grabs my behind. "Shut up. You're wrecking it."

Drop.

Drop.

Drop, drop. From my deep slumber, I hear rain as it sprinkles onto the tent.

Drop, drop, drop. It gets heavier.

321

"Don't fucking tell me," Jameson whispers from beside me.

Crash sounds the thunder, and we both jump in fright as the forest flashes white.

"You can't be serious," he mutters into the darkness.

My back is to Jay, and I bite my lip to try to stop myself from laughing. He had a complete meltdown when we got into bed over the sound of the animals in the forest keeping him awake—in fact, he's had about ten meltdowns.

This will be the icing on the cake.

The rain really begins to come down, and thunder begins to crack repeatedly.

"Well, this is just fucking great," he huffs.

I smile and roll over to face him. "It's fine. Tents are waterproof. Just go back to sleep."

The tent continually lights up an iridescent white as lightning flashes through the sky.

He sits up and feels around the tent in the dark. He's foraging for a long time on his hands and knees.

"What are you doing?"

"Looking for a fucking light!"

I laugh out loud.

"How do you find this funny? Not one fucking thing about this is funny, Emily."

He finally finds the light and puts it on his head and switches it on and looks at me.

His hair is all mussed and sticking up everywhere, and his eyes are wide and crazy.

Unable to help it, I get an uncontrollable fit of the giggles.

"What?"

"If you could . . ." I have to stop talking because I'm laughing so much. "If you could just see yourself."

He smirks, and then a crash of lightning hits so close it sounds like it hit a tree right next to us.

"We're going to fucking die tonight," he stammers in a panic.

The rain hammers down, and I unzip the tent. We both peer out into the apocalyptic storm.

It's really pouring down, and I zip the tent back up. "It's fine. The tent is waterproof, and we'll just have to try to sleep through it."

"Have you lost your fucking mind?" he snaps. "Who could sleep through this?"

"Me—I could." I lie back down and pull the sleeping bag blanket over me.

I smile when I remember Jameson's earlier meltdown that he couldn't touch me in my sleeping bag. In an hour-long operation, he unzipped both of our bags and put one underneath us and one over the top of us so that we could cuddle while we sleep. He's super cute.

The tent begins to sway side to side as the windstorm picks up.

"Holy fucking . . . here we go," he mutters as he looks at the ceiling of the tent.

One end of the tent lifts up in the wind, and he pounces over and holds the tent to the ground.

I burst out laughing again.

"Not helping," he cries.

I jump up in my fits of giggles and grab his jacket and begin to put it on.

"What are you doing?" He frowns.

"I have to hammer the tent pegs back in." I put my headlamp on my head.

His mouth drops open in horror. "What?"

"It's the only way the tent will stay up."

"You're not going out there. It's dangerous," he whispers angrily.

"Somebody has to do it." I pick up the hammer.

He snatches the hammer from me. "This will fucking do me in."

I laugh.

"Goodbye, Emily." He unzips the tent. "It was nice knowing you." He disappears out into the storm.

"This is why you're the CEO." I giggle as I hear the metallic bangs as he hammers the tent pegs back in.

The rain really begins to pour down, and the wind is ferocious. Honestly, what are the chances?

Damn you, weather.

I unzip the tent and peer out into the pouring rain. He's struggling to stay on his feet from the wind as he bends down and hammers tent pegs into the ground, headlamp still firmly in place. He's muddy and sopping wet. I get the uncontrollable giggles once more, and unable to help it, I grab my phone and take some photos of him. Surely one day he'll find this funny.

After ten minutes, he comes back in. He's panting, wet, and covered in mud from the splashing of the rain. I grab a towel and begin to dry his hair. I peel his shirt off him and slide down his track pants. "Just get dry. It's going to stop soon," I say to try to calm him.

The sound of the rain is deafening above us, and he dries himself.

I shuffle through his bag and find him some dry clothes, and the tent begins to sway again as he hops around half-wet, trying to get dressed.

The tent lifts again.

"Get fucked," he snaps.

Oh my God—this really is horrendous.

We hear a loud rip in the roof, and our eyes widen.

"Oh no . . . the tent," I whisper. "We can't damage the tent—it's Michael's."

"I'll buy the poor prick a camper. This is fucking intolerable," he splutters.

Rip. The tent rips in half. "Ah," I scream as our things go flying everywhere in the wind. I scurry to the ground as I try to throw everything into bags.

Some kind of sanity rubber band breaks inside him, and he puts his hands on his hips, tips his head back to the sky, and bursts out laughing.

"This isn't funny. Get our bags to the truck," I cry.

He laughs . . . and laughs . . . and laughs.

I scramble to keep our phones dry and run to the truck with our bags.

"Jameson," I yell. "Do something."

He turns to me and takes me in his arms in the pouring rain and kisses me. Our headlamps hit together, and I laugh too.

"This is ridiculous," I whisper.

"Hotel?"

"Please."

"Hello." I smile at the receptionist of the tourist center. "Have you got any B and Bs available for two nights, please?"

The woman behind the desk types away.

We stayed in a hideous hotel last night, and Jameson refuses to stay there again. He said we can only stay the full weekend if I find somewhere half-decent for the next two nights. He's chasing coffee outside for us.

The rain is gone, and at some stage we have to go back and pick up the camping stuff from the Armageddon storm last night. We just got our things and left. There was nothing we could do in the middle of the night in those conditions anyway.

"I only have a farmhouse." She types and then reads. "Arndell is the property."

I frown as I listen.

"It's available for two nights, and you can have that at a discounted rate if you want."

I smile. I love that she thinks we need a discount. "Okay, that sounds good. Thank you." I slide over Jameson's credit card, and she does the paperwork.

"Here are the keys." She hands me a map. "Go down to Falls Road, and then the property has its own road in on the right."

"Oh, how big is it?"

"The house is on three hundred acres. The land is gorgeous. The house is a little tired, but the location is stunning."

I smile. "Cool, okay."

I bounce out to the pickup to see my poor disheveled man. He looks like he's been to hell and back, and funnily enough, I think it's the most relaxed I've ever seen him. It's as if that sanity rubber band that broke in him last night released some of his tension.

"Okay, we got a farmhouse."

He reaches over and puts his hand on my thigh and hands me my coffee. He shifts the gears on the steering wheel and pulls out.

I smile out the window as I ride in the bumpy truck.

"Do you know we haven't passed a car?" he says as he keeps his eyes on the road.

"It's nice, isn't it?"

He shrugs. "Different."

We follow the directions, and ten minutes later we get to a big stone entryway with the sign.

ARNDELL

326

"This is it."

We turn up the driveway, and I smile. The road is lined with huge trees that create a canopy. Rolling green hills are as far as you can see.

"Oh, look at this place." I smile in wonder. "She said the land was beautiful." For five minutes, we drive through until we get to the top of a hill and find a big old house. It's white with a sweeping veranda around the edge. The roof is made of shingles, and it must be a hundred years old.

Jameson's eyes find me.

"Don't say anything." I smirk.

He holds his hands up in the air as if crying defeat.

We climb out and open the front door and peer in. I smile broadly. Wide-timber floors, a huge fireplace, and great big windows with views out over the property. You can see for miles from up here. The furniture is dated, but that doesn't matter to us.

I take Jay's hand as we walk through and look around. A large living area, a formal dining room, a big kitchen, a bathroom, and a bedroom are downstairs. There's an old timber staircase, and we go up to find five bedrooms and another bathroom.

I turn to Jameson and wrap my arms around his neck. "Is this better, Mr. Miles?"

He smiles as he bends to kiss me. "This will do."

We lie on a blanket in the grass, and the sun is warm on our faces. It's Sunday afternoon, and we are in a sleepy haze.

Last night was heaven. We lit the fire, and Jay humored me and helped me carry the mattress out so that we could sleep next to it.

Today we have explored the property and went into town to grab some groceries in our light-blue pickup truck.

Jameson is relaxed for the first time since we met.

I'm happy . . . so happy.

I roll to face him. "Tell me about your relationship with Claudia."

He frowns and rolls to his side toward me. "What do you want to know?"

"Everything."

He reaches up and brushes his finger over my bottom lip. "It wasn't like what we have."

"How so?"

"Well, we were friends for a long time. There was never this instant attraction or . . ." His voice trails off.

"No, go on," I urge. "I want to know."

"She did some stories for us, and we got to know each other. Then . . . over time we built a friendship."

I watch him.

"I thought . . ." He hesitates and plays with the blanket underneath him as he thinks for a moment.

"You thought what?"

"I thought she was the love of my life. She was like me. Driven." He shrugs. "She got me."

My stomach twists in jealousy.

"We were together for three years. Engaged."

I frown. "You were engaged?" I didn't know this. It was on her bio but not his, and I was hoping it was wrong.

"Yes."

My eyes hold his. "What happened?"

He exhales heavily. "She was offered the job as editor in chief for British *Vogue*. It was a huge thing, and she had worked so hard to get it."

I watch him as he speaks.

"She moved and . . ." His voice trails off.

"What?"

"We tried the long-distance thing, and I struggled with no sex. It's not who I am."

I frown.

"So we made a pact that we would be with other people but try again in a few years. We had a five-year plan of getting back together."

My heart sinks. *He still loves her.*

"But then a year ago I met this girl on a plane."

I smirk.

"And she was everything that I wasn't looking for."

Our eyes are locked, and the air crackles between us.

"But I couldn't pursue her because of my promise to Claudia." He takes my face in his hand, and his thumb dusts back and forth over my bottom lip. "I wanted to. I desperately wanted to. I felt a physical connection with her from the word *go*. I was hard the entire plane trip, and our night together was insane." He smiles softly. "There was something about her that I couldn't forget. She lingered in the back of my mind. I compared all sex and women with her since then." He pauses as he tries to articulate his thoughts. "They always fell short . . . even Claudia."

I smile as hope blooms in my chest.

"Recently I'd been thinking about her a lot, and I had even contacted the airline and found out her name."

"You had?" I whisper. *This is news.*

He nods. "I got a photocopy of your passport emailed to me just six weeks before you started working for us. I'd planned on contacting you, but with everything going on at work, I hadn't got around to it yet. I had no idea that you were coming to work for Miles Media."

"That explains it, then." I smirk.

"Explains what?"

"Why you never called. I look like a prisoner in that photo."

He chuckles. "This is true." He leans in and kisses me softly. "Tell me about your past loves."

My eyes search his. "I can't."

He frowns.

"Since I met you, I've realized that I've never been in love before."

He smiles softly. "What about the guy with Backseat Barbie?"

I giggle. "You remember him?"

"Yes." He smirks as he pulls me over his body and holds me tight.

"What I felt for them, Jay, and what I feel for you is incomparable."

We lie in silence for a while and stare up at the trees as they sway over us.

"I love you," I whisper.

He kisses my temple. "Good, because I don't camp in hell for just anyone."

I giggle as I hug him. This man kills me.

We stare at the fire as it flickers. It sporadically cracks as the wood burns. Emily is in front of me on our makeshift bed on the floor. We've just made love and are in a sleepy, relaxed state.

Home tomorrow.

To be honest, I could stay here with her forever.

She makes anywhere home.

Emily smiles up at me. Her long dark hair is splayed across the pillow, and her big eyes offer me a deep comfort. My hand slides down over her full breast and lower over her stomach. I turn her head and take her lips with mine. Our tongues dance in a slow erotic dance.

I'm so in love with this woman. When we're alone, nothing else matters.

"Thank you," I whisper.

Her eyes search mine. "For what?"

"For finding me."

She rolls toward me and takes my face in her hands. "We were always going to find each other," she whispers. "Soul mates do that."

I smirk as I tuck a piece of her hair behind her ear. "You don't really buy into that soul mate mumbo jumbo thing, do you?"

"I didn't." She kisses me softly. "Until I met you."

We stare at each other in the flickering light, and if I could bottle this moment, I would.

Never have I had something so raw and pure in my life.

Her love is a light . . . my light.

"Jay," she murmurs as she runs her fingers through my stubble. Her eyes search mine.

"Yeah, baby?"

"Can we come back here next weekend?" she asks hopefully.

"Really?" I whisper.

She nods with a soft smile. "I love this old house."

I smirk. If the truth be known, I'm kind of keen on it myself. "Maybe."

She snuggles against my chest. I feel her relax in my arms, and after a while, the gentle pattern of her breathing notifies me that she's drifted off to sleep. I inhale deeply into her hair and smile as I watch the fire.

This is it. I can stop searching.

I've found her.

Chapter 20

Jameson

I walk into the apartment right at seven to the delectable aroma of gourmet food cooking. I smile, drop my laptop bag, and make my way to the kitchen to find Emily dancing with her back to me as she cooks. I stand at the doorway and watch her for a moment. She's wearing a black skirt and a white shirt, her long dark hair is in a ponytail, and her naturally beautiful face is glowing.

A warm feeling of comfort runs through me at her obvious happiness.

All is right in my world when she's here.

This is the weirdest thing I've ever experienced. I don't want to be anywhere but here with her. From three o'clock every afternoon I start to watch the clock, waiting for the time I get to come home.

I watch as she picks up her wineglass and sips it; her burgundy lipstick marks the glass in a perfect lip shape, and I smile—even her lipstick on the glass does things to me.

I would never want to wash it again; I'm like a starstruck schoolboy.

Her behind moves sexily to the beat, and I watch her, transfixed by the beautiful woman in my kitchen. She turns and catches sight of me and smiles sexily. "Hello."

She comes to me, and I wrap her in my arms.

"How's my man?" she asks as she kisses me softly.

"Good now that I'm home."

Our lips touch again and again, and I sit her up on the counter and stand between her legs as we kiss.

"Are we having an entrée before our meal, Mr. Miles?" she breathes against my lips.

I unzip my fly. "Looks like it."

It's Thursday and crazy around here. We are preparing reports for our board meetings tomorrow. It feels good to be back at it without the added pressure of all the other shit that's been going on around here. Tristan and I are at my desk, discussing the new advertising budget we have set, when there's a knock on my door.

"Come in," I call. The door opens, and a familiar face comes into view. My face falls, and I stand immediately. "Claudia."

Tristan's eyes widen, and he looks to me as he stands. "Hi, Claud." He rushes to her and kisses her on the cheek. "How are you?" he asks.

She forces a smile. "Good, thank you . . . and you?"

"Great." Tristan's eyes meet mine across the room. "I have some things to do. See you later, Claud."

"Goodbye." Her smile fades, and her nervous eyes come to me. "Hello, Jameson."

"Hello." I walk around and kiss her on the cheek; her familiar perfume permeates around me, and I frown at the memories it evokes. "How are you?" I ask.

She clutches her purse. "I've resigned from *Vogue*. I'm coming home to New York."

I stare at her, lost for words.

"I've missed you too much, Jameson. I can't live without you," she whispers.

My heart drops. "Claud, no . . ."

Her eyes fill with tears. "You said it was distance."

Empathy fills me. I can't stand seeing her upset, and I take her into my arms.

"It's not the distance anymore," I murmur into her hair. The door opens, and Emily bounces in. Her face falls, and she stops on the spot when she sees Claudia in my arms.

"Oh . . . I'm—"

"Come in, Emily," I say.

Claudia pulls out of my arms, and her crazy eyes go to Emily.

"Claudia, this is Emily . . . my girlfriend," I introduce them.

Emily's eyes flick between us, and then she holds out her hand. "Hello, Claudia. Nice to meet you." She smiles kindly.

Claudia shakes her hand. "Hello." She turns her attention back to me.

Emily looks between us again. "I'll give you some privacy."

"Thank you," I whisper as my eyes stay fixed firmly on Claudia. I hate hurting her.

"Goodbye," Emily says. "Nice to meet you."

Claudia's eyes fill with tears anew as the door quietly clicks closed. "Does she even know who I am?" she whispers.

"Yes."

"And she found me in your arms and is happy to leave you here with me?" she mutters sarcastically.

My eyes hold hers, annoyed that she thinks Emily has reason to be insecure. "She knows where my heart lies."

Claudia's eyes fill with tears, and I internally kick myself for being an ass. "I'm coming home to New York, Jameson. We can get back together."

"No, we can't."

Her eyes search mine.

"I'm marrying her, Claud."

"Don't say that," she whispers. "She's just easy for you because she's no challenge."

"You're wrong; she's the love of my life."

She clenches her jaw in anger. "You bastard."

"I'm sorry." I step back from her. "But there's no other way to put it."

Her anger erupts. "So . . . what happens when I see you out?" she snaps.

"You say hello."

"Do you think you can replace me so easily?" she stammers.

I stare at her, sad that she's hurting.

"I love you, Jameson. Come back to me," she pleads as she takes my hand in hers.

"You need to go, Claud."

"You're kicking me out?" she shrieks.

"No. I'm asking you to leave."

"That's the same thing."

I exhale heavily; this isn't going to end well. I need to end it before an all-out war begins. I kiss her on the forehead and walk to the door and open it. "Goodbye, Claudia."

She angrily swipes the tears from her eyes and storms past me. I close the door and stare at the carpet for a moment as I feel the tectonic plates move another notch closer to goal. I go back to my desk and dial Emily's number.

"Hi," she answers.

"Hi."

"I came up to see if you wanted to go out to lunch today."

I smile softly. I love this woman—not an inch of insecurity.

"I do. Meet you in the foyer at one."

Emily

It's just around three in the afternoon.

I turn to Aaron. "Wish that damn cheesecake Uber would show up about now."

"Ha, right?" he mutters.

"I'll go make the coffees." I stand and make my way to the kitchen. I make Aaron's and then Molly's, and then as I'm making mine, Jake walks into the kitchen.

"Hi, Emily."

"Oh, hi." I stir the coffee.

"Holy shit, get ready for a media storm tomorrow."

"Why?"

He looks around and leans in as if not wanting anyone to hear what he has to say. "You should see what Ferrara is putting to print tomorrow."

"What?" I frown.

"You can't tell anyone," he whispers.

"I wouldn't."

"They have new dirt on Jameson Miles. The shit is about to hit the fan."

My eyes widen. "What? How do you know?"

"Our insider in their office has just called it through."

"What is it?"

He looks around. "Apparently—"

Someone else walks into the kitchen, and we both step back from each other guiltily. The guy begins to make idle chitchat with Jake, and if I wait around, it will be too obvious that I am waiting to talk to him alone. Shit, I'll come back in a minute.

I make my way back to my desk with my heart in my throat. What dirt do they have on Jay?

Oh hell, I need to find out what it is.

I keep an eye on the kitchen, and as soon as I see Jake go back to his desk, I make my way over to him, and his eyes light up when he sees me. "Hi."

"Meet me in the photocopy room, please?" I whisper.

"Sure."

I walk in and wait, and moments later he follows me in.

"What the hell is going on?" I whisper.

"I can't tell you here; it's too risky," he says as he looks around.

"Just tell me," I almost beg.

"Meet me after work, and I'll tell you everything over a quick drink."

I stare at him. "What time?"

"Six thirty?"

I think for a moment. That would still give me time to go to Tristan if I need to. "Just tell me now."

"No way. I'll tell you it all tonight; it's too in depth."

Damn it, I don't want to meet this idiot, but if I don't, how would I know what Ferrara is up to? If I find out, then maybe we can get an injunction and stop the story from going to print.

"Okay, fine. Where?"

"Harry's Bar, six thirty."

"Okay, see you there."

I go back to my desk and look around guiltily. My heart rate is going through the roof. What dirt do they have on Jameson?

Oh no, my poor man.

Molly and Aaron are both not at their desks, and I know I have to ring Jay and let him know I'm going to be late when they can't hear me lie and use them as my alibi.

I nervously dial his number.

"Hi," his sexy voice purrs down the phone.

"Hi." I begin to break into a sweat as I prepare to lie. "I'm going to go out to dinner with Molly and Aaron tonight." I screw up my face. "Aaron is a bit down, and we're going to try and cheer him up."

"Oh." He seems surprised.

"Is that okay?" I reply nervously.

"Of course it is."

"I'll come over as soon as I finish, and it won't be late."

"Okay, babe."

"What will you eat?" I frown. I hate that I won't be cooking for him. Looking after Jameson has become my favorite thing.

"I'll find something; don't worry about me."

"Oh, okay." I fall silent, feeling guilty.

As if sensing my inner turmoil, he asks, "Is everything all right, Emily?"

"Yes, of course. I love you. See you tonight." I hang up in a rush before I confess my lie.

Six thirty on the dot I walk into Harry's Bar. I've been here before with Aaron and Molly, so I know where it is.

Jake is in the back corner, and he waves happily when he sees me.

I smile awkwardly and make my way over to the table. A glass of wine sits there waiting for me.

"Hi." I sit down opposite him.

"Hi. You look beautiful." He smiles as he looks me up and down. I frown. I went home and showered and changed quickly. I hope he doesn't think it was for him. I changed for Jay for when I see him later.

"You ordered me a drink?" I ask.

"Yes." He smiles warmly. "I hope you like it—cab sav."

"Thanks." I sip it. "What's the story about Jameson?"

He opens the menu. "Should we get something to eat?"

"I'm really not hungry," I reply. I just want to get the information and get the hell out of here.

He keeps reading the menu. "I might get some wedges."

"Tell me what you know," I ask again.

"Well, it's a tangled web."

I sip my wine as I watch him. I'm so nervous about what he's about to tell me that I feel sick.

"Apparently there is a huge story coming out tomorrow."

I sip my wine. "About?"

"Well . . ." He pauses. "I think I'm going to get the wedges; do you want wedges?"

"Fine, get the wedges," I snap.

He keeps looking at the menu, and I'm about to explode. *Pick some food, you damn fool.* "I'll get the wedges," I say as I stand in a rush. "Is that it? Is that all you want?"

"Uh-huh."

I march to the counter. "Can I have a bowl of wedges and a trio of dipping sauces, please?"

I exhale heavily as I try to calm myself down. *Just be calm.*

"Emily." I hear a voice behind me.

"Is that all?" the waiter asks me.

"Yes, please." I smile as I turn back toward the voice that just called me.

Jake grabs my hand and kisses me on the lips.

I step back, shocked. "What are you doing?"

"Kissing you." He smiles as he leans in to kiss me again.

I jump back and out of his reach. "What the hell, Jake? I don't like you like that," I snap as I wipe my mouth.

"I thought that since we were on a date . . ."

"What?" I stammer, horrified. "I came here to find out about Jameson."

He smiles a broad, cheeky smile and then winks.

I glare at him. "There's no breaking story, is there?"

He shrugs. "We could make the story about the wild night we spend together."

"You're a fucking idiot," I snap. "I am not interested in you."

"Oh, but you should be." He grabs my hand again, and I push him hard in the chest.

"Stop it."

"That will be twenty-two dollars," the poor waiter says as he looks between us.

"I'm not paying for this imbecile's wedges," I snap. "Goodbye, Jake," I say as I storm toward the door.

"Emily . . . come on. We would be great together," he calls.

I stumble out of the bar, furious, as steam shoots from my ears. I've been stressed out all day, and for what?

Stupid Jake's lie to get me on my own.

The guy's a fucking sleazebag. And now I can't even go home because I lied to Jay about where I am.

I walk into a Thai restaurant, and the waiter approaches me.

"Can I have a table for one, please?" I ask sadly. I'll just eat dinner alone and then go home to my man.

I can't believe I fell for that trick. What an asshole.

At least there's no story.

I bend and kiss Emily on the forehead in the dark. She's still sleeping. "I'm going, babe."

"Hmm." She wraps her arms around me and pulls me down on top of her. "No, don't go. Play hooky today."

I smile in her arms. "I can't; I have a meeting this morning." I sigh. I have so much damage control to do. Even though the immediate story-leak threat has come to an end, this battle with Ferrara is nowhere near over. If anything, I feel it's about to come to a head. "Two days until we go away," I remind her.

She smiles with her eyes closed. "Two days is too long, Mr. Miles. One of these days I'm going to kidnap you."

We kiss softly, again and again, and I can feel my arousal grow between my legs. I pull back from her. "I've got to go," I whisper into her hair. "If I stay here, I'm going to fuck you and be late."

"Good." She smirks. "Fuck me and be late."

I chuckle against her lips, and with one long, last, lingering kiss, I get up and stare at her lying in my bed, which is all messed up. She smiles up at me, and my heart constricts. Nothing has ever looked so perfect . . . or felt so right. Even with all this shit going on, Emily instills in me a sense of calm, as if the whole world is still all right because we have each other. "I love you."

"I love you more." She smiles as she sits up and makes a last-minute attempt to drag me back to bed.

It's so fucking hard to leave when she's like this.

I make my way downstairs and see my trusty friend Alan standing beside the car.

"Morning." I smile.

He gives me a sad smile, and I frown. "Everything all right?"

He opens the door of the limo, and Tristan, Christopher, and Elliot are in the back, waiting for me.

I frown. "Hi." My eyes flick to Alan in question. "What's going on?"

"Get in." Elliot sighs.

I glance between them; their faces are solemn, and I know something has happened. "Is Dad all right?" I ask.

"Dad's fine."

"Mom?"

"She's great. Get in."

I get in and close the door, and the limo pulls out into the traffic.

"I want you to know that we don't believe anything about this, and we are simply here for you," Tristan says.

"What's going on?" I snap as agitation washes over me.

Elliot hands me the paper. I stare at it for a moment, and it takes a few seconds for my brain to process what I'm seeing.

The front page of the *Gazette* is a huge image of Emily kissing Jake the investigator.

She's holding his hand and smiling as his lips press to hers. It looks as though it's in a restaurant or something.

I frown as my chest tightens. "What the fuck is this?" I snap angrily as I flick the paper.

I scan the story.

Jameson Miles—Media Guru's Fall from Grace

In what appears to be the final nail in Jameson Miles's media coffin, his fiancée, Emily Foster, has been having a secret affair. The two have been spotted in various locations and were snapped holidaying in Italy two months ago. Leaked bank statements released today prove that Jameson Miles has been embezzling money and transferring it to an offshore account. The board is expected to fire him as CEO of Miles Media today, and criminal charges will be laid. Looks like Emily Foster jumped ship just in time.

Chapter 21

I look up to my brothers, speechless.

I stare back down at the photo of Emily. She's wearing her yellow dress . . . the same one she was wearing yesterday. My eyebrows rise by themselves as I try to make sense of this. "When was this taken?"

"No idea, but it had to be lately. She has the bracelet on that you bought her."

I glance down to her arm, and sure enough, the diamond-and-gold bracelet is on her arm.

Can it be?

I frown—a clusterfuck of questions . . . not my Emily, *no*.

"We know it's not you," Elliot says. "You've been hacked; we will prove it. I promise you."

"What?" I frown, unable to string a sentence together. I drag my eyes up to my brothers in confusion.

"There've been transfers, Jameson. Millions of dollars have left our bank accounts with your password," Christopher says solemnly.

I narrow my eyes. "What are you talking about?" I whisper. "I don't understand." I glance back down at the image. "When was this photo taken?"

"This is a setup; I'm sure of it," Tristan snaps. "Emily wouldn't do this."

"What?" I frown, unable to believe what I'm hearing. I run my two hands through my hair as I begin to perspire; adrenaline rushes through my bloodstream.

"That's bullshit, and you know it," Elliot snaps. "The timing of this image going to print is no coincidence."

I frown as my eyes come to Elliot.

"Has Emily been in your apartment alone?" he asks.

I stare at him, my mind a clusterfuck of confusion.

"Has she had access to your computers, Jameson?" Christopher snaps.

I screw my face up. "Yes . . . but . . ."

They all sit back in their seats as if collectively coming to a conclusion.

I look between them. "What?" I whisper.

"I think Emily's working with Gabriel Ferrara. It's all a little bit too coincidental, if you ask me. She's been sent in to keep you occupied while he planned your demise."

"What?" I snap. "That's preposterous."

"Yes, it is," Tristan agrees. "Fucking ridiculous."

"Think about it," Elliot snaps. "She conveniently shows up here and, within weeks, has you by the balls."

"What?" I screw up my face. "Fucking bullshit."

I reread the story as fury rages inside of me like never before.

Elliot hits the paper with the back of his hand. "What's this fucking photo, then?"

"A setup," Tristan snaps.

I stare at the image; she's holding Jake's hand and smiling as he kisses her . . . it looks like she's happy to be there. My eyes flick to Tristan in question.

I have no idea what to think . . . what the actual fuck *is* going on here?

"I'm telling you, man, it's a camera angle; you know better than anyone that the right angle can tell a completely different story," Tristan says.

"Bullshit. Where there's smoke there's always fire," Elliot growls. "Nevertheless, Emily Foster is fucking irrelevant right now. Deal with her later. You're being accused of embezzlement. You could go to jail, Jameson."

I run both of my hands through my hair as I bring my focus back to the facts.

I feel a surge of adrenaline rush throughout my body as my skin prickles.

"What's happened?" I ask. I can hear my angry heartbeat in my ears.

"We're not sure. Huge bank transfers have been coming out of the accounts, and nobody noticed," Christopher replies.

"Going to where?" I frown.

"An offshore account."

"How the fuck am I implicated in all of this?" I glance back down at the image of Emily kissing Jake, and I want to kill somebody . . . *Gabriel Ferrara*. "I don't understand." I drag my eyes to my brother to try and focus on the facts.

"It's coming up that the transfers were made from your log-in details."

"What?" I screw up my face in question. "That's impossible; I haven't been into our business accounts for months. I have no reason to."

"That's what I said," Tristan snaps. "I handle the money side of things; you all know that."

"We have the accounts and legal team meeting us at the office at eight," Elliot replies.

My eyes flick to him. "Does Dad know?"

"Yeah." He exhales heavily. "He's meeting us there."

I clench my jaw and stare out the window as we fly through the streets of New York.

Anger, confusion, and betrayal are all that I see.

I drag my hand down my face and inhale deeply as I try to slow my heart rate down. I feel crazier than ever before.

My reputation . . . my business.

My girl.

I stare out the window, and moments later we arrive at the Miles Media building. It's just 7:20 a.m., and we make our way to the top floor. I need to be alone before the craziness begins.

I walk into my office, shut the door, and drop into my chair at my desk.

The room is silent . . . and empty.

Through my windows I can see bustling New York below as the city prepares for the day. Everything down there seems so normal . . . so in order.

My temper is simmering like a volcano and dangerously close to exploding.

I don't know if I'm going to smash something or burst into tears.

Either way, I feel completely unstable.

With my elbows on the desk, I drop my head into my hands; my breath quivers on the intake as I try to calm myself down.

She told me she was going out with Molly and Aaron last night. I go over the conversation we had when she got home.

"How were your friends?" I asked.

"Great . . . it was good to see them," she replied.

She lied.

I was at home missing her . . . and she was out with another man.

I get a lump in my throat as reality sets in.

I've been over here falling madly in love with her . . . while she's been seeing someone else.

The door clicks, and I close my eyes to try and block out Tristan—I know it's him.

He knows me better than anyone.

I hear him go to the bar and drop ice into two glasses, then the comforting sound of scotch being poured. He places one in front of me, and my heavy eyes rise to meet his.

He clinks his glass with mine as it sits in my hand. "Well, this day fucking sucks already." He leans on my desk with his behind.

"You think?" I mutter as I take a sip. I feel the burn as it glides down my throat.

"When was the photo taken?" he asks.

"Last night."

He frowns.

I clench my jaw as I stare out the window, ashamed that the woman I love doesn't love me back. "She said she was out with Molly and Aaron."

He sips his scotch and raises his eyebrows as if surprised that she lied. "I thought she was the one."

I frown, my chest constricting once more. "That makes two of us."

Silence hangs between us.

"Let's just get through this day and prove your innocence." He sighs as he drains his glass.

I nod.

He watches me for a moment, and eventually he asks, "You okay?"

I nod once, unable to push the lie past my lips.

"We will prove that you're innocent, Jay." He puts his reassuring hand on my shoulder. "I promise you."

I drain my glass and go to the bar for a refill.

He watches me once more, and I know he's choosing his words wisely. "Tell me that you're all right."

I roll my lips, and my eyes rise to his. "I'm all right."

"Why do I get the feeling that you're about to lose your shit and kill someone?"

"If you want to save a life today, get rid of Jake Peters."

"It's already done. I called and fired him this morning at five a.m., as soon as I saw the story."

I take a sip of the amber fluid; it heats my throat as it goes down.

He pauses before he asks, "Do you want me to fire Emily?"

I stare out the window and over the city. "No."

"I was thinking . . . ," he continues.

"Get out," I bark.

"But—"

"Now."

The door clicks quietly behind him, and I stand and move to the window and stare out over the city.

Adrenaline surges through my body, and I feel the earth's tectonic plates move beneath me. I sip my scotch as a cold, detached determination takes its place in my soul.

Nobody fucks with me like this and gets away with it.

Get ready to meet your maker, Mr. Ferrara.

Your day is near.

I bounce out to the waiting limo and see trusty Alan standing beside it. He opens the door. "Good morning, Alan."

He nods. "Morning."

I frown and get in. He's not in a very good mood today. The door closes behind me, and I look around for the paper.

Hmm . . . Jameson must have taken it with him this morning. I'm still sleepy and lethargic. There's a lot to be said for morning exercise—it definitely wakes you up for the day. I put my head back and close my eyes as we roll through the traffic.

What feels like ten minutes later, the car comes to a halt and switches off. I glance up. We are out in front of my apartment building. Huh?

Alan opens the door.

"What are you doing?" I ask.

"Mr. Miles instructed me to drop you here this morning."

"What . . . why?"

"He suggested that you have the day off." He gestures with his hand for me to get out of the car.

"Huh?" I frown. "What's going on, Alan?"

"I'm not sure, but Mr. Miles said that he didn't want you to come into the office and that he will be in touch."

I screw up my face. "Be in touch—what does that mean? Why can't I go to the office? I'm confused."

"You need to get out of the car, Emily," he asserts.

"What?"

He gestures again with his hand, and I get out in a huff.

"Has something happened?" I stammer as I brush past him. "Is Jameson all right?"

"You need to speak to him, Emily."

"Fine, I will," I snap as I take out my phone and dial his number.

"Goodbye, Emily," Alan says before getting into the limo and quickly pulling out.

Jameson's phone rings out. I call again . . . it goes straight to voice mail. He's switched it off.

"What the fuck?" I whisper, annoyed.

I go to call Sammia, his PA, but then realize that it's only eight o'clock—she isn't even at work yet.

What the hell is going on? I cross the street and half walk, half run to the corner paper stall. I see the front page of the *Gazette*, and the blood drains from my face as I see a half-page picture of Jake and me kissing.

"Dear God," I whisper. I read the story.

Jameson Miles—Media Guru's Fall from Grace

In what appears to be the final nail in Jameson Miles's media coffin, his fiancée, Emily Foster, has been having a secret affair. The two have been spotted in various locations and were snapped holidaying in Italy two months ago. Leaked bank statements released today prove that Jameson Miles has been embezzling money and transferring it to an offshore account. The board is expected to fire him as CEO of Miles Media today, and criminal charges will be laid. Looks like Emily Foster jumped ship just in time.

What?
My hand goes over my mouth in horror.

Oh my God, poor Jameson. "I'm not his fiancée, you fuck-ing idiots," I sneer. "How many things can you possibly fuck up in one story?"

I turn and begin to storm back to my apartment as I redial his number with a sense of urgency.

"Hey," the paper man calls out to me. "You didn't pay for that."

"Oh, I'm sorry," I apologize as I rush back to pay. "I was distracted. Thank you."

Jameson's phone goes straight to voice mail once more.

What do I do? What do I do? My shoulder slams into a man as he walks past.

"Hey, watch where you're going," he calls.

"Sorry," I stammer.

I dial Tristan's number.

"Hi, Em."

"Tristan, what the hell is going on?" I cry.

"We're in meetings; I'll call you later."

"What?"

He hangs up.

"Ahhh," I cry. My eyes fill with tears of frustration.

He wouldn't believe it. Surely, he knows it's not true . . . but there's a photo as evidence.

I dial Molly's number.

"Hey, chick, do you want a coffee?" she asks chirpily.

"Molly," I cry in relief that someone answers their damn phone. "Oh my God, it's all lies." I stop on the spot on the busy sidewalk and move to the side up against the building to talk.

"What's wrong?"

"The *Gazette*," I stammer. "Google the *Gazette*. There's an image on the front page of me kissing Jake, and it says we are having an affair."

"What?"

"Somebody must have been following me, or . . ." I shake my head as I try and think of a logical explanation. "What the fucking hell is going on?" I whisper angrily.

"Holy shit." She pauses. "I see it. Wait . . . when the fuck did you kiss Jake?"

"He kissed me last night," I stammer. "I didn't kiss him back, for fuck's sake. Do you—"

"Hang on; I'm reading," she interrupts me.

I put my hand over my face as I wait for her to read.

"Oh my God," she whispers.

"Alan brought me back to my apartment and told me not to come into work today."

"What?"

"He said that Mr. Miles will contact me later."

"Well, what did Jameson say?" she asks.

"He won't answer his phone. I called Tristan, but he said they are in meetings, and he'll call me later."

"Holy . . . fucking . . . shit. This *is* bad."

"You think?" I cry.

"What are you going to do?"

"I don't know. What do I do?"

"Well, if Jameson told you to stay home, maybe you should."

"Why?"

"Because he doesn't need more attention; it says here he's been accused of theft."

My eyes widen as I imagine the media storm that's going to come from this.

"But what if he believes this?" I stammer. "I've never been with Jake. This is complete bullshit. I love *him*."

"He said he will be in touch . . . he will be."

I listen as my mind runs at a million miles an hour.

354

"You're just going to have to wait."

I screw up my face in tears. "You don't think I should come in?"

"God, no. He doesn't have time to worry about you too."

"But I didn't do this," I whisper.

"I know. I'll go up and see him in his office and tell him everything."

"You will?" I whisper hopefully.

"If you come in, Em, the whole building is going to attack you."

I put my hands over my face in horror as I imagine everyone waking up to this story this morning. I'm going to be Miles Media's public enemy number one.

"I'm going to get into work and find out what the hell is going on, and I'll call you back, okay?" she says.

I nod, my eyes filled with tears. I can't believe this is happening. "Okay."

"Go back to your apartment and wait. I'll be in touch."

"Thank you," I whisper as I wait on the line. "Wait, what are you going to say to Jameson?"

"I'm just going to tell him the truth. I'll call you back in half an hour."

My shoulders slump. "Okay, thanks." I hang up.

I walk from my kitchen and back to the living area. I turn and walk back the same route. It's been forty minutes.

Jameson still isn't answering his phone, and Molly hasn't called me back.

What the fucking hell is going on over there?

I text Jameson a message.

Jay
I don't know what the hell is going on.
That photo is a setup.
You know I love you and would
never do that.
Call me back, please.
I'm freaking out!!!

I throw my phone onto the lounge and continue my pacing. Why isn't anyone calling me back?

I wait twenty minutes and then text Jameson again. My phone rings, and I scramble to answer it. It's Molly.

"Hello."

"Hi."

"What happened?"

"I couldn't get in to see him; he was in a meeting with the solicitors," she whispers. "He's got bigger things to worry about at the moment, Em. He could go to prison."

I frown. What? "Oh my God."

"Management is going nuts down here. I have to get off the phone before I get fired."

"What?" My eyes fill with tears . . . *I didn't do this.* "I couldn't give a rat's ass about the company right now. I need him to know that I didn't do anything with Jake. That whole story is bogus."

"I know. I'll go back up in my lunch break. But for now, hang tight."

I put my hand over my mouth as a roll of nausea fills my stomach.

"I'll call you back as soon as I speak to him."

I wait on the line, hoping for a miracle answer to come to us.

"Okay?" she asks.

"Yeah, okay," I whisper before hanging up the call.

I begin to pace once more with a new sense of urgency. What if he believes this?

What if the board believes that he stole the money?

What if he's charged . . . and goes to prison?

Oh my God. I text him again.

I'm serious.

Call me back NOW!!

I'm losing my mind over here.

Another thirty minutes pass as I continue to pace. I can't deal with this waiting. I call Molly, and it goes straight to voice mail. I hang up in a fluster and call Aaron. His phone rings out.

"What the actual hell!" I cry through tears. "What's going on over there?"

I text Jameson again.

Call me now, or I'm coming into the office!!!!!!!!

I'm getting angry, you must know I'm frantic.

My phone rings, and the letter *J* lights up the screen. I pick up a rush. "Oh my God, Jay."

"Hi," he answers, monotone.

"What's going on?" I whisper. "Jay. I can't believe the lies. He kissed me once, and I slapped him across the face. I promise you that I'm not seeing that slimeball."

He stays silent.

A sense of dread fills me. Why is he so quiet? "Jay."

"You didn't think to tell me about this?"

"It only happened last night."

"You said you were with fucking Molly!" he screams.

My eyes fill with tears at the sound of his anger. "I know I did, but he said he had some information about the case, and I knew you wouldn't want me to meet him alone."

"I wonder fucking why?" he bellows.

I screw up my face. "Don't be angry with me," I whisper. "That picture is . . ." I shake my head as I try to articulate what it is that I want to say. "It's taken out of context, I promise you."

"I have to go. Stay out of sight. I don't need to worry about you too."

"What?" I stammer.

"I'm too busy."

"Don't go," I plead. "Jay, we need to talk about this. I'll come to your office now."

"Don't you dare," he sneers.

My eyes widen. "What do you mean?"

"There are a million and fucking one people in my office right now, and I don't have the fucking time to deal with your shit," he growls.

I cringe . . . God, I've never heard him so angry. "Will I see you tonight?" I whisper.

"Goodbye, Emily." The line goes dead.

I drop to the couch and stare at the wall . . . a sick sense of dread begins to sink in . . . he believes it.

Holy fuck.

Eight o'clock that evening

I sit on the lounge and listen to the sound of a movie as it plays on the television.

I can't watch the news. I had to turn it off. It's going on and on about the evidence building against Jameson and the embezzlement case.

358

My mind is miles away. Jameson hasn't called me back all day, and I don't know what's going on over there at Miles Media, but I know it's a media circus.

I'm torn between giving him the space that he needs and running to him as fast as I can. I've decided that I'm going to do as he asked and just stay here and sit tight. He will call me as soon as he can. I know he will, and he's right—me being out and about will only add fuel to the fire. He really doesn't need to worry about me, too, at the moment.

The magnitude of the situation has finally sunk in. What's going to happen if they can't find out who transferred that money?

How long can Jameson deal with this type of pressure?

With a lump in my throat I begin to pace. My carpet must be nearly threadbare after today's pacing activities. I can't remember ever being this stressed.

At eleven o'clock at night, I haven't heard from Jameson, and I am sick with worry, literally.

I've thrown up twice. I decide to call him one last time . . . *where is he?*

With shaky fingers, I dial his number, and it rings and then goes to voice mail.

He's declined the call. My heart sinks, and my eyes fill with tears.

"This is Jameson Miles; leave a message," the recorded message plays.

"Hello." I pause. "Jay," I whisper. "Baby." I get a lump in my throat. "I'm sorry for lying. I was trying to find out about the case, and then he kissed me and . . ." My voice trails off. "I know how this looks, but you have to believe me. I don't even like Jake as a friend; you know that." I walk to the window and stare out over the traffic. "I'm going out of my mind here . . . I love you." I stay silent, unsure what to say. "Don't let them poison your mind, Jay. You're the only person who knows what we have," I whisper through tears. "Come home to me, where you belong." I pause, hoping that I'm getting through to him. "I don't even want to hang up . . . I need you. Please come over . . . I'm begging."

The other end stays deathly silent, and I screw up my face in pain.

"I love you," I whisper. The beep sounds, and I am cut off. I throw the phone onto the lounge and begin to cry.

What the hell is happening?

With my heart in my throat, I walk into the Miles Media building. It's eight thirty in the morning, and I'm coming to work.

Jay didn't call me back last night, and I can't say that I blame him.

I cried myself to sleep . . . well, I didn't really sleep, so I don't think it counts. I've got this sick lead ball in my stomach, and it won't go away.

I have no one to blame for this fucking mess but myself. I lied to my love, and it backfired, and now he thinks the worst. So I'm here today to do the best job that I can of making it up to him.

He's hurt . . . I know he is.

My poor man seemingly has the whole world against him, and I'm so worried about him. How much stress can a man take before he cracks?

I get into the elevator and swipe my security card to the top floors, and a red light comes up. I frown. No. I swipe it again, and the red light flickers again.

"No, Jay . . . don't do this," I whisper through tears. "Don't you fucking lock me out."

I swipe it again; the red light flickers once more. "You son of a bitch," I whisper angrily. I hit the fortieth-floor button, and the green light appears. My heart begins to hammer hard in my chest. He's blocked my access to his floor.

I take out my phone and text him.

Are you serious?
You can't even talk to me?

The elevator doors open, and I stride out onto my floor as I try to calm my anger down.

I know he's got a lot going on, but he knows this is hurting me, and he doesn't seem to care.

Is this how he works? He's just going to cut me from his life without even letting me explain? I sit at my desk and stare into space. My leg bounces in anger . . . what do I do? How do I make him understand that this is all a misunderstanding if he won't even talk to me?

A group of girls walk out of the elevator and begin to walk down the corridor, and then they all stop on the spot when they see me, as if shocked. I stare at them, and they exchange looks and then smirk to each other. "Hi." One of them fakes a smile.

"Hi," I reply. I turn and switch on my computer. Great. Now I'm the office gossip as well—can this fucking situation get any worse?

"Yay, you're here," Molly's familiar voice sounds from behind me.

I swing in my chair toward her, and her face falls when she sees mine. "Oh, baby," she whispers as she puts her arms around me. "Are you all right?"

"He's blocked my access to his floor," I whisper against her shoulder.

"What?" she whispers as she fixes my hair. "He's just . . ." She hesitates. "God, I don't even know what to say, Em."

I stare sadly at my computer.

"Let's just get our work done, and we can brainstorm over lunch." She smiles as she rubs my shoulder.

"Yeah, I guess."

Over the next half hour, I watch on as everyone arrives for their day, sees me, and then proceeds to whisper to the person next to them.

I'm not only the office gossip; I'm the office slut. The idiot who played upon the CEO with the company douche . . . I'm embarrassed, I'm ashamed, and this is appalling.

It's four o'clock, and Jameson hasn't answered any of my calls. I think I'm losing my mind.

Aaron thinks I should give him time. Molly thinks I should be dropped onto his floor by a helicopter . . . either that or bomb the whole floor.

Me . . . I just want to crawl under a rock and hide.

Molly returns from the photocopy room and smiles sweetly over at me.

"What?"

"Say, 'Thank you, Molly. You're a lifesaver.'" She smirks.

I frown.

She passes me over a security card, and I stare at it in my hand. "What's this?"

"It's Melissa's card to get to the top floors. I stole it."

My eyes widen. "You stole her card?" I whisper as I look around guiltily.

"How else are you going to get to see the stupid fuck?" she murmurs.

I smile at her perfect choice of words. "Thanks." I go to the bathroom and stare at my reflection in the mirror.

I look like shit. I drop my shoulders and inhale deeply as I steel myself. Let's do this.

I take the elevator to the top floor, with my heart hammering hard in my chest. I have no idea what's going to be awaiting me, but bring it the fuck on, because I'm getting angry now.

How dare he not even let me explain?

The elevator opens, and Sammia's face drops as she sees me. "Emily," she stammers as she stands. "Mr. Miles isn't here."

I storm past her and down the hall and open his door in a rush . . . and there he sits behind his desk, his cold, calm persona firmly in place.

Elliot is sitting with him, and his eyes snap up. "How did you get up here?"

My eyes find Jameson's across the room, and I can see the hurt from here. "Can you give us a moment, please?" I ask.

"No," Elliot snaps. "Leave now."

My anger bubbles. "With all due respect, this is none of your business," I snap.

Elliot narrows his eyes and stands. "How dare you—this is entirely my business!"

"Oh, I dare all right," I fire back.

Jameson clenches his jaw, and Tristan comes into the office. His step falters when he sees me. "Emily." He frowns as he looks between the three of us.

"Tristan, I need a moment with Jameson, please," I ask him hopefully.

"Of course." He forces a weak smile. "Out, Elliot."

Elliot glares at me.

"Now," Tristan repeats.

Elliot and Tristan leave the office, and we are left alone. Jameson stands and goes to the window, turning his back to me.

Oh God, how do I fix this? "Jay," I whisper as I walk toward him. "Baby, I didn't do this . . . you have to believe me. I know how this looks."

He remains silent.

"He kissed me, and I slapped him, and I had no idea that someone took a photo," I stammer.

Silence. I see his jaw clench from the side as he stares out over New York.

"Are you at least going to talk to me?" I cry. "Why did you block my access to this floor?"

He turns, angered. "Because I don't trust you."

I step back, shocked. "What?"

"You heard me. I don't trust you. Get out."

My face falls. "Jameson, I know you're under a lot of pressure."

"This has nothing to do with the fucking pressure I'm under!" he screams.

I wither. "You can trust me, I promise you."

"Where did you tell me you were on Thursday night, Emily?" he sneers.

I stare at him through tears. "I was trying to find out information."

"By lying to me?"

I nod. "I know it sounds like . . ."

"Like I can't trust you." He turns his back and lifts his chin skyward in defiance. "I have more to worry about at the moment than dealing with a deceitful girlfriend."

"Jameson," I whisper.

"We have nothing to further talk about, Emily . . . get out," he says calmly.

"No," I plead. "I'm not leaving. I love you."

He turns, and his cold eyes hold mine. "Did you practice that speech?"

My heart drops . . . oh, he's so hurt.

"Jay . . ."

"If you won't leave . . . I will." He strides toward the door, and it closes quietly behind him.

I close my eyes in the silence and inhale through my shaking chest.

Did he just end us?

This can't be happening.

It's six o'clock, and I'm sitting at the café across the street from Miles Media. I'm watching the media circus gather as they wait for Jameson to leave the building.

This embezzlement scandal is news . . . big news, and while the rest of the world is hanging on to the story, I've been on the edge of tears all day.

I don't know what to do or how to reach him. He's put his defenses up, and with everything else going on for him at the moment, I don't know how hard I can push without him completely losing it.

I don't want to stress him out further, but he needs me more than ever at the moment. I put my head into my hands. Why the hell did I go and meet Jake?

What the fuck was I thinking? How was that ever a good idea?

I go over that night in my head, and I can hear myself lying straight out to Jameson when I got home . . . *why?* At the time, I thought I was protecting him. I know better now. This is one big mess, and I have no idea how to fix it. My mind goes to the money that has been stolen from the accounts. They all think it's Ferrara, but why would Ferrara, a man who already makes billions of dollars a year, risk it all to take down a competitor? It just doesn't make sense to me.

In my eyes, the person who has stolen the millions needs the millions.

But who is it, and how the hell did they get access to Jameson's banking details?

There's more to this case than meets the eye.

Molly, Aaron, and I are having a crisis breakfast meeting tomorrow, and hopefully together we can brainstorm a plan of action. I hear a flurry of excitement, and I look up to see Jameson walk from the building, flanked by security as the reporters clamber around him, shouting his name and clicking photos. He keeps his head down and doesn't comment and then climbs into the back of his limo.

It pulls out from the curb and whisks him away into the night . . . and farther away from me.

An overwhelming sadness seeps into my bones.

How can I help him?

"Okay, so here are the facts," Molly states. We're at breakfast trying to dissect my mess of a life. I'm more zombie than human, having not slept for two nights. I'm on my second coffee, and it's seven o'clock. "You lied to Jameson about where you were going and went out to dinner with Jake," Molly says.

I roll my eyes.

"You got home and then lied again to Jameson about where you had been."

I blow out a deep breath. "Correct."

"Now," she continues, "Jameson's whole life is falling apart, and he is being accused of a crime that he didn't do."

"Yes," I snap before I sip my coffee.

"The entire world is watching, and you are public enemy number one."

"How is this fucking helping me?" I stammer.

Aaron and Molly make eye contact across the table. "This doesn't look good," Aaron says.

"I know." I put my head into my hands. "I don't know how to help him. I've completely screwed everything up. I'm the villain in this story, and I want to be the hero."

Silence falls across the table as we sip our coffees.

Aarons eyes light up. "I've got it."

"Huh?"

"I know how you could be the hero."

I roll my eyes. "How?"

"Solve the case . . . you're a reporter; you've done this shit before."

I sit up, suddenly interested.

"Those private investigators are obviously fucking useless; they are doing nothing."

"That's true." I frown. "But I don't know anything about computers. Where would I even start trying to track those transfers?"

"I don't know, but finding out where that money has gone yourself does seem like the only way you are getting Jameson out of this." Molly shrugs. "We could help?"

I think about it for a moment. Why couldn't I do this myself? I've cracked cases before—big cases too.

"You know what—you're right." I feel a fire start in my stomach. "I am going to find out who's doing this."

Molly and Aaron smile.

"And when I do"—I punch my hand into my fist—"they will wish they were fucking dead for messing with my man."

"Attagirl." Molly smiles. She and Aaron high-five each other.

I smile as I sip my coffee, and for the first time in days, I feel hopeful. I hold my coffee cup up, and we all clink cups. "To Operation Hero."

I run down the street as fast as I can, my mind a clouded fog. With every step that I run . . . the better I feel. It's been three days since I've seen her . . . three days incarcerated in hell.

I can't see her. I can't put myself in that position ever again.

Nobody is worth feeling this bad for . . . nobody.

I turn the corner and run past a row of restaurants and get to a park, and I see a person up ahead in the darkness.

Their stance seems familiar, and I squint my eyes to try and see.

As I run, a cold sense of realization hits me as to who it is. Gabriel Ferrara. He's on the phone and smoking a cigar as he leans on his black Ferrari. He hasn't seen me.

I stop running and pant as I approach him. *Fucking dog.*

I'm furious that he put that photo of Emily on the front page of his paper. It was a direct attack on me . . . and it hit the target.

Turning, he sees me, and his face falls. "I've got to go." He hangs up his call.

"Look what crawled out of the gutter," I pant.

He smirks as he inhales on his cigar. "Miles."

I glare at him.

"How's that girl of yours?" he asks with a wink. "You should put her on a leash."

I glare at him.

He flicks his cigar at me; my fury begins to bubble.

I step forward.

"You know she made a move on me. Seems like you've lost your edge with everything: the company, the bank accounts.

Sex. How does it feel to have your woman search for someone who can satisfy her needs?"

All I can see is red . . . blinding anger.

I lose control and punch him hard in the face, and then I hit him again and again in quick succession.

He falls to the ground beside his car, and I hear someone yell, "Call the police!"

"Fuck . . ." I look down to his slumped body and the blood pouring from his nose.

What have I done?

I turn and sprint as hard as I can into the darkness. I run down a block and cut through a park as I hear a police siren in the distance.

Fuck.

I run across the street, and a car comes out of nowhere.

Bright lights, car horn, blurred vision.

It hits me, and I go flying into the air.

Darkness . . . nothing.

Chapter 22

Emily

On my laptop, I scroll through the information that I've collected today. I have nothing to go on other than Hayden. He's the only person who has a shady past and the only person I can think of who would double-cross Miles Media.

But selling shitty stories is a far cry from stealing millions of dollars from a global company. I don't think he's capable of something like this.

So why is my gut telling me that he is somehow involved?

I check my phone . . . no messages.

Please call me.

I get a vision of my Jameson all alone in his big apartment, and my heart aches. I've decided that I'm going over there tomorrow night and knocking the door down.

I can't give him the space that he needs . . . I need him.

The door buzzes, and I jump up, excited. Jameson. I run to the telecom to see two police officers on the screen. I push the button. "Hello?"

"Is that Emily Foster?"

"Yes."

"Can we come up, please?"

"What's wrong?" I whisper. Oh my God, what's happened?

"We need to talk to you."

"Has something happened?" I stammer.

"Let us in, please."

"Okay." I push the button with my heart pumping hard.

Moments later they knock on the door, and I open it in a rush. "Hello."

Two solemn-looking police officers force a smile. "Are you Emily Foster?"

"Yes." My heart begins to race.

"Can we talk to you for a moment, please?"

I stand back. "Yes, please come in."

"We would like to talk to Jameson Miles, please." They look around my apartment and then turn their attention back to me. "Is he here?"

"No, he isn't." I feel my heart begin to pump harder in my chest. "What's this about?"

"He's wanted for questioning in regards to an assault earlier this evening."

"What?" I frown.

"Gabriel Ferrara was attacked tonight outside a restaurant by Mr. Miles. A warrant has been issued for his arrest."

"Is he all right?"

"Mr. Ferrara has significant facial injuries and has been taken to the hospital."

I put my hand over my mouth in horror.

"What happened?" I ask.

"Mr. Ferrara was getting into a car when Mr. Miles approached him in the dark. A fight broke out, and Mr. Miles assaulted him."

"Where was this?"

"Out in front of Bryant Park, opposite Lucina's."

"Oh my God," I whisper. "Is Jameson all right?"

"Witnesses say he ran off through the park."

I close my eyes in relief . . . *thank God.*

"You have the wrong person," I stammer. "Jameson would never attack someone. He's the CEO of a company, not a pub brawler." That's a complete lie; I know Jameson would love to beat Ferrara to a pulp . . . "I don't know where he is," I assert with renewed determination.

"Can we search your apartment?" the policeman asks.

"Of course. He's not here, though." I stand back to allow them access.

The police search the apartment and come back to me in the living area. They hand me a business card. "As soon as you hear from him, you need to call us. If you don't, you may be charged with obstruction of justice. Hiding a person of interest from authorities is a very serious offense."

"Okay." I storm to the door and open it in a rush. "Good night." The officers leave, and I close the door behind them with a slam.

I put my two hands over my mouth in horror and dial the number.

Jameson's phone rings out . . . he wouldn't answer my call anyway. "Damn it."

In a panic, I call Tristan.

"Hello."

"Tristan," I stammer. "Do you know where Jameson is?"

"What's wrong?" he says.

"The police were just here, and Jameson apparently assaulted Ferrara. They've issued a warrant for his arrest. Do you know where he is?"

"What?"

"He's not answering my calls, and witnesses said he ran off across the park."

"What the fuck?"

"What do I do?"

"I'll try calling him and call you back."

"Okay." I hang up and begin to pace . . . *where are you?*

Moments later Tristan calls back. "He's not answering. I'll come over."

"Thank you."

An hour later Tristan and I walk through Bryant Park. We haven't talked other than about finding Jameson. He's angry with me about Jake and obviously doesn't want to discuss it.

I'm angry with me.

It's one o'clock in the morning, and now I'm getting frantic. My eyes roam over the park in the darkness. "Where could he be?" I whisper.

"I don't know. Try calling him again," he says.

I dial his number and keep walking through the darkened park when we hear something.

Tristan's eyes widen, and he holds up his hand. "Shh, listen."

From the darkness, we can hear a faint ringtone. It goes silent, and I redial his number.

We both look around frantically, and then we see the white glow as the screen lights up. "Here." I run over to the side and see a phone lying in the grass. My eyes widen in horror as Tristan picks it up. He swipes it on and puts in the code, and the screen lights up.

His eyes rise to meet mine. "It's Jameson's phone."

We both look up across the darkened park as a sense of fear sweeps through me. "What the hell has happened to him?" I whisper.

It's four o'clock in the morning, and Tristan and I are frantic. We've walked for hours. Alan, Elliot, and Christopher are all out looking for Jameson.

"He's probably just hiding out from the police somewhere. He'll be fine," Tristan tries to comfort me. I'm in full-blown tears now; there's no hiding my distress.

"This is all my fault," I whisper as we walk. "If I didn't go to that setup, none of this would have happened."

"What do you mean, setup?"

"Jake told me that he had information on a story that Ferrara was publishing the next day about Jameson and that he would tell me out of work. I didn't want to worry Jameson, so I lied and went to meet him. He just wanted to get me alone, and he kissed me. I slapped him across the face and left, and then the next day . . ." I shrug. "You saw the pictures."

He frowns. "So you weren't seeing Jake?"

"No," I snap. "I'm in love with fucking Jameson, you idiot." I sob. "And he won't let me explain."

"Fucking hell, what a mess." His phone rings, and he quickly answers. "Hello."

He listens. "Yes." He listens some more. "Is he all right?" He gasps. He puts his hand over his chest. "Thank God."

"What?" I mouth.

"Thank you. I'm on my way." He hangs up.

"What?" I whisper.

"Jameson is in the hospital."

"What happened?"

"He was hit by a car."

My hands fly over my mouth in horror.

"He's okay—just a concussion."

"Oh, thank God."

"I'm going to go get him."

"I'm coming," I demand.

"Em . . ." He pauses. "I don't think that's a good idea. The paps will be everywhere after this Ferrara bullshit, and Jameson doesn't need more publicity. Who knows what reporters are at the hospital? Jameson specifically wants you kept out of the spotlight. Let me talk to him, and I'll call you when we get home."

Hope blooms in my chest. *Is he trying to protect me?*

"But I didn't do anything wrong, Tristan. I want to see him."

Empathy wins, and he takes me in his arms. "Let me get him home safely, and I'll call you." He pulls back and holds me by the arms as he studies me. "I promise I'll call you. I'll drop you home and then sort him out, and then I'll call you. You have my word." His eyes search mine.

"Okay."

We walk for a moment in silence.

"I'm going to find out who stole the money if it's the last thing I do," I whisper.

"Emily, that's a bad idea. Leave it to the detectives. You're tired and emotional. Let's get you home."

I nod, knowing that he is right about everything and hating it even more.

I watch the nurse take my pulse as she holds my hand, and I inhale deeply. She's older and motherly, the kind you want looking after you.

"How's the headache?" she asks.

"Still there."

She smiles and gets her flashlight and shines it in my eyes to inspect my pupils. "You have a serious concussion. You're very lucky to be alive, young man."

I hear chatter from outside, and Tristan appears at the door. "Hey."

"Hi." I smirk at the worry on his face.

He rushes to my side. "Are you all right?"

"I'm fine."

"He is not fine," the nurse interrupts. "He got hit by a car. He could have been killed. As it is, he has a very serious concussion."

Tristan drags his hand down his face. "Jesus."

"He's staying in for the night, and as long as all his preliminary tests come back clear in the morning, he can go home."

"Okay . . . thanks." Tristan slumps into a seat beside the bed.

"I'll be back in an hour with some pain medication." She smiles.

"I don't need it," I reply.

"I'll be back anyway."

I roll my eyes, and she leaves us alone. "Sorry," I whisper.

"Fucking hell, Jay, we've been out of our head with worry. Searching for you all night."

I puff air into my cheeks.

"The police came to Emily's, and then she called me, and then we found your phone in Bryant Park."

"Emily?" I frown. "Why did you involve her?"

"She's frantic, Jameson. She wanted to help find you."

I roll my eyes. "I seriously doubt that."

"You know, I don't think she is on with that fuckwit Jake. This was a misunderstanding."

"Shut up," I dismiss him.

"No. You shut up. Why won't you even talk to her?"

"Because she lied to me. Straight to my face about seeing another man."

He watches me.

"And I don't need that fucking shit in my life. I have enough going on, if you didn't notice."

"She wants to see you."

"Yeah, well, I don't want to see her," I snap.

"Then you need to end it with her; she's frantic."

I screw up my face in annoyance. "Just fucking go home. I'll get Alan to pick me up tomorrow."

"Why won't you even talk about this?"

"Because this is none of your business. Emily and I are over. It was over the moment she started lying to me."

The nurse reappears. "I'm tired," I announce.

She smiles. "Yes, okay." She turns her attention to Tristan. "We will call you in the morning when he's ready for release."

"Yeah, okay," Tristan replies. His eyes hold mine, and I know that he knows I'm not tired at all.

The nurse goes into the bathroom.

"And what am I supposed to tell Emily? She's waiting for my call," he whispers angrily.

"I don't give a fuck what you tell her—she's not my problem."

He drags his hand down his face. "You're a selfish son of a bitch sometimes."

"And your point is?"

He stares at me for an extended time. "See you tomorrow."

Emily

My phone dances across the coffee table, and I pick it up in a rush.

"He's okay." Tristan sighs.

"Thank God." I close my eyes in relief. "Can I see him?"

"He has a bad concussion and is going to be in the hospital for a few days."

"What?"

"He said it's best that you don't come down; he doesn't want the media circus."

My eyes fill with tears. Damn it. It feels like all I do is cry at the moment.

"He's sleeping now."

"Did he say anything? About me?" I pause as I try to articulate my thoughts. "How do I get through to him, Tristan?"

He exhales heavily. "I don't know. He's got a lot of shit going on, Em. I don't think he's thinking straight at the moment. I'll try and talk to him tomorrow."

I screw up my face in tears. "Okay," I whisper. "Can you call me . . . please?" God, I sound like the world's biggest loser, but I don't know what else to do. "I'm so worried about him, Tristan."

"We all are, Em. I'll call you tomorrow. Just try and get some sleep."

"Okay, good night." I hang up and get into the shower, and tears of relief begin to fall.

At least he's okay, and tomorrow is another day. He will come back to me. I know he will.

I slide down in my chair as I peer across the street. I'm on Operation *Spies Like Us*.

Hayden is my stalking subject. I don't know why, but I can't let this go with him.

I called in sick to work. I figure this story may be the most important story of my entire career to crack.

I still haven't spoken to Jameson, and with every day that passes, I lose a little more hope.

It's seven o'clock in the evening. I'm wearing a blonde wig and dark glasses, and I have even rented a car. I've been sitting here for eight hours, with no sign of stupid Hayden.

He lives in a busy part of town in a nice apartment block; the street is bustling, and people are everywhere. I have to concentrate on not missing anything.

Damn it, come out already.

I've eaten all my snacks. I'm hungry and dying to go to the bathroom, but damn it, I want a lead or something . . . anything . . . throw me a bone here.

I look down the darkened street and back up the other way. God, Hayden's probably on his way to Istanbul by now. That's what I would do if I got fired from my job for stealing. Although apparently, he has no idea he's still being investigated. He thinks being fired is as far as it's going to go.

I lie back in the chair and let out a deflated breath. I glance over my shoulder and see Hayden stopped and talking to a woman on the sidewalk.

Shit.

I scoot down in the chair. They must be getting back from somewhere. They seem to be deep in a serious conversation, and she has a large bag over her shoulder. I take out my phone and snap a picture of the two of them. I zoom in and take a few shots. Who is she? Is that his girlfriend?

I text Aaron and Molly in a group chat and send them the picture.

Do you know this girl?

I keep watching as they continue to talk. For five minutes, I watch them, and then Molly texts back.

I've seen her before, but I don't know where from?
Does she work in a café or something??

Hmm. I text back.

I have no idea?

A text comes back from Aaron.

Yes, she used to work for Miles Media.

My eyes widen, and I text back.

How long ago?

He writes back.

No idea,
I haven't seen her for a while though.

Shit. I send the photo to Tristan and text him.

Tristan, this girl apparently worked for Miles Media,
can you find out who she is from HR, please?

A reply immediately bounces back.

Sure thing, are you okay?

I reply.

Yes, I'm on operation stakeout.

He texts back.

Do you want me to come and help you?

I smirk.

I thought you thought this was a bad idea.

He replies.

I do, I don't want you in danger.

I text back.

No, can you just text HR for me now, please?

He replies.

Ok.

I wait and wait and wait, and finally a text comes back.

**Her name is Lara Aspin.
HR are searching for her job title in the morning,
I'll keep you posted.**

I smile, excited that I at least have a little lead. I have no idea what it means, but I guess it's something. I text back.

Thanks.

I check my phone . . . no missed calls.

I turn the car on and pull out into the traffic, and a sense of dread begins to hang over me.

Nighttime is the worst; my bed without Jameson is cold. There's a void where he's supposed to be.

My heart is aching.

I'm losing hope for us . . . I miss him.

I lie on the couch and stare at the television. The cushion beneath my head is wet with tears.

It's been three days since Jameson was hit by a car.

Six days since I've seen him . . . I can't eat. I can't sleep.

I'm in hell.

To make matters worse, I embarrassed myself last night by going to his apartment and crying into the security camera, begging for him to let me in.

He didn't, and after half an hour his doorman ushered me out of the building.

I'm ashamed.

I don't know what to do . . . he won't see me; he won't speak to me.

All the love and laughter we shared, reduced to nothing.

It's like I never meant anything to him . . . maybe I didn't?

I knew he had a reputation for being cold, but this . . . this coldness is next level.

How could he watch me on camera sob and beg and not even let me in?

I pick up my phone and text him.

I miss you.

I stare at my phone, and then I see the dots. I sit up . . . he's typing something. My heart begins to race. This is the first time. I watch the dots roll as I wait . . . and then they stop.

Wait . . . what? Where is the text?

I wait.

The dots start again, and I smile through tears . . . yes. He's replying. I wait and wait.

Then the dots stop once more.

"Send the text, damn it," I snap.

I wait, and nothing comes through for half an hour. My anger starts to bubble. How dare he not even acknowledge me? Who the fuck does this asshole think he is?

I angrily text back.

At least have the guts to say what you want to.

A text immediately bounces back.

Move on, I have.

I read the message and then read the message again through tears . . . *what?*

Just like that . . . move on?

Fucking asshole.

I get up and throw my phone as hard as I can. The screen smashes on the coffee table. I'm so fucking furious that I have absolutely no control of the situation. I storm into the bathroom, I get under the shower, and, unable to help it, I cry . . . and cry . . . and cry. Howling sobs, and my chest is heaving hard as I hold myself up against the tiles.

Tears of anger, tears of frustration, tears of heartbreak.

I knew it was coming . . . deep down, all along, I knew it was coming, but holy fuck . . . it hurts.

I drop my shoulders in the back of my limo as I steel myself for what I'm about to do.

"Are you sure about this?" Alan asks as he opens the door.

"Yes. It is what it is; I'm not hiding any longer," I say as I climb out of the car. I look up at the New York Police Department sign above the door, and I walk through.

The policeman at the front desk smiles. "Can I help you, sir?"

"Yes, my name is Jameson Miles, and I would like to hand myself in."

The policeman's face falters. "You are wanted?"

"I was involved in a fistfight with a man named Gabriel Ferrara and then went to the hospital. I was unaware until late last night that you were looking for me. My apologies for taking so long to get here."

The policeman smiles. "Thank you for coming in." He opens a door at the side of reception. "Please come this way."

Five hours later, I stand on the pavement outside the Ferrara building and look up to the top floors. I dial a number that I've had for years but have never called.

"Gabriel Ferrara," the deep voice answers.

"It's Jameson Miles. I'm out in front of your building. Get down here now."

I hang up and inhale deeply. I lean my behind on my limo.

After having spent the last five hours in the police station, I am not in the mood to wait for this prick, but I need to say what I need to say, or it's going to keep festering inside of me.

I told the police that my punch on Ferrara was self-defense and that they need to check the security footage. I'm not sure if it will stick, but it will give me some time. The police were actually okay and told me that seeing as he flicked the cigar at me first, I will probably only be charged with common assault and given a good behavior bond.

That, I can deal with.

Gabriel Ferrara appears through the front door, flanked by four security guards.

His eye is black and his cheekbone swollen. I smirk as I see his fucked-up face.

"You look like shit."

"Yeah, well, a madman attacked me," he mutters dryly.

I step forward as my anger resurfaces. "I know what you're doing."

He glares at me.

"You don't scare me. It's laughable how underhanded you have become."

He rolls his eyes. "Fuck off, Miles."

"If you think that underhanded criminal behavior can take down Miles Media, you can think again," I sneer.

He narrows his eyes.

"Miles Media has been the market leader for thirty years, and we will continue to dominate. Tell me, does your father know what you've stooped to?"

He lifts his chin in defiance. "Criminal behavior—what the hell are you talking about? That hit and run has left you delusional."

"You know exactly what I'm talking about."

We glare at each other; hate hangs in the air like poisonous pollution.

"I know what you're doing," I whisper.

His eyes hold mine.

"And as soon as I prove it, I'm going to fry your fucking ass in court."

"I'd like to see you try."

I stare at him as I remember how good it felt to hit this fucker. "Is your cheekbone broken?"

He glares at me, and I know it is.

"Let me tell you this—disrespect Emily Foster again, and next time . . . I won't just break your cheekbone. I *will* kill you," I sneer.

He raises his eyebrow as if surprised by my statement. "Is that a threat, Miles?"

"That's a fucking promise," I growl. "Leave her out of this."

I turn and get into my limo, and we pull away. I watch Gabriel Ferrara storm back into the building, flanked by his security.

The day I bring that asshole down is going to be a sweet victory.

I run down the street in the dark. It's just midnight. I haven't been here in a while, and for some reason, tonight I need to be.

Emily's apartment building.

I count the windows until I get to her apartment, and I stare up at it.

What's she doing?

Is she missing me as much as I'm missing her?

I get a vision of ringing the doorbell and asking to come up, and we would hug, and I would feel happy . . . like I used to.

But then I remember the hurt I felt last week when she lied to me, the out-of-control feeling that I have whenever I'm with her.

The way my enemies are using her to get to me, the way she's handing them the ammunition like candy.

And I know that nothing could bring me undone . . . except her.

She's my only weakness.

And weakness is something that I can't afford to have.

Not now, not ever.

I stare up at her apartment for a long time, and then with a heavy heart, I turn and begin the depressing run home.

I've never been so alone.

Emily

I stare at the coffee in front of me; the thought of drinking it turns my stomach. It's been four days since I got the dreaded four-word text from Jameson.

Move on, I have.

Four days is a long time to walk around with a broken heart . . . it's weak and barely clinging to life. I keep hoping and praying that he's going to come back with a grand gesture and hold his arms out, and I run into them, and this nightmare will all be forgotten.

If only that were true.

My mind is clouded with memories of the man I thought I knew. The hole in my life seems so large, and I just don't understand how you can fall so hard in love with someone in such a short period of time.

I should have stayed with Robbie, because in hindsight, Robbie was safe.

There was never a chance of him hurting me this deeply . . . but then, I wouldn't have met Jameson and found out what it was like to have this all-consuming love inside of me. No matter how it ended, I wouldn't trade that feeling for anything. Even if it was only mine for just a little while.

The only thing keeping me going at the moment is Molly and Aaron. They've been wonderful. Cheering me on from the sidelines, reminding me of why I came to New York in the first place. It would be so easy to run home right now with my tail between my legs.

"Are you going to eat the rest of that?" Molly gestures to my half-eaten sandwich.

I crinkle up my nose. "No, do you want it?"

"Just forget you ever met him, Em." Aaron sighs. "No man is worth this heartache."

I force out a weak smile. "He'll come back, Aaron. I know he will."

"You know you keep saying that, Em, but where is the fucking asshole?" Molly replies.

"He's just . . ." I shrug as I try to articulate my thoughts. "Lost at the moment."

"No, what he is is a self-absorbed fucking asshole," she huffs. "Good riddance, I say; you dodged a bullet."

There is absolutely no love lost between Aaron and Molly as far as Jameson is concerned. "Maybe." I sigh sadly.

"Come on; we have to get back." Aaron stands. "Lunch break is over."

We make our way back out onto the street and are walking toward the Miles Media building when Molly stops on the spot. "Fuck," she whispers.

"What?"

"Look."

We all glance up and see Jameson walking down toward us with a woman. He's in his customary navy suit and looking all immaculate, and they are deep in conversation.

"He's at work today?" I frown as I stare at him. I didn't even know he came back to work yet. He hasn't seen us and is talking as he walks. "Who's the woman?" I ask. She looks familiar, but I can't place her.

Molly grabs my arm with a sense of urgency. "Come on; let's go this way." She tries to pull me into a shop.

"Who's the woman?" I repeat as they get closer.

"Claudia Mason."

The air leaves my lungs . . . *his ex.*

He's with his ex?

I begin to hear my heartbeat in my ears as the ground sways beneath me.

"Let's go; we don't want him to see us," Molly urges as she grabs my arm once more. I pull out of her grip and stand strong.

As he gets to us, he glances up and sees me. His step falters, and then he clenches his jaw and doesn't make eye contact.

Tears well in my eyes as I watch him walk past.

He stops with his back to me, and I hold my breath.

Turn around . . . turn around.

After a moment, he falls back into stride beside the woman and disappears up the street without looking back.

A searing pain lurches through my chest as I fight tears. I drop my head in sadness.

There's my answer.

That's it . . . we're done.

It's Friday night, and I slide down in the seat of my rental car as I peer across the darkened street. I've completely thrown myself into solving the case, if not for any reason other than to distract me. I'm outside Hayden's apartment, and I know that I'm probably clutching at straws by being here, but what else am I going to do?

Crying and staring at the wall is getting old. A text comes through on my phone, and I glance down and see the letter *J*.

I read the text and nearly drop the phone in shock.

One last stop over.
JFK Airport. Sat, 8pm.

JFK Clubhouse Bar.
I need to see you.

J

xxx

I sit up. What?

He needs to see me . . . *he needs to see me?*

Hope blooms in my chest. Oh my God. I immediately call Molly.

"Hello," she answers.

"Jameson just texted me. He wants to meet tomorrow night!" I blurt out in a rush.

"What?" she snaps. "Did you tell him to go fuck himself?"

"No."

"Why not?"

"Because." I try to think of a perfect explanation. "Maybe seeing Claudia snapped him out of this, and I want to see him too, Moll. This is what I've been wanting all along."

"Oh God, can you hear yourself? Why would you want to see him? He's been a complete douchebag."

"I know, but he's been under so much stress, Molly. I just need to talk to him."

"For the record, I think this is a bad idea." She sighs.

I smile. She's wrong . . . this is a great idea. I text him back.

See you there.

x

I smile goofily out the windshield and look over to see Hayden talking to that same girl who used to work at Miles Media.

Lara Aspin . . . something is up with her too. I want to know more about her; so far, I've been unable to dig up anything, not

394

even an address. She finishes her conversation with Hayden and begins to walk down the street. My eyes flick between her and Hayden. Shit, what do I do?

I watch Hayden disappear into his building.

Well, I already know where Hayden lives. If I let her go, I may never find her again.

I really do need to know where she lives.

I watch her as she walks down the street. Damn it. I jump out of the car and cross the street and fall in behind her on the sidewalk.

She walks down the subway stairs, and I hesitate. It's dark, and God knows where she's going . . . shit.

I watch her disappear down the stairs, and I brace myself. Damn it. I have to follow her. We wait on the platform for a while, and then she gets onto a train, and I get on after her. I stand by the doors and stare out the window while I keep her in my peripheral vision.

Adrenaline is surging through my body, and I have to admit, this is actually kind of fun. I should have been a cop.

We go four stops, and then she gets up and stands by the door. The stop is Central Station, and I let out a sigh of relief—at least it's safe there.

We get off the train, and I drop back so she doesn't get suspicious. We walk, and we walk, and we walk . . . damn it, where is she going?

She disappears into a crowd, and I jump up to see if I can see her. I walk farther, and I can't see her. She's disappeared into thin air.

Damn it.

I turn and look back down the street we just came from. Where did she go?

I walk back a little way, and then I catch sight of her in a shop.

Thank God.

I duck in and then notice it's a pawnshop. I pretend to look at something in the back as she talks to the man on the desk.

"Well, it's not worth much," he says.

"I would like five hundred dollars for it. It's in perfect working order," she replies.

"You're dreaming. No way."

I peer through a gap in a bookcase and see a MacBook. Shit . . . she's selling her computer.

Why would she be selling a computer?

My mind begins to race as the two of them haggle over the price. The shop attendant wins in the end, and he hands over two hundred dollars. I watch her disappear out the door, and I wait for a moment and go to the desk.

"Hello." I smile casually.

"Hey," the overweight pawnshop man mutters as he counts his till up.

This may just be the craziest thing I've ever done, and I've done some pretty crazy things in my life. "I would like to buy that computer, please."

He frowns as he glances up. "What one?"

I point to the one she just sold him.

"Nah, I haven't cleaned it up yet. Go to the cabinet on the left, and find another one."

"No, it has to be that one."

"Not for sale yet. Come back in two days."

If I come back in two days, it will be wiped. "Name your price," I assert, feeling brave.

He stills, and his eyes come to mine. "A thousand dollars." He raises an eyebrow in a silent dare.

"You just paid two hundred for it—are you crazy?" I stammer.

He shrugs and goes back to what he's doing.

I stare at the computer on the desk, and I don't know why, but my gut is telling me to buy it. "Damn it, okay, fine. As it is, right now, for a thousand dollars."

He smiles a slimy grin. "Okay, honey."

I hand him over my mother's credit card, the one I have for emergencies . . . sorry, Mom.

I pay the thousand dollars and take the computer and walk out the front door.

My phone rings. Tristan's name lights up the screen. Perfect timing.

"Hello," I answer.

"Sorry I took so long to get back to you. That girl's name is Lara Aspin, and get this—she used to work in accounts," he blurts out.

"What does that mean?" I frown.

"She had access to the bank account details."

"Oh my God, Tristan," I whisper as I look around guiltily. "I just followed her on the train, and she sold her computer to a pawnshop, and I know this is crazy, but I just bought it for a thousand dollars."

"What? You have it? You actually have her computer?"

I smile proudly. "Uh-huh."

"Where are you? I'm coming to get you now."

I walk through the airport with my heart in my throat. I'm pulling my small carry-on suitcase so that I look the part of a tired traveler . . . or perhaps I'm just trying to pretend to myself that this isn't a bad idea.

Because I know it is; deep in my gut I know that I shouldn't be playing this dangerous game with him. I should be sitting down and having a civilized grown-up conversation.

But desperation has brought out my weakness, and I'm hoping that tonight Jameson and I can talk . . . and he can apologize and beg for me to come back, and then I can punish him, and we can begin to get back on track.

I haven't seen Claudia again, so I have no idea what is going on with her, but the fact that Jameson wanted to see me tonight tells me that it's nothing.

I hope it's nothing . . . God, I hope it's nothing . . . *stop it.*

I duck into the bathroom to give myself one last pep talk. I reapply my red lipstick, Jameson's personal favorite, and I stare at my reflection in the mirror. My long dark hair is out and wavy. I wanted to wear a dress but didn't want to seem too eager, so I finally decided to wear black fitted capri pants and a black silk shirt with the top button strategically undone. My black lace bra is just peeking through if I move the right way. I'm wearing his favorite fragrance and think I look sexy without trying to be sexy . . . is that even a thing?

God knows. I guess I'll soon find out.

Don't be needy . . . don't be whiny . . . and don't be overdramatic, I remind myself. Be sexy and alluring . . . like I was when we first met.

Right, I can do this.

I drop my shoulders, take a deep breath, and steel myself for the night ahead. This is literally a make-or-break situation. I need to remind him why he fell in love with me in the first place . . . how the hell has he forgotten?

That in itself is an issue . . . I close my eyes in disgust. *Stop overthinking this.*

I walk down the corridor and into the Clubhouse Bar. It's busy and bustling. I walk in and take a seat in the corner at a bench-seat table for two. If he wants to see me, then he can find me. I'm on a stopover and totally oblivious to anything around me.

I take out my laptop and open my emails.

"Can I get you a drink?" the waiter asks as he approaches my table.

"Yes, please." I smile as I hand him my credit card. "A top-shelf margarita, please."

He smiles and, with a cheeky wink, walks away. Damn it, that Jameson Miles has spoiled me. I seem to have an addiction to top-shelf shit, and it just rolls off my tongue a little too easy now.

I turn my attention back to read my emails and pretend that they're fascinating.

They're not.

And what I really want to be doing is giving this place the once-over with an eagle eye . . . is he here?

The waiter returns with my drink. "Here you are, a top-shelf margarita." He places it down onto the table. "And the gentleman at the bar asked that I deliver these to you." He places a large bowl of strawberries and a dipping bowl of hot chocolate on the table.

My eyes rise to where he gestures, and I see Jameson sitting at the bar. He's wearing dark denim jeans and a white shirt that I bought him. His dark hair is messed to perfection. Our eyes lock, and he raises his glass and then takes a sip.

My stomach rolls in excitement. He hasn't looked at me like that in a long time.

"Thank you," I reply to the waiter, completely distracted by the beautiful specimen at the bar.

I sip my margarita as I try to keep the goofy smile from my face, and I turn back to my emails to act uninterested.

Strawberries with hot chocolate; there's no way to eat them without slurping them up and looking like an animal.

I smirk . . . maybe that's what he wants?

Game on.

With my eyes locked onto my computer screen, I pick up a strawberry and dip it into the hot chocolate and lick it and then place it seductively in my mouth. I suck the chocolate and rub it back and forth over my lips.

I take a sip of my margarita and then repeat the move.

I smile to myself . . . what the actual hell am I doing? I'm in an airport bar when I'm not flying anywhere, pretending not to know someone while he watches me go down on a fucking strawberry. This really is beyond bizarre.

If Molly and Aaron could only see me now.

The waiter arrives with another margarita. "Compliments from your friend at the bar."

"Thank you." I keep my eyes down as I play the game and refuse to look at him.

Ten minutes later, I take the final sip of my margarita and allow my eyes to drift to the man at the bar; his dark eyes are on me, and heat blazes between us.

I know that look . . . *I'm going to fuck you . . . so damn good.*

I feel my arousal begin to thump, and with my eyes locked on his, I pick up a strawberry and lick it.

He stands as if summoned by my tongue. With our eyes locked, I suck, and he walks toward my table. "Mind if I take a seat?" his deep, sexy voice purrs.

"Not at all." My eyes drop to the bulge in his pants, and I raise my eyebrow.

"Don't judge." He smiles as he falls into the bench seat beside me. "I just watched the best damn strawberry porn that I've ever seen."

"Really?" I smirk. I feel the heat from his close proximity, and I have to fight not to lean toward him.

He holds out his hand. "I'm Jim."

My heart free-falls from my chest, *exactly like the first time.* I take his hand, and electricity shoots up my arm like an electric shock. "Hi, Jim. I'm Emily."

So we're playing that game, are we? Pretending we don't know each other. This really is like a stopover do-over. I'll do whatever it takes to break the ice between us.

With his elbows resting on the table, he steeples his hands under his chin. His eyes dance with mischief. "Where are you flying to, Emily?"

"London." I sip my drink. "You?"

"Dubai. My flight's been delayed."

"Mine too."

With locked eyes, we both sip our drinks. The air is electric, and regardless of the love that I have for this man, there is no denying that the sexual chemistry we have is out of this world.

"Thanks for the drink." I smile softly.

"You're welcome." His eyes are dark and hooded, and I can feel his arousal from here.

"What do you do for a living?" I ask.

"I'm a tour guide," he replies without hesitation.

"Really? What kind of tours do you run?"

"Camping."

I snort my drink up my nose as I giggle. "Oh." I cough. "So . . . you're the outdoor type?"

"Totally." He sips his margarita. "I'm at one with nature." He crosses his two fingers to show me just how close.

I try and fail to hide my broad smile. "That's good to know. Cavemen are such a turn-on."

His eyes dance with delight; he likes this game.

I do too.

"What do you do?" he asks.

"I'm a psychic."

He bursts out laughing. Oh, it feels good to see him laugh again. "A psychic?" His eyes widen in surprise.

"Yes."

"So . . . you read minds?"

"I do."

"All right." He looks around the bar and gestures to a woman with his drink. "Tell me what that woman's saying over there."

I look over and see an older woman who looks like she is scolding her husband as he drinks his beer. "She's telling him that he had better hurry up and put on his compression socks before the flight and that he's had enough. They won't let him on the plane if he's drunk."

"Hmm." He smirks as he looks around. "What about him?"

I look over to the man who is looking at his phone. "He's googling prostitutes for his business trip."

"And him?"

"Wondering if his wife is sleeping with her boss."

His smile broadens. "You're good."

I cock my head. "I know."

"And her?"

I look over at a girl staring at her phone with a worried look on her face.

"Googling fungal infections. She's worried that she caught something from her wild and condomless Saturday night."

His eyes dance in delight as he looks around the bar, and then his eyes come back to meet mine. "What about me?"

"What are you thinking?"

"Yes."

Our eyes lock . . . shit, I promised myself that I wouldn't be a drama queen tonight, and that is a surefire question to wind me up. I could go to town on what a jackass he's been . . . and I will later. "Right now?" I ask.

"Yes." His eyes are dark as he watches me.

"It's good to see you."

He gives me a slow, sexy smile and leans toward me. "It is." He cups my face in his hand, and my heart stops. "Although that wasn't all I was thinking."

"No," I breathe. "I know."

He smiles as if fascinated, our faces only millimeters apart. "Why don't you tell me what else I was thinking?" His eyes drop to my lips.

"You were wondering what the chocolate on my lips tastes like," I whisper. How am I supposed to string two words together when he's looking at me like that?

In slow motion, he leans in and licks my open lips. My sex clenches in appreciation.

Oh God . . .

"Are you flirting with me, Jim?" I whisper.

He licks me again. "I am. How am I doing?"

Goose bumps scatter up my spine, and I swallow the lump in my throat. "Okay."

"Just okay?"

I nod, breathless from his touch.

"What about when I do this?" In slow motion he kisses me; his strong tongue slides through my open mouth and tenderly caresses mine.

"That could probably work," I murmur against his lips.

"And this?" His kiss deepens, and I feel my arousal waken from its dormant sleep.

I close my eyes as emotion rushes through me . . . this is not good. One kiss, and I'm about to burst into tears.

How could you treat me so badly?

Don't be a wimp . . . I need to keep my emotions in check . . . at least for now.

Tomorrow is a different story, but tonight is about celebrating what we have with each other.

I pull out of his kiss. "I don't know what kind of woman you think I am, Jim, but I can assure you—picking up camping tour directors in an airport bar is not my style." I sit back and straighten my shirt and sip my margarita.

He rolls his lips as if amused with the game and picks my hand up and brings it to his lips. He begins to kiss it, and then he turns it over and, with his strong tongue, licks the palm of my hand.

My sex clenches in appreciation . . . *fuck*. I'm losing control of this situation.

Fast.

I glance over and see two girls sitting near us, transfixed and watching him with their mouths hanging open.

What must we look like? A gorgeous man sitting here making out with my hand while I act totally uninterested. *Act* being the operative word.

"You're making a scene," I murmur as I watch him.

"I can't help it," he murmurs against my skin. "It's been too long."

"How long?" I ask.

"Fifteen days." He kisses my hand again. "Fifteen long days."

That's how long we've been apart . . . he knows how long we've been apart to the day. He wants to break the ice between us too. He's missed me; I know he has. Suddenly I don't want to play hard to get. I want him . . . hard . . . and fast.

I pull my hand away from his lips. "Buy me another drink, and then perhaps I'll put you out of your misery."

His eyes flicker with arousal, and his hand immediately goes up as he summons the waiter. "Yes, sir."

"Two—"

"Four," I interrupt him. He frowns, probably deterred by the extra time it's going to take to drink those.

"Four margaritas, please," he replies to the waiter.

"Yes, sir."

"Please make it fast," he adds.

The waiter frowns at his apparent desperation. "Yes, sir, of course." He rushes to the bar.

We stare at each other as electricity thrums between us—no words are needed. We both can feel this magnetic pull to each other; it's too strong to deny.

"It really . . . is good to see you, Em," he whispers.

An hour later we walk down the hotel corridor, hand in hand. We are both quiet, lost in our own thoughts.

My heart is beating so fast, and I know what's about to happen . . . I'm looking forward to what's about to happen.

He opens the door and leads me into the penthouse. I look around and am instantly reminded of who I'm with. It's easy for me to forget his wealth, but it never goes away. The door closes behind us, and he turns me to him. We stare at each other, and then he wraps his arms around me and holds me tight as he puts his head into the crook of my neck. He holds me and holds me . . . as if scared to let me go.

The love between us is palpable—so much emotion . . . so much regret—and I find myself tearing up.

I want to blurt out that I love him, that he hurt me, and that I'm angry, but I want to let the moment just be. Let the feelings between us speak for themselves; words seem irrelevant to what's between us.

He pulls back, and his eyes search mine. "I've missed you," he whispers.

I cup his face in my two hands, and I kiss him long and slow and just how he likes it.

He smiles against my lips as he slowly unbuttons my shirt and throws it to the side. He takes off my bra and cups my breasts. His thumbs dust back and forth over my hardened nipples. Our lips are locked, and he undoes my pants and slides them down and takes them off.

He drops to his knees, and I hold my breath as he slides my panties down my legs and takes them off.

He leans in and inhales my sex deeply; his eyes close in pleasure as he kisses me there.

Oh . . . I've missed him.

I think back to the first night we had together on our stopover, and it was so different to this. His touch back then was filled with lust; his touch now is filled with adoration and love.

He lifts my leg over his shoulder and licks me in my most private part, the one that nobody but he knows. My hands instinctively go to the back of his head.

This is insane. I haven't touched him once, and he's on his knees in front of me, completely dressed . . . having the time of his life.

His tongue finds a rhythm, and my body begins to move by itself, guiding his tongue just where.

I begin to shudder, and I close my eyes to try and block him out. He's been touching me for all of four minutes, and I'm about to come . . . *hold it.*

My knees go weak, and I shudder against him, and I feel him smile into me. He laps me up and lays me on the bed. He arranges me how he wants me and spreads my legs open for his gaze. "So . . . fucking perfect," he whispers to himself.

With urgency, he tears his shirt over his head and slides his jeans down. His cock hangs heavy and hard between his legs.

He's so beautiful . . . the perfect male specimen.

I smile up at him, and then he goes to his pocket and takes out a condom. Uneasiness fills me. "What are you doing?"

"I want you more than once, and I don't want to lose the sensitivity."

I frown as I watch him roll it on . . . that's weird; in the past he always made me roll them on him as if he was unable to.

He lies beside me on the bed and runs his fingers through my hair as he looks down at me. I can't read him tonight at all. He seems . . . intense.

"You're seeming very sentimental tonight, Mr. Miles," I whisper.

"Maybe I am."

I reach out and cup his face in my hand. He seems so lost. "Are you all right?"

"Tonight I am." He leans down and kisses me, and I can feel the emotion behind it. It's as if he's channeling all his love through his lips, and I lose all coherent thought.

He lies over me, and our bodies take on an agenda of their own as they writhe together.

Our kiss turns frantic, and he lifts one of my legs and slides in deep. I feel the stretch of his possession; there's no forgetting his size. It's unapologetic.

We both moan in pleasure, and he slides out and slowly back in. I'm wet, so wet, and the sound of my arousal hangs in the air.

"Jesus fucking Christ, Emily," he whispers as he loses control and slams in hard, knocking the air from my lungs.

And then we're hard at it. The bed is hitting the wall with force; our eyes are locked on each other's . . . silent . . . and in awe. This is a higher level of frequency.

Our bodies were made to fit together. *We* were made to fit together.

He screws up his face as if in pain. "I can't hold it, babe," he pants.

I smile. I love that he can't hold it. "Let go," I breathe against his lips. "We have all night. Give me everything."

I roll over and feel the dull ache deep inside, and I wince.

Oh man . . . my body is wrecked.

Jameson Miles fucked me all night long. Hard and every which way, and today I'm going to pay for it. I turn toward him. He's lying on his side, perched on his elbow, watching me. "Hi." I smile softly, embarrassed by what he must have seen.

"Hi." He leans in and kisses me before taking me in his arms and holding me tight.

"I'm sore," I whisper.

"That makes two of us." He smirks.

I close my eyes against his chest, and we lie in peaceful bliss for another half hour, dozing.

I get up to go to the bathroom and notice the trash can full of condoms . . . hmm, he wore condoms all night. I didn't notice at the time.

I get back into bed beside him and snuggle back against his chest. "Why did you wear condoms last night?"

I feel his body stiffen beneath me, and I instantly know it was purposeful. He stays silent.

"Jim?" I frown as I sit up.

"Don't." He goes to pull me back down onto his chest. "Let's just have a nice morning together."

I stare at him. "Why would you wear condoms when I know how much you hate them?"

He exhales heavily as if annoyed and gets out of bed. "I don't want any accidents."

"What?"

He exhales heavily as if frustrated.

I sit up. "You think I would trap you by getting pregnant?"

He rolls his eyes.

"What the hell?" I snap as I jump out of bed. "Are you serious?"

"We're not together, Emily. I would have to be a fucking idiot to not take precautions."

My face falls. "What was last night?"

His eyes hold mine. "It was goodbye."

"What?" I can feel the tears of shock welling in my eyes.

"Don't be upset," he stammers.

"Don't be upset?" I cry as I begin to lose control. "You summoned me here to meet you with absolutely no intention of us getting back together?"

He stares at me.

"Is that true?" I yell.

"I'm not the man for you, Emily," he replies calmly, and I know that this is a practiced speech.

I frown as the walls begin to close in around me. "What?" I whisper.

"You're in love with Jim."

I angrily swipe the tears as they roll down my cheeks.

"I'm Jameson. Jim doesn't exist, Emily. He's a figment of your imagination, the man you want me to be."

"What the fuck are you talking about?" I cry.

"You're better off without me."

"If this is about Jake—" I stammer.

"This isn't about Jake, although I'm fucking furious with you for lying to me."

"I swear to you that nothing happened," I cry.

"I know it didn't."

"Then why?" I whisper. "I don't understand. We belong together, Jay."

"I can't." He closes his eyes and pauses for a moment as if steeling himself to push the words past his lips. "I don't want marriage and babies. I don't want the same things as you. I'm not cut out to do normal, Emily. I'm married to my job. It will never change. I've thought long and hard about this."

I step back from him as horror dawns. I can hear my own heartbeat in the silence.

"I will always love you," he whispers.

I stare at him through tears . . . what the fuck is happening right now?

He brushes past me and goes into the bathroom, and the door closes. I stare at a piece of carpet on the floor, shocked to my core. After the beautiful night we had together . . . this is how he treats me?

He reappears fully dressed, and his eyes find mine. "Can I give you a lift somewhere?"

"If you walk out that door now, we are over forever," I whisper.

His eyes hold mine. "I know." He steps forward and kisses me softly as he cups my face in his hands. Our faces screw up against each other's. "This is for the best; another man can make you happier."

I step back, furious. "Don't you dare throw that shit at me."

"Do you want a lift or not?"

"Go to hell," I spit.

His haunted eyes hold mine. "I'm already there." He turns and walks out the door. It clicks quietly behind him.

I sob out loud into the silence as I hold my poor heart.

Chapter 23

I sit on the carpet cross-legged, with my back resting against the couch, and flick my phone. I watch it spin until it slows in momentum, and I spin it again.

It's been a weird day today—one of realization and the closing of a chapter in my life.

I'm not crying. I don't have any tears left for Jameson Miles.

To be honest, I'm just angry, mostly with myself for meeting him last night and being his puppet once again.

Magic Mike XXL is on Netflix, and I'm watching it again. It's ironic, really, that we started our love affair watching this movie, and now I'm watching it again on our demise.

I've been deep in thought. I've got some decisions to make—big decisions.

About where I'm going with my life . . . my career and my future at Miles Media.

I already know what I need to do. I glance up to the television, and it's a campfire scene on the beach, and the men are talking about a woman one of them loved.

"When someone shows themselves to you . . . believe them."

My chest constricts at the significance of that statement.

For weeks now, I've refused to believe that Jameson Miles was coldhearted.

He is, though; no matter how the man I thought I knew presented himself . . . his reality is a lie.

"Jim doesn't exist," he said.

My phone rings, and the name *Tristan* lights up the screen. I frown. "Hello."

"Oh my God, Em. They think they've found it."

I sit up. "What?"

"Lara Aspin's computer—there's evidence on there that it was used to log in to our bank accounts."

"What?" I whisper, wide eyed.

"We don't have details yet, but the computer analysts just called to let us know that the history is very promising."

I smile. "That's great."

"I'll see you in the office in the morning? Come up to the top floor as soon as you get in."

"Yeah, sure." I pause on the line. "Hey, thanks for letting me know."

"See you in the morning," he says chirpily down the line.

I hang up and, with a sad smile, stare into space for a moment. I get up and open my laptop at the kitchen table, and I begin to type.

I believe you, Jameson . . . I finally believe you.

"Oh my God, Em, did you hear?" Aaron smiles happily as he spins on his chair toward me.

I've just arrived at work for the morning and put my handbag down onto the desk. "What?"

"The headlines today say that they have made an arrest over the embezzlement."

"Really?" I fake a smile. "That's great." I look around. "Is Moll here yet?"

"No, she'll be here soon." He turns on his computer.

"Okay, I'll be back in a moment." I take the envelope from my bag and swipe my card to get to the top floor. Funnily enough, it works today.

The doors open, and Sammia smiles broadly as if she's happy to see me. "Good morning, Emily."

"Hi." I look around. "Is Tristan here?"

"Yes, he's in Jameson's office. Just go through."

My stomach drops. "Okay, thank you." I walk across the tiles and make a mental note of the sound. My shoes don't click on the tiles anymore, and I think back to a time when they did. I look out over the view and take a picture in my mind. I do love this building—so many exciting memories of when I started coming up to this floor. I knock on the door and hear Jameson's strong voice. "Come in."

Here we go.

I swallow my nerves and open the door, and Tristan's face lights up. "Here she is. The hero of the day."

"Hi." My eyes find Jameson's across the room.

"Hi." He dips his head as if ashamed.

"The evidence is all on the computer, Em." Tristan beams. "You did it; you solved the case. I don't know why you kept following her, but boy, am I glad that you did."

"Happy I could help."

"Thank you." Jameson frowns as if pained. "I'm very grateful for your dedication to solving the case."

Tristan looks between us and must sense the tension between us. "I'm going to leave you two alone. We need to celebrate . . .

413

tonight," he calls as he rushes from the room in an excited flurry. It must be such a relief to him to have the case against Jameson coming to an end.

I close my eyes. Damn it, just get this over with. I hand Jameson the envelope, and he stares at it in his hand. "What's this?" he asks.

"My letter of resignation."

He frowns as his eyes hold mine. "No, Em." He shakes his head. "I can't accept this."

Emotion overwhelms me, and I blink so that I don't cry. "I can't work here, Jameson."

"You love Miles Media—working here was your dream," he whispers.

"No. You're wrong. I loved you . . . and you were my dream. I've taken a position with Athena, the place I did my internships. I start next Monday."

His eyes search mine. "Em . . ."

A tear escapes onto my cheek, and I wipe it away with a nervous smile. "You know, I watched *Magic Mike XXL* last night."

He listens.

"And there was this poignant line that finally made everything make sense to me."

"Which was?"

"When someone shows themselves to you . . . believe them."

He frowns, not understanding.

"I finally believe you, Jameson."

"Believe what?"

"That you're a coward."

He clenches his jaw.

"That you're too scared to love me."

Our eyes are locked, and an undercurrent of anger runs between us.

"And I deserve someone who knows that I'm worth the risk."

He clenches his jaw as he watches me.

"You're just not brave enough to love me."

"That's not fair," he whispers.

"No." I shake my head softly. "Falling in love with you is what isn't fair. I never stood a chance . . . you knew that all along. You keep your heart in a tightly sealed Miles-High icebox, only to be looked at."

His face falls, and I turn and walk from his office. I close the door quietly on my way out, and I stare at it for a moment as I gather the gumption to walk out of his office for the last time. In a strange kind of irony, this has been the best and worst time of my life.

Goodbye, Mr. Miles.

I will always miss you.

With a tight chest, I watch Emily leave the office. The door clicks closed, and the walls begin to close in around me.

On autopilot, I pour myself a scotch and walk to the window. I stare out over New York as I fight an overwhelming sense of sadness.

She's gone.

Knock, knock. Tristan appears and smiles broadly as he sees my drink. "We celebrating already?"

"Seems that way."

He looks around. "Where's Emily?"

"She left." I sip my scotch and feel the warmth of the amber fluid. I stare at it in the glass. "She resigned. Effective immediately."

"What?" His face falls. "You can't be serious."

"It's for the best."

"What the fuck? How is it for the best?"

"We were never going to work, Tris; you knew that." I pause. "There's always going to be an asshole like Ferrara prepared to step on her to bring me down. I don't want her dragged through the mud any further."

"Is that what you're telling yourself?" he huffs.

I stare out the window.

"I don't fucking get you, man; you're madly in love with her. Why are you really letting her go?"

I pause as I contemplate his question. "She deserves better than the life I can give her."

"Fuck off," he scoffs. "She couldn't get a better life than the one you could give her. She would never want for anything."

"It's not the money she wants," I mutter dryly.

"What does she want?"

"Things . . ." I frown as I try to articulate my thoughts. "Things . . . I'm incapable of giving her."

"Like what?"

"Time."

He stares at me, lost. "But you committed to Claudia no problem."

I raise my eyebrows as I sip my scotch.

"What does that mean?"

"I didn't care if Claudia was waiting at home for me. I didn't care how much time I spent away from her. I could travel, work, focus . . . I was content to put her fourth or fifth in line, and she never expected anything different." I exhale heavily. I feel the weight of the world on my shoulders. "Claudia was easy."

"Because you didn't really love her?"

I shrug, unable to put a label on my feelings.

He puts his hand on my shoulder. "You're more than a CEO, Jameson. You deserve to be happy too. Why do you think it has to be one or the other?"

I frown, pained.

"Don't let the love of your life walk away because you're scared that you're going to lose her."

"It's inevitable, Tristan . . . eventually, *she* will leave. Her hand will be forced."

"And then what will you be?" he snaps. "A lonely, stressed-out, alcoholic CEO?"

My eyes rise to meet his.

"Oh, wait." He gestures to my drink. "That's already happening." He shakes his head in disgust. "When I find my woman, I'll move heaven and hell to keep her."

"Get out." I sigh. "You have no idea what you're fucking talking about."

"Actually, I'm kind of glad I'm getting to watch you fuck up your life," he calls as he walks toward the door. "Now I know what *not* to do."

I sip my scotch as the door slams hard behind him.

My buzzer on my desk sounds, and I push the button. "Yes, Sammia."

"The detectives are here to see you, sir."

I drain my glass . . . good, a distraction. "Thank you, send them in."

"A toast." Molly smiles as she holds her glass up.

Aaron and I hold our glasses up to touch hers.

"To new beginnings."

"To new beginnings," we all repeat.

"You're going to be great." Aaron smiles. "You watch—you'll be taking over the news floor within no time."

We're out to dinner in a bar and celebrating. I start my new job tomorrow. It's been a week since I left Miles Media.

Feels like a lifetime ago.

I was going to go home and see my parents, but I just didn't have the mental energy. I stayed home for some self-love instead. I needed time alone to lick my wounds and heal. I had a few massages, got some Reiki done to calm my heartache, ate healthy, and went for two runs a day to exhaust myself so that my body had no choice but to sleep at night.

I'm okay . . . empty, but doing okay.

I've stopped reading the paper so that I don't have to see his name. On my runs, I go the other way so I don't have to see the Miles Media building or restaurants or anything that would remind me of him or our time together.

Him . . .

I can't even bring myself to say his name.

He's been put into the vault, and nobody dares mentioning him to me. It's like he never existed . . . and maybe he never did.

"What are you wearing tomorrow?" Molly asks as she cuts into her steak.

"I thought my navy suit." I chew my food. "I want to look professional and smart."

"No gray skirt?" Aaron smirks.

I wipe my mouth with my napkin. "I threw that fucker out."

"What?" Molly shrieks. "I loved that skirt! I would have had it."

"That was a troublemaking skirt," I reply. "Trust me; you don't want that kind of negativity in your life."

"Here, here." Aaron lifts his glass, and we clink again.

"Michael asked me out on a date on Saturday night," Molly says casually.

My knife and fork hit the plate with a clang as my eyes rise to meet hers. "What?"

She shrugs. "I don't know what to make of it, really."

"Did he ask you out for a casual dinner? Are you sure it's a date?" Aaron frowns.

"No, his exact words were, 'Would you like to come out on a date on Saturday night?'"

I smile. "Are you going to go?"

"I don't know." She sighs. "So much water has passed under the bridge between us. We've just got to a place of trust and friendship again. I don't want to ruin it."

"By fucking him?" Aaron smirks as he bites into his food.

"Well, if I did fuck him, and he didn't use double Viagra on me, I would be mortally offended. I know what tricks he has in his toolbox now."

We all giggle.

"God, that night was funny," I add, remembering him passing out from all the blood in his dick.

Molly rolls her eyes. "For you, maybe."

We fall silent as we eat.

"Good luck for tomorrow, babe," Aaron says.

"Thanks, guys." I smile. "You are the best two things about New York."

"God, you're so right," Molly mutters into her glass. "And these margaritas." She raises her glass to show me. "So should I go out with Mike?"

"Yes," Aaron and I gasp. "Go."

"Emily." Athena smiles as she wraps her arms around me. "It's so good to see you. Welcome."

"Hi." I smile nervously.

"You're going to love it here." She pulls me through the office by the hand. "Here is your office."

I smile, surprised. "I get my own office?"

"Of course you do."

I look around the little office. It's definitely no management top floor, but it suits me just fine. There's a window and a desk and a chair in the corner. It's kind of homey. I turn to her. "Thank you for taking me on. I am so grateful."

Athena smiles and rubs my arm. When I called her asking for a job, she never once asked what happened with Miles Media or my relationship with Jameson. But I know that she knows that I'm probably broken with nowhere else to go, and running home with my tail between my legs isn't an option.

She's right.

I'm going to make it up to her; I'm going to be the best damn reporter that she has ever had.

"I'll leave you to it." She smiles. "Staff meeting at ten to introduce you to everyone. We have welcome doughnuts."

I smile. "Thanks, that would be great."

She disappears down the corridor, and I take a seat at my new desk and look around the lonely space.

I miss Molly and Aaron . . . and the buzz of Miles Media.

"With this projection here, the forecast is a growth of ten percent over the next eighteen months." Harrison from finance taps the graph on the projector whiteboard as he addresses the board meeting.

The table is alive with chatter and enthusiasm. The comeback strategy from the drama over the last four months is alive and well.

Me . . . I'm miles away.

I can't concentrate . . . I can't think . . . I feel like I can't breathe.

Maybe I'm not okay.

Emily started her new job today, and I wanted to call her and wish her luck.

I couldn't sleep thinking about it and even picked up the phone a few times. I drop my head.

But what's the point . . .

I wonder if she ran this morning. Did she wear her runners that she said have motors on them? I smile softly to myself as I remember Elliot thinking I was talking about Zuckerberg having the motorized runners.

Idiot . . .

I twist in my chair to stretch my back. I need a massage.

Emily doesn't like me getting massages. I think back to the kind of massages I used to get, and it seems like another lifetime ago.

BE—Before Emily . . . *stop it.*

"Jameson will be addressing that in the morning."

I look up, lost. What are they talking about?

The board members around the table all stare at me as they wait for my reply. My eyes flick to Tristan for guidance.

"When you fly to Seattle tonight." He raises his eyebrows as a gentle reminder.

"Yes." I nod. "That's right."

Tristan is limping me through work at the moment, well aware of my state of mind.

The meeting continues, and I sip my water to try and bring my mind back to where it needs to be. This isn't good enough, Jameson.

Focus.

I walk onto the plane.

"Good evening, Mr. Miles. Your seat is here, sir. 1A."

"Thank you." I fall into the seat in the front row of first class.

The plane slowly boards, and I stare out the window. Flying never used to bother me. I hate it now.

I hate that it reminds me of her . . . of how we met. Of the night we had together.

Of how badly things turned out in the end.

With my elbow leaning on the armrest, I pinch the bridge of my nose. I just want to get there and go to my hotel and sleep. I'm tired and not in the mood for this shit.

"Can I get you anything, Mr. Miles?"

"Scotch, please."

An elderly man takes the seat next to me. He nods. "Hello."

"Hi." I smile. I turn my attention out the window to the baggage crew down on the tarmac, all doing their job and rushing around doing the safety checks.

They're driving on carts, flashing lights, and waving flags.

I wouldn't even care if the plane fucking crashed.

Burning in hell would be better than this.

Four days later

I smile at Alan as he stands next to the limo at the airport. "Hello, sir. Did you have a nice trip?"

"It was fine; thank you." I smile as I get into the back seat.

"Would you like to do the normal route, sir?" he asks through the door.

"Yes, please."

He smiles. "Very well." He shuts the door, and moments later, the car pulls out into the traffic.

Half an hour later, he slows down as we drive past Emily's apartment, and I peer through the window.

Is she there?

We do this every night on the way home—my own stupid way of saying good night to her . . . if I don't, I end up running back here later.

Who am I kidding? I run back here most nights anyway. I hold my breath as we drive past, hoping to catch a glimpse of her . . . I've never seen her once.

My heart drops; she's not here.

I look back through the back window as we disappear down the street.

Emily . . . where are you?

Emily

I sit on the bus on my way home from work and read my Kindle. It's dark and just around six o'clock in the evening. I'm happier . . . stronger. I've been at my new job for three weeks, and I love it. I did the right thing. People are all really lovely, and thankfully, I'm not the office gossip anymore, and I have a more integral role than I did at Miles Media. I still see Molly and Aaron all the time for drinks and dinner, and I've planned to go home for the weekend.

I'm running a lot . . . funnily enough I don't need to pretend a man with an ax is chasing me. I'm so angry that I can't help but sprint.

Gleeful jogging is no longer in my repertoire. The bus slows. I close my Kindle and stand as I wait for the bus to stop. I climb down the steps and begin to walk the two blocks to my apartment. The season is getting colder. Fog puffs as I breathe, and I wrap my large coat around me for warmth as I stride it out.

I might have Indian for dinner. *No . . . stick to your budget; there are leftovers in the fridge from last night.* I approach my building and fumble around in my bag for my keys.

"Hello, Em," a voice says from behind me.

I turn, startled. Jameson stands before me, and the sight of him tightens my chest. "What are you doing here?"

His eyes search mine. "I had to see you."

The sight of him brings an unexpected wave of emotion that I previously thought I had under control. I stare at him through tears.

He carefully steps forward. "How are you?"

Suddenly, I'm furious . . . like a raging bull, and I drop my head and fumble through my bag. I need to get away from him.

Where are my fucking keys? "Fine," I snap. I find my keys and turn toward the door.

"I miss you."

I stop and close my eyes.

"I can't . . ." He pauses. "I can't move on until I know we're okay."

I frown and turn back toward him.

His face is pained, and he appears nervous.

Our eyes are locked, mine filled with tears . . . his with regret. He turns back and looks at his car, which I didn't notice parked in the dark. "I brought you something."

He nearly runs to the car and then retrieves a huge bouquet of yellow roses and walks back and passes them to me.

I stare at him in confusion. "Yellow roses?"

He smiles softly. "Yellow roses are supposed to symbolize friendship."

"You want to be my friend?"

He nods hopefully. "We can start fresh?"

Something snaps deep inside of me. "You've got a fucking nerve," I sneer.

His face falls.

"You waltz back here after breaking my fucking heart and give me yellow fucking roses!" I scream.

He steps back, shocked by my venom.

"I wouldn't be friends with a selfish prick like you if you were the last fucking person on earth!" I yell as the angry tears run down my face. I completely lose control and start ripping the roses to shreds, and I break the heads and smash them up and then throw them on the ground and jump and stomp on them. I want to hurt these stupid roses like he's hurt me.

His haunted eyes watch on.

Adrenaline is coursing through my body, and still unsatisfied with the state of the roses, I pick them up and walk out to the road and throw them as hard as I can out onto the asphalt. A passing bus runs them over.

"That's what you can do with your friendship," I sneer as I stomp past him.

I open the door and walk into the building without looking back. I hit the elevator button with force, and I can see him standing at the glass door, watching me, in my peripheral vision. Tears are streaming down my face, and I'm furious that I let him see how crazy I am.

How crazy he's made me.

The elevator doors open, and I march in and hit the door button.

The doors close, and I screw up my face in tears and sob out loud.

Damn you, Jameson Miles . . .

Chapter 24

There are moments in your life that you know you will remember forever.

Certain situations that are poignant and have shaped who you are.

Last night was one of them.

What kind of psycho rips roses to shreds with her bare hands while screaming like a lunatic? Shame runs through me.

This . . . is the level I've stooped to.

Strangely enough, last night was the first time I've slept well in weeks. As if releasing a little of the steam in the pressure cooker has somehow calmed my soul.

I don't feel guilty for being so mean . . . normally, I would. But Jameson Miles is an enigma all of his own . . . one that I can no longer pity.

"I wouldn't be friends with a selfish prick like you if you were the last person left on earth," I said . . . screamed actually. It was a mean thing to say—the worst—but he got what he fucking deserved. The doors of the elevator in my building open, and I step out into the foyer and walk out into the street.

"What the hell happened here?" I hear the woman in front of me mutter under her breath as she stops and looks around at the carnage.

There are yellow rose petals strewn everywhere; flower buds that are squashed and bruised lie on the concrete. Out on the road the carcass of the flattened bouquet with the big cream satin bow lies.

Jesus . . .

I drop my head and stomp past the crazy. I glance up at the ceiling to see where the cameras are. I wonder if anyone saw it on the security footage.

I hope not . . . how embarrassing.

I get on my bus and open my Kindle. I'm not reading my usual rom-com genre. I can't stand the thought of all that love bullshit. I'm mixing it up and reading *Pet Sematary*—maybe that's it. Maybe Steven King is taking me to the dark side. The side where you don't take shit, and payback on yellow roses is due.

Good for him . . . bring it the fuck on. I swipe to the next page.

Every dog has its day.

I sip my coffee as I sit in the café across the street from Miles Media. I've been coming here the last few days before work. Alan told me that Emily used to come here with her friends. I'm hoping to run into one of them.

Why? I don't know.

Emily's words from last night are playing over and over in my mind.

I wouldn't be friends with a selfish prick like you if you were the last person on earth . . . I wouldn't want to be friends with me either if I were her.

I've never seen her so angry . . . or thin. She's lost a lot of weight. I hate that I've put her through this shit.

I sip my coffee, and I feel a hand rest on my shoulder.

"Hey," Tristan says as he sits down beside me on a stool.

"Hi."

"Looking for Emily?" he says casually.

"Nope."

"Liar," he replies with a cheeky grin. "Hey, the boys and I have organized a trip to Vegas for us this weekend. The jet's all lined up."

I screw up my face. I could think of nothing worse.

"It'll be great. Drinking, gambling. Add some beautiful women to the Miles-High Club. You need to snap out of this and get back on the horse. I'm thinking a blonde or two . . . forget about the brunettes for a while, and besides, we need to celebrate your innocence. Elliot and Christopher fly in on Friday." He winks as he tries to sweeten the deal.

"Yeah, that sounds completely shit," I mutter dryly.

"I don't care what you say. You're coming."

I stare straight ahead. I've lost the ability to get excited about anything lately.

He falls serious. "I'm worried about you, Jay."

I roll my eyes.

"We all are. You're acting completely out of character."

"I'm fine," I murmur into my coffee. I look around once more, remembering why I'm here.

"Why don't you just go to her house if you want to see her?" he says.

"I tried that last night."

"How did it go?"

I puff air into my cheeks. "She went postal and . . ." I pause as I try to explain the situation. "I took her yellow roses, and she smashed the fuck out of them like a madman."

"Yeah?" He smirks and then smiles broadly as if impressed. "Why would you take her yellow roses and not red ones?"

"I thought . . ." I exhale heavily. "I thought yellow was safe, signifying friendship so that she would talk to me. I just wanted to talk to her."

"You didn't tell her that, though, did you?"

"Yeah."

He gives a subtle shake of the head as if I'm stupid. "How did that go down?"

"That's about the time she turned into the Hulk."

"I don't blame her, to be honest."

My eyes flick to him in question.

"You well and truly fucked her over."

"I did not fuck her over," I spit. "I'm trying to protect her."

"Listen, you can lie to yourself all you want to. But don't bother lying to me. You're a bad liar . . . the worst."

"Fuck off, man; it's too early for this shit." I sigh.

"Tristan," the girl behind the counter calls. He stands and gets his coffee and slaps me on the back. "You staying here, being a miserable prick?"

"Fuck off," I grunt. He smiles and leaves without another word.

I exhale heavily and stare back down at my coffee. I get a vision of the hurt on Emily's face last night, and my chest constricts. I keep going over and over it in my mind, and I just want to know that she's all right. Maybe then I can forgive myself and stop thinking about her every minute of every day. I take out my phone. I'll call her.

No, she will only hang up. I'll text . . . what will I write?

Good morning.
Murder any roses today?

I hit send and wait. I drink my coffee and stare at my phone as I wait for her to reply . . . she doesn't.

Twenty minutes later, I text her again.

Please talk to me.

I order another coffee as I wait. It's 8:15 a.m., and I know she hasn't started work yet. I also know that she would have her phone on her and is purposely ignoring my texts.

Fuck this. I dial her number, and it rings . . . I close my eyes as I wait.

It rings and then declines.

Fuck. She hit reject.

I text her.

Answer your phone or I'm coming over there.

My text doesn't go through . . . huh? I call again, and the call won't connect. What's going on? I try again . . . nothing. For ten minutes, I continue to try to get through. I can't. What's going on?

I type into Google, "Why can't I text or call someone?" The answer bounces back that cuts to the bone.

"You've been blocked."

She blocked my number? *What the fuck?*

Anger surges through me; nobody has ever blocked me before. Not in business or personal . . . and never a woman.

She really doesn't want to be friends with me . . . in any shape or form.

My heart sinks. How the hell did I fuck this up so badly?

I stare at the Miles Media building through the window, and the thought of going there today and playing the facade that everything's okay is just too much.

I text Tristan.

I'm taking the day off.
See you tomorrow.

I sit and finish my coffee, and a song comes on—"Bad Liar" by Imagine Dragons.

I listen . . . Tristan just called me a bad liar, and ironically, the lyrics ring true. With a sad damnation to hell, I drag myself out of the café and into a cab.

"Where to?" the cab driver asks.

"Park Avenue."

The cab pulls out into the traffic, and I put my headphones in, hit Spotify, and listen to the song again.

"Bad Liar" . . . my new anthem.

433

I flick through the travel images on Google. I'm going to take a skiing trip.

Switzerland, I think.

I need to get away. New York is just too small . . . or suffocating . . . or life threatening . . . or something that I just can't quite put my finger on. Either way, I'm getting the hell out of here.

She blocked me.

I might work from London for a while . . . yeah, I could do that. Would make sense.

And I would get to spend more time with Elliot and Christopher. My heart drops as I remember someone else who lives in London. I'd be closer to Claudia, and I broke her heart the other day again too.

She wanted me back, and I told her that I don't think I ever loved her . . . she got angry, and basically, it's a fucked-up situation all around.

No, I can't work out of London . . . too complicated. Scratch that idea.

How long will I go to Switzerland for? I go over the dates. Maybe a month?

Hmm . . . I bring up my work diary and begin to go through it. I'm owed a lot of holidays, and I guess I may as well take some.

As soon as I step into my apartment, my security phone goes off, and I answer. "Hello."

"Good afternoon, Mr. Miles. Mrs. Miles is here in the foyer to see you."

I close my eyes. Shit. "Yes, thank you. Please let her in."

Moments later the elevator doors open, and my mother steps out. Her face lights up when she sees me. "Hello, darling."

"Hi, Mom."

She takes me into her arms and holds me close for a moment as if sensing something is off.

"What are you doing here?" I smile as I pull out of her arms.

"I should ask you the same thing," she replies as she follows me and sits down on the couch.

"I just . . ." I pause as I try to articulate my lie. "I just need some time off after all that embezzlement shit."

Her eyes hold mine. "Good, I'm glad."

"Can I get you anything?" I stand, uncomfortable lying to her.

"Some tea, please, darling."

I walk into the kitchen and begin to make her tea. I take out her fine china pink-and-gold teapot and cup, the one she always drinks from when she's here. She follows me and sits at the kitchen counter.

"Did Tristan send you?" I ask with my back to her.

"He's worried about you."

"I'm fine, Mom."

"I'll be the judge of that. What's going on with Emily?"

"Nothing."

"Why not?"

"Emily and I aren't together anymore."

"Because?"

I keep making the tea.

"Look at me, Jameson."

I drag my eyes to hers.

"Why aren't you with Emily anymore?" she asks.

"Emily deserves better."

She watches me.

"Ferrara." I frown as I get my wording right. "I don't want this life for her."

"You don't want her being with a workaholic, you mean?"

I shrug as I pass her the cup of tea.

"So, you ended it with her . . . for her?"

I purse my lips as I remain silent.

"Well that proves it, Jameson."

"Proves what?"

"That she's the one."

I frown.

"You know, ever since you were a tiny little boy, you've done this."

"Done what?" What is she talking about?

"When you were very little, maybe three or four years old, you used to have this little pale-blue pickup truck."

I listen.

"You loved it. It fit in the palm of your hand, and you always carried it around. It was your pride and joy."

I smile softly.

"The thing is, Tristan loved it too. He had his own, but yours was the special one. And even though you loved that truck with all of your heart, the moment that Tristan got upset about anything . . . you would give it to him. You couldn't stand seeing him upset, and you felt responsible to make him happy."

I frown.

"As you grew up, I watched you do this many times, Jameson, with many things. To the outside world you were aloof and cold, but for the ones you loved, you would do anything to make them happy. You have more heart than sense."

My eyes hold hers.

"Why do you think that Emily wouldn't be happy with you?"

I stare at her for a moment as a clusterfuck of emotion runs through me. "Because eventually, I'm going to let her down," I whisper.

Her face softens. "Jameson darling, how? By working too hard? By being too honorable to your family business?"

I close my eyes.

"I'm in love with a man just like you, Jameson. You know him well, your father. He, like you, is a workaholic."

"How . . . ?" I frown. "I don't know how to do both, Mom."

"Then work it out."

I stare at her.

"Emily loves you, Jameson, not your money . . . or your company. She loves you . . . just you."

I drop my head.

"Stop being so damn selfless, and do what you want to do."

"I don't know what that is anymore," I whisper.

"Oh, nonsense," she snaps. "Tell me something. If you were on a deserted island, who would you want by your side?"

"Emily," I whisper without hesitation.

"Being in love is like being on a deserted island, Jameson. You focus on them and them only, and you make everything else fit around that person."

I inhale deeply.

"If you don't want to travel into the future with her, don't. But don't you dare pull away from your own happiness to protect her."

I clench my jaw as I listen.

"How one man can be so ruthless in business and so giving to those he loves, I will never understand . . . but, the fact that your father is your carbon copy, I know it's possible." She cups my face in her hand. "The man I love and the man that the world knows are two very different men . . . and that's just how I like it. I like that I'm the only one who gets his softness."

I smile softly.

"I am your father's world, Jameson; he made it work around the company. Never once have I felt neglected or unloved. I have always come first to him."

I stare at her as her words roll around in my head.

"The man that Emily loves and the one that you think you are are two very different men. You need to allow yourself to be who you are with Emily *and* be the Jameson Miles that the world knows. It's not one or the other like you think it is. The fact that you have put Emily's happiness ahead of your own cements that she is the one who has been chosen for you."

"She won't speak to me," I whisper.

She stands. "Then make her listen." She takes me into her arms. "Go and get your love, and grab her with both hands . . . and never let her go." She kisses me on the cheek and, without another word, leaves my apartment.

My mother's words ring home, loud and clear.

You need to allow yourself to be who you are with Emily and be the Jameson Miles that the world knows. It's not one or the other like you think it is.

It's five o'clock in the morning, and I lie and stare at the ceiling of my living room from my couch. I'm still fully dressed in the clothes I wore yesterday. I haven't slept all night.

My mother's words keep going over and over in my head.

She thinks that I can be both the man that Emily wants and the man that I need to be.

As I see it, I have three options. The first is to walk away from Miles Media so that I can be a man worth being with. The second is to let Emily leave my life forever. My stomach twists as I imagine living my life without her.

The third is to try to be both . . . is it truly possible to live as two men?

I stand, and for the first time in a long time, I have crystal-clear clarity.

Fuck this.

I'm going to try, and if I can't make it work, I will leave Miles Media.

I'm getting my girl back.

She comes first.

Chapter 25

Emily

I close down my computer and pack up my desk and make my way to the elevator. I'm one of the last to leave the office. It's been a long day, but I achieved a lot. It's the weirdest thing—blocking Jameson yesterday was the most satisfying thing I've done since I murdered his roses.

In some kind of sick and twisted way, being mean to him is releasing some of my anger. Hurting him is like the best kind of therapy. I must really be messed up at the moment; either that, or payback is just surprisingly satisfying. I watched the movie *John Wick* last night, and I smiled the whole way through it . . . that in itself says a lot about my current headspace.

I take the elevator and walk out onto the street. It's dark and cold, and I pull my heavy coat around my shoulders for protection.

"Emily," I hear a voice from behind me.

I stop on the spot . . . shit. Jameson . . . what's he doing here? I put my head down and keep walking.

"Emily," he repeats.

I spin toward him. "What, Jameson?" I snap.

"Can I talk to you?"

"No. Go away." I turn away from him and start to storm to my bus stop.

He follows me as I walk. "I just want five minutes of your time."

I stay silent.

He runs to catch up with me. "I know I fucked up . . . bad."

I glare at him as I imagine punching his stupid, handsome face. I get a vision of his head snapping back as I connect the hit.

"Please," he stammers as he runs after me. "I need to explain why."

"I'm not interested." I march forward.

He follows me for a while longer as if not sure what to say. "I'm going to follow you until you talk to me. Can we get a drink or something?"

"No."

"Dinner?"

"Go. Away. Jameson."

"I'm not leaving you," he stammers as he runs to keep up with me.

"You already did. Get out of my face."

He runs in front of me and walks backward facing me. "I mean, I'm not leaving you again . . . ever."

"Then it's going to be a one-sided relationship because I want nothing to do with you. Ever again."

His face falls. "Don't say that."

A man runs into him as he walks backward. "Watch out," the man snaps as he brushes past.

"I just want ten minutes of your time," he stammers.

"No." We arrive at my bus stop, and I stand in line. He stands next to me.

"Alan can come and get us, you know?" He looks at the long line of people. "We don't have to catch the bus."

I glare at him, unimpressed. *Spoiled brat.*

He smiles. "You're still gorgeous when you're angry . . . you know that?" he says loudly, and other people in the bus line begin to look over.

Red steam shoots from my ears at him making a scene. "Jameson, go the fuck home," I whisper angrily.

"No." He folds his arms in front of him like a petulant teenager. "I'm not leaving without you."

People around us are all watching. I take out my Kindle and open it . . . anything to block him out.

"What are you reading?"

I remain silent as I pretend to read.

Damn him . . . he thinks he can turn up here and demand to see me . . . he can kiss my ass.

"I'm reading a good book at the moment," he continues.

I keep reading.

"It's called . . ." He pauses as he thinks for a moment. "It's called 'how to get your girl back after a midlife crisis.'"

The girls behind me snicker.

I twist my lips to try and hide my amusement. *Don't get fucking cute now, asshole.*

"Chapter one is called 'bus duty,'" he continues.

I bite the inside of my cheek.

"Yes, it says to follow her to the bus stop and keep talking aimlessly until she gets sick of the sound of your voice and has to talk to you . . . even if that first word is *shut up* . . . that's something, right?"

I flick the page of my Kindle over as I stop myself from playing into his hands and saying the words *shut up.* The girls behind me snicker again. I glare at my Kindle. I won't be surprised if the screen breaks under the pressure.

"What does chapter two say?" the girl behind me asks as the bus arrives and pulls to a stop. I jump on.

"Get on the bus," I hear him say from behind me.

I walk on and take a window seat at the back, and he comes and sits beside me.

Are you kidding me?

"This is a great seat," he whispers. "I like it."

"Stop talking to me," I growl.

"I can't. You see, I've finally worked it out. And I need you to listen to me so that we can sort this mess out."

I stare out the window.

"I mean, how can we fix this if you won't speak to me?"

"We won't. That's the point," I mutter dryly.

"Don't say that, FB."

I glare at him as a glow of red covers the sky . . . don't fight; don't give him the satisfaction.

He smiles sweetly, totally oblivious to my rage. "It's so good to see you."

I roll my eyes and look back out the window . . . don't talk to him . . . not one word . . . don't give in to him.

"God . . . I've missed you, Em," he whispers.

Something inside of me breaks.

"You don't get to say that," I snap.

"But it's true."

"Shut up, Jameson. The time for talking is over." The bus pulls up to my stop, and I get up and brush past him. He runs after me as I storm up the pavement.

"I'm not leaving until you talk to me."

I keep walking.

"I'll wait out here all night."

I keep walking.

"Em, come on," he sighs.

I keep walking.

"How can you be so cold?" he demands.

I turn like the devil himself. "Don't you dare call me *cold*, you hypocrite. You're the only fucking cold one here."

"There she is." He smiles as if proud of himself for getting me to say something.

My face falls at my own weakness. "Jameson," I whisper.

"Babe." He grabs my two hands in his. "Please talk to me. I miss you, and I know you miss me too. I need to make this right between us; we can make it through this."

Tears well in my eyes at his touch, and I'm angry with myself for letting him get this close. "I can't." I brush past him.

"Please, Em," he calls from behind me. "I'll beg."

I keep walking.

"Do you want me to get on my knees right here? Because I will."

I keep walking, and he runs up behind me. "Tell me how to make this right? Tell me what to do, and I'll do it."

I turn to him. "Move on . . . I have."

His face falls. "Okay . . . I deserved that."

"I didn't." I push through tears as I brush past him and keep walking.

"I know, Em," he calls. "I'm so sorry. That guy . . . that guy was crazy to let you go. I was out of my fucking head."

I get to my building, and he comes up behind me as I open the door with my key. He slides his arm around my waist from behind and pulls me close. "Please," he murmurs into my hair. "I love you."

I close my eyes in pain at the feel of his touch . . . *I miss him.*

I pull out of his grip. "Don't touch me," I spit. "What makes you think you can come back here and say that?"

His eyes search mine. "Because you love me . . . and two wrongs don't make a right. If you don't let me make this right between us out of stubbornness, which is a real possibility . . ." He pauses as he tries to get the wording right. "We will both regret it forever; you know we will."

I stare at him for a moment as his words roll around in my head. I turn and walk into my building and close the door behind me. He watches me through the glass.

I hit the elevator button, and the doors open straightaway. I dive in and hit the buttons to close the doors as my tears well in my eyes.

Bastard.

I walk out of my building right at eight o'clock in the morning. I haven't slept much, and I keep seeing Jameson's sad face when I left him last night. I hate that I care about him. His words kept playing over and over in my head all night. I hate that he said them. I hate that they made sense.

"Because you love me . . . and two wrongs don't make a right. If you don't let me make this right between us out of stubbornness, which is a real possibility . . . we will both regret it forever; you know we will."

God, what a mess.

"Good morning," I hear a chirpy voice from behind me.

Jameson is standing beside my door in his navy suit, looking all dapper and not at all discouraged like he should be.

"What are you doing here?"

"Waiting for you." He smiles as he takes my gym bag from me and puts it over my shoulder. "Are we catching the bus today?"

I look at him deadpan. "I'm catching the bus. What you're doing . . . I have no idea."

"I'm following you around until you agree to have dinner with me."

"It's not happening, Jameson."

"Okay," he says as he begins to walk to the bus stop. "I'll just be following you around for forever, then." I stare at him, and he gives me a slow, sexy smile. "You look beautiful today."

"Stop it."

"No."

I walk to the bus stop with him beside me. I'm staying silent, and he is jabbering.

"Did you run this morning?" he asks. "I did."

I stare at him.

"I'm actually quite fit at the moment—all this heartache has me running at record speed," he continues.

That makes two of us . . . I keep my mouth tightly closed. I don't want him to know that I've been angry running too.

We catch the bus. I'm silent, and he's carrying on like we are long-lost best friends.

"Do you want to go camping this weekend?" he asks as he opens his paper.

"No. I'm going to my parents this weekend," I reply flatly.

"Oh." His face falls. "Well, that's going to be uncomfortable."

"What is?"

"When I follow you to your parents."

"You are not coming to my parents," I scoff.

"Watch me." His eyes dance with mischief. "You won't talk to me; I'm going to keep following you until you do."

"I don't want you to follow me. In fact, I don't want anything to do with you."

"No need to be snarky," he says casually as he turns the page of his paper. "It's unbecoming."

I glare at him. "You know what's unbecoming?" I whisper angrily. "Jerks who break girls' hearts and think that they can snap their fingers and get her back at the drop of a hat."

He smirks down at me. "Yes, I have to agree. Although if they are meant to be together, and he was under the impression that he was doing the right thing by her at the time . . ."

"Oh, please," I huff. "Can you hear yourself?"

"Have dinner with me tonight."

"No."

The bus pulls up at my stop, and he stands and grabs my gym bag and puts it back over his shoulder. I watch him walk up the aisle of the bus to get off, and I smile to myself. Has he ever caught a bus before?

Idiot.

We walk up the road in silence, and I turn and catch sight of the limo parked across the street. Alan is leaning up against it, and he smiles and waves over at me.

"Alan knows you're here?" I whisper in mortification.

"Everyone knows I'm here," he says casually as he hands my bag over. "It's no secret that I want you back. I have stated my intentions loud and clear."

I stare at him.

"See you this afternoon."

"Jameson," I sigh.

"I'm not giving up on us, Em . . . ever." He smiles softly. "We were made for each other."

I scratch my head in frustration.

"Have a nice day." He watches me with his hands in his pockets, keeping a safe distance.

"Bye." I turn and walk into my building. My phone beeps a text. It's from an unknown number.

Have a good day.
This is my burner phone
in case of an emergency.

Jameson. He's got another phone, one that I haven't blocked. I get into the elevator and find myself smirking at the ground. *Stop it* . . . he's an asshole . . . never forget that.

It's three o'clock, and I'm finishing a report for publication this week. I love this job. I mean, not as much as I loved Miles Media, but that ship has sailed—may as well make the most of it. The staff are all really friendly and nice and have welcomed me with open arms.

"Delivery for Emily Foster," I hear.

I look up and see a man walking through the floor with a white box. What the hell?

"Oh, she's in that office over there," I hear someone say.

He knocks on my door. "Are you Emily Foster?"

"Yes."

"I have a delivery for you." He hands over the white box.

I take it from him. "Thank you."

"Um." He smirks, shuffling awkwardly in place. "It's from the Kung Fu Panda."

"What?"

"I was told to tell you that the Kung Fu Panda sent it."

I try to hide my smile and fail miserably. "Thank you." He leaves, and I open the box to find a huge caramel cheesecake and a small white card.

Cheesecake for my cheesecake.
xoxoxo

I close the box and smirk. He's an idiot, and I'm not a cheese-cake . . . if he thinks he can weasel his way back into my good book by being cute, he has another thing coming.

Kung Fu Panda . . . where the hell does he get this shit?

A girl from the office next door pops her head around the corner. "What's that?"

"Cheesecake, want some?"

"Hell yeah, I'll get the plates." She disappears to the kitchen.

I stare at my phone for a moment. Should I text him and say thank you?

No, this is why he did it—to get a reaction. He knows I've got good manners and would never receive a gift without thank-ing him. He'll be waiting for my call.

Well, too bad for the stupid Kung Fu Panda. More fool him.

He created this beast; he can live with my rudeness. He's in the freezer.

At six o'clock in the evening, I make my way downstairs. I may have fixed my hair and applied some lipstick . . . not that I'll ever admit to it.

I walk out of the building and out onto the street to see Jameson standing and leaning up against the wall. He's wearing his gray suit, the one that I love. His dark hair hangs over his fore-head, and his chiseled jaw does things to my insides. He smiles broadly and pushes off the wall when he sees me coming. How long has he been standing there? "Good afternoon, Ms. Foster."

"I didn't know that you knew kung fu," I say as I walk past him.

449

"Oh, I do," he says as he falls into step behind me. "There are a lot of things about me that you don't know. Did I tell you that I'm becoming an extreme sportist?"

I keep silent as I walk. It's hard to keep a straight face when he's in this mood.

"Yes, I thought I might start hiking up mountains and camping there and stuff. Making fire with my bare hands and whatnot."

I smirk as I walk in front of him, unable to help it. "Really?"

"Uh-huh. You see, I'm becoming one with nature."

"You. One with nature. I'd like to see that," I mutter dryly.

"Okay, we can hike up a mountain this weekend. How's Mount Kosciuszko?"

"I'm busy," I say as I keep walking.

"Oh, that's right; we are going to your parents this weekend."

"You're not coming, Jameson."

"Your mother said I could when I spoke to her earlier."

I spin on the spot toward him. "You called my mother?"

"No, but I will if you don't have dinner with me." He smiles hopefully.

I stare at him. "Jameson, if you think the Kung Fu Panda sending me a cake and calling me a cheesecake can reverse the damage you have done, you are seriously deluded."

He takes my two hands in his. "I don't, Em, but please . . . just let me say what I need to say."

I stare at him.

"And then if you don't want to see me again, I'll stop following me." His eyes hold mine. "We need to talk about this; you know we do."

I roll my eyes.

"Please?" He bats his eyelashes to try and be cute; it's annoying that he is.

"Fine. You have ten minutes." I sigh.

"Where do you want to go?" He smiles.

"Wherever is easiest."

"Okay." He looks around. "How about that Italian restaurant across the street?"

"Fine." He tries to take my hand, and I snatch it away. "You have got to be kidding," I snap.

"Jesus, calm down," he mutters.

I follow him across the street and into the restaurant, and we take a seat at the back of the restaurant. It's small and darkened with candles on the tables. Red tablecloths decorate the tables. It's nothing like the usual upmarket Italian that he takes me to, but it will have to do.

"Can I get you some drinks?" the waiter asks.

Jameson smirks and gestures to me. "I'll have what she's having."

I stare at him for a moment and open my menu. "All right, we'll have a bottle of the Henschke Hill of Grace, please."

"Yes, ma'am." The waiter disappears out the back to the bar.

Jameson's eyes come to me, and he smiles softly and takes my hands over the table.

"Do you know how much I've missed you?" he whispers.

I stare at him in some kind of strange detached state.

"Did you miss me?"

Instantly I'm overwhelmed with emotion. I stay silent as I battle the lump in my throat. I hate that he makes me feel so weak and vulnerable. I pull my hands out of his grip. I need to create some distance between us.

"Em." He frowns. "I . . ." It's clear that he has no idea what to say. "When I saw that image of you kissing Jake—"

"Jameson," I stammer.

He holds his hand up to signify silence, and I close my mouth. "Something snapped inside of me. I was so thrown that it upset me so deeply that I . . ." He frowns as he remembers it. "I was furious—firstly with you, but then with myself."

Our eyes are locked.

"I was going through so much shit at work, and the very last person on earth that I thought would lie to me . . . was you."

I drop my head in shame.

"And then when I calmed down after a few days and realized that you had been set up, the future mapped itself out to me."

I frown.

"There is always going to be someone like Ferrara who is prepared to step on you to hurt me."

My heart drops.

"And I don't want that for you."

"Jay," I whisper sadly.

"I don't want you to be married to a workaholic who has to travel all the time and is stressed out of his head. I don't want you to have to remind your husband not to drink too much or stop being rude to people because he's too busy to care. I don't want you to have to remind your husband that he's neglecting you."

"Your bottle of wine." The waiter appears out of nowhere. He opens it and pours us both a glass.

"Thank you," I reply. My eyes go back to meet Jameson's.

The waiter leaves us alone.

"I don't want you to come second to Miles Media. I don't want you to *ever* come second to anything."

"But—"

"Let me finish, please," he demands.

I sit back in my chair, annoyed that he wants to speak first.

"The thing is, if you're with me—married to me—your life is going to be all those things."

The lump in my throat gets big.

"I love you too much to let you live that life, Em."

452

He's ending it again. My eyes fill with tears.

He takes my hand over the table and lifts it to his mouth and gently kisses it. "Don't cry. I hate that you've cried over me."

I blink to try and get rid of these stupid tears.

"I made a decision to protect you from that life. To push you away. Because I knew that one day, you would eventually be unhappy . . . and I just can't live with that."

"It wasn't your decision to make," I whisper angrily.

He frowns. "My job is to look after you and make the hard calls, ones that you can't make for yourself."

"Jameson." I stare at him through tears.

"But something happened while I was away from you." He leans in and cups my face in his hand. "I realized that I didn't want any of those things either."

My eyes search his.

"I can't live without you, Em. I've been so fucking miserable that it's been unbearable."

He leans in and kisses me softly; his eyes search mine as he dusts his thumb over my bottom lip. "If you don't want me as I am now, I'll resign from Miles Media immediately, and we can move to bumfuck nowhere and, I don't know, live in a fucking tent somewhere."

I smirk. "You idiot," I whisper.

He smiles as he holds my face in his hand.

"I love you how you are. I don't want you to change anything."

"You do?"

"But I don't . . ." I pause as I try to articulate my feelings. "How can I move on from how you've treated me?"

"I don't know."

"I can't just pretend that this hasn't happened, Jameson. You've hurt me too deeply."

453

"I know; I don't want you to," he stammers. "But can't we just . . ." He shrugs. "Start dating again? Take it slow."

I stare at him as confusion fills me.

"I know it's going to take time to get back to where we were, but we have the rest of our lives. We can date and get to know each other properly this time."

I sit back as I consider his proposal, and I sip my wine. "You know, I always imagined that I would find my dream guy and fall in love, and then it would come to this big cheesy climax."

He scrunches up his nose. "Cheesy climax? That just sounds wrong."

I giggle as I imagine what he must be thinking about. "No, I meant proposal."

"You want a cheesy proposal?" He frowns. "Wouldn't you want a romantic proposal?"

"Not really. My point is, this isn't how I imagined things would go."

"Me neither." He takes my hands in his. "Far from it. I'm officially an idiot. Give me another chance, Em. I won't fuck it up, I promise."

I stare at him.

"I love you; you love me." He shrugs. "We can work through this, and then hopefully in time, you can forget it ever happened, and you can live happily ever after with an outdoorsy Kung Fu Panda." He smiles hopefully.

"You're an idiot, Mr. Miles."

"Who's hopelessly in love with you." He leans over and kisses me softly, and I feel my resistance fade. "I love you, cheesecake," he whispers.

"Don't call me fucking cheesecake."

He chuckles against my lips. "Too far?"

"Way too far."

Chapter 26

We walk down the street toward my apartment, hand in hand. Jameson is being overattentive and talking nonstop, and I am quiet. I'm annoyed that with just one dinner meeting, I find myself here with him.

I'm officially a pushover.

Weak as water.

His phone beeps with a text, and he shuffles around in his pocket to retrieve it and smiles. "Tristan." He reads the text out loud "How did it go?"

I roll my eyes. "Text back, 'Not out of the woods yet. Still may be found dead in a ditch tomorrow.'"

Jameson smirks. "No, I'm not writing that. If it actually happens, I don't want you to go to prison." He turns to face me and tucks a piece of my hair behind my ear. "You wouldn't kill me." He leans in and kisses me softly.

My eyes hold his. "Wouldn't I?"

He smiles and then takes my hand as we walk toward the door. I stop on the spot. "Good night," I announce.

"What?"

"You're not coming in."

"Why not?"

"Jameson, I am still eighty percent pissed off with you."

"Yes. I know. Let me make it up to you." He smiles darkly.

I pull out of his arms and step back from him. "There is nothing sexual that you could do that would make up for how you have treated me."

His face falls.

"When I agreed to try again, it was just that . . . to try again. I'm not promising anything, and I don't know how this is going to turn out. I honestly don't know if we can get back what we had. The morning you left me after the second stopover, you broke something between us. I have never been so upset in all of my life. It was devastating for me. Having sex with you now is the very last thing that I want to do."

"Em," he whispers. "I couldn't talk to you because it killed me to push you away. I was battling myself over it."

"Good night, Jameson."

He looks around in a fluster. "Well, when will I see you again?"

I shrug. "It's Thursday, and I'm away for the weekend, so next week, I guess."

"Next week?" he huffs. "That's like four days away."

"Is it?" I reply flatly as I begin to dig in my bag for my keys. I really do need to get a better system in this damn handbag; it's like the fucking Bermuda Triangle in here.

"Well, that's too long," he stammers. "I haven't seen you for a month. I need more time with you."

"Take it or leave it," I reply.

"Em?"

I turn and kiss him softly on the lips, and he snaps his arms around me. We stay still for a few minutes in each other's arms, holding on tight and needing the closeness that the other provides. I've missed him desperately, and it would be so easy to take him upstairs right now.

No . . . I have serious trust issues that I need to deal with. *He needs to deal with.*

"I'll sleep on the lounge," he whispers. "I can't be away from you for one more night. Don't ask that of me."

I pull away, knowing where this is going if I stay in his arms. "Good night, Jameson."

His eyes search mine as he silently begs to come upstairs.

I force a smile and open my door as he stands on the pavement. I give him a wave and disappear into the elevator as he watches on. The elevator doors close, and I blow out a breath of relief.

Good girl . . . stay strong.

I put my lipstick on and smile at my reflection in the mirror. Jameson called me when he got home last night to say good night. It feels strangely good to have him back in my life . . . *but for how long?*

I have this annoying little voice in my psyche that keeps reminding me what he did and how badly he treated me. I'm trying to listen to his reasoning and trust what he's saying, but it's hard to pretend that nothing has happened between us.

It wasn't nothing; it was Armageddon, and my entire world crashed at my feet. I don't like the way I depend on Jameson Miles for my happiness.

It won't happen again; I won't allow it . . . even if that means holding him at arm's length for the rest of my life . . . or however long we're together.

See, there it is again.

Negative thoughts . . . ugh.

I make my way downstairs with my luggage for the weekend with me and out the front doors to see Jameson leaning up against the wall—navy suit, gorgeous face, and a swoony smile . . . just for me. "Good morning, my beautiful girl."

"Hi." I smile up at him.

He leans down and takes my face in his hands and kisses me, and I feel my knees weaken underneath me. "How did my girl sleep?" He takes my hand in his and takes my suitcase from me.

"Fine, thanks."

"Can we get a civilized lift to work today?" he asks.

I glance over and see Alan and the limo parked at the curb across the street. "Um." I frown. "You go with Alan. I want to catch the bus."

He raises an eyebrow as if unimpressed. "Okay, bus it is."

"You don't have to walk me to work, Jameson. I'm quite capable of getting myself there."

"I know; I just want to spend the twenty minutes with you. I'm not seeing you all weekend, remember?" He gives me a sexy wink, and my stomach does a nervous flip. We walk to the bus stop hand in hand.

"Have you heard anything more about Lara Aspin and Hayden?"

"No. They've been charged, but the court case won't be for a while. I can't believe you solved it. You don't know how grateful I am to you."

I smile, feeling proud of myself.

"How do you like your new job?" he asks.

I shrug. "It's great."

His eyes hold mine. "Great as in 'really great,' or great as in 'it will do'?"

"Great as in 'I'm getting used to it.'"

"Why don't you come back to Miles Media?"

"No. I'll be keeping our work lives separate from now on."

"Hmm." He frowns, unimpressed. "We'll see."

The bus arrives, and we make our way on. It's crowded today, and I find a seat, but Jameson has to stand. He's squashed between a smelly man and a woman who looks like she has rabies. I sit and watch him and the horror on his face as he watches the people around him. I have to bite my lip to stop myself from laughing. Eventually the bus pulls to our stop, and he gets off in a rush.

"That's it," he scoffs as he brushes his suit off like the snob that he is. "No more fucking buses. We need to be disinfected right now. Did you see the people on that fucking bus?"

I giggle. "That was just a bad trip."

"I mean it, Emily," he snaps. "No more fucking buses. Alan is now your driver. Over my dead body are we catching another bus."

"Yes, boss." I smile as he takes my hand in his, and we begin our walk to work.

"What time does your flight leave tonight?" he asks.

"Three."

His face falls. "You're going early?"

"Yes. I have a half day today."

"I was going to take you to the airport." He frowns as he stares down at me. "I have a board meeting at four; I can't get out of it."

"That's fine."

"Shit . . . maybe I can cancel?"

"Jameson, it's fine. You are not canceling a meeting to take me to the airport. Stop it. You will see me when you see me."

He stares at me as he processes my words. "Alan will collect you."

I nod, knowing that if I don't agree, he will in fact cancel his meeting. "Okay."

We arrive at my work, and he turns me toward him. "You'll call me the minute you land?"

"No."

"Why not?"

"I'll call you before I go to bed."

He stares at me.

"What are you doing this weekend?" I ask.

"My brothers are all going to Vegas tonight."

"Are you?"

"No."

"Why not?"

"They're chasing booze and wild women."

My face falls.

He wraps his arms around me. "I already have my wild woman; I'm not interested in what they are looking for."

I smile up at him, surprisingly grateful that he's not going.

"Will you miss me?" he whispers.

"Probably not."

"You probably could try and be flirtier in our conversations, you know?"

"Could I?" Our lips touch, and he kisses me softly.

"Are you sure you have to go?" he murmurs against my lips.

"Yes, Jameson."

"I love you," he whispers.

My heart somersaults in my chest at hearing those precious words. "Have a nice day."

"That's not what I wanted to hear."

"But that's all you're getting." I kiss him quickly and pull out of his arms. "Please stop pressuring me. I'll call you tonight."

He puts his two hands into his suit pockets and smiles sexily as he watches me walk into the building.

I get into the elevator with a hammering heart and flushed cheeks.

Why is he so damn gorgeous?

I walk out of work just after one o'clock and see the limo and Alan standing beside it. He smiles warmly and opens the back door as if gesturing for me to get in. I smile and make my way over to him. I haven't heard from Jameson all day and wasn't sure if Alan was in fact coming to collect me. "Hello."

He smiles warmly. "Hello, Emily. It's so lovely to see you."

I get into the back of the limo and find a lone red rose on the back seat, waiting for me.

Oh.

I smile and inhale it deeply; a beautiful perfume fills the space. The car pulls out from the curb, and I get a vision of myself stomping on the yellow roses the other night. *Maniac.*

I was half hoping that Jameson would be in the car waiting for me. Should I even be going away right now? Isn't sorting this out with him more important?

No.

You had these plans before he decided to waltz back in . . . stick to them.

I should call and thank him, though. I dial his number.

"Hello," his sexy voice purrs down the line.

My stomach flutters at the sound of his voice. "Hi," I breathe. "Are you with Alan?"

"I am. Thank you for my rose."

"So red is better?"

"Seems that way." I feel my face blush in embarrassment.

"Mental note to never buy anything yellow ever again."

I giggle, embarrassed.

"You have a good weekend," he eventually replies.

"You too."

"I'm not going to call you this weekend."

"Why not?" I ask.

"Your words are playing on my mind."

"What words?"

"You told me not to force this between us."

I listen.

"I'm stepping back."

My heart drops. "You're giving up?"

"No. Just the opposite; I'm making plans for our future. But I understand that you need time. Me forcing you to forgive me before you're ready may not be the smartest move."

I smile softly as I listen, hope blooming in my chest.

"You just call me whenever you want to speak to me," he says.

"Okay."

"And that could be fifty times a day. I'll be waiting for your call like a lovesick schoolboy."

I smile as I hang on the line . . . I really do want to see him this weekend.

No.

"Okay."

"Goodbye, Emily."

"Goodbye," I whisper. I hang up, smell my rose, and smile sadly out the window as New York flies by. I feel like I'm in a subspace. Caught between two men, each with their own memory—one of Jameson Miles's coldhearted dismissal and the other of playful Jim's overwhelming love. Each time I feel myself leaning toward one, the other jumps in my way. I'm not sure how to turn this off, but I need to work it out . . . and sooner rather than later.

Half an hour later the limo pulls up at the airport, and Alan opens my door. I clutch my rose in my hand, knowing that I can't take it in.

Alan retrieves my bag from the trunk. "Would you like me to carry this in for you?" he asks.

"No, thank you." I look down at my rose. I feel strangely attached to it and can't stand the thought of it dying. "Would you be able to put the rose in some water for me, please?" I ask him.

He smiles warmly. "Of course." He takes it from me. "I'll put it in water at Mr. Miles's apartment for you."

"Thank you." I shrug, suddenly feeling stupid. "Goodbye, Alan."

"I'll see you on Sunday when we pick you up."

"Okay." With a meek wave, I make my way to the check-in desk, and surprisingly there's no line today. "Hello. I have a booking for Emily Foster." I slide my license across the desk to the check-in clerk.

"Hello." She types my name into her computer. "Ah yes, Ms. Foster. I see you have amended your booking to first class."

I frown. "No."

She rechecks the details. "Yes, your two tickets were upgraded late last night."

"Two tickets?"

"Yes, a second was booked, and then they were both upgraded."

Jameson.

"Oh, I see. Okay, thank you." I collect my ticket and walk through security and make my way to the bar. I have nearly two hours before my flight leaves.

"What will it be?" the bartender asks as I take a seat.

"A margarita, please."
I text Jameson.

> **Mr Miles, thank you for the upgrade.**
> **It is very much appreciated.**
> **Tell me, was the second seat for you or to make sure I didn't sit next to someone else?**

My drink is delivered, and a text bounces back.

> **My dear Miss Foster, I am outraged that you would think I could be so calculating.**
> **Of course, I don't want you sitting next to anyone else.**
> **I know how irresistible you are.**
> **xoxox**

I smile as I sip my drink, and another text arrives.

> **Although, if I wasn't playing hard to get and being non-pushy. I would have taken you on the company jet and initiated you to the real Miles High Club.**
> **You wouldn't walk for a week.**
> **Enjoy the peaceful silence.**
> **xoxox**

I roll my lips to hide my smile, and I text back.

> **Goodbye Jameson.**
> **Glad that your deviant behavior is still alive and well.**
> **I was getting worried.**
> **xoxoxo**

A text comes straight in.

You have no idea.
And no watching Magic Mike, watch Grumpy Old
Men instead.
It will make me more appealing.
xoxox

I sip my drink and find myself smiling goofily into space.

Things *are* going well . . . for the first time in a long time, I feel myself become a little excited for what's to come.

Let's see what happens.

I stare at the ceiling in the darkness from my bed. It's midnight. My old bedroom brings a surprising comfort that I didn't know I needed.

It's great being here with my family, but New York seems so very far away.

I didn't call Jameson like I said I would; in fact I haven't spoken to him all night.

Being here with people who love me makes me realize how fragile I've been. I was completely alone and heartbroken in New York. I mean sure, I had Molly and Aaron, but I've known them all of three months. It's not the same as having family around, the ones who will stand by your side through thick and thin.

I don't know where I'm going with Jameson, only that I didn't want to speak to him tonight. Why?

Maybe I'm never going to let go of this hurt; maybe he's done irreversible damage.

Maybe I'm too good for him and his shit . . . there's no *maybe* in that sentence—I know I am.

My phone vibrates on the side table, and I frown as I see the letter *J* light up.

I exhale heavily and answer, "Hello."

"Hi." He pauses for a moment. "You weren't calling me tonight?"

"I got distracted."

Silence down the phone. Eventually he speaks. "Em."

"Yes."

"Did you go there to get away from me?"

I roll my eyes in frustration. "No, Jameson," I whisper angrily. "Why is everything about you? I booked this trip two weeks ago."

"Okay, I just asked. Jesus. Why are you so angry?"

Tears form in my eyes. "You really have to ask?"

"You tell me why."

Suddenly a volcano that I didn't even know was there erupts inside of me. "Because I'm in love with a selfish fucking asshole, and I don't know how to turn it off, and I'm waiting for the other shoe to drop and for you to walk away again," I blurt out in a rush.

He stays silent.

"And the way you just march back in and demand my forgiveness pisses me off."

He listens.

"And you could have any woman in the world; they are lining up for you. So why are you putting me through this shit? I don't want the heartache, Jameson."

"Is that what you think? That I want any woman in the world?"

Tears roll down my face, and I swipe them away angrily. "I have no idea what you want anymore, Jameson."

466

"Cut the fucking shit, Emily," he snaps. "You listen, and you listen good. I don't want anyone else. I've been promiscuous since I was eighteen years old. I've slept with a lot of women . . . and I mean a lot of women. You are the only person I have ever had this connection with. The only woman I have loved like this. So don't you dare throw that shit at me about wanting someone else. Have I ever given you any reason to doubt me?"

"Your masseuse," I snap.

"Was before I fucking met you," he growls. I can hear the anger in his voice. "If you don't want me, then fine, I'll leave. But don't let me hold out and try desperately to make things work when you're obviously not going to let me in."

My face contorts with tears.

"Only you can decide if you want this, Emily. Forgiveness is a choice."

I stay silent.

"Do you want to walk away from me, or do you want to try and make this work?"

I don't answer him.

"Well?" he demands.

"You know I want to try," I whisper.

"Then stop thinking of the bad shit, and think of the good between us."

"I can't."

"Why not?"

"Because you scare me."

He falls silent. "You're scared of me?"

"Yes." I nod through tears.

"Baby," he whispers as empathy floods his voice. "Don't be scared of me. Please, don't ever be scared of me. I love you."

"I'm trying." I sob. "But I can't help it."

We both stay silent for a while, lost in our own thoughts.

"I want you to take this weekend to think about us. I was serious about what I said—if you don't want to live in New York, we can move. I'll resign from my position immediately."

"Jameson," I sigh. "Why would you do that?"

"Because I want you to know that you come first to me now. All of this shit—my money, my apartment, my job, New York— it means nothing if I'm fucking miserable, Emily. And believe me, I am fucking miserable without you. If you want to live in a tent in the back of bumfuck nowhere, we can."

I get a vision of Jameson living in a tent and being eaten by mosquitos on the daily. "You idiot." I smile softly. "I don't want to live in a tent. I love New York. I love you running Miles Media. I wouldn't change anything about you. Why would you think that I would?"

"Because I'm a lot to take on, I know that. You said to me once before that to love is to be brave. I need you to be brave, Emily, and move forward from all this. Please think about it. Come back to New York and back to me one hundred percent, and we can start working on a new life together. Holding me at arm's distance isn't the way to navigate this. We won't be able to work it out if we're not together."

"I know," I whisper.

"Will you think about what you really want?"

I stay silent.

"Please, Em?"

"Yes, okay. I will. I promise." The line falls silent for a moment, and I want to change the subject. "What are you doing tomorrow?" I ask.

"Shopping."

"Shopping—you? What are you shopping for?"

"Well, where do you get the tents with bathrooms in them?"

I smile. "Bumfuck nowhere."

He chuckles, and it's a beautiful sound; it does things to my insides. It's been a long time since I heard him laugh.

"Em . . . I'm not going to speak to you again until I pick you up from the airport on Sunday night. I want you to really think about your future and who you want in it. Either you come back to me with open arms, and we give this a red-hot go, or you end it."

My heart drops.

"It has to be this way. If I can't have all of you, I would rather be without you."

I listen as my mind begins to go into overdrive . . . he's giving me an ultimatum.

All or nothing.

I honestly don't know if I can give him my all. I don't think my all exists anymore.

"I'll see you then?" he asks hopefully.

"Okay."

"I love you." He hangs up, and the line goes dead.

I roll over in the darkness and exhale heavily.

What *do* I want for my future? Do I give him away . . . ? Or give him everything? Or what's left of my heart, at least. It's been smashed to smithereens.

I literally have no idea.

Chapter 27

Jameson

I tap my foot as I crane my neck to look at the traffic backed up in front. Shit.

I press the buzzer to the front of the limo. "Are we going to be late?" I ask Alan.

"No, sir; we're an hour early. Plenty of time."

"I don't want to miss her flight. Go the back way."

"You won't. Relax."

I sit back and try to control my nerves. Emily hasn't contacted me all weekend, and I'm pretty sure she's coming home to end it between us. I've run and run and run. The only time I have had any semblance of peace is when I've pounded the pavement around New York.

I can't accept the possibility that I won't be in her life, that she won't be in mine . . . the thought sickens me. *How could I have been so fucking stupid?*

I've been trying to pull a logical argument together in my head as to what I'm going to say if she ends it . . . so far I've come up empty.

The limo pulls up at the airport, and I climb out in a rush. "You'll be here?" I ask.

"No, I'll circle. Let me know when you have her, and I'll come back around. You still have fifty minutes before her plane lands."

"Yes, yes, I know." I pat down my pockets as I look around nervously. "Do I have everything?" I'm flustered and vague.

"Yes, sir."

I drop my shoulders and exhale heavily. "Wish me luck."

Alan smiles broadly and, with a jovial nod, says, "Good luck, sir."

I walk into the airport and up to the arrival gate of her plane. I still have forty minutes. I look over to the bar, and it calls my name in a sweet song.

A scotch would be so good right now . . . take the edge off.

No.

I need to cut that shit out. I haven't allowed myself to have a drink all weekend. Emily deserves more than a drunk.

With nerves racing through my body, I walk to one end of the airport and then back to the arrival lounge. I glance at my watch. Thirty-five minutes to go. I do it again and again.

I can't sit still.

Not when I know what's coming.

Emily

I walk with the crowd into the arrivals lounge. My flight has just landed, and my heart is beating hard in my chest.

I've dug into the bottom of my soul this weekend, searching for the answers.

Trying to work out what to do with my life and who to do it with.

One thing is clear: the only thing that is clear . . . is who I love.

I can't deny it.

Jameson Miles is etched into my heart, and as petrified as I am of him hurting me again, his words keep coming back to me. "*To love is to be brave.*"

I'm going to swallow my pride and be brave. I'm going to let myself go . . . and hope to God I'm doing the right thing, because I can't go through this again.

He comes into view, and he smiles as our eyes lock. Excitement fills me, and I do a little skip and begin to run, and I jump into his waiting arms. We cling to each other tightly, locked in an embrace. We don't speak; we don't kiss; we just hold on.

Clinging desperately to the hope that we can get past this.

My shadows are chased away for a little while.

"I missed you," he whispers into my hair.

"I missed you too."

He bends, and his lips take mine as we forget where we are. His tongue slowly strokes through my open lips, and he holds my face in his two hands as we get lost in the moment. His kiss is tender and, more importantly, familiar.

With him, I am home.

An hour later, we walk into my apartment, hand in hand.

We hardly spoke on the way home. I sat on his lap, tucked safely in his big arms, and enjoyed the closeness. His lips dusted back and forth over my temple as he held tight, as if not believing I was here with him.

I've missed the closeness. *Our closeness.*

It's not even about the sex with us anymore. I mean, it was in the beginning. But my heart has eclipsed any physical need that my mere body desires . . . and I know he's the same.

He turns me toward him, and his eyes search mine. "Em . . ." He pauses as if trying to get the wording right in his head. "I swear to you, from this moment on . . . you are my everything. Our new life together . . . starts right now."

I smile up at him as my eyes fill with tears anew. "I love you."

"I love you too." We kiss, and unlike the tenderness we have shared over the last hour, a new desperation fills us.

Suddenly I want him . . . all of him. "Take me to bed."

He scoops me up and carries me into the room like a bride and stands me before him. His lips drop to my neck, and I smile at the ceiling as goose bumps scatter over my skin. He bites me with an edge I remember so well.

Oh, I've missed him.

I lift his shirt over his head and throw it to the side, and he does the same to mine. We become animals as we tear each other's clothes away. There is nothing between us now. Only skin . . . and love.

His lips tenderly take mine as he lays me back on the bed, and his lips go to my neck and then start to go lower, and I cling to him. "No, I need you up here with me."

We stare at each other in some kind of otherworldly experience. *This is special.*

I wish I could bottle this moment.

"Now, Jim," I whisper, "I need you now."

His eyes close in pleasure as he lies on top of me; our lips are locked, my legs open and cradling his large body as it rocks against mine, searching for its own release.

With one deep purposeful thrust, he slides home deep, and we both moan in pleasure.

"Fuck, Em," he whispers into my neck.

I cling to him as I ride the pleasure wave between us. "I know, baby, I know."

He pulls out and pushes back in, my body rising to meet his.

The need for more overwhelms us, and I begin to thrash beneath him. "Fuck me," I whimper. "God, give it to me hard."

He pulls out and slams back in, knocking the air from my lungs. He repositions my legs over his shoulders and, with dark eyes watching me struggle to take him, begins to ride me.

Long, sharp, punishing hits—the bed begins to hit the wall, and I can do nothing but watch the perfect male specimen in all his glory.

Jameson Miles is the most sexual being I have ever known.

Everything about him screams "fuck me."

Watching him in the throes of passion, where he is grappling for control, is every woman's ultimate fantasy; he's like a sexual time bomb waiting to explode. Perspiration dusts his skin; his dark hair hangs over his forehead, and his breath begins to quiver as he struggles to hold off his orgasm.

His pumps become piston fast, and the burn of his possession overtakes me as I fall into the abyss. I cry out as an earth-shattering orgasm rips me to shreds.

My body contracts hard around his.

"Fuck, fuck, fuck," he pushes out as he slams repeatedly into me. The sound of the bed hitting the wall with force echoes through the apartment.

He tips his head back, holds himself deep, and moans loud as he comes hard, deep inside of me.

And then we kiss, and my whole world returns to good. To the place I've missed so, so much.

The emotion between us is so strong that it brings tears to my eyes.

"Welcome home, fuck bunny," he whispers against my lips. "Welcome home."

One week later

"We need to do a follow-up story, a where-are-they-now kind of thing," Athena says as we stand together at the printer.

"Yes, I know. I'm going to go over the notes this afternoon as soon as I get a chance."

The office is a hive of activity today; news has broken overnight. A married senator has been caught in a scandal with his secretary, and the phones are ringing off the hook.

People are everywhere as they try to decipher the truth as the rumor mill spins into overdrive.

I'm having trouble concentrating, if I'm honest. I'm on a Jameson high. I think I can successfully say I've joined the Miles-High club.

This last week has been . . . *magical.*

I'm completely and utterly in love with this man. We moved me into his apartment on the weekend. Any trepidation that I had has finally gone.

I hear an unusual sound coming through the office, and Athena and I look up as the office watches on. I hear "The Piña Colada Song," and I frown as Jameson comes into view through the desks.

Tristan is with him and holding an old-fashioned tape deck, and the familiar tune is blasting through the office.

> If you like piña coladas,
> And getting caught in the rain.

"What in the world?" I frown.

Jameson smiles hopefully as he approaches me. His eyes search mine.

The office falls silent as they watch on.

"Emily Foster," he says.

"Yes?"

He drops to his knee, and the office collectively gasps. My hands fly over my mouth.

"Will you marry me?" He opens a black box and holds out a solitaire diamond ring.

I stare at him for a moment as my brain misfires.

Is this real?

I look over to Tristan. I'm in complete and utter shock.

"I'm the DJ." Tristan grins as he taps the tape recorder as if very proud of himself.

"You are crazy," I whisper.

"This proves it," Jameson mutters dryly as he looks up at me from his knee.

My eyes are wide. I'm shocked to my very core.

"Answer the question," he says.

I nod through giggles as "The Pina Colada Song" echoes through the office. "Yes."

He slides the ring on my finger. It's an oval diamond on a thin gold band, and I stare at it, still completely in shock.

I bend to him, and we kiss as the office breaks into laughter and cheers. They clap as we laugh into our kiss.

I can't believe this is happening.

He stands and takes me into his arms. "Cheesy enough for you?" He smiles down at me.

I giggle as I hold him tight. "Next level cheese—and perfect. I love you, Mr. Miles."

The song finishes, and Tristan presses play, and the song begins to repeat. The workers all cheer.

Jameson laughs in embarrassment and leans in to kiss me. "The things I would do for you, Emily Foster, the things I would do."

Epilogue

I read the story in the paper.

> Hayden Morris and Lara Aspin were officially charged today with the embezzlement of seven million dollars from Miles Media.
>
> In what has been described as a modern Bonnie and Clyde story, the two, who have been dating for five years, carried out the fraud over a period of three years. The crime may have gone unnoticed, and they were only caught when Morris was fired by Miles Media.
>
> Fueled by a need for revenge, they stupidly decided to frame Jameson Miles for the crime. In the backfire of all backfires, this decision sealed their fate. The pair will be serving prison time of ten years in different state prisons.

> Jameson Miles has been cleared of any wrong-
> doing. Miles Media reached a new height today
> on the stock market since April 2018.

I smile broadly. It seems so long ago now that this all happened—a lifetime, if I'm honest.

Thank heavens it's all over.

We have a wedding to plan. He's given me three months.
We have so much to do, so many decisions. Where will we get
married? I have no idea. Jameson has said that I have to pick
the destination because as long as I'm there, he doesn't care
where it is.

I wait on the curb in the underground parking lot. It's
Friday afternoon. "What did he say he was doing?" I frown
at Alan.

"I think you will be pleasantly surprised." He smirks.

I frown as I consider the possibilities. Jameson has been
acting weird all week. Taking secret phone calls and being all
pleased with himself. Maybe he's secretly booked the wedding
venue?

I hope so—helps me out.

I hear a crunch of gears, and I look up and frown. Bessie is
bunny hopping toward us with Jameson behind the wheel, and
Alan bursts out laughing.

My mouth falls open in shock. "What in the world?" I
whisper.

He pulls up beside me, and I open the door.

"Going my way?" He smiles with a sexy wink.

I laugh out loud. "What are you doing?"

"Taking you away for a few days."

"You are?"

"Your things are already in the trunk."

"In Bessie?" I stammer.

"Yes, in Bitchy. I borrowed her from Viagra Mike. Although I must tell you, I've ordered you a new Range Rover. Bessie is unbearable."

"You snob." I giggle, then turn and hug Alan in excitement.

He laughs. "Have a great weekend, Ms. Foster," he says as he helps me into the car. I lean over and grab Jameson and kiss his face. I love that he borrowed Bessie for me.

He honks the horn. "Goodbye, Alan," he calls as he does an overexaggerated wave.

I laugh out loud at his un-Jameson-like behavior. "Goodbye, Alan."

We bunny hop out of the parking lot, and he takes my hand in his and kisses the back of it. "Where do you want to go, my little fuck bunny?"

I smile over at my beautiful man. "Bumfuck nowhere."

Two hours later

Jameson pulls into the driveway of Arndell, and I bounce in my seat. "We are going to our house?" I shriek in excitement.

"Yes, I booked it for the weekend."

I unclip my seat belt and slide over and begin to smother his face in kisses as we drive up the driveway while he chuckles at my childlike behavior. We arrive at the old house, and I bounce out of the car before the car even stops and run up to the front door. I turn and stare out over the view of the beautiful grounds.

"Oh, Jameson, I just love this place." I smile dreamily as he walks up behind me.

"I know." He hands me a key ring with a red ribbon bow tied to it.

I frown as I stare down at it in my hand.

"That's why I bought it for you."

My eyes meet his. "What?"

"Uh-huh. I thought we could live here on the weekends and on holidays."

"You want to be a swamp person with me?" I whisper in surprise.

He stands and takes me in his arms. "I could be anything, Emily Foster . . . as long as I'm with you."

Desperate to know more about the Miles brothers? Read on for an exclusive first chapter of the next book in the series, *The Takeover*, out very soon . . .

Chapter 1

The phone buzzes on my desk. "Hello," I answer.

"Hi, Tristan Miles is on line two for you," Marley replies.

"Tell him I'm busy."

"Claire." She pauses. "This is the third time he's called this week."

"So?"

"Pretty soon, he's going to stop calling."

"And your point is?" I snap in exasperation. I love Marley, but damn it, I wish she would mind her business. Sometimes, it really blows having your best friend as your receptionist.

"My point is we paid the staff out of the overdraft this week. And I know you don't want to admit this, but we are in trouble, Claire. You need to hear him out."

I exhale heavily and drag my hand down my face. I know she's right: our company, Anderson Media, is struggling. We're down to our last three hundred staff members, having downscaled from the original six hundred. Miles Media has been circling like wolves for months, watching and waiting for the perfect time to move in for the kill. Tristan Miles: the head of acquisitions and the archenemy of every struggling company in the world. Like a leech, he takes over companies when they're at their lowest, tears them apart, and then with his never-ending funds, turns them into huge successes. He's the lowest snake in the snake pit. Preying on weaknesses and getting paid millions of dollars a year for the privilege. He's a rich, spoiled bastard with a reputation of being acutely intelligent, hard as nails, and conscience-free.

He's everything I hate about business.

"Just listen to what he has to say—that's all. You never know what he might offer," Marley pleads.

"Oh, come on," I scoff. "We both know what he wants."

"Claire, please." She pauses. "You can't lose your family home. I won't let that happen."

Sadness rolls over me; what a mess I've made of everything. "Fine." I sigh, defeated. "Schedule a meeting."

"Okay, great."

"Don't get excited," I snap. "I'm just doing this to shut you up, you know?"

"Good, mouth officially shut from here on out. Cross my heart."

I roll my eyes. "If only. Will you come with me?"

"Yes, for sure. We'll stick Mr. Fancy Pants's checkbook where the sun doesn't shine."

I giggle at the idea. "Okay, deal."

I hang up and go back to my report, wishing it were Friday and I didn't have to worry about Anderson Media and the bills.

I'm tired . . . so tired.

Thursday morning Marley and I power down the street on the way to our meeting. "Why are we meeting here again?" I ask.

"He wanted to meet somewhere neutral. He has a table booked at Bryant Park Grill."

"That's odd—it's not a date," I scoff.

"It's probably all part of his grand plan." She holds her hands up and does an air rainbow. "Neutral ground." She widens her eyes in jest. "While he tries to fuck us up the ass."

"With a smile on his face." I huff. "Oh god, I hate him already."

"So remember the strategy." She coaches me as we walk.

"Yes."

"Tell me it again . . . so I remember it."

I smile. Marley is an idiot. A funny idiot nonetheless. "Stay calm; don't let him ruffle my feathers. Don't say an outright no—just keep him on ice in the background as an insurance policy."

"Yes, that's a great plan."

"It should be . . . you thought of it." We arrive at the restaurant. I take out my compact and reapply my lipstick. My dark hair is twisted up into a loose knot. I'm wearing a navy pantsuit with a cream silk blouse, closed-toe high-heeled patent pumps, and my pearl earrings. Sensible clothes—I want him to take me seriously. "Do I look okay?" I ask.

"You look hot."

My face falls. "I don't want to look hot, Marley. I want to look hard."

She scowls as she falls into character. "Totally hard." She punches her hand with her fist. "Iron maiden snatch style."

I smirk at my gorgeous friend; her bright-red zany hair is short and punky, and her pink cat-eye glasses are in full swing. She's wearing a red dress with a bright-yellow shirt underneath with red stockings and shoes. She's so trendy that she's actually scruffy. Marley is my best friend, my confidante, and the hardest worker in our company. She hasn't left my side for the last five years; her friendship is a gift, and I have no idea where I would be without her.

"Are you ready?" she asks.

"Yes. We are twenty minutes early—I wanted to get here first. Get the upper hand."

Her shoulders slump. "When I ask you if you're ready, you're supposed to answer with, 'I was born ready.'"

I roll my eyes. "This isn't a fucking Rocky Balboa movie, Marley," I snap as I push past her. "Let's get this over with."

We drop our shoulders, steel ourselves, and walk into the foyer. The waiter smiles. "Hello, ladies. How can I help you?"

"Ah." I glance at Marley. "We are meeting someone here."

"Tristan Miles?" he asks.

I frown. How did he know that? "Yes . . . actually."

"He has the private dining room booked upstairs." He gestures to the stairs.

"Of course he does," I mutter under my breath.

Marley curls her lip in disgust, and we make our way up the stairs. The top floor is empty. We look around, and I see a man out on the balcony on his phone. Perfectly fit navy suit, crisp white shirt, tall and muscular. His hair is longer on top, dark brown with a curl. He looks like he belongs on a modeling shoot, not the snake pit at all.

"Holy fuck . . . he's hot," Marley whispers.

"Shut up," I stammer in a panic that he will hear her. "Act fucking cool, will you?"

"I know." She hits me in the thigh, and I hit her back.

He turns toward us and flashes a broad smile and holds up a finger, gesturing he will be just a moment. I fake a smile, and he turns his back to us to wrap up his call. I glare at his back as my anger rises. How dare he make us wait. "Don't speak," I whisper.

"Can I whistle?" she whispers as she looks him up and down. "I totally want to wolf whistle the fuck out of this guy. Asshole or not."

I pinch the bridge of my nose—this is a disaster already. "Please, just don't speak," I remind her again.

"Okay, okay." She does a zip-her-lips-closed gesture.

He hangs up his call and walks toward us, confidence personified. Smiling broadly, he holds out his hand. "Hello, I'm Tristan Miles." He's all dimples and square jaw and white teeth and . . .

I shake his hand like a truck driver, hard and emotionless. "Hello, I'm Claire Anderson. Nice to meet you." I gesture to Marley. "This is Marley Smithson, my assistant."

"Hello, Marley." He smiles. "Nice to meet you." He gestures to the table. "Please take a seat."

I sit down with my heart in my throat—great. As if I wasn't ruffled already, he didn't have to be good looking as well.

"Coffee, tea?" He gestures to the tray. "I took the liberty of ordering us morning tea."

"Coffee, please," I reply. "Just cream."

"Me too," Marley adds.

He carefully pours us our coffees and passes them over with a side plate of cakes.

I clench my jaw to stop myself saying something snarky, and finally he takes a seat opposite us. He undoes his suit jacket with one hand and sits back in his chair. His eyes come to me. "It's nice to finally meet you, Claire. I've heard so much about you."

I raise my eyebrow in annoyance; I hate that his voice is husky and sexual. "Likewise," I reply.

I glance down and notice the black onyx-and-gold cufflinks and the fancy Rolex watch; everything about this guy screams money. His aftershave wafts between us. I try my hardest not to inhale, but it's otherworldly. I glance over at Marley, who is smiling goofily as she stares at him . . . totally besotted.

Great.

He sits back, relaxed and confident, cool and calculating. "How has your week been?"

"Fine, thanks," I reply, my patience being tested. "Let's just cut to the chase, Mr. Miles, shall we?"

"Tristan," he corrects me.

"Tristan," I reply. "Why do you want to meet with me so badly? What could possibly warrant you calling me five times a week for the last month?"

He brushes his pointer over his big lips as if amused, and his eyes hold mine. "I've been watching Anderson Media for some time now."

I raise my eyebrow, angered by his tone. "And do tell: what have you learned?"

"You are letting staff go every month."

"I'm downsizing."

"Not by choice."

"I'm not interested in what you're offering, Mr. Miles," I snap. I feel a sharp kick under the table to my ankle, and I wince in pain. *Oww* . . . that hurt. I glance at Marley. She widens her eyes in a shut-up-now signal.

"How do you know I want to make you an offer?" he replies calmly.

How many times has he had this conversation? "Don't you?"

"No." He sips his coffee. "I would like to buy your company, but I'm not offering a free pass."

"Free pass," I snap.

Marley kicks me again . . . oh shit, that hurt. I throw her a dirty look, and she fakes a broad smile. *Happy, happy,* she mouths.

"And what do you mean by a free pass, Mr. Miles?"

"Tristan," he corrects me.

"I'll call you whatever I want," I snap.

He gives me a slow, sexy smile as if loving every minute of this. "I can see you're a passionate woman, Claire, and that's admirable . . . but come on. Let's be serious here."

I roll my lips, willing myself to stay silent.

"The last three years your company has run at a massive loss. You're losing advertising accounts left, right, and center." He steeples his hand on his temple as he stares at me. "I'm guessing the financials are a nightmare."

I swallow the lump in my throat as we stare at each other.

"I can take everything off your hands, and you can take a hard-earned break."

Anger begins to pump through my blood. "You would love that, wouldn't you? Play Mr. Nice Guy and take everything off my hands . . . come in on your horse and save the day like a white knight."

His eyes hold mine, and a trace of a smile crosses his face.

"I will hold on to my company if it's the last thing I do." I feel a swift kick, and I jump, losing the last of my patience. "Stop kicking me, Marley," I snap.

Tristan breaks into a broad smile as he looks between us. "Keep kicking her, Marley," he says. "Kick some sense into her."

I roll my eyes, embarrassed that my assistant is kicking the shit out of my ankles.

He sits forward, his purpose renewed. "Claire, let's get one thing straight. I always get what I want. And what I want is Anderson Media. I can take it now from you for a good price that will protect you. Or"—he shrugs casually—"I can wait for six months until the liquidators move in and get it for next to nothing, and you can face bankruptcy." He steeples his hands on the table in front of him. "We both know the end is near."

"You self-conceited prick," I whisper.

He tilts his chin to the sky and smiles proudly. "Nice guys come last, Claire."

My heart begins to beat faster as my anger begins to build.

"Think about it." He takes out his business card and slides it across the table.

TRISTAN MILES
09488449467

"I know this is not how you want to sell your company. But you need to be a realist," he continues.

I stare at him, sitting there all cold and heartless, and I feel my emotions bubbling dangerously close to the surface.

Our eyes are locked. "Take the offer, Claire. I'll email you a figure this afternoon. You will be taken care of."

My sanity rubber band snaps, and I sit forward. "And who will take care of my late husband's memory, Mr. Miles?" I sneer. "Miles Media sure as hell won't."

He twists his lips, uncomfortable for the first time.

"Do you know anything about me and my company?"

"I do."

"Then you'll know that this company was my husband's labor of love. He worked for twenty years to build it up from the ground. His dream was to hand it down to his three sons."

His eyes hold mine.

"So . . . don't you fucking dare"—I slam my hand on the table as my eyes fill with tears—"sit there with that smug look on your face and threaten me. Because believe me . . . Mr. Miles, whatever you're dishing out isn't half as bad as losing him." I stand. "I've already been to hell and back, and I will not have some rich, spoiled bastard make me feel like shit."

He rolls his lips, unimpressed.

"Don't call me again," I snap as I push back in my chair.

"Think about it, Claire."

"Go to hell," I snap. I begin to storm to the door.

"She's just having a bad day. We'll definitely think about it," Marley splutters in embarrassment. "Thanks for the cake—it was yummy."

I angrily wipe the tears from my face as I run down the stairs and out the front doors. I can't believe I was so unprofessional. Shame fills me, and I screw up my face with tears anew.

Marley runs to keep up with me. She wisely stays silent and then looks up and down the street. "Oh, screw this, Claire—let's not go back to work. Let's go get drunk instead."

I stand at the window and stare over New York. My hands are in my suit pockets, and a strange feeling is burning a hole in my stomach.

Claire Anderson.

Beautiful, smart, and proud.

No matter how many times I've tried to wipe her out of my mind over the last three days since our meeting, I can't.

The way she looked, the way she smelled, the curve of her breast through her silk shirt.

The fire in her eyes.

She is the most beautiful woman I've seen in a long time, and her heartfelt words are playing on repeat.

"So . . . don't you fucking dare sit there with that smug look on your face and threaten me. Because believe me . . . Mr. Miles, whatever you're dishing out isn't half as bad as losing him. I've already been to hell and back, and I will not have some rich, spoiled bastard make me feel like shit."

I take a seat at my desk and roll the pen beneath my fingers as I mentally go over what I have to say. I have to call her and follow up on our meeting, I'm dreading it. I exhale heavily and dial her number. "Claire Anderson's office."

"Hello, Marley. It's Tristan Miles."

"Oh, hello, Tristan," she replies happily. "Are you after Claire?"

"Yes, I am. Is she available."

"I'll put you straight through."

"Thank you."

I wait, and then she answers. "Hello, Claire speaking."

I close my eyes at the sound of her voice . . . sexy, husky . . . enticing.

"Hello, Claire. It's Tristan."

"Oh." She falls silent.

Fuck . . . Marley didn't tell her it was me.

An unfamiliar feeling begins to seep into my bones. "I just wanted to see if you were okay after our meeting. I'm sorry if I upset you." I screw up my face . . . *What are you doing? This is not in the plan.*

"My feelings are no concern of yours, Mr. Miles."

"Tristan," I correct her.

"How can I help you?" she snaps impatiently.

My mind goes blank . . .

"Tristan?" she prompts me.

"I wanted to see if you would like to have dinner with me on Saturday night." My eyes close in horror . . . what the fuck am I doing right now?

She stays silent for a moment and then replies in surprise. "You're asking me out on a date?"

I screw up my face. "I don't like the way we met. I would like to start again."

She chuckles in a condescending tone. "You have got to be kidding. I wouldn't go out with you if you were the last man on earth." She whispers, "Money and looks don't impress me, Mr. Miles."

I bite my bottom lip . . . *Ouch.* "Our meeting was nothing personal, Claire."

"It was very personal to me. Go and find a bimbo to wine and dine, Tristan. I have no interest in dating a soul-sucking cold bastard like you." The phone clicks as she hangs up.

I stare at the phone in my hand. Adrenaline is pumping through my system at her fighting words.

I don't know whether I'm shocked or impressed.

Perhaps a bit of both.

I've never been rejected before and definitely never been spoken to like that.

I turn to my computer and type into Google:

Who is Claire Anderson?

Read on for the first chapter of T L Swan's backlist title, *Mr. Masters*, available to buy now!

ALINA MASTERS 1984–2013

WIFE AND BELOVED MOTHER. IN GOD'S HANDS WE TRUST.

Grief. The Grim Reaper of life.

Stealer of joy, hope, and purpose.

Some days are bearable. Other days I can hardly breathe, and I suffocate in a world of regret where good reason has no sense.

I never know when those days will hit, only that when I wake, my chest feels constricted and I need to run. I need to be anywhere but here, dealing with this life. My life.

Our life. Until you left.

The sound of a distant lawn mower brings me back to the present, and I glance over at the cemetery's caretaker. He's concentrating as he weaves between the tombstones, careful not to clip or damage one as he passes. It's dusk, and the mist is rolling in for the night.

I come here often to think, to try and feel.

I can't talk to anyone. I can't express my true feelings.

I want to know why.

Why did you do this to us?

I clench my jaw as I stare at my late wife's tombstone.

We could have had it all . . . but, we didn't.

I lean down and brush the dust away from her name and rearrange the pink lilies that I have just placed in the vase. I touch her face on the small oval photo. She stares back at me, void of emotion.

Stepping back, I drop my hands in the pockets of my black overcoat.

I could stand here and stare at this headstone all day—sometimes I do—but I turn and walk to the car without looking back.

My Porsche.

Sure, I have money and two kids that love me. I'm at the top of my professional field, working as a judge. I have all the tools to be happy, but I'm not.

I'm barely surviving; holding on by a thread. Playing the facade to the world.

Dying inside.

Half an hour later, I arrive at Madison's—my therapist.

I always leave here relaxed. I don't have to talk, I don't have to think, I don't have to feel.

I walk through the front doors on autopilot.

"Good afternoon, Mr. Smith." Hayley, the receptionist, smiles. "Your room is waiting, sir."

"Thank you." I frown, feeling like I need something more today. Something to take this edginess off. A distraction.

"I'll have someone extra today, Hayley."

"Of course, sir. Who would you like?"

I frown and take a moment to get it right. "Hmm. Hannah."

"So, Hannah and Belinda?"

"Yes."

"No problem, sir. Make yourself comfortable and they will be right up."

I take the lift to the exclusive penthouse. Once there I make myself a scotch and stare out the smoke-glass window overlooking London. I hear the door click behind me and I turn toward the sound. Hannah and Belinda stand before me smiling. Belinda has long blonde hair, while Hannah is a brunette.

There's no denying they're both young and beautiful. "Hello, Mr. Smith," they say in unison.

I sip my scotch as my eyes drink them in.

"Where would you like us, sir?"

I unbuckle my belt. "On your knees."

Chapter 1

Brielle

Customs is ridiculously slow and a man has been pulled into the office up ahead. It all looks very suspicious from my position at the back of the line. "What do you think he did?" I whisper as I crane my neck to spy the commotion up ahead.

"I don't know, something stupid, probably," Emerson replies. We shuffle toward the desk as the line moves a little quicker.

We've just arrived in London to begin our yearlong working holiday. I'm going to work for a judge as a nanny, while Emerson, my best friend, is working for an art auctioneer. I'm terrified, yet excited.

"I wish we had come a week earlier so we could have spent some time together," Emerson says.

"Yeah, I know, but she needed me to start this week because she's going away next week. I need to learn the kids' routine."

"Who leaves their kids alone for three days with a complete stranger?" Em frowns in disgust.

I shrug. "My new boss, apparently."

"Well, at least I can come and stay with you next week. That's a bonus."

My position is residential, so my accommodation is secure. However, poor Emerson will be living with two strangers. She's freaking out over it.

"Yeah, but I'm sneaking you in," I say. "I don't want it to look like we're partying or anything." I look around the airport. It's busy, bustling, and I already feel so alive. Emerson and I are more than just young travelers.

Emerson is trying to find her purpose and I'm running from a destructive past, one that involves me being in love with an adulterous prick.

I loved him. He just didn't love me. Not enough, anyway. If he had, he would have kept it in his pants, and I wouldn't be at Heathrow Airport feeling like I'm about to throw up.

I look down at myself and smooth the wrinkles from my dress. "She's picking me up. Do I look okay?"

Emerson looks me up and down, smiling broadly. "You look exactly how a twenty-five-year-old nanny from Australia should."

I bite my bottom lip to stop myself from smiling stupidly. That was a good answer.

"So, what's your boss's name?" she asks.

I rustle around in my bag for my phone and scroll through the emails until I get to the one from the nanny agency. "Mrs. Julian Masters."

Emerson nods. "And what's her story again? I know you've told me before but I've forgotten."

"She's a Supreme Court judge, widowed five years ago."

"What happened to the husband?"

"I don't know, but apparently she's quite wealthy." I shrug. "Two kids, well behaved."

"Sounds good."

"I hope so. I hope they like me."

"They will." We move forward in the line. "We are definitely going out at the weekend though, yes?"

"Yes." I nod. "What are you going to do until then?"

Emerson shrugs. "Look around. I start work on Monday and it's Thursday today." She frowns as she watches me. "Are you sure you can go out on the weekends?"

"Yes," I snap, exasperated. "I told you a thousand times, we're going out on Saturday night."

Emerson nods nervously. I think she may be more nervous than I am, but at least I'm acting brave. "Did you get your phone sorted?" I ask.

"No, not yet. I'll find a phone shop tomorrow so I can call you."

"Okay."

We are called to the front of the line, and finally, half an hour later, we walk into the arrival lounge of Heathrow International Airport. "Do you see our names?" Emerson whispers as we both look around.

"No."

"Shit, no one is here to pick us up. Typical." She begins to panic.

"Relax, they will be here," I mutter.

"What do we do if no one turns up?"

I raise my eyebrow as I consider the possibility. "Well, I don't know about you, but I'm going to lose my shit."

Emerson looks over my shoulder. "Oh, look, there's your name. She must have sent a driver."

I turn to see a tall, broad man in a navy suit holding a sign with the name Brielle Johnston on it. I force a smile and wave meekly as I feel my anxiety rise like a tidal wave in my stomach.

He walks over and smiles at me. "Brielle?"

His voice is deep and commanding. "Yes, that's me," I breathe.

He holds out his hand to shake mine. "Julian Masters."

What?

My eyes widen.

A man?

He raises his eyebrows.

"Um, so, I'm . . . I'm Brielle," I stammer as I push my hand out. "And this is my friend Emerson, who I'm traveling with." He takes my hand in his and my heart races.

A trace of a smile crosses his face before he covers it. "Nice to meet you." He turns to Emerson and shakes her hand. "How do you do?"

My eyes flash to Emerson, who is clearly loving this shit. She grins brightly. "Hello."

"I thought you were a woman," I whisper.

His brows furrow. "Last time I checked I was all man." His eyes hold mine.

Why did I just say that out loud? Oh my God, stop talking. This is so awkward.

I want to go home. This is a bad idea.

"I'll wait over here." He gestures to the corner before marching off in that direction. My horrified eyes meet Emerson's, and she giggles, so I punch her hard in the arm.

"Oh, my fuck, he's a fucking man," I whisper angrily.

"I can see that." She smirks, her eyes fixed on him.

"Excuse me, Mr. Masters?" I call after him.

He turns. "Yes."

We both wither under his glare. "We . . . we are just going to use the bathroom," I whisper nervously.

With one curt nod, he gestures to the right. We look up and see the sign. I grab Emerson by the arm and drag her into the bathroom. "I'm not working with a stuffy old man!" I shriek as we burst through the door.

"It will be okay. How did this happen?"

I take out my phone and scroll through the emails quickly. I knew it. "It says woman. I knew it said woman."

"He's not that old," she calls out from her cubicle. "I would prefer to work for a man than a woman, to be honest."

"You know what, Emerson? This is a shit idea. How the hell did I let you talk me into this?"

She smiles as she exits the cubicle and washes her hands. "It doesn't matter. You'll hardly see him anyway, and you're not working weekends when he's home." She's clearly trying to calm me. "Stop with the carry on."

Stop the carry on.

Steam feels like it's shooting from my ears. "I'm going to kill you. I'm going to fucking kill you."

Emerson bites her lip to stifle her smile. "Listen, just stay with him until we find you something else. I will get my phone sorted tomorrow and we can start looking elsewhere for another job," she reassures me. "At least someone picked you up. Nobody cares about me at all."

I put my head into my hands as I try to calm my breathing. "This is a disaster, Em," I whisper. Suddenly every fear I had about traveling is coming true. I feel completely out of my comfort zone.

"It's going to be one week . . . tops."

My scared eyes lift to hold hers, and I nod.

"Okay?" She smiles as she pulls me into a hug.

"Okay." I glance back in the mirror, fix my hair, and straighten my dress. I'm completely rattled.

We walk back out and take our place next to Mr. Masters. He's in his late thirties, immaculately dressed, and kind of attractive. His hair is dark with a sprinkle of gray.

"Did you have a good flight?" he asks as he looks down at me.

"Yes, thanks," I push out. Oh, that sounded so forced. "Thank you for picking us up," I add meekly. He nods with no fuss.

Emerson smiles at the floor as she tries to hide her smile. That bitch is loving this shit.

"Emerson?" a male voice calls. We all turn to see a blond man, and Emerson's face falls. Ha! Now it's my turn to laugh. "Hello, I'm Mark." He kisses her on the cheek and then turns to me. "You must be Brielle?"

"Yes." I smile then turn to Mr. Masters. "And this is . . ." I pause because I don't know how to introduce him.

"Julian Masters," he finishes for me, adding in a strong handshake.

Emerson and I fake smile at each other.

Oh, dear God, help me.

Emerson stands and talks with Mark and Mr. Masters, while I stand in uncomfortable silence. "The car is this way." He gestures to the right.

I nod nervously. Oh God, don't leave me with him. This is terrifying.

"Nice to meet you, Emerson and Mark." He shakes their hands.

"Likewise. Please look after my friend," Emerson whispers as her eyes flicker to mine.

Mr. Masters nods, smiles, and then pulls my luggage behind him as he walks to the car. Emerson pulls me into an embrace. "This is shit," I whisper into her hair.

"It will be fine. He's probably really nice."

"He doesn't look nice," I whisper.

"Yeah, I agree. He looks like a tool," Mark adds as he watches him disappear through the crowd.

Emerson throws her new friend a dirty look, and I smirk. I think her friend is more annoying than mine, but anyway . . .

"Mark, look after my friend, please?" He beats his chest like a gorilla. "Oh, I intend to."

Emerson's eyes meet mine. She subtly shakes her head and I bite my bottom lip to hide my smile. This guy is a dick. We both look over to see Mr. Masters looking back impatiently. "I better go," I whisper.

"You have my apartment details if you need me?"

"I'll probably turn up in an hour. Tell your roommates I'm coming in case I need a key."

She laughs and waves me off, and I go to Mr. Masters. He sees me coming and then starts to walk again.

God, can he not even wait for me? So rude. He walks out of the building into the VIP parking section. I follow him in complete silence.

Any notion that I was going to become friends with my new boss has been thrown out the window. I think he hates me already.

Just wait until he finds out that I lied on my résumé and I have no fucking idea what I'm doing. Nerves flutter in my stomach at the thought.

We get to a large, swanky, black SUV, and he clicks it open to put my suitcase in the trunk. He opens the back door for me to get in. "Thank you." I smile awkwardly as I slide into the seat. He wants me to sit in the back when the front seat is empty.

This man is odd.

He slides into the front seat and eventually pulls out into the traffic. All I can do is clutch my handbag in my lap. Should I say something? Try and make conversation? What will I say?

"Do you live far from here?" I ask.

"Twenty minutes," he replies, his tone clipped.

Oh . . . is that it? Okay, shut up now. He doesn't want a conversation. For ten long minutes, we sit in silence. "You can drive this car when you have the children, or we have a small minivan. The choice is yours."

"Oh, okay." I pause for a moment. "Is this your car?"

"No." He turns onto a street and into a driveway with huge sandstone gates. "I drive a Porsche," he replies casually.

"Oh."

The driveway goes on and on and on. I look around at the perfectly kept grounds and rolling green hills. With every meter we pass, I feel my heart beat just that bit faster. As if it isn't bad enough that I can't do the whole nanny thing . . . I really can't do the rich thing. I have no idea what to do with polite company. I don't even know what fork to use at dinner. I've got myself into a right mess here. The house comes into focus and the blood drains from my face.

It's not a house, not even close. It's a mansion, white and sandstone with a castle kind of feel to it, with six garages to the left.

He pulls into the large circular driveway, stopping under the awning.

"Your house is beautiful," I whisper.

He nods, as his eyes stay fixed out front. "We are fortunate."

He gets out of the car and opens my door for me. I climb out as I grip my handbag with white-knuckle force. My eyes rise up to the luxurious building in front of me. This is an insane amount of money. He retrieves my suitcase and wheels it around to the side of the building. "Your entrance is around to the side," he says. I follow him up a path until we get to a door, which he opens and lets me walk through. There is a foyer and a living area in front of me. "The kitchen is this way." He points to the kitchen. "And your bedroom is in the back-left corner."

I nod and walk past him, into the apartment.

He stands at the door but doesn't come in. "The bathroom is to the right," he continues.

Why isn't he coming in here? "Okay, thanks," I reply.

"Order any groceries you want on the family shopping order and . . ." He pauses, as if collecting his thoughts. "If there is anything else you need, please talk to me first."

I frown. "First?"

He shrugs. "I don't want to be told about a problem for the first time when reading a resignation letter."

"Oh." Did that happen before? "Of course," I mutter.

"If you would like to come and meet the children . . ." He gestures to a hallway.

"Yes, please." Oh God, here we go. I follow him out into a corridor with glass walls that looks out onto the main house, which is about four meters away. A garden sits between the two buildings creating an atrium, and I smile as I look up in wonder. There is a large window in the main house that looks into the kitchen. I can see beyond that into the living area from the corridor where a young girl and small boy are watching television together. We continue to the end of the glass corridor where there is a staircase with six steps leading up to the main house. I blow out a breath, and I follow Mr. Masters up the stairs. "Children, come and meet your new nanny."

The little boy jumps down and rushes over to me, clearly excited, while the girl just looks up and rolls her eyes. I smile to myself, remembering what it's like to be a typical teenager.

"Hello, I'm Samuel." The little boy smiles as he wraps his arms around my legs. He has dark hair, is wearing glasses, and he's so damn cute.

"Hello, Samuel." I smile.

"This is Willow," he introduces.

I smile at the teenage girl. "Hello."

She folds her arms across her chest defiantly. "Hi," she grumbles.

Mr. Masters holds her gaze for a moment, saying so much with just one look. Willow eventually holds her hand out for me to shake. "I'm Willow."

I smile as my eyes flash up to Mr. Masters. He can keep her under control with just a simple glare.

Samuel runs back to the lounge, grabs something, and then comes straight back. I see a flash. Click, click.

What the hell?

He has a small instant Polaroid camera. He watches my face appear on the piece of paper in front of him before he looks back up at me. "You're pretty." He smiles. "I'm putting this on the fridge." He carefully pins it to the fridge with a magnet. Mr. Masters seems to become flustered for some reason. "Bedtime for you two," he instructs, and they both complain. He turns his attention back to me. "Your kitchen is stocked with groceries, and I'm sure you're tired."

I fake a smile. Oh, I'm being dismissed. "Yes, of course." I go to walk back down to my apartment, and then turn back to him. "What time do I start tomorrow?"

His eyes hold mine. "When you hear Samuel wake up."

"Yes, of course." My eyes search his as I wait for him to say something else, but it doesn't come. "Good night then." I smile awkwardly.

"Good night."

"Bye, Brielle." Samuel smiles, and Willow ignores me, walking away and up the stairs.

I walk back down into my apartment and close the door behind me. Then I flop onto the bed and stare up at the ceiling.

What have I done?

It's midnight and I'm thirsty, but I have looked everywhere and I still cannot find a glass. There's no other option; I'm going to have to sneak up into the main house to find one. I'm wearing my silky white nightdress, but I'm sure they are all in bed.

Sneaking out into the darkened corridor, I can see into the lit-up house.

I suddenly catch sight of Mr. Masters sitting in the armchair reading a book. He has a glass of red wine in his hand. I stand in the dark, unable to tear my eyes away. There's something about him that fascinates me but I don't quite know what it is. He stands abruptly, and I push myself back against the wall. Can he see me here in the dark?

Shit.

My eyes follow him as he walks into the kitchen. The only thing he's wearing is his navy-blue boxer shorts. His dark hair has messy, loose waves on top. His chest is broad, his body is . . .

My heart begins to beat faster. What am I doing? I shouldn't be standing here in the dark, watching him like a creep, but for some reason I can't make myself look away.

He goes to stand by the kitchen counter. His back is to me as he pours himself another glass of red. He lifts it to his lips slowly and my eyes run over his body. I push myself against the wall harder. He walks over to the fridge and takes off the photo of me.

What?

He leans his ass on the counter as he studies it. What is he doing? I feel like I can't breathe.

He slowly puts his hand down the front of his boxer shorts, and then he seems to stroke himself a few times.

My eyes widen. What the fuck?

He puts his glass of wine on the counter and turns the main light off, leaving only a lamp to light the room. With my picture in his hand, he disappears up the hall. What the hell was that?

I think Mr. Masters just went up to his bedroom to jerk off to my photo.

Oh. My. God.

Knock, knock.

My eyes are closed, but I frown and try to ignore the noise. I hear it again. Tap, tap. What is that? I roll toward the door and I see it slowly begin to open. My eyes widen, and I sit up quickly. Mr. Masters comes into view. "I'm so sorry to bother you, Miss Brielle," he whispers. He smells like he's freshly showered, and he's wearing an immaculate suit. "I'm looking for Samuel." His gaze roams down to my breasts hanging loosely in my nightdress, and then he snaps his eyes back up to my face, as if he's horrified at what he just did.

"Where is he?" I frown. "Is he missing?"

"There he is," he whispers as he gestures to the lounger. I look over to see Samuel curled up with his teddy in the diluted light of the room. My mouth falls open. "Oh no, what's wrong?" I whisper. Did he need me and I slept through the whole thing?

"Nothing," Mr. Masters murmurs as he picks Samuel up and rests his son's head on his strong shoulder. "He's a sleepwalker. Sorry to disturb you. I've got this now." He leaves the room with his small son safely asleep in his arms. The door gently clicks closed behind them.

I lie back down and stare at the ceiling in the silence. That poor little boy. He came in here to see me and I didn't even wake up. I was probably snoring, for fuck's sake. What if he was scared? Oh, I feel like shit now.

I blow out a deep breath, lift myself up to sit on the edge of the bed, and I put my head into my hands. I need to up my game. If I'm in charge of looking after this kid, I can't have him wandering around at night on his own. Is he that lonely that he was looking for company from me—a complete stranger?

Unexplained sadness rolls over me, and I suddenly feel like the weight of the world is on my shoulders. I look around my room for a moment as I think.

Eventually, I get up and go to the bathroom, and then walk to the window to pull the heavy drapes back. It's just getting light, and a white mist hangs over the paddocks.

Something catches my eye and I look down to see Mr. Masters walking out to the garage.

Wearing a dark suit and carrying a briefcase, he disappears, and moments later I see his Porsche pull out and disappear up the driveway. I watch as the garage door slowly closes behind him. He's gone to work for the day.

What the hell?

His son was just found asleep on my lounger and he just plops him back into his own bed and leaves for the day. Who does that? Well, screw this, I'm going to go and check on him. He's probably upstairs crying, scared out of his brain. Stupid men. Why don't they have an inch of fucking empathy for anyone but themselves? He's eight, for Christ's sake!

I walk up into the main house. The lamp is still on in the living room and I can smell the eggs that Mr. Masters cooked himself for breakfast. I look around, and then go up the grand staircase. Honestly, what the hell have I got myself into here? I'm in some stupid rich twat's house, worried about his child who he clearly doesn't give a fuck about.

I storm up the stairs, taking two at a time. I get to the top and the change of scenery suddenly makes me feel nervous. It's luxurious up here. The corridor is wide, and the cream carpet feels lush beneath my feet. A huge mirror hangs in the hall on the wall. I catch a glimpse of myself and cringe.

God, no wonder he was looking at my boobs. They are hanging out everywhere, and my hair is wild. I readjust my nightgown over my breasts and continue up the hall. I pass a living area that seems to be for the children, with big comfy loungers inside it. I pass a bedroom, and then I get to a door that is closed. I open it carefully and allow myself to peer in. Willow is fast asleep, still scowling, though. I smirk and slowly shut her door to continue down the hall. Eventually, I get to a door that is slightly ajar. I peer around it and see Samuel sound asleep, tucked in nice and tight. I walk into his room and sit on the side of the bed. He's wearing bright blue and green dinosaur pajamas, and his little glasses are on his side table, beside his lamp. I find myself smiling as I watch him. Unable to help it, I put my hand out and push the dark hair from his forehead. His bedroom is neat and tidy, filled with expensive furniture. It kind of looks like you would imagine a child's bedroom being set out in a perfect family movie. Everything in this house is the absolute best of the best. Just how much money does Mr. Masters have? There's a bookcase, a desk, a wingback chair in the corner, and a toy box. The window has a bench seat running underneath it, and there are a few books sitting in a pile on the cushion, as if Samuel reads there a lot. I glance over to the armchair in the corner to his school clothes all laid out for him. Everything is there, folded neatly, right down to his socks and shiny, polished shoes. His school bag is packed, too.

I stand and walk over to look at his things. Mr. Masters must do this before he goes to bed. What must it be like to bring children up alone?

My mind goes to his wife and how much she is missing out on. Samuel is so young. With one last look at Samuel, I creep out of the room and head back down the hall, until something catches my eye.

A light is on in the en suite bathroom of the main bedroom. That must be Mr. Master's bedroom. I look left and then right; nobody is awake. I wonder what his room is like, and I can't stop myself from tiptoeing closer to inspect it. Wow.

The bed is clearly king-size, and the room is grand, decorated in all different shades of coffee, complimented with dark antique furniture. A huge, expensive, gold and magenta embroidered rug sits on the floor beneath the bed. The light in the wardrobe is on. I peer inside and see business shirts all lined up, neatly in a row. Super neatly, actually. I'm going to have to make sure I keep my room tidy or he'll think I'm a pig. I smirk because I am one according to his standards of living.

I turn to see his bed has already been made, and my eyes linger over the velvet quilt and lush pillows there. Did he really touch himself in there last night as he thought of me, or am I completely delusional? I glance around for the photo of me, but I don't see it. He must have taken it back downstairs.

An unexpected thrill runs through me. I may return the favor tonight in my own bed.

I walk into the bathroom. It's all black, gray, and very modern. Once again, I notice that everything is very neat. There is a large mirror, and I can see that a slender cabinet sits behind it. I push the mirror and the door pops open. My eyes roam over the shelves. You can tell a lot about people by their bathroom cabinet. Deodorant. Razors. Talcum powder. Condoms. I wonder how long ago his wife died. Does he have a new girlfriend?

It wouldn't surprise me. He is kind of hot, in an old way. I see a bottle of aftershave and I pick it up, removing the lid before I lift it up to my nose.

Heaven in a bottle.

I inhale deeply again, and Mr. Master's face suddenly appears in the mirror behind me.

"What the hell do you think you're doing?" he growls.

ACKNOWLEDGMENTS

There are no words meaningful enough to thank my wonderful team.

I don't write my books alone. I have an army.

The best army in the world.

Kellie, the most wonderful PA on earth.

You are amazing. Thank you for all that you do for me.

Keeley, not only are you an amazing daughter, but you're now a wonderful employee. Thank you for wanting to work alongside me. It means a lot.

To my wonderful beta readers: Mum, Vicki, Am, Rachel, Nicole, Lisa K., Lisa D., Nadia, and Charlotte. Thank you. You put up with a lot and never whine, even when I make you wait for the next chapter. How I got so lucky to have you come into my life and to be able to call you my friends, I will never know.

To Rena, you came into my life like a breath of fresh air and somehow adopted me. Thank you for believing in me. You're the yin to my yang, or the ting to my tang.

Vic, you make me better, and your friendship is so valued.

Virginia, thank you for everything you do for me. It is so appreciated.

To my motivated mofos. I love you to bits. You know who you are.

To Linda and my PR team at Forward. You have been with me since the beginning, and you will be with me until the end. Thank you for everything.

To my homegirls in the Swan Squad. I feel like I can do anything with you girls in my corner. Thanks for making me laugh every single day.

This year I'm adding someone new to my list.

Amazon.

Thank you for providing me with an amazing platform to bring my books to life.

I am my own boss.

Your belief and support of my work this last year have been nothing short of amazing.

And to my four reasons for living, my beautiful husband and three children.

Your love is my drug, my motivation, and my calling.

Without you, I have nothing.

Everything I do is for you.

Gratitude.

The quality of being thankful.

Readiness to show appreciation for and to return kindness.

Trust in the universe.

It always delivers.

ABOUT THE AUTHOR

A psychologist in her former life, T L Swan is now seriously addicted to the thrill of writing and can't imagine a time when she wasn't. She resides in Sydney, Australia, where she's living out her own happily ever after with her husband and their three children.